My Heart Stood Still

"Written with poetic grace and a wickedly subtle sense of humor . . . the essence of pure romance. Sweet, poignant, and truly magical, this is a rare treat: A romance with characters readers will come to care about and a love story they will cherish."
—*Booklist*

"A totally enchanting tale, sensual and breathtaking . . . An absolute must-read."
—*Rendezvous*

If I Had You

"Kurland brings history to life . . . in this tender medieval romance."
—*Booklist*

"A passionate story filled with danger, intrigue, and sparkling dialogue."
—*Rendezvous*

The More I See You

"Entertaining . . . The story line is fast-paced and brings to life the intrigue of the era . . . wonderful."
—*Midwest Book Review*

"The superlative Ms. Kurland once again wows her readers with her formidable talent as she weaves a tale of enchantment that blends history with spellbinding passion and impressive characterization, not to mention a magnificent plot."
—*Rendezvous*

Another Chance to Dream

"Kurland creates a special romance between a memorable knight and his lady."
—*Publishers Weekly*

"[A] wonderful love story full of passion, intrigue, and adventure . . . Lynn Kurland's fans will be delighted."
—*Affaire de Coeur*

The Very Thought of You

"[A] masterpiece . . . this fabulous tale will enchant anyone who reads it."　　　　　　　　　　　　　—*Painted Rock Reviews*

This Is All I Ask

"An exceptional read."　　　　　　—*Atlanta Journal-Constitution*

"Both powerful and sensitive . . . a wonderfully rich and rewarding book."　　　　　　　　　　　　　　　—Susan Wiggs

"A medieval romance of stunning intensity. Sprinkled with adventure, fantasy, and heart, *This Is All I Ask* reaches outside the boundaries of romance to embrace every thoughtful reader, every person of feeling."　　　　　—Christina Dodd

"In this character-driven medieval romance that transcends category, Kurland spins a sometimes magical, sometimes uproariously funny, sometimes harsh and brutal tale of two people deeply wounded in body and soul who learn to love and trust each other . . . Savor every word; this one's a keeper."
　　　　　　　　　　　　—*Publishers Weekly* (starred review)

"Sizzling passion, a few surprises, and breathtaking romance . . . a spectacular experience that you will want to savor time and time again."　　　　　　　　　—*Rendezvous*

A Dance Through Time

"An irresistibly fast and funny romp across time."
　　　　　　　　　　　　　　　　—Stella Cameron

"One of the best . . . a must-read."　　　　　—*Rendezvous*

"Lynn Kurland's vastly entertaining time travel treats us to a delightful hero and heroine . . . a humorous novel of feisty fun and adventure."　　　　　　　　　　—*A Little Romance*

"Her heroes are delightful . . . A wonderful read!"
　　　　　　　　　　　　　　　—*Heartland Critiques*

Love Came
Just in Time

Lynn Kurland

BERKLEY SENSATION, NEW YORK

THE BERKLEY PUBLISHING GROUP
Published by the Penguin Group
Penguin Group (USA) Inc.
375 Hudson Street, New York, New York 10014, USA
Penguin Group (Canada), 90 Eglinton Avenue East, Suite 700, Toronto, Ontario M4P 2Y3, Canada
(a division of Pearson Penguin Canada Inc.)
Penguin Books Ltd., 80 Strand, London WC2R 0RL, England
Penguin Group Ireland, 25 St. Stephen's Green, Dublin 2, Ireland (a division of Penguin Books Ltd.)
Penguin Group (Australia), 250 Camberwell Road, Camberwell, Victoria 3124, Australia
(a division of Pearson Australia Group Pty. Ltd.)
Penguin Books India Pvt. Ltd., 11 Community Centre, Panchsheel Park, New Delhi—110 017, India
Penguin Group (NZ), Cnr. Airborne and Rosedale Roads, Albany, Auckland 1310, New Zealand
(a division of Pearson New Zealand Ltd.)
Penguin Books (South Africa) (Pty.) Ltd., 24 Sturdee Avenue, Rosebank, Johannesburg 2196,
South Africa

Penguin Books Ltd., Registered Offices: 80 Strand, London WC2R 0RL, England

This is a work of fiction. Names, characters, places, and incidents either are the product of the author's imagination or are used fictitiously, and any resemblance to actual persons, living or dead, business establishments, events, or locales is entirely coincidental. The publisher does not have any control over and does not assume any responsibility for author or third-party websites or their content.

LOVE CAME JUST IN TIME

A Berkley Sensation Book / published by arrangement with the author

PRINTING HISTORY
Berkley trade paperback edition / June 2001
Berkley Sensation mass market edition / October 2005

Copyright © 2001 by The Berkley Publishing Group.
"The Gift of Christmas Past" by Lynn Kurland copyright © 1996 by Lynn Curland from *The Christmas Cat*.
"The Three Wise Ghosts" by Lynn Kurland copyright © 1997 by Lynn Curland from *Christmas Spirits*.
"And the Groom Wore Tulle" by Lynn Kurland copyright © 1999 by Lynn Curland from *Veils of Time*.
"The Icing on the Cake" by Lynn Kurland copyright © 2000 by Lynn Curland from *Opposites Attract*.
Cover art by Bruce Emmett.
Cover design by Lesley Worrell.

ISBN: 0-425-20693-9

BERKLEY® SENSATION
Berkley Sensation Books are published by The Berkley Publishing Group,
a division of Penguin Group (USA) Inc.,
375 Hudson Street, New York, New York 10014.
BERKLEY SENSATION and the "B" design are trademarks belonging to Penguin Group (USA) Inc.

PRINTED IN THE UNITED STATES OF AMERICA

10 9 8 7 6 5 4 3 2 1

Dear Friends,

When my editor told me that Berkley was planning to issue my previously published novellas in a single volume, I was thrilled by the news. While I was excited by the thought of see-ing some of my favorite characters together in a single book, what I found most appealing about the idea was the opportu-nity to include a personal note as a preface.

Writing is a great joy in my life, made all the more so by the readers I've come in contact with as a result of it. A hearty thank you goes to everyone who has been so supportive of my work and let me know it either by letters, E-mail, or just con-tinuing to shell out hard-earned money for my stories! You've made it possible for me to do something I love. I hope that in some small way I've been able to adequately return your in-vestment.

I'm often asked why I do novellas (mostly by my husband who knows how hard it is for me to keep my verbosity down to one hundred pages). The primary reason is that these are characters who have intrigued me in some way with their little quirks, but haven't seemed quite ready for the prime-time spot-light of a full book. For those of you who have felt that they deserved more stage time, rest assured they will no doubt show up again in the future—probably in more than one place!

Take Abigail and Miles, for instance, in "The Gift of Christmas Past." They find each other in medieval England thanks to Abby's trip down through Murphy's Pond and up through Miles's very pungent moat. They were left celebrating a lovely Christmas with their family, but that certainly didn't answer many questions about their future. It seemed only right to have another peek into their lives in The More I See You.

Megan and Gideon de Piaget were aided in their quest for love by three ghosts in "Three Wise Ghosts." Not only will the newlyweds return, but those matchmaking ghosts will be back as well. (So many matches to be made, so few centuries in which to make them. . . .)

I've had numerous complaints about having left Ian MacLeod languishing in a Scottish dungeon. (Nobody really thought I was going to leave him there forever, did they?) In "And the Groom Wore Tulle" *he finds his true love and the rest of his family several centuries in the future. (For his prehistory, consult* A Dance Through Time.*) And don't be surprised if he and the colorful Jane make future appearances. There are strange things always going on at that MacLeod keep. . . . No doubt Ian will be in on much of the action.*

"The Icing on the Cake" *features a modern-day MacLeod named Samuel and his unlikely bride. He has siblings (they all seem to!), and I'm just certain they have stories as well just waiting to be told.*

If you're wondering how all these characters fit together, don't think you're alone! When even my editor and I scratched our heads once or twice over who went where, we decided that a genealogy chart was definitely in order. It's an easy way to keep track of marriages, siblings, and foster siblings, though it is somewhat simplified in the interest of space. I can only imagine the poor printer's headache in a few years with a dozen more characters to find room for!

It is my greatest hope that somewhere in these stories you'll find something to make you laugh, make you cry, or simply be entertained for an hour or two. Thank you again for making a place in your hearts and bookcases for some of my favorite characters.

Happy reading!

Contents

ROMANTIC ROOTS

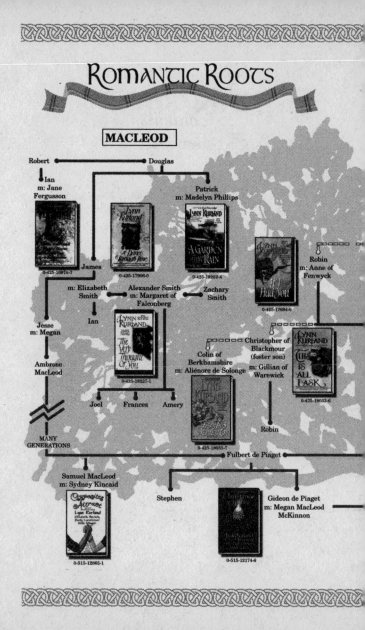

MACLEOD

Robert — Douglas

Ian
m: Jane
Fergusson

Patrick
m: Madelyn Phillips

0-425-16970-7

0-425-17906-0

0-425-18202-4

Robin
m: Anne of
Fenwyck

0-425-17694-0

James

m: Elizabeth
Smith

Alexander Smith
m: Margaret of
Falconberg

Zachary
Smith

Ian

Jesse
m: Megan

0-425-18237-1

Colin of
Berkhamshire
m: Aliénore de Solonge

Christopher of
Blackmour
(foster son)
m: Gillian of
Warewick

THIS
IS
ALL
I ASK

0-425-18033-6

Ambrose
MacLeod

Joel   Frances   Amery

MANY
GENERATIONS

0-425-18685-7

Robin

Fulbert de Piaget

Samuel MacLeod
m: Sydney Kincaid

Stephen

Gideon de Piaget
m: Megan MacLeod
McKinnon

0-515-12965-1

0-515-12174-6

family lineage in the books of
LYNN KURLAND

DE PIAGET

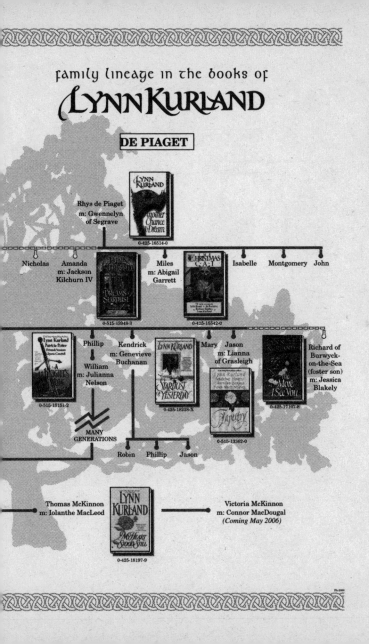

Rhys de Piaget
m: Gwennelyn
of Segrave

Another Chance to Dream
0-425-16514-0

Nicholas   **Amanda**
m: Jackson
Kilchurn IV

Dreams of Stardust
0-515-13948-3

Miles
m: Abigail
Garrett

A Christmas Cat
0-425-16542-0

Isabelle   **Montgomery**   **John**

A Knight's Vow
0-515-13151-2

Phillip

William
m: Julianna
Nelson

Kendrick
m: Genevieve
Buchanan

Stardust of Yesterday
0-425-18238-X

Mary   **Jason**
m: Lianna
of Grasleigh

Tapestry
0-515-13362-0

The More I See You
0-425-17107-8

**Richard of
Burwyck-
on-the-Sea**
(foster son)
m: Jessica
Blakely

**MANY
GENERATIONS**

Robin   **Phillip**   **Jason**

Thomas McKinnon
m: Iolanthe MacLeod

My Heart Stood Still
0-425-18197-9

Victoria McKinnon
m: Connor MacDougal
(Coming May 2006)

The Gift of
Christmas Past

Prologue

"DAMES," BRUNO SAID, with a regretful shake of his head. "Whatcha gonna do wit 'em?"

Sir Maximillian Sweetums swished his tail twice, settled himself more comfortably on his cloud, and admitted to himself that he quite had to agree with his companion—as indelicately put as the sentiment had been.

"Ah, dear Bruno," Sir Sweetums said, "there's the rub. Women don't like to be 'done with.' Especially The Abigail. A most forthright and independent spirit, she is."

"It ain't like you ain't tried, Boss," Bruno offered. "Before you, uh, I mean while you was still, uh—"

Sir Sweetums held up his well-manicured white paw to spare the blushing bulldog further embarrassment.

"Yes, I understand." It was very impolite to mention to a feline that his nine lives were up, but Sir Sweetums overlooked the faux pas. After all, he'd lived his turns to the fullest, using his considerable wits and wiles to their best advantage.

He'd had a different charge during each of his nine lives, and he'd seen eight of those mortal charges successfully settled. It was Number Nine who had, and continued, to elude his superior matchmaking skills. The Abigail. He'd tried, oh, how he'd tried.

He'd made an unmentionable deposit into the toolbox of a less-than-desirable handyman The Abigail had taken a fancy to. He'd leaped off the back of the couch over an insufferable attorney, snatching the man's hairpiece and wresting it to the ground. Snags in gabardine trousers, bloodcurdling yowls, sneak attacks from the bushes—they had served only to keep the undesirables from The Abigail. But a suitor to suit? Sir Sweetums wrinkled his aristocratic nose disdainfully. Nary a one, dear reader, nary a one!

That was before. Two years into his post-ninth life and subsequent Guardian Feline Association membership, Sir Sweetums had found the Right One for The Abigail.

Now it was just a question of bringing them together.

"Hey, Boss, uh, is you ready to go yet?"

Sir Sweetums tucked a bit of stray fur behind his left ear. "Yes, my friend, I believe the time has come. You saw to the details?"

"Yeah, Boss. Dat movie's on right now. Only how come dey don't have no parts for no Guardian Animals in dat one?"

"Perhaps The Capra was allergic."

A thoughtful expression descended onto the bulldog's pudgy face. "Yeah," he said, nodding slowly. "Maybe dat's it." He looked up at Sir Sweetums and snapped to attention when he saw the feline was poised to jump. "Anyting else, Boss, befores you go? Some Tenda Viddles? A sawsah of haf n' haf?"

Sir Sweetums was already leaping down athletically from the cloud. "No time, dear Bruno," he called back. "We mustn't keep Fate waiting any longer!"

"Good luck, Boss! You's gonna need it," Bruno added, in an undertone. "Dames," he said, with a slow shake of his head. "Whatcha gonna do wit 'em?"

Chapter One

IT *WASN'T* A wonderful life.

Abigail Moira Garrett stood on the bridge and stared down into the murky waters below her. She couldn't even find a decently rushing river to throw herself into. The best she could do was Murphy's Pond and the little one-lane bridge that arched over the narrow end of it. Instead of meeting her end in a torrent of water, she'd probably do no better than strangle herself in the marshy weeds below. It was indicative of how her life had been going lately.

It had all started last Monday. Her power had gone off during the night, causing her to sleep until ten A.M. The phone call from her boss had been what had woken her. He'd told her not to bother coming in. Ever.

If only it had stopped there. But it hadn't. And why? Because she'd uttered the words, "It can't get any worse than this." Those were magical words, guaranteed to prove the utterer wrong, words that drew every contrary force in the universe to zero in on the speaker with single-minded intensity.

Tuesday she'd been informed that because of a glitch in the system, it would take several weeks to collect unemployment.

Wednesday she'd been informed that she wouldn't be getting any unemployment because her Social Security number didn't exist. If she wanted to take it up with the Social Security office, their number was . . .

Thursday, her landlord had told her he wanted her out.

Being between jobs, she had now become a freeloader and he wasn't taking any chances on her.

Chest pains had begun that night.

On Friday her fiancé, whom she had always considered boyishly charming, boyishly mannered, and boyishly handsome, had left her a note telling her that since she no longer had a job and wouldn't be able to support him in the style to which he wanted to become accustomed after they married, he was moving on to greener pastures. To the woman in the apartment next door, to be exact.

And now, on top of everything else, Christmas was three days away. Christmas was meant to be spent with family, basking in the glow of friendship, food, and hearthfire. All she had to bask in was the odor of sweat socks that permeated her apartment, despite her attempts to dispel it. She had no family, no hopes for posterity anytime soon and, most especially, no cat.

She dragged her sleeve across her eyes. This was her second catless Christmas. She should have been used to it by now, but she wasn't. Just how was one to make the acquaintance of Sir Maximillian Sweetums, live with him for ten years, then be expected to live without him? One day he'd been there and the next, *poof,* he'd been gone. She'd cried for days, looked for weeks, hoped for months. But no Sir Sweetums.

And now that darned movie had just made matters worse. She had watched George Bailey lose it all, then regain it in the most Christmassy, heartfelt of ways. It certainly had been a wonderful life for him. All watching it had done for her was make her realize just exactly what she didn't have. Good grief, she didn't even have a Social Security number anymore!

She stepped up on the first rung of the railing and stared down into the placid waters. All right, now was the time to get ahold of herself and make a few decisions. She had no intentions of jumping—not that she would have done herself much harm anyway. Well, short of getting strangled in Mr. Murphy's weeds, that is. No, she had come to face death and figure out just what it was she had to live for.

She threw out her hands as a gust of wind unbalanced her. Okay, so maybe this was a little drastic, but she was a Garrett and Garretts never did things by halves. That's what her father had always told her and she had taken it to heart. Her dad ought to have known. He'd fallen off Mt. Everest at age seventy.

She stared out over the placid pond and contemplated her situation. So, she'd lost her job. She didn't like typing for a living and she hated fetching her boss coffee. She would find something else. And her apartment was hazardous to her sense of smell. She could do better.

Her fiancé Brett could be replaced as well. What did she need with a perpetual Peter Pan who had three times as many clothes as she did, wore gallons of cologne, and deep down in his boyish heart of hearts was certain she should be supporting him while he found himself? Maybe she'd look for a different kind of guy this time, one who didn't mind working and wouldn't hog all her closet space. She crossed her heart as she made her vow. *No one who dresses better, smells nicer, or works less than I do.*

So maybe her life was in the toilet. At least she was still in the bowl, not flushed out on her way to the sewer. She could go on for another few days.

Oh, but Sir Sweetums. Abby swayed on the railing, shivering. He was irreplaceable. Even after two years, she still felt his loss. Who was she supposed to talk to now while she gardened in that little plot downstairs? Who would greet her at the end of each day with a meow that said, "and just where have you been, Miss? I positively demand your attention!" Who would wake her up in the morning with dignified pats on her cheek with his soft paw?

Meow!

Abby gasped as she saw something take a swan dive into the pond. She climbed up to the top of the railing for a better look. That had to have been a cat. It had definitely meowed and those headlights had most certainly highlighted a tail.

Headlights? A very large truck traveling at an unsafe speed rumbled over the one-lane bridge, leaving behind a hefty gust of wind. Abby made windmill-like motions with her arms as she fought to keep herself balanced on that skinny railing.

"Hey, I wasn't through sorting out my life!" she exclaimed, fighting the air.

It was no use.

Darkness engulfed her. She didn't see the pond coming, but she certainly felt it. Her breath departed with a rush as she plunged down into the water. She sank like a rock. Her chest burned with the effort of holding what little breath she still possessed.

Time stopped and she lost all sense of direction. It occurred to her, fleetingly, that Murphy's Pond wasn't that deep. Maybe she had bonked her head on a stiff bit of pond scum and was now hallucinating. Or worse.

An eternity later, her feet touched solid, though squishy, ground. With strength born of pure panic, she pushed off from the gooey pond bottom and clawed her way to the surface. She started to lose consciousness and she fought it with all her strength. No halves for this Garrett.

She burst through the surface and gulped in great lungfuls of air. She flailed about in the water to keep afloat, grateful she was breathing air and not water. Finally, she managed to stop coughing long enough to catch her breath.

And then she wished she hadn't.

The smell was blinding. Her teeth started to chatter. Maybe she had died and been sent straight along to hell. Was this what hell smelled like?

Well, at least there was dry land in sight. It was possible she had just drifted to a different part of Mr. Murphy's pond. Things floated by her, but she didn't stick around to investigate. Pond scum was better left unexamined at close range. She swam to the bank and heaved herself out of the water. She rolled over onto her back and closed her eyes, content to be on *terra firma,* still breathing, still conscious.

She had to get hold of herself. Life just wasn't that bad. Lots of people had it worse. *She* could have had it worse. She could have married Brett and watched her closet space dwindle to nothing. She could have been fetching Mr. Schlessinger coffee until she was as personable as the cactus plants he kept on his windowsill. Life had given her the chance to start over. It would be very un-Garrett-like not to take the do-over and run like hell with it.

She took a last deep breath. She needed to get up, find her car and go home. Maybe she'd stop at the Mini Mart and get a small snack. Something chocolate. Something very bad for her. Yes, that was the ticket. She sat up, pushed her hair out of her eyes and looked back over the pond, wondering just where she'd wound up.

She froze.

Then her jaw went slack.

It seemed that the moon had come out. How nice. It illuminated the countryside quite well. She blinked. Then she rubbed her eyes.

She wasn't sitting on the bank of Murphy's Pond. She was sitting on the bank of a moat.

She looked to her left. What should have been the bridge over the narrow end of the pond, wasn't. It looked like a drawbridge. She followed it across the water, then looked up. She blinked some more, but it didn't help.

All right, so maybe she *had* died and gone to hell. But she'd always assumed hell was very warm, what with all that fire and brimstone dotting the landscape. She definitely wasn't warm and she definitely wasn't looking at brimstone. She was looking at a castle.

She groaned and flopped back onto the grass. *Faint, damn it!* she commanded herself.

Shoot. It was that blasted Garrett constitution coming to the fore. Garretts never fainted. But did they lose their minds? Abby turned that thought over in her head for a few minutes. She didn't know of anyone in the family having lost it. Lots of deaths of Garretts of grandparent vintage driving at unsafe speeds, skiing down unsafe hills, climbing up things better admired from a distance. But no incontinence, incapacity, or insanity.

Meow.

Abby sat up so fast, she saw stars. She put her hand to her head. Once the world had settled back down to normal rotation, she looked around frantically.

"Sir Sweetums?" Abby called.

Meow, came the answer, to her left.

Abby looked, then did a double take. "Sir Sweetums!" She jumped to her feet. "It's you!"

There, not twenty feet from her, sat her beloved Sir Maximillian Sweetums, staring at her with what could only be described as his dignified kitty look. He flicked his ears at her.

Abby took a step forward, then froze. What did this mean? Surely Sir Sweetums hadn't been packed off to hell. But she had the feeling he just couldn't be alive. Did that mean she was dead, too?

Without further ado, she pulled back and slapped herself smartly across the face.

"Yeouch!" she exclaimed, rubbing her cheek. Well, that answered a few questions. Though Sir Sweetums might have left his corporeal self behind, she certainly hadn't.

But, whatever his status, His Maximillianness was obviously in a hurry to be off somewhere. He gave her another meow, then hopped up on all fours, did a graceful leap to change his direction, and headed toward the drawbridge.

"Hey," Abby said, "wait!"

And Sir Sweetums, being himself, ignored her. That was the thing about cats; they had minds of their own.

"Sir Sweetums, wait!"

The blasted cat was now on the drawbridge and heading straight for the castle.

The castle?

"I'll deal with that later," Abby promised herself.

Later—when she figured out why the moonlight was shining down on walls topped with towers and those little slits that looked just about big enough for a man to squeeze through and either shoot something at you, or fling boiling oil at you. Later—when she'd decided just what she was: dead or alive, in heaven or hell. Later—when she'd had a bath to remove the lovely fragrance of *eau de sewer* from her hair and clothes.

"Hey, stop!" Abby exclaimed, thumping across the drawbridge. She pulled up short at the sight of the gate. It looked suspiciously like something she'd seen in a documentary on medieval castles. Abby took a deep breath and added that little detail to her list of things to worry about later. Now she had to catch her fleeing feline before he slipped through the gate grates.

She made a diving leap for Sir Sweetums's tail. She wound up flat on her face in a puddle of mud, clutching a fistful of what should have been cat hair.

She jumped to her feet and took hold of the gate, peering through the grates. They were about ten inches square—big enough for her to see through, but definitely not big enough to squeeze through.

"Sir Sweetums," she crooned, in her best come-here-I-have-some-half-and-half-in-your-favorite-china-bowl voice.

Nothing. Drat.

"Come on, Max," she tried, in her best aw-shucks-cut-me-some-slack voice.

Not even a swish of a tail to let her know she'd been heard.

"Get back over here, you stupid cat!" she hollered.

That wasn't working either. No cat. No castle owners either. Well, maybe they were asleep.

She thought about waiting for morning to call for help but all it took was one good whiff of herself to decide that *that* wasn't an option. Maybe that was all part of hell, too. Phantom cats, sewer-like stench clinging to one's clothes, delusional surroundings.

She rubbed her muddy cheek thoughtfully. It was still sore. She felt far too corporeal for the afterlife. Nope, she wasn't dead. Totally in control of her faculties was debatable, but she'd give that more thought later.

What she wanted now was a hot bath and a mug of Swiss Miss with mini marshmallows. She was a damsel in definite distress. Maybe there was a handsome knight inside ready to rescue her from her less than best-dressed self.

She started to yell.

Chapter Two

MILES DE PIAGET shifted in his chair, shoved his feet closer to the fire blazing in the middle of the great hall, and tried to fall asleep. He had a bed, but he'd shunned it in favor of the hard chair. He likely could have contented himself with merely choking on the abundance of smoke in his hall, but somehow this dual torture had suited him better. Of course had he remained at his sire's keep, he could have been sitting in a more comfortable chair, enjoying the festivities of the season in a smokeless hall. Artane was a thoroughly modern place, with hearths set into the walls and flues to carry the smoke outside.

But Miles had sought discomfort and Speningethorpe certainly provided him with that. It was, politely, a bloody sty. Miles knew he was fortunate to have arrived and found the place possessing a roof. But he'd wanted it. He'd all but demanded it. He'd wanted a place of refuge. What with the pair of years he'd just survived, peace and quiet was what he'd needed, no matter the condition of the surroundings.

He never should have made the journey to the Holy Land. Aye, that was the start to all his troubles. Now, staring back on the ruins of his life, he wondered why his reasons had seemed so compelling at the time. It wasn't as if he'd had to prove himself to his sire, or to the rest of the countryside, for that matter. He vaguely remembered a desire to see what his father and brothers had seen on their travels.

Perhaps the tale would have finished peaceably if he'd

been able to keep his bloody mouth shut on his way home. Soured and disillusioned after returning from Jerusalem, he'd let his tongue run free at the expense of a former French Crusader. If he'd but known whom he'd been insulting!

He shook aside his thoughts. It did no good to dwell on the past. He'd escaped France with his flesh unscorched and he had his grandfather to thank for that. He'd been home for four months already; it was past time he sent word and thanked the man for the timely rescue. He would, just as soon as he'd brooded enough to suit himself. That time surely wouldn't come before the celebrations were over. Had he ever possessed any desire to celebrate the birth of the Lord, he had it no longer. He'd seen too many atrocities committed for the sake of preserving holy relics. Nay, what he wanted was silence, far away from his family, far away from their joy and laughter. He had no heart for such things.

His father hadn't argued with him. But then, Rhys of Artane had had his own taste of war and such, and he understood. He'd asked no questions, simply given in to Miles's demand for the desolate bit of soil without comment. His only action had been to see stores sent along after the fact by a generously-manned garrison. Miles had kept the foodstuffs, but sent the men back. He would hear about that soon enough. He smiled grimly. His father would be provoked mightily by the act. Hopefully his mother had the furnishings secured well.

The wood popped, startling him. He shifted in his chair, then paused. Was that a voice?

Surely his father wouldn't have ridden from Artane so soon. Miles frowned. He would have to investigate, obviously. He pushed himself to his feet, feeling far older than his score and four years. The saints pity him if he ever reached his sire's age. He was exhausted already by living.

He walked to the hall door, then unbolted it by heaving a wooden beam from its iron brackets. He set the beam aside and pulled the heavy door back.

There was most definitely someone at the gates. Miles sighed heavily and returned to his chair for his sword. It would have been wise to don at least a mail shirt, but he had no squire to aid him, nor any energy to arm himself alone. A sword and a frown would have to suffice. He snatched a torch from a sconce on the wall and left the great hall. Perhaps he'd been too hasty in his decision to leave the servants behind. It was much easier to ask who was at the gates than to discover the truth of the matter for oneself.

Miles walked toward the lone gatehouse in the bailey wall. There were times he wondered why anyone had bothered with even the one wall surrounding the keep. Speningethorpe was very assailable, a fact he didn't think on overmuch. Who would want the place?

"Open up, damn it!"

Miles stopped in the gatehouse tunnel, too surprised to do anything else but stare. There was some sort of creature pounding on his portcullis, babbling things in a rapid, obviously irritated manner.

The creature stopped its tirade and then hopped up and down.

"Oh, someone's home! Great. Can you open this gate? I lost my cat inside. At least I think it's my cat. He looks like Sir Sweetums, but I don't know how that can be." The being stopped speaking suddenly and looked at him.

Miles looked back. He took another step closer, holding out the torch.

"Am I in hell?" the creature asked, uncertainly.

Miles almost smiled. "Near to it, certainly."

"Really?" This was said with a gasp.

Miles took another step forward. The being before him was covered with muck. He frowned. Perhaps it was a demon come to torment him. The saints knew he deserved it. He'd committed enough sins in his youth to warrant a legion of demons haunting him for the rest of his days.

But did demons smell so foul? That was a point he wasn't sure on. He considered it as he gave the mud-covered harpy before him another look. It had to be a harpy. He'd heard of such creatures roaming about in Greece. They were part woman, part bird. This being certainly chirped like the latter. She spoke the peasant's tongue, poorly, and her accent was passing strange. Miles frowned. Had she truly come from Greece? Then how had she come to be standing outside his gates?

"Look, can't you at least open up? I'm freezing and I stink."

Miles considered. "Indeed, there is a most foul odor that attends you."

"I went for a swim in your moat."

"Ah," he said. "That explains much."

The harpy frowned at him. Miles took a step closer to her. She was a very plump harpy, indeed. Her arms were excessively puffy, as was her middle. She had scrawny legs, though. No doubt in keeping with her bird-like half. He stared at her legs thoughtfully. She wore very strange hose. Even stranger shoes. He leaned closer. Her foot coverings might have been white at one time. It was hard to tell their present color by torchlight, but he had little trouble identifying the stench.

"Hey," the being chirped at him, "would you just let me in already?"

He hesitated. "Are you truly a harpy?"

The creature scowled at him. "Of course not. Who are you? The gatekeeper of hell?"

Miles laughed, in spite of himself. "You insult both me and my fine hall, and now I am to let you inside?"

The woman, who claimed not to be a harpy, looked at him with a frown. "Hall?"

"Speningethorpe," he clarified.

"And just where is that?" she demanded.

He shrugged. "It depends on the year, and who is king. 'Tis nearer Hadrian's wall. Some years it finds itself in England, some years in Scotland. A lovely place, really, if you've no use for creature comforts."

The woman swayed. "England? Scotland?"

"Aye," Miles said.

The woman sat down with a thump. "I'm dreaming."

Miles wrinkled his nose. "Nay, I think you aren't. I know I'm not."

The woman looked up at him. He thought she might be on the verge of tears. It was hard to tell with all that mud on her face.

"I'm having a very bad day," she whispered.

"Demoiselle, your wits are most definitely addled. 'Tis no longer daytime. 'Tis well past midnight."

She nodded numbly. "You're right."

Miles looked down at her and, despite his better judgment, felt a small stirring of pity. She was shivering. What she truly was, he couldn't tell, but she had come banging on his gates in the middle of the night seeking refuge. How could he refuse her?

He jammed the torch into a wall sconce, then turned back and looked at her.

"Are you alone?"

She nodded again, silently.

"No retainers lie in wait, ready to storm my keep and take it by force after I let you in?"

She looked up at him and blinked. "Retainers?"

"Men-at-arms."

"No. Just me and my stinky self."

Miles almost smiled. "Very well, then. The both of you may come in. I'll raise the gate just far enough for you to wriggle under, agreed?"

"Whatever you say."

Miles propped his sword up against the wall and trudged up the steps to the upper floor of the gatehouse. For all he knew, the woman could be lying. She could very possibly be a decoy some Lowland laird had sent to prepare the way for an assault.

He found himself cranking up the portcullis just the same.

"Are you inside?" he called down.

He heard a faint answer in the affirmative. He released the crank and the portcullis slammed home. Miles thumped down the circular steps. He realized as he retrieved his sword and the torch that he was relieved to find both still in their places. The years had taken their toll, he thought with a regretful sigh.

Well, at least the woman was still alone and not accompanied by two score of armed men. That wouldn't have done much for his mood. His guest was standing just inside the gate. She smiled at him, seemingly a little self-conscious.

"I'm sorry to barge in on you like this. I need a bath and then I'd like to look for my cat."

"Cat?" His nose began to twitch at the very thought of such a beast. He rubbed the possibly offended appendage almost without thought. "Cat, did you say?"

"You're allergic?" she asked.

"Allergic?"

She looked at him closely. "You know, you sneeze when you smell one?"

"Aye, that I do, demoiselle. If your beastie has wandered into my keep, I daresay we'll have no trouble locating him."

She laughed. Miles found himself smiling in response.

Saints above, he was going daft. He'd just let a stranger inside his gates without demanding to know aught of her business save that she was seeking a missing feline. Her person did nothing to recommend her—especially since it was all he could do to breathe the same air she occupied. But her laugh was enchanting.

Without warning, Miles felt a surge of good humor well up in him. 'Twas true he could have remained at Artane and joined in the festivities eventually, but if he had, he wouldn't be standing at his gates with this woman. Beyond reason, he couldn't help but think he'd made the right choice.

He made her a small bow. "Miles of Artane, lately of Speningethorpe, your servant." He straightened and gave her his best lordly look. She didn't respond. He cleared his throat. Perhaps she merely needed something else to be impressed by. No sense in not making use of his connections. "My sire is Rhys de Piaget," he said. "Lord of Artane."

She looked at him blankly.

"You know him not?" Miles asked, surprised. His father's reputation stretched from Hadrian's wall to the Holy Land. And what reputation Rhys hadn't managed to spread, Miles's older brothers Robin and Nicholas had seen to. Surely this woman knew something of his family.

Her mouth worked, but nothing came out.

"Saints, lady, even the lairds in the Lowlands know of my sire."

She swallowed. "I think I'm really losing it here."

Miles frowned. "What have you lost?"

"My mind." She shook her head, as if that would somehow solve the problem. It must not have helped, because she gathered herself together and gave the whole of her a good, hard shake.

Miles hastily backed up to avoid wearing what she'd shaken off.

"Look," she said with a frown, "I'm confused. Now, am I in hell, or not? Telling me the truth is the least you can do."

"Nay, lady, you are not in hell," he said. "As I said before, you are at Speningethorpe. 'Tis in the north of England, on the Scottish border."

"And you're Miles of Ar-something, lately of this other Spending place, right?"

Close enough. "Aye."

She shook her head. "Impossible. I can't be in England. I was in Freezing Bluff, Michigan, half an hour ago. I fell into a pond." She was starting to wheeze. "I couldn't have resurfaced in England. Things like this just don't happen!" Her voice was growing increasingly frantic.

"Perhaps the chill has bewildered you," he offered.

"I'm not bewildered! I smell too bad to be bewildered!"

He had to agree, but he refrained from saying so.

"England! Geez! And backwoods England at that!"

"Backwoods?" he echoed.

"Backwoods," she repeated. She looked at him accusingly. "I bet you don't have running water, do you?"

Miles gestured apologetically toward the moat. "I fear the water runs nowhere. Hence the less than pleasing smell—"

"Or a phone?"

"Phone?" he echoed.

"Oh, great!" she exclaimed. "This is just *great!* No phone, no running water. I bet I'll have to haul my own water for a bath too, right?"

"Nay, lady. I will see to that for you." Let her think he was being polite. In reality, he didn't want her moving overmuch inside. She was sopping wet and he didn't want moat water being dripped all over his hall, sty that it was. Having the cesspit emptied into the moat had seemed a fine deterrent to attackers at the time, but he wondered about the wisdom of it now.

"Look," she said, planting her hands on her fluffy waist, "I appreciate the hospitality, such as it is, but what I really need from you is a bath, some hot chocolate and a bed, pretty much in that order. Sir Sweetums will have to wait until tomorrow. Things will look brighter in the morning."

She said the last as if she dared him to disagree with her.

So he nodded, as if he did agree with her.

"And then I'll figure out where the hell I am."

He nodded again. Whatever else she planned, she certainly needed a bath. Perhaps her wits would return with a bit of cleanliness.

"Garretts never have hysterics," she said sternly, wagging her finger at him.

"Ah," he said, wisely. "Good to know." The saints only knew what hysterics were, but he had the feeling he should be relieved the woman before him never had them.

"You are a Garrett?" he surmised.

"Abigail Moira Garrett."

"Abigail," he repeated.

"Right. But don't call me that. Only my grandmother called me that, and only when I was doing something I shouldn't have been. Call me Abby."

"I like Abigail better," he stated.

She gave him a dark look. "Well, we'll work on that later. Now, let's go get that bath, shall we?"

Miles watched her march off toward the stables. He smiled in spite of himself. The saints only knew from whence this creature had sprung, but that didn't trouble him. He'd seen many strange things in his travels. He liked her spirit. She made him smile with her bluster and babble.

"Miles?"

"Aye, Abigail?"

"I can't see where I'm going," she said, sounding as if that were entirely his doing.

"That shouldn't matter, as the direction you've chosen is the wrong one. The great hall is this way."

She appeared within the circle of his torchlight again. "Great hall? What's so great about it? Do you have central heat? What, no phone but a great furnace?"

Miles didn't even attempt to understand her. He inclined his head to his right. "This way, my lady. I'll see to a bath for you."

He led her to the hall, ushered her inside and rehung the torch. He set the bar back across the door. That was when he heard her begin to wheeze again.

"Garretts do not faint. Garretts do not faint."

"I'll be back for you when the tub is filled," he said, giving her his most reassuring smile. "Things will look better after a bath."

She nodded. "Garretts do not faint," she answered.

Miles laughed to himself as he crossed the hall to the entrance to the kitchens. If she continued to tell herself that, she just might believe it.

Chapter Three

ABBY SAT IN a crude wooden washtub and contemplated life and its mysteries. It gave her a headache, but she contemplated just the same. Garretts didn't shy away from the difficult.

No phone, no electricity, and no Mini Mart down the street. Things were looking grim. She looked around her and the grimness increased. Had she stumbled upon a pocket of backwoodsiness so undiscovered that it resembled something from the Middle Ages? The fire in the hearth gave enough light to illuminate a kitchen containing stone floors, rough-hewn tables and crude black kettles. Not exactly *Better Homes and Gardens* worthy.

Abby stood up and rinsed off with water of questionable cleanliness. She wasn't sure she felt much better. Even the soap Miles had given her was gross. She decided right then that she was a low fat person, especially when it came to soap. At least she thought she'd just washed with a glob of animal fat. She filed that away with half a dozen other things she would digest later. On the brighter side, though, at least she didn't smell so much like a sewer anymore. She'd splurge on a fancy bar of soap when she got home.

She dried off with a completely inadequate piece of cloth, then looked at what Miles had given her to wear: coarse homespun tights and a coarse linen tunic. Not exactly off-the-rack garments, but they would do. She put the clothes on, *sans* her dripping wet underthings, and found, not surprisingly, that Miles' hand-me-downs were much too large. They might have fit if she'd kept her oversized down coat on under them, but there was no wearing that at present. She kept the tights hitched up with one hand while she dumped her clothes and coat into the washtub with the other. She'd let them soak for a while. She didn't want to wash her leather Keds, but she had no choice. She dunked them in the tub a few times with everything else.

"Hachoo!"

The sneeze echoed in the great hall. Abby dropped her shoes in the tub and ran for the doorway. She slipped and skidded her way out into the large gathering hall. Miles was standing by the wood piled high in the middle of the room, sneezing for all he was worth. He looked at her and scowled.

"Dab cat," he said, dragging his sleeve across his furiously tearing eyes.

"Where?" Abby said, looking around frantically. "Sir Sweetums! Here, kitty, kitty."

She saw a flash of something head toward the back of the hall.

"Damn cat," she exclaimed, taking a firm grip on her borrowed clothes and giving chase. "Come back here!"

"Abigail, wait!"

Oh, like Miles would be any help in catching the spirited feline. Abby scrambled up the tight, circular stairs, almost losing her balance and the bottom half of her clothes.

"Here, kitty, kitty—whoa!"

She would have fallen face first into nothingness if it hadn't been for that arm suddenly around her waist, pulling her back from the gaping hole that was the top of the stairs.

"We're missing some of the passageway and a good deal of roof," Miles said, panting. "By the saints, woman, you frightened me!"

His fingers investigated a bit more around her waist. Abby would have elbowed him, but her situation was too precarious.

"What happened to your middle?" he asked. "And your arms?" He frisked her expertly. "Saints, I thought you were excessively plump!"

"That was my down coat, you creep. Stop groping me!"

"Hrumph," he said. His fingers stilled, but he didn't move.

"Just what manner of woman are you, Abigail Garrett?"

"One on the verge of heart failure—if Garretts had heart failure, which we do not. Now, can we please go back downstairs? It's really drafty up here." She looked out into the shadows. "And I've lost Sir Sweetums again." She had the most ridiculous urge to sit down and cry. "Just when I thought I had him. But how can I have him? He's gone." An unbidden tear slipped down her cheek. "I'm losing it." She sighed heavily. "I'll be the first in my family to go that way, you know. Garretts never lose it. We die in flamboyant, reckless ways. We never go quietly. Except me. I'm such a familial failure."

"The only place you are going, Abigail, is to a chair before the fire. You'll catch the ague here in this night air."

"Don't call me Abigail."

He grunted. "Turn around and keep hold of my hand. These stairs are steep."

Abby followed him, because he had her hand in his and didn't seem to want to let go. She didn't want to go downstairs. She wanted to keep her eyes peeled for her cat, who should have been chasing butterflies in heaven. Instead, he was causing an allergic reaction to an inhabitant of hell.

"I'm tired," she said.

And with that, she pitched forward. She felt herself be caught and lifted.

"Saints, woman, but you are a mystery."

"I can't handle any more tonight," Abby whispered.

She felt herself lowered onto something relatively soft.

"Then take your rest, slight one. Things will look better in the morning."

Abby thought they just might, especially since the last thing she heard was a sneeze.

ABBY WOKE, STRETCHED, and shuddered. What a lousy night. And what an awful dream! Too many chocolate chips eaten straight from the bag. She'd have to coat them in cookie dough the next time around to diffuse the impact.

She rolled out of bed with her eyes closed, mentally halfway to the shower before her feet hit the floor.

"Oof!" the floor exclaimed.

Abby stumbled as the floor under her feet moved. She

would have hit the ground if it hadn't been for those hands that came out of nowhere and caught her. How it happened she couldn't have said, but she soon found herself sprawled out over a long, impressively muscled form, staring down into dark eyes. She looked into them for several moments before she figured out their color. Gray. Dark gray. Like storm clouds.

So, it wasn't a dream. Miles of Spend-whatever held her up just far enough for her to get a good look at his face. She really felt as though she should be polite and get up, but she found she just couldn't.

The torchlight from last night just hadn't done justice to this guy. Maybe she'd been distracted at the time by the clamoring her sense of smell had set up. She must have smelled *very* badly. It was the only possible reason she could have done anything besides gape at the man she was currently using as a beanbag.

She propped her elbows up on his chest and took advantage of her vantage point. He was a stunner, even if he was a little bit on the unkempt side thanks to an abundance of shaggy dark hair and a stubble-covered chin. He was beautiful in a rough, mountain man kind of way. He probably lived off the land for months at a time. No fighting for mirror space with this guy, no sir. Abby felt her blood pressure increase at the thought. He probably limited his toilette to dragging his hands through his hair a few times each day and shaving when his face got too itchy. She had the feeling he didn't use hairspray or mousse—which meant her feet wouldn't stick to his bathroom floor. Oh, yes, this was her kind of man. Handsome *and* low-maintenance.

"Hmmm," she said.

"Hmmm," he replied.

He was giving her the same once-over. He reached up and fingered her hair. It was unruly hair, she knew, and she opened her mouth to make an excuse for the riot of auburn curls, when he met her gaze and smiled.

"You have beautiful hair, Abigail."

Okay, if he wanted to like it, he was welcome to.

"Indeed, you clean up very passably."

"What do you mean I clean up just passably?" she demanded. "I was giving you much higher marks than that."

He grinned. "Indeed."

Abby tried to hold onto her annoyance, but it didn't last long against the dimple that appeared in his cheek.

"Oh, you *are* cute," she said, feeling a little breathless.

"I take that to mean you find me tolerable to look at."

"Who, you? Of course not. I was just talking about your dimple. The rest of you isn't even passable."

He laughed. "Disrespectful wench. You've no idea whom you're insulting."

"At least I gave you credit for one decent feature," she grumbled. She started to move off him, then got a good look at his floor. "Geez, Miles, what's the deal with your living room here? Are you planning on bringing barnyard animals inside anytime soon?"

He sighed. "I know the rushes need changing."

"Yeech," she said, climbing gingerly onto the bed. It was then she realized that she'd slept on a bed while he'd slept on a blanket on the floor. On the rotting hay, rather. She frowned at him. "Why didn't you just go sleep in another bed?"

"There is no other bed."

"Well," she said, slowly, "I appreciate the gallant gesture, but you wouldn't have had to make it if you didn't run such a lousy hotel. You know, inn," she clarified at his blank look.

He shook his head, with a small smile. "This is no inn, my lady."

"Spend-whatever. If that isn't a name for an inn, I don't know what is."

"Speningethorpe. 'Tis the name of my hall. I know 'tisn't much, but it gave me peace and quiet."

"Until last night."

He shrugged. "Perhaps too much peace and quiet isn't a good thing."

"All right," she said, crossing her legs underneath herself, "if you don't run an inn, what do you do? Is it just you here?" At that moment a surprisingly distressing thought occurred to her. "Are you married?" she demanded. She looked around. "Is there a wife hiding in here somewhere? This is all I need—"

A large hand came to rest over her mouth. Miles sat up, then took his hand away.

"Nay, no wife. Women do not like me."

"Really?" she asked, looking at him and finding that very

hard to believe. "Good grief, is everyone blind here in back-woods England?" She clapped her own hand over her mouth when she realized what she'd said. "I meant—"

He was grinning. "I know what you meant, Abigail. And I thank you for the compliment. But even though I am a knight with land of my own, women don't care overmuch for my past accomplishments."

"And just what would those be?" Great. Out of all the places she could have resurfaced, she'd resurfaced in the moat of someone with questionable past accomplishments.

But at least he had accomplishments. And what was this business about being a knight? Maybe that was why he carried a sword. Abby looked at him thoughtfully. It couldn't hurt to reserve judgment until she found out more about him. She realized that she was already stacking him up against her Ideal Man list, but she could hardly help herself. After all, he had given her the only bed in his house. He was easily the most appealing man she had seen in years. He liked her hair. He had a great accent. He wasn't much of a housekeeper, but that could be fixed. The first thing to do was move the barn-like *accoutrements* outside—

"—burn me at the stake—"

"Huh?" she exclaimed, tuning back in. "Run that one by me again."

He looked at her with a frown. "Haven't you been listening?"

"No. I've been cataloging your good points. I don't think this is one of them."

He shook his head with a slow smile. "I was telling you that I'd just recently escaped being burned at the stake. For heresy."

"For *what?*"

"Heresy—which was a lie, of course. I had simply made the grave error of expressing my views on the Crusades," Miles said. "I was traveling through France this past fall, hav-ing just returned from the Holy Land, where I saw and heard tell of ruthless slaughter. To be sure, I could find nothing to recommend the whole Crusading affair. One night I sought shelter at an inn. I slipped well into my cups, but came back to myself a goodly while after I'd already disparaged my table companion, a man I soon learned was a former Crusader and a powerful French count."

"And what did he do to you? Threaten a lawsuit?" Trouble with the law, Abby noted. That could definitely be a mark in the negative column.

Miles smiled. "The law had nothing to do with it, my lady. He sent for his bishop, threw together an impromptu inquisition—of souls without any authority, I might add—and convicted me of both heresy and witchcraft."

"Witchcraft?" Abby eased herself back on the bed. There was no doubt about *that* being a red flag.

He snorted. "Aye, if you can stomach that. The count's witnesses—paid for handsomely, of course—claimed they had seen me conversing with my familiar."

"And that would be?"

"A fluffy black cat."

Abby laughed. "Oh, right. That would have been a pretty one-sided conversation, what with you sneezing your head off."

Miles smiled. "I laughed as well, at first. I sobered abruptly when I saw the wood piled high around the stake and one of the count's men standing there with a lit torch."

"Good grief," she said, "they really weren't going to do it, were they? What kind of backwater town were you in, anyway? Hadn't they ever heard of Amnesty International? Human rights activists would have been all over this."

"I daresay the count's men had heard of many things, yet they fully intended to do the man's bidding. They secured me to the post, but not without a goodly struggle on my part."

Abby was speechless. What was the world coming to? She made a mental note to avoid rural France as a travel destination.

"The count had taken the torch himself and was giving me a last fanatical spewing forth of religious prattle when a miracle occurred."

Abby found she was clutching the edge of the bed with both hands. "What?" she breathed. "A downpour?"

Miles laughed. " 'Twould have been fitting, to be sure. Nay, 'twas my grandsire, whom I had been traveling to meet. His men overcame the count's, he set me free and I fled like a kicked whelp, not even bothering to offer him a kiss of peace. Needless to say, my journeying in France was thereafter very short-lived."

"Did you tell the police about that guy? What a nutcase!"

"Police?" he echoed, stumbling over the word. "What is that?"

Abby frowned. "You know, the authorities."

"Ah," Miles said, nodding, "you mean Louis. Nay, I did not think it wise to chance a visit to court. My grandsire sent word a fortnight after I arrived home telling me that he'd seen the matter settled." Miles said pleasantly. "The sly old fox has something of a reputation. I daresay he applied the sword liberally, as well as informing the king of what went on."

"Sword?" Well, Miles seemed to have one handy. Maybe his entire family had a thing about metal. "And what do you mean he informed the king?" she asked. "What king?"

"Louis. Louis IX, King of France."

"But France doesn't have a king," she pointed out.

"Aye, it does."

"No, it doesn't. It has a president."

"Nay, it has a king. Louis IX. A good king, as far as they go."

Abby scrambled to her feet, careful to keep them on blanket-covered floor. As an afterthought, she made a grab for her tights to keep them from falling to her knees.

"France does *not* have a king," she insisted.

Miles jumped to his feet just as quickly.

"How can you not know of King Louis?" he asked.

"What is he, some fringe guy trying to overthrow the government?"

"He's the bloody king of that whole realm!" Miles exclaimed. He looked at her as if she'd lost her mind. "Next you will tell me that you know nothing of Henry."

"Henry who?"

"Henry III, King of England!"

"No, no, no," she said, shaking her head. "Henry isn't king. There's little prince *Harry,* but he's just the spare heir. Elizabeth is queen."

"Elizabeth? Who is Elizabeth?"

He was starting to sound as exasperated as she felt.

"All right," she said, taking a deep breath. "Let's start from the beginning. And can we go sit by the fire? I'm cold."

"Gladly," Miles said. He shoved his feet into boots, then

clomped over to the pile of logs in the middle of the room and built up the fire.

Abby tiptoed gingerly into the kitchen and put on her Keds. They weren't as dry as they could have been, but it beat the heck out of wearing more of Miles's floor on the bottoms of her tights than she was already. She squished her way over to the fire to face her scowling host.

Miles folded his arms across his chest. "Let us see if we cannot untangle this snarl inside your head."

"My head?" she said. "I'm not the one who's confused."

"Aye, but you are!"

"I am not! France does *not* have a king, and neither does England. England has a queen and her name is Elizabeth!"

"It has a king and his name is *Henry!*"

Abby smirked. "I'd say let's turn on the TV and see what the local newscaster says, but I'll bet you don't have a TV either, do you?"

"Nay, I do not," he said, stiffly. "Nor would I have one."

"Ha," she said. "You don't even know what a TV is."

He scowled fiercely. "Aye, I do."

"Do not."

"How would you know what I do and do not know?"

"You don't have any electricity, bucko. It's a dead giveaway."

He growled at her. "You are a most infuriating woman."

"Really?" she said, surprised. She smiled suddenly. "How nice. I've always wanted to be infuriating. It looks like the Garrett blood is really coming out. My grandmother would be so proud."

"I think I'd like to wring it all from you, for 'tis most— ha . . . ha . . . hachoo!"

Abby barely stepped aside in time to avoid the product of his violent sneeze. She grabbed his arm.

"Hush," she whispered, frantically. "Sir Sweetums has to be nearby."

Miles panted through his mouth. "Sir Sweetubs? What kind of a nabe is that for a bloody cat?"

"It's a term of endearment. Like this: sweetie pie, honey bunch, snookums." She tickled him under the chin for effect. "See?"

Miles scowled. "I see noth—ha . . . ha—"

Abby put her finger under his nose to plug it. "Don't even think about it, toots. We've got a kitty to find. Don't make any sudden moves."

She kept her finger under his nose as they turned slowly in a circle.

"See anything?" she whispered.

"Nay."

"Keep looking."

They turned another circle and Miles froze suddenly. "There," he said, softly.

Sir Sweetums was sitting next to the hall door.

"Perhaps he will cobe if you call to hib," Miles said, breathing through his mouth. He was obviously fighting his sneeze.

"Here, kitty, kitty," Abby said. She beckoned. "Come here, Sir Sweetums. Miles won't hurt you. He likes cats."

Miles muffled a sneeze in his sleeve.

"All right, his nose doesn't, but the rest of him does."

Abby took a step forward. Sir Sweetums got to his feet, gave her a meow she couldn't quite interpret, turned on his heel and, with his tail held high, walked through the door.

Through the closed door.

Miles staggered. He threw his arms around her and clutched her.

"Merciful St. Michael," he breathed. "I did not see what I just saw."

Abby would have felt the same way, but she had inside information. It was hard to swallow, but she had the feeling Sir Maximillian Sweetums was a ghost. She held onto her shaking host and wondered just how to break the news to him.

"Things of this nature do not happen," Miles said, his voice hushed. "'Tis a modern age. I do not believe what I have just seen."

Abby looked up at him. "Honey, I think you're living in the past. Everyone else has indoor plumbing."

"How much more modern an age can it be?" he asked, returning her look, his eyes wide. "I don't care overmuch for his politics, but King Henry is a most forward-thinking monarch."

She rolled her eyes. "Oh, brother. Not that again."

"Aye, that again," he said, some of the color returning to

his face. He released his deathgrip on her and stepped back a pace. "Saints, woman, where have you been?"

"Out to lunch," she returned, "obviously."

"Henry rules England," he insisted.

"No, he doesn't."

"By the very saints of heaven, you are a stubborn maid! Have you forgotten the bloody year? Who else would sit the throne in 1238?"

Abby blinked. "Huh?"

Miles clapped his free hand to his head. "That swim addled your wits, Abigail."

"What did you say before?" she managed. "What year?"

"1238. The Year of Our Lord 1238!"

Abby kept breathing. She knew that because she had to remind herself to do it. In, out, in, out. Twelve-thirty-*eight,* twelve-thirty-*eight.* She breathed in and out to that rhythm.

It couldn't be true. She looked around her at the stone room. There weren't any fireplaces; just Miles's bonfire in the middle of the room. No electricity, no central heat, no carpet. The walls were bare, leaving their stone selves fully open to perusal. No twentieth-century construction job there.

She looked down. There was stone beneath her feet, what she could feel of it beneath the layer of scum and hay. She looked around again. There were a pair of crude wooden tables near the walls, and chairs that looked rustically crafted. But that was the extent of the furniture. She took a deep breath. Well, the place certainly *smelled* like 1238.

She looked up at Miles. He stood in homespun clothing exactly like hers, wearing a very medieval frown. He didn't have the benefit of modern grooming aids, if his finger-combed hair and non-ironed tunic were any clue. He'd definitely been packing a sword the night before. He'd said he was a knight. Could that be true too?

Abby looked toward the door. Maybe if she stepped outside into the fresh air, she might have a different perspective on things.

She wanted to saunter across the great hall casually, but she had the feeling it had come out as more of a frantic get-me-the-hell-back-to-my-century kind of run.

She struggled with the heavy wooden beam that obviously

served as a dead bolt in 1238. Heavy hands came to rest on her shoulders.

"Abigail—"

"Let me out!" she shrieked.

"Abigail—" he said, starting to sound a bit concerned.

Abby wasn't just a bit concerned. She was on the verge of having hysterics—and she was starting not to care just exactly what Garretts did and did not do.

"Please!" she begged.

Miles heaved the beam aside and opened the door, in spite of her attempts to help. She ran outside.

It was raining. She slogged straight into three inches of muck.

"Yuck!" she exclaimed.

She would have run anywhere just to be running, but she couldn't seem to get her feet unstuck from the goo.

"Abigail."

Before she could tell Miles just what had her so frantic, she found herself turned around bodily and gathered against a very firm, very warm body. Without giving his good or bad points any more thought, she threw her arms around him and clung.

"Oh, man," she said, feeling herself beginning to wheeze again. It was a nasty habit she'd gotten into lately. She was certain wheezing was something no respectable Garrett ever found herself doing. "Oh, man, oh, man," she wheezed again.

"By the saints, you're trembling," Miles said, sounding surprised. He stroked her back with his large hand. "There's nothing to fear, Abigail."

"It's 1238!" she exclaimed against his very rough, very un-department-store-like shirt.

"See?" Miles said, obviously trying to sound soothing. "You've remembered the year. 'Tis a most encouraging sign. I'm certain 'twas simply a bit of chill that seeped into your head and addled your wits for a time. Reason is most definitely returning to you."

Abby felt her tights beginning to slip and she made a grab for them before they migrated any further south. She tilted her head back and looked at Miles.

"It really is 1238, isn't it?" she whispered. "And you really are Miles of Spendingthorn—"

"Speningethorpe—"

"Whatever, and you really are a knight, aren't you?"

"For what it is worth, aye, I am."

Well, stranger things had happened. Like Sir Sweetums walking through a thick, wooden plank of a door.

Then there was her trip down into Murphy's Pond the night before to consider. That had taken an awfully long time, hadn't it?

But seven hundred years?

She rested her nose against Miles's chest and contemplated. Garretts didn't faint. Garretts didn't run away from difficulties. Garretts didn't lose their marbles.

Funny, she'd never heard anything about Garretts not time-traveling.

She looked up at Miles. "You don't believe in witches, do you?"

He smiled faintly. "Having come within scorching distance of a healthy bonfire myself, I would have to say nay, I do not believe in witches."

"Then I think you should sit down."

"Why?"

"Because you're going to fall down when I tell you what I have to tell you. It'll hurt less if you're closer to the ground."

Miles looked at her archly. "The de Piagets of Artane do not faint."

Abby reached up and patted him on his beautiful cheek. "There's a first time for everything, toots."

"Toots? Why do you persist in calling me that?"

Abby took his hand and pulled him back inside the hall. He'd just have to trust her on this one.

And she definitely hoped he'd meant what he'd said about the witch thing, or she was certain her revelations would land her in the fire.

Chapter Four

MILES FROWNED TO himself as he allowed Abigail to pull him back inside his hall. Something had obviously troubled her deeply, if her frantic flight from his fire was any indication. But what? She had looked at him as if she were seeing a ghost.

He realized abruptly that he was allowing himself to be led and he dug in his heels. Abigail stopped and looked at him with that same, almost frantic look. Miles held his ground.

"Whatever you have to tell me, you may most certainly tell me while we are standing. Indeed, I insist upon it."

He looked down at her as he said it, and wondered if *she* shouldn't be the one sitting down. She was very pale. Saints, had she suffered some sort of injury that had damaged her mind so that she barely remembered the date?

He lifted his hands and cupped her face, rubbing his thumbs gently across her cheeks. Her skin was so soft and fair. Perhaps she was a nobleman's daughter who had become lost and wandered into his moat. Never mind how she was dressed. It was possible her sire employed seamstresses with very odd ideas on fashion. He should have questioned her sooner about her family, but he'd been too bemused by her actions the night before, then too unsettled by the appearance and disappearance of her cat today to think too deeply.

She caught his right hand and looked at it. "You have more calluses on this hand than the other."

"Of course," he said.

"Why?"

"'Tis my swordarm, Abigail." He put his callused hand to her brow. She wasn't feverish. Indeed, she was chilled. "Perhaps we should repair to the fire," he said, pulling her in that direction, "then you should tell me of yourself. Forgive me for not having asked sooner. Your sire will no doubt be grieved over your loss. I will take you to him as soon as may be—"

"Honey," she said, "I think you should sit."

"Why do you call me honey?" he asked, finding himself being urged toward a chair. He sat to humor her.

"It's a term of endearment."

"Like Sir Sweetums?" he asked. "Saints, what a name!"

He would have expressed himself further on that, but Abigail had pulled up a stool in front of him and sat. The tunic he had given her to wear fell off one of her shoulders. It was exceedingly distracting.

He looked at her face and instantly ceased to mark what she said. He knew her lips were moving, but he couldn't concentrate on her strangely-accented words. There were surely a score of things that puzzled him about her, but he couldn't seem to focus his thoughts on a bloody one of them. All he could do was gaze at the woman before him and marvel.

Saying she cleaned up passing well was an understatement. Where she had come by that riotous mass of hair he did not know, but it certainly suited her. He could almost hear her saying it: "Garrett hair is never obedient." He smiled at the thought. Indeed, Abigail's hair seemed to be a reflection of the woman herself—beyond the bounds of reason or propriety.

And if her spirit hadn't intrigued him, her comeliness certainly would have. He found himself entirely distracted by thoughts of running hands and mouth over that bit of shoulder she couldn't seem to keep covered up. He followed the curve of her shoulder out to her arm and down to her hand. It was then he realized she was snapping her fingers at him.

"The lights are on but nobody's home," she was saying.

"Ah," he stalled, "I was thinking on your words."

She jerked up her tunic over her shoulder. *His* tunic—his clothing that was covering her lithe body, much as he wanted to be doing. Miles was on the verge of allowing himself to be distracted by that thought when Abigail waved at him.

"Come on, Miles," she said, sounding exasperated. "Pay

attention. I'm trying to tell you something very important."

He blinked at her. "Oh."

She sighed with exaggerated patience. "Are you with me now?"

"Indeed, we are sitting here together."

She dropped her face to her hands and laughed. Miles couldn't help himself. He reached out and ran his hand over her hair. It was pleasingly soft to the touch. It was not so dark as his, and with somewhat of a reddish tint to it. It was hair he wished he could sink his hands into as he sank another part of himself—

"Good grief!" Abigail exclaimed, jerking back upright. "Can't you just concentrate on what I'm saying for five minutes?"

"I'd rather concentrate on kissing you, if it's all the same to you," he offered.

"No," she said, firmly. "I'm serious about this."

And, suddenly, the truth struck him like a blow. He sat back and felt the blood leave his face. She was betrothed. How could he not have seen it before? Either that, or she was wed. She was no simpering maid who had to rely on her sire for every breath she took and every word to come out of her mouth. Abigail was far too sure of herself. She was likely of an age with his own score and four years, surely old enough to have been wed several years.

"Go ahead," he said, flatly, "Tell me of him."

"Who, Brett? How do you know about Brett?"

Damn. Knowing he had surmised correctly was no consolation.

"I assumed," he said curtly.

He should have stayed at Artane. What in hell's name had possessed him to come here? To hold Abigail Moira Garrett in his arms and feel himself falling in love with her unruly hair and indomitable spirit? What had made him think she might even be free? What fool would let her go, once he had her?

And who had he been to think she might want him? Lord of his own hall though he might have been—but what a hall! The farmland surrounding his keep had lain fallow for years. The forests were likely thick with thieves. And it wasn't as if he could go to the continent to better his situation. There was most certainly no welcome for him in France, despite how

generous Louis might be with his understanding. He had been
accused of witchcraft. What would Abigail want with a husband of that ilk?

"—and when I lost my job, he broke up with me and took
off. Next door, to be exact. To Bunny Ann Bartlett's apartment."

But, oh, to have had the chance to try to win her. He looked
at her and, to his surprise, felt himself longing for the chance
like he'd longed for nothing else in years, save his knight's
spurs. To hear his name come from those lush lips with the
same tones of love as she used when speaking of her husband—

"—a total putz. He kept bottles of hairspray and mousse at
my apartment for emergency touch-ups. There were times I
had to take a putty knife to the bathroom floor just to get the
stuff up—"

To be the one she gazed at with longing, to be the one she
welcomed to her bed each night—

"—of course, I think it's because I wouldn't sleep with
him. Garretts don't do that until after marriage, you know.
So, he left me. Bunny probably hit the sheets with him the
minute he walked through her door."

Miles blinked. He realized he hadn't heard everything
she'd said. And he'd understood even less.

"Bunny?" he asked.

"Brett's new girlfriend. They're getting married soon."

"Your husband is marrying someone else?"

Abigail looked at him as if he'd lost his mind. "Husband!
Are you kidding? I never would have married that creep! I
only got engaged to him because I was so miserable after Sir
Sweetums met his unhappy kitty end. I knew Brett never really wanted to marry me. He was just using me for my ultra
hold mousse."

Miles shook his head, feeling mightily confused. "Then
you aren't wed?"

"Of course not!"

"Oh," he said.

Then he understood.

"Aaahh," he said, feeling himself start to smile. He
couldn't help it. A feeling of relief started at his toes and
worked its way upward until it settled on his mouth. "The
saints be praised for that!"

Abigail leaned forward and felt his forehead. "You aren't feverish," she muttered.

"Indeed, I am most certainly not," he said, grasping her hand and hauling her onto his lap. He beamed at her. "And you are not wed."

"Boy, nothing gets by you, does it?"

He ignored her mocking tone in favor of contemplating his next action. "I believe I've heard enough," he announced. "I'm going to kiss you now."

She eluded his lips and managed to slip out of his arms and plant herself back on her stool. Miles frowned.

"Perhaps I was unclear—" he began, reaching for her again.

"Miles!"

"What?" he said, feeling his frown settle into a scowl.

"You can't kiss me. You haven't heard what I have to tell you."

"You aren't wed. What else could I possibly need to know?"

She clapped her hands on her knees, then rose with exaggerated care. "I am having a serious case of low blood sugar and you are *not* helping matters. I need something to eat. I don't suppose you have anything with chocolate in it, do you?"

"Chocolate?"

"Of course not," she groaned and walked off toward the kitchen. "It's too early in time for chocolate."

Miles followed after her grumbling self into his pitifully kept kitchen. He watched her rummage through the stores his father's men had unloaded onto one of the tables, and found himself wondering just what it was she had to tell him. Had she left her home without permission? There was her former fiancé to consider. The betrothal had been broken, obviously, but was that enough to have made her flee her home?

"Abigail," he said, "perhaps then you should tell me of your sire. I will no doubt need to get word to him that you are well." There, now he would have the entire tale.

She turned around with a loaf of bread in her hand. "You can't," she said, softly. "He's dead."

"Oh," Miles said, quietly. "Forgive me."

She smiled. "You couldn't have known."

Miles moved to stand next to her. He broke off a hunk of bread. "Did he die well?"

"He fell off the side of a mountain. My mother fell off trying to catch him."

"A glorious and astounding finish, as is right. I'm sorry, though, Abigail. You must miss them very much."

She shrugged and chewed slowly.

"No other family? Uncles? Aunts? Siblings?"

She swallowed and looked up at him. "They're a bit too far away to contact."

"Word can be sent."

She shook her head.

He frowned. "The world is not that large, Abigail, and I have seen a great deal of it. Now where is this place you come from—Frozen Muff?"

"Freezing Bluff. It's in Michigan."

That was surely no place he'd ever heard of, but he was loath to admit his ignorance.

"Scotland," he guessed.

"Not even close."

"Hmmm," he said, frowning. "Where exactly is Freezing Bluff, if not in the north?"

Abigail set her bread aside. She took Miles's bread away from him and put it on the table, too. Then she looked up at him slowly.

"*Where* isn't exactly the right question." She paused for a goodly while, then looked at him soberly. "*When* is, though."

He frowned. "What mean you by that?"

She clasped her hands behind her back. "I think you're right about Henry. He probably was king in 1238."

"I see you've finally come to your senses—what mean you was? He still *is*."

"If you're living in 1238."

"Which I am." Saints, perhaps that swim *had* truly addled her wits.

"Which I wasn't—yesterday."

Miles shook his head. "I don't understand."

"Elizabeth is queen in my day."

"Your day?"

"1996."

"1996?" he whispered.

"The Year of Our Lord 1996," Abby said, slowly and distinctly. "Seven hundred years in the future."

Miles blinked. He looked at her head. No horns. He reached out and put his hands on her shoulders. She looked perfectly sane. She felt perfectly normal.

"1996," he repeated. The very numbers felt foreign on his tongue.

He looked at Abigail again. Was it possible? Could she have been living and breathing in another time one moment, then found herself alive in his time the next? Saints above, the thought left him with his head spinning.

Indeed, the entire room seemed to be spinning.

"Miles!"

He felt Abigail throw her arms around him. It didn't help. The stone of the kitchen floor came up to meet him. Abruptly.

"Oof," he managed, as Abigail landed on his stomach.

"I saved your head," she panted.

"My gratitude," Miles said, realizing that indeed her fingers were between his head and the unyielding floor. "Truly."

"I thought men from Artane didn't faint."

Miles could only manage a grunt. Words were beyond him. He was lying on his kitchen floor with a woman sprawled over him who supposedly lived in a time well past when the world should have ended. With great effort, he flopped his arms around her and held on. She felt like a true woman. She spoke a bit strangely, and used words he had to puzzle out, but now knowing her background, he could understand it. Background? Saints, her background was his foreground. Her past was his future. He groaned. He didn't spare much effort in doubting her. If he could believe he'd seen her cat walk *through* his hall door, he could believe this. But, by the saints, the very thought of it hurt his head.

And then the truth of the matter struck him with the force of a charging horse.

He couldn't keep her.

He groaned again, from deep within his soul. Merciful St. Christopher, he could not keep her! How could he, when she belonged in another time so completely foreign to his? She had a life there, a life that should be lived. How could he sentence her to a life at Speningethorpe? It wasn't even Artane, with its modern comforts, that he offered. His hall was no better than a stable. Surely she was used to luxuries he couldn't imagine. How could he rob her of that?

He pushed her gently away and struggled to sit up.

"I'll find a way to send you back," he said, flatly. "Today."

"What?"

"Back home!" he snapped, looking at her with a glare. "I'll find a way to get you back to your home. Damnation, Abigail, I'll do it as soon as I've caught my breath."

"You'll send me back?" she asked.

Miles gritted his teeth. "Of course!" He lurched to his feet and grasped the table for support. "As bloody quick as I can!"

She was silent for several moments, long enough for him to catch his breath and regain his balance. His vision cleared just in time to see her expression of hurt change to one of anger. He hardly had time to unravel the mystery of that change when he was assaulted by a barrage of words.

"Oh, great!" she exclaimed, scrambling to her feet. "This is just great! You don't want me either!" She started to pace in front of him. "First it's my boss who gives me the old heave-ho, though I hated that job and his stupid cactus plants anyway. Then my landlord wants me out. Peter Pan takes a hike because I can't pay for his upkeep anymore. Hell's bells, not even the Social Security office wants anything to do with me! Just what's wrong with me, anyway?" She stopped, looked at him with another accusing glance, then poked him sharply in the chest. "You tell me that, Mr. I-just-barely-escaped-the-Inquisition knight from Spendingthorn."

"Speningethorpe."

"Whatever," she snarled.

"Ah . . . ," he began.

"Never mind," she said, her eyes blazing. "I don't want you either. Your house is a mess. You don't even have a job. I'm *not* going to work my fingers to the bone to feed and clothe another boyfriend. Forget it. I'm finding my cat," she said, sticking her nose up in the air, "and *going*." She turned away from him smartly. "Sir Sweetums, get over here *right now!*"

Miles watched with open mouth as she stomped from his kitchen. And, much as he hated to admit it, he hadn't understood a thing she'd said. Except for the part about the Inquisition.

Oh, and that she thought he didn't want her.

Which had to mean, and he congratulated himself on the ability to deduce this, that she wanted *him*.

And while he was indulging in realizations, he realized that while she might have only come to want him recently, he'd wanted her from the moment he'd clapped eyes on her formerly fluffy self standing at his gates. Harpy or no, he had very much wanted to understand all there was to understand about Abigail Moira Garrett. He wanted it even more now. And if it meant keeping her in the glorious Year of Our Lord 1238, then so be it.

He stepped out into the great hall and watched as she hitched up her hose and stomped across the great hall, hollering for her bloody cat. What an enchanting woman. Hell, he didn't care if she was an enchant*ed* woman. He wanted her.

And Miles de Piaget always got what he wanted.

He would invite her to stay. Indeed, he would all but demand that she stay.

He strode forward. It took four long strides to catch up to her, another to position himself properly, and half another to sweep her squeaking self up into his arms. He looked down into her beautiful face and gave her his most lordly look. He knew it wasn't as convincing as his sire's, but since Abigail had nothing to compare it to, it would do.

"The future will just have to go on without you," he announced.

She blinked. "I beg your pardon."

"Petered pain is something you'll not have to bear again."

"Petered pain?"

"Aye," he said, firmly.

"Oh," she whispered. Then she smiled, a gentle smile. "You mean Peter Pan."

"Whatever," he said, with an imperious look. "And that so-shall sec . . . sec—"

"Social Security," she supplied.

"Aye, that. You'll have no need of it. Whatever it is," he added. "You will have me."

"I will?"

"Whether you like it or no."

"I see."

He grunted. "So you do."

He stalked back to the fire. Abigail's arms stole around his neck and it broke his heart. How could she think no one wanted her?

He set her down on her feet near the fire, put his hand under her chin, and lifted her face up.

"I assume this agrees with you," he stated.

She looked up at him solemnly. "I didn't think you were giving me any choice in the matter."

"I'm not. I intend to woo you fiercely. I am merely assuming the idea agrees with you."

A small smile touched her mouth, "I suppose the future isn't all it's cracked up to be."

"Especially when the glorious Year of Our Lord 1238 provides one with such exceeding luxuries," he said, indicating his pitiful hall with a grand sweep of his arm.

"Well . . . now that you mention it—"

He didn't wish to hear what she intended to mention, so, like the good soldier he was, he marched straight into the fray without hesitation. He lowered his head and covered her mouth with his.

She shivered.

And then she kissed him back.

Miles's senses reeled. He gathered Abigail close and wrapped his arms around her. He smiled to himself as he remembered his first sight of her and how plump a harpy she had seemed. She was definitely not fluffy now. He could work on that later. Visions of half a dozen little Abigail-like creatures scampering about his hall calling "here, kitty, kitty," sprang up in his mind. He lifted his head and blinked.

"Miles, I think—"

He captured her mouth again. Thinking was not something he wanted to do much more of for the moment. Later he would give thought into little dark-haired, gray-eyed waifs and their mother running roughshod over his hall and his heart. For now, he was far too lost in Abigail's arms.

Miles could hardly believe the events of the past several hours. He'd come to Speningethorpe a se'nnight before, determined to wither away to an intolerable, bitter old man. Without warning, Abigail had come splashing down into his moat and changed his life completely. Perhaps there was more to Sir Sweetums than met the eye.

Whatever the case, Miles knew he had made the right choice. Perhaps the sailing would be a bit rough at first, what with them both coming from different worlds. Already her cat had done damage to his nose. The saints only knew what wreckage Abigail would leave of his heart. But surely it would be worth the effort.

The smell of something burning finally caught his attention. And that warmth on his backside he had thought to be Abigail's hand had suddenly turned into something else entirely.

"Merde!" he shouted.

"Drop and roll!" Abigail said, shoving him. "Drop and roll, you idiot!"

He dropped and she rolled him. He soon found himself face down on the floor. There was a fine draft blowing over his backside.

"The fire got your tights, too, I'm afraid," Abigail said. "What a shame. Your bum is looking kind of red—"

Miles whipped over so he was sitting, bare-arsed, on the floor. He felt furious color suffuse his cheeks. Abigail laughed.

"Oh, Miles," she said, shaking her head.

He grunted and scowled to save his pride. Abigail leaned forward and kissed him on the cheek.

"You're very cute."

Well, he knew that was a compliment. A pity he'd had to scorch his arse to wring one from her! To soothe his burned backside and assuage his bruised ego, he hauled her into his lap and looked at her purposefully.

"I will need to be appeased," he announced.

She put her arms around his neck. "And just how is that done in 1238?"

"I will show you."

"I had the feeling you would."

Miles kissed her. In time he forgot the pain of his toasted backside. He forgot that, by the saints, he was some seven hundred years older than the woman in his arms. He was almost distracted enough to bypass giving thought to what he would tell his father about her when he took her to Artane.

"Hey," Abigail said, looking at him with a frown, "keep your mind on the task at hand. Really, Miles. It can't be that taxing."

He threw back his head and laughed. Perhaps this was truly the gift he'd needed most for Christmas—a woman who had no reason to tread lightly near him. He looked at Abigail and smiled.

"My lady, you amaze me."

"Of course I do. What other twentieth-century girls have you met lately?"

He smiled and kissed her again. She was certainly the only one, the saints be praised. He doubted he would survive the wooing of another.

His nose began to twitch, but he stuck his finger under it and kept his mouth pressed tightly against Abigail's. With any luck that blasted cat would keep his distance until Abigail was properly wooed.

And if Miles ever caught up with Sir Sweetums, he would offer him a cup of the finest meade in gratitude.

Chapter Five

ABBY SAT CROSS-LEGGED on the table in the kitchen and watched Miles cut up vegetables for a stew.

"Do you know what you're doing?" she asked, doubtfully.

He looked up from under his eyebrows. "I cooked many a meal for myself in my travels. We will not starve."

"But how well will we eat?"

Miles very carefully set the knife down, crossed the two steps that separated her resting place from his working area of the table, and stopped in front of her.

"Oh, no you don't—"

She wasn't fast enough. She didn't even get a chance to give him her kissing-won't-solve-all-our-problems speech before a very warm, very firm mouth came down on hers. She shivered. It was a mouth minus its previous surrounding accompaniment of whiskers. Miles had shaved once he'd learned modern guys did it every day. Abby had vowed solemnly to herself not to overuse that keep-up-with-the-twentieth-century-Joneses strategy too often. But it was worth it for this. Kissing a be-whiskered Miles was great, but this was earth-shattering.

And he'd dispensed early on with that closed-mouthed kissing business. He was going straight for the jugular and didn't seem to care which way he got there, inside her mouth or out. Abby thought he might be wishing he could just crawl inside her and this was the best he could get for the moment. She hadn't given him her Garretts-don't-do-it-before-marriage speech, but they hadn't gotten that far yet. She sincerely hoped they got that far eventually.

Abby blinked when Miles lifted his head.

"Finished?" she croaked.

"Do you doubt my skill in the kitchens?"

She shook her head, wide-eyed.

He smiled in the most self-satisfied of ways and returned to his chopping. Abby rubbed her finger thoughtfully over her bottom lip. Maybe kissing *would* solve quite a few things.

Abby looked at Miles chopping diligently. Just how had she gotten so lucky? She had been rescued by a fantastic-looking man who got so distracted by kissing her that he set his own clothes on fire. He was stacking up oh-so-nicely against her Ideal Man list. It was almost enough to make her forget about going home.

Home. She turned the thought over in her mind. Modern conveniences waltzed before her mind's eye and she examined each in turn. Somehow they just didn't seem that appealing. Phones were noisy, fast food was unhealthy, and life in the corporate world spent basking under fluorescent lights gave her headaches. She'd always liked camping, which was a good thing, since Miles's castle was about on that same level of civilization.

And there probably wasn't any use in thinking about it. She had no guarantee that diving into Miles's moat would leave her resurfacing in Murphy's Pond.

On the other hand, what future did she have in the past? Miles certainly hadn't mentioned marriage. He was definitely shaping up to be someone she could share her life with, but was he free to choose his wife? Her knowledge of the marital practices of medieval nobility was scant, unfortunately. Even if could choose, who was to say he'd want her?

"Where go you?"

Abby hadn't realized she had gotten off the table until Miles spoke.

"Just out," she said, moving toward the kitchen door. Maybe a little distance would soothe her smarting feelings. She was losing it. Why in the world did she think—

"You sound as if you need to be convinced to stay," he stated, snagging her hand. "Come you back here, my lady, and let me see to it."

Abby let him pull her back, turn her around, and gather her into his arms.

"Abigail," he said softly, "what ails you?"

She put her arms around him and shook her head. "Nothing."

"Do you miss your home?"

"No."

He lifted her face up. Abby met his dark gray eyes and almost wanted to cry. Why be dumped here if she couldn't have him?

"Saints, but you Garretts are a stubborn lot," he said, smiling down at her. "You are resisting my wooing. You leave me with no choice but to pour more energies into it. Perhaps without the distractions of supper to prepare."

Well, wooing sounded good. Maybe it was best to just give things a few more days. After all, she might find out she really didn't like him very much.

He released her, dumped the rest of his vegetables into the pot, hung it over the fire, then turned back to her with a purposeful gleam in his eye.

"Is that all that needs to go in there?" she asked.

He shrugged and advanced.

"What if it tastes lousy?"

"You'll never notice."

"Why not?"

"Because you'll be too distracted by my surliness if you do not give me your complete attention."

"One of these days, Miles de Piaget, kissing me into submission isn't going to wor—"

But, oh, it was working at present. With her last coherent thought, Abby knew the day she decided she didn't like him would be the day they'd need snow tires in hell.

AN HOUR LATER, Abby held up a dollar bill to the firelight. "This is George Washington. He was the first president of the United States."

"No king?"

"Nope. That's why we said 'no thank you' to England in the 1700s. We're all for life, liberty and the pursuit of happiness without a monarchy to tell us how to go about it."

Miles looked with interest at her wallet that sat between them on the blanket near the fire. Abby had appropriated his sleeping blanket as a carpet. The chair was too uncomfortable for sitting, and the floor too disgusting for intimate contact.

"What else have you in that small purse?" he asked.

"Not as many things as I would like," Abby said with a sigh.

She had her little wallet on a string, her gloves, and her keys. Her sunglasses had been stuffed inside her coat. The only other things she'd had in her pocket were a plastic bag of gourmet jelly beans and some soggy lint. But he'd been fascinated by it all. She'd been fairly certain he'd believed her when he'd hit the floor in the kitchen, but there was nothing like a bit of substantial evidence to slam the door on doubt.

He'd examined her jeans closely, seemingly very impressed by the pockets and copper rivets. Her down coat was still dripping wet, but she had the feeling they'd be fighting over that once it was dry. Her underwear and bra she'd finally had to rip out of his hands. It was then she'd given him her Garretts-don't-do-it-before-marriage speech. She'd expected protests. Instead, she'd gotten a puzzled look.

"Of course you don't," had been his only comment.

So, now they were sitting in front of his bonfire, examining the contents of her wallet and munching on Jelly Bellies.

"Aaack," Miles said, chewing gingerly. "What sort is this one?"

She leaned forward and smelled. "Buttered popcorn, I think."

"Nasty." He swallowed with a gulp. "Is there this chocolate you spoke of?" he asked, poking around in the bag hopefully.

"I wish," she said with feeling. She'd had one lemon jelly bean and given the rest to Miles. Unless sugar found itself mixed in with a generous amount of cocoa, she wasn't all that interested. Now, if it had been a bag of M&M's she'd been packing, Miles would have been limited to a small taste and lots of sniffs. "Chocolate doesn't even get to England until the seventeenth century. Trust me. *This* is history I know about."

"Where does it come from?"

"They grow it in Africa."

"Oh," he said, sounding almost as regretful as she felt. "A bit of a journey."

"You didn't see any on your travels?"

He shook his head. "Not that I remember."

Abby leaned back against the chair legs. "What made you decide to go to Jerusalem?"

"I wanted to see the places my father had been in his youth, I suppose. My father had gone on the Lionheart's crusade, first as page, then squire to a Norman lord. My brothers followed in his footsteps to the Holy Land, even though there was no glorious war for them to wage." He smiled faintly. "I think I simply had a young man's desire to see the world and discover its mysteries. Instead, I saw cities ravaged by war, women without husbands, children without fathers." He shrugged. "I don't think fighting over relics was the message the Christ left behind Him. Perhaps I found it even more ironic because I overlooked the city of Jerusalem on Christmas day."

"I take it that count you insulted didn't feel the same about it?"

Miles smiled. "Indeed, he did not. And I am not shy about expressing my opinions, whether I am in my cups or not."

"Was your grandfather upset with you?"

"Nay. You see, of all his grandsons, he says I remind him overmuch of himself." He smiled modestly, then continued. "My eldest brother, Robin, would rather grumble and curse under his breath. Nicholas is a peacemaker and rarely says aught to offend. My younger brothers are giddy maids, talking of nothing but whatever ladyloves they are currently wooing." He smiled again. "I, on the other hand, am surly and moody and generally make certain others know that."

"Oh, boy, surly *and* moody," she said, with delight. "And to think I could have landed in the moat of someone who was merely agreeable and deferring."

"And how dull you would have found him to be," he said with a grin. "My grandsire shares my temperament. I am his favorite, of course."

"Of course," she agreed, dryly. "You were just lucky he happened by when he did."

"It is perhaps more than luck. I learned later one of his servants had been passing by and heard me telling the count rather loudly that he was a mindless twit."

"Oh, Miles," she laughed. "You'd make a terrible diplomat."

"Aye," he agreed. " 'Tis fortunate I'll never pursue that calling."

"Then what is it you intend to pursue?" She knew it was a loaded question, but she couldn't stop herself from asking it.

His smile deepened. "I intend to pursue you, of course."

"Really?" she squeaked. She cleared her throat and tried again in a more dignified tone. "Really," she said, hoping it sounded casual.

He nodded. "Aye. But how is a twentieth-century girl wooed? Gifts?"

"Well, it is almost Christmas."

He frowned. "And you plan on making me participate in the festivities?"

"If I can do it, so can you." She had her own reasons for finding Christmas difficult, but she managed each year. Miles could, too. "We could spruce up the place a little."

"Aye," he agreed, sounding reluctant.

"Come on, grumpy. It'll be fun."

"Fun?" he echoed doubtfully.

"As in enjoyable, entertaining. We'll do some cleaning and sprucing and you'll feel much better about the season. Trust me. And while we're cleaning, I'll tell you the story of Ebeneezer Scrooge." She laughed. "Talk about the Ghost of Christmas Past! Boy, this puts a whole new spin on that one."

Miles only blinked at her.

"We may have to forgo the gifts," she continued. "I would have put those Jelly Bellies in your stocking, but you ate them all."

Miles burped discreetly. "And they were delicious. Is that how 'tis done in your day? Sprucing and giving?"

"Pretty much."

He reached over, put his hand behind her head and pulled her toward him. "You are the best gift I could have asked for," he murmured against her lips. "I need nothing else."

Abby closed her eyes as he kissed her. Was it possible to fall in love with someone so soon?

It was much later that she managed to catch her breath enough to ask if he thought the stew was finished.

"Do you care?" he asked, with a twinkle in his eye. "My appetite is running more toward more of your mouth. I can guarantee it is more tasty than what boils in yon pot."

"Who needs food?" Abby managed.

And that was the last thing she said for a very long time.

Chapter Six

MILES STRUGGLED TO fashion the soft straw into a bow. "Will this do?" he asked, holding it up.

"Well, it isn't raffia, but we'll survive."

Miles handed her the bow, then leaned his elbows on the table and watched her rummaging through his stores for other appropriately Christmassy items, as she called them.

He'd slept poorly the night before. He'd been tempted to blame it on his stew. It had been, in a word, inedible. More than likely it had been sleeping so close to Abigail and not touching her. Garretts didn't do that sort of thing before marriage—not that he'd expected anything else. He wouldn't take her until he'd wed her. The thought of it sent a thrill of something through him; he wasn't sure if it was excitement or terror. He'd always known he would take a wife sooner or later. It had certainly suited his brothers well enough, though the wooing of their ladies had been tumultuous.

Miles stole a look at Abigail and wondered if the courting of her would take such a toll on him. He didn't think so. She looked fairly serene as she sifted through his things. Perhaps she would accept him well enough as time went on.

He watched her and couldn't help but smile. It seemed a better thing to do than shake his head, which was what he had been doing since she'd started telling him future things the eve before. Airplanes, cars, trains, microwaves; the list was endless. It would take him a lifetime to draw from her all the things she took for granted, things he hadn't even imagined, well-traveled though he might have been.

"Abigail, what sort of work did you do in your day?" he asked.

"I was a secretary for an insurance salesman," she said, frowning at a bow. She flashed him a brief smile. "People paid this man a certain amount of money each month just in case they died or their house went up in flames. If that happened, then he would replace the house or pay the family money to compensate for the deceased. I wrote out all his correspondence and things on a machine called a computer. And I watered his plants. I hated it."

"What would you rather have been doing?"

"Anything but that." She fingered a fig. "I always wanted to be a gardener. I love to watch things grow. A family would have been nice, too."

"I see," he said. No wonder she had found Brett so lacking. The man obviously didn't share her sentiments about marriage. But why was she so concerned with sprucing and giving? Was that all part of it?

"Why is this Christmassy fuss so important to you?" he asked.

He might not have noticed her hesitation if he hadn't been watching her so closely. But he noticed it, and he certainly noticed the false smile she put on for his benefit.

"'Tis the season, ho, ho, ho, and all that," she said, brightly.

"Hmmm," Miles said, thoughtfully. She was lying, obviously. He looked at her sad little pile of straw bows, then back up at her.

"How did you celebrate in your time?"

"Oh, there's a lot to it. You have to decorate the house with a tree and ornaments and greenery. All the family gets together and there's lots of food and laughter." She gave another piece of straw a hard yank. "It's the family togetherness thing."

Miles reached out and put his hand over hers. "Abigail, I want to know how *you* celebrated."

She looked away. "I went to my grandmother's. Until she and my granddad died."

"Then it must have been quite festive. Tell me of your siblings. What a clan you must have been with a houseful of Garretts."

"Oh, it was a houseful, all right," she said. "I don't have any brothers or sisters, but I have lots of cousins and aunts and uncles. They would all show up with gifts and things."

"And what of your parents?"

Abby shrugged. "They usually took me there and left me. They never stayed." She smiled at him briefly. "They always had other things to do."

Miles's chest tightened. He tried to pull her into his arms, but she wouldn't come.

"I was something of a surprise," she said, walking over to the kitchen hearth. "They had me after they'd been married almost twenty years. They had never wanted children and it was too inconvenient to fit me into their lifestyle, I guess."

"Oh, Abigail," Miles said softly.

"Don't," she said, holding up her hand. "I didn't tell you so you could feel sorry for me. I've had a great life. My grandparents were wonderful. I didn't need my mom and dad to make my life any better than it was."

He digested that for a few minutes. This obviously went deeper than that.

"So these Christmassy items remind you of your grandparents?"

She shrugged. "I suppose. Or maybe I just want what they had."

Miles understood. His father worshipped his mother and she him. They had their disagreements, surely, but there had never been a time that Miles had doubted their love for each other. Not that every household in England ran thusly. Most marriages were made to form alliances and were likely devoid of love. Miles knew his parents were something of an exception. Abigail obviously wanted such an exceptional marriage. Miles smiled to himself. And him right there to give it to her. Life was indeed miraculous.

"I want the whole enchilada," she was saying. "I want a husband who loves me. I want children. I want real Christmases with lights and a tree and my own family there around me. I want a fireplace."

Miles considered the last. 'Twas obvious improvements would have to be made to the hall.

"And while we're talking about marriage, let me be perfectly clear on this. I want a husband who will stick by me when things get rough, who won't bail at the first sign of trouble." She shot him a challenging look.

"Bail?"

"Leave. Run away."

"Ah, I see."

"So you do."

She had planted her hands on her waist again. Miles had the feeling she was gearing up for battle. He was beginning to suspect he might be the enemy.

"Then you don't want a man who would run off when things became difficult," he offered, wanting to make sure he understood.

"That's right, bucko."

"Anything else?"

She held up her hand and began using her fingers to tick off her items of importance.

"He can't dress better than I do, he can't smell better than I do, and he has to have a job."

"A job?"

"An occupation. He can't just sit around the house watching TV all day and expect me to pay all the bills."

Miles clasped his hands behind his back. "And?"

She was silent for a moment. "He has to love me," she said, quietly.

Well, that was done easily enough. Miles suspected he'd fallen in love with her the first time she'd begun to wheeze.

The occupation item was a problem. Miles leaned back against the worktable and stared thoughtfully at the ceiling. He could build Speningethorpe up and turn it into a profitable estate, but would that be enough for Abigail? 'Twas certain he would have to do something with his hands so as not to appear idle. Perhaps he would send for his hounds. He'd bred them in his youth, as he'd managed to keep himself home until he was almost two-and-ten. Aye, there was always a market for a finely-trained hound.

And if hounds weren't substantial enough, he would look to horses. His mother had a fine eye for horseflesh. When he took Abigail to Artane, he would seek his mother's opinion on the matter.

Miles considered Abigail's other items. It was certain he wasn't dressed better than she; he was wearing his oldest pair of hose. They were worn through at the knee, but better bare knees than a bare arse, to his mind. He was quite certain she smelled far better than he did. She certainly would once he took to cleaning out the kennels.

All in all, he thought he just might suit.

He flashed her a brief smile and started toward the great hall. There was no time like the present to see the future accounted for. It was just barely midday. If he rode hard, he could be to Seakirk Abbey and back by dawn. The abbot would likely be there for the Christmas celebrations. Miles had no qualms about using whatever tactics were necessary to see the man on a horse heading north with him. No doubt his own reputation as a convicted heretic would serve him. His elder brothers had already spread the tale from one end of the isle to the other, embellishing it with each retelling. Miles had been livid at first, especially since they had found it to be such a fine jest. Now, he thought the blot on his past just might serve him well.

"Where are you going?"

The desperate tone of Abigail's voice made him pause. He looked at her as he threw his cloak around his shoulders and pulled on his gloves.

"I've things to see to."

Her jaw went slack. "Just like that?"

"Abigail, I've a task to see to—"

"I bare my soul to you," she said, sounding irritated, "and all you can do is walk away?"

"Abigail—"

"Great!" she exclaimed. "This is just *great!*"

He paused and considered. If he told her what he was about, heaven only knew what she would say. She might say she thought he should take a swim in his moat. Worse yet, she might leave.

He couldn't bring himself to think about that. Only last night he had begun to realize just what he would be asking her to give up to remain with him.

He couldn't bear the thought of having her say him nay.

Aye, 'twas best he had the priest handy when he informed her of his intentions. Garretts never did things by halves, and neither did de Piagets.

"There's wood enough for the fire," he said, "so you shouldn't freeze—"

"It's about the sex thing, isn't it," she demanded.

"Well, aye," he said, with a nod, "that's part of it, surely." He certainly wouldn't take her 'til he'd wed her and the sooner he'd wed her, the happier he would be.

"Ooohh," she said, grinding her teeth. She picked up a piece of wood and heaved it at him. "You're such a jerk!"

Miles ducked, his eyes wide. "Abigail—"

"Go," she shouted, pointing to the door. "Just leave if you're going!"

Miles thought it best to do just that, while he was still in one piece. And when Abigail reached for another heavy stick of wood, he did the most sensible thing he could think of.

He bolted for the door.

He'd barely pulled the hall door to when he heard the thump of wood striking it on the other side. So he'd left his dignity behind. He would smile as he told his children how difficult it had been to woo their mother. It would make a fine tale.

He was halfway to the stables before he realized in how precarious a situation he was leaving his lady. He couldn't allow her to remain in a keep with an unbarred door and no men to protect her.

He turned back to the hall and pushed on the door. There was no budging it. Abigail had obviously made use of the crossbeam. Well, perhaps that would do. He would make as much haste as possible. The sooner he was home, priest in tow, the better he would like it.

Assuming, however, he didn't have to break down his own door to get to his bride.

He smiled as he strode to the stables. What a fine life it promised to be!

Chapter Seven

ABBY THREW ANOTHER log onto the fire, then dragged her hand across her eyes.

"What a jerk," she said, with a snuffle against her sleeve. "He's no better than the rest of them."

She could hardly believe Miles had just walked out, leaving her behind to ponder the reasons for his hotfooted departure. Maybe her soul-baring had scared him. Abby scowled. Coward. And he'd flat-out admitted that part of it was the sex thing. And after how readily he'd accepted it before, as if he would have been surprised by anything else! She scowled again. For all she knew, he'd just been toying with her.

Abby moved closer to the fire, with a muttered curse. It had been a very bad day. After Miles had left around noon, she'd spent the afternoon pacing and raging. Then she'd cried. When she'd tired of that, she had retreated to Miles's chair. She'd been sitting there since dusk, cursing both his inadequate bonfire and the day she'd landed in his moat. After slandering his hall and his person to her satisfaction, she'd simply sat and pondered life and its mysteries, shaking her head. Her grandmother had always shaken her head a lot. Abby was beginning to understand why.

Miles's actions baffled her. She had been prepared for him to lose it when she'd told him where and when she'd come from. But when she had told him her tiny little dream of home and hearth to call her own, not only had he not given her dream the proper respect and attention it deserved, he'd walked out on her. And on Christmas Eve, of all times! Tonight was the night to have people around her who cared for her. All she had was an empty castle. She had no Christmas tree, no twinkling lights, and no presents. Hell's bells, she didn't even have any fruitcake to worry about disposing of!

But that wasn't the worst of it. Much as she didn't want to admit it, what she didn't have was what she wanted the most.

Miles.

She'd always wondered if there were such a thing as meeting a person and knowing immediately he was the Right One. She'd never experienced it before. She was very familiar with attraction to the Wrong One. She would meet a man, think he was handsome, then ten minutes later start making excuses for his glaring flaws. But no amount of fiddling had ever turned any of those men into the Right One.

With Miles, it had been completely different. One minute she'd been chewing him out for not having indoor plumbing, the next she'd been comparing him to her Ideal Man requirements and finding nothing lacking. Until today. Running out on her was a big check mark on the Red Flag side of the list. If he didn't love her enough to stay, he just wouldn't do.

Besides, what did she want with primitive old medieval England anyway? No running water, no phone, and no History Channel on cable. Hell, she was *living* the History Channel.

She needed modern comforts. Hot showers. Soap, that came pre-wrapped and contained moisturizers with long, scientific names. Craft stores, where she could buy makings for Christmas decorations. Good grief, even simple things like flipping a switch for lights, indoor plumbing, central heat . . . the Mini Mart!

Well, time was awastin'. She jumped to her feet purposefully and headed toward the door. She'd just go home. There wasn't anything there for her either, but at least she'd be miserable in comfort. It was definitely a step up from being miserable in a drafty old castle that was ratty even by *medieval* standards!

She put her shoulder under the crossbeam and gave it a shove over to her left. It took several tries, but finally she managed to slide it far enough to one side that all it took was a good push upward to tip it out of the remaining bracket. She took hold of the iron door ring and started to pull.

"Meow."

Abby paused, then shook her head. "That's not going to work this time. I'm late for my date with the moat."

"I say, old girl, *meow!*"

Abby whirled around, fully expecting to see someone behind her.

She was alone.

This was way too spooky. She took a few hesitant steps out into the middle of the room, searching the shadows. Then she squeaked in surprise.

Sir Sweetums sat on the bottom step of Miles's circular stairway. He swished his tail impatiently, then turned and disappeared upward into the shadows.

"I'm going to regret this," Abby muttered under her breath.

She crossed the room, then climbed up the circular stairs. She waited until her eyes had adjusted fully. The moon was full, which helped. But one of these days Miles was really going to have to do something about a roof over this part of his castle—

"Really, my dear, you are the most stubborn of women."

Abby shrieked and jumped back. All she succeeded in doing was smacking herself smartly against the stone of the stairwell.

"Who's there?" she said, her voice warbling like a bird's.

"'Tis I," a cultured voice said from the darkness. "Your beloved Sir Sweetums."

Against her better judgment, Abby strained to see into the shadowy hallway across from her. What she really needed to be doing was getting up and looking for a weapon, not peering into the shadows to catch a glimpse of a ghostly cat who seemed to be having delusions of conversation. Maybe that big cleaver in the kitchen would be protection enough.

And then, before she could gather her limbs together and move, Sir Sweetums himself appeared across the gaping hole that separated the stairwell from what should have been, and likely would be again, a hallway leading to bedrooms.

Abby sank down onto a step and gaped at him in amazement. "Sir Sweetums?" she managed.

"But of course," he said, giving his paw a delicate lick and skimming said paw alongside his nose. He finished with his ablutions and looked at her. "Who else?"

"Ooooh," Abby said, clutching the rock on either side of her. "I've really lost it this time. Garretts aren't supposed to hallucinate!"

"No hallucination, dearest Abigail," Sir Sweetums said placidly. "Just me, come to bring you to your senses. I've been trying for years, since the moment you lost your wits over that pimply-faced chap named Mad Dog McGee when you were twelve."

Garretts never whimpered. Abby thought moaning might not be a blot against her, so she did it thoroughly.

"No vapors, I beg of you!" Sir Sweetums exclaimed, holding up his paw.

"You're talking," Abby said, hoarsely. She shook her head. "I'm talking to a cat. I can't believe this."

"We've talked before," Sir Sweetums pointed out. "I have many fond memories of conversing whilst I stalked the butterfly bush and you puttered amongst the hollyhocks—"

"That was different. You were using words like 'meow' and 'prrr.' You weren't going on about me puttering amongst my hollyhocks." Abby glared at him. "This is unnatural!"

"'Tis the season for giving, my dear, and this is the gift given to animals each year from midnight on the eve of the Christ Child's birth to sunrise the next morning."

"But you aren't alive," Abby whispered. "I know you aren't."

"Ah," Sir Sweetums agreed, with a nod, "there's the heart of it. I wished I could have come to you and told you, but once a feline enters the Guardian's association, he cannot go back. Unless he has further work to do." Sir Sweetums cocked his head to one side. "And to be sure, I had further work to do with you, my girl!"

Abby leaned back against the stone and shivered once. When it had passed, she took a deep breath and let it out again.

"All right," she said. "I can handle this." She laughed, in spite of herself. "I'm living in 1238. If I can believe that, I can believe I'm talking to you." She looked at her very beloved Sir Sweetums and felt her eyes begin to water. "I missed you so much."

Sir Sweetums coughed, a little uncomfortably it seemed to her. "Of course, my dear."

"Did you miss me?"

"Of course, my dear," he said, gently. "Out of the mortals I had charge of during my nine lives, you were my favorite. Didn't you know?"

Abby smiled through her tears. "No, I didn't know. But thanks for telling me."

Sir Sweetums smiled, as only a cat can smile. "My pleasure. Now, on to the reason I am here. You really must get hold of yourself in regards to The Miles. He is a perfectly acceptable human. Indeed, I would have to say he is the best of the matches you could have made."

"He's a total jerk," she grumbled.

"Strong-willed," Sir Sweetums countered. "Sure of himself and unafraid to speak his mind."

"He may speak, but he doesn't listen. I told him my most precious dream yesterday morning and he didn't even acknowledge it!"

"Maybe he was giving thought to your words."

"Hrumph," she said, unappeased. "If that's true, why did he leave?"

"When he returns, you'll ask."

"I'm not going to be here when he gets back."

"Tsk, tsk," Sir Sweetums said. "My dearest Abigail, you don't think I brought you all the way here just to have you leave, do you?"

"You?" she screeched. "*You're* the one responsible for this?"

"Who else?" he said, with a modest little smile.

"Why?" she exclaimed. "Why in the world did you drag me all the way here?"

"Because this is where you need to be," he said, simply.

"Right. Without chocolate, my superfirm mattresss, and running water. Thanks a lot."

Sir Sweetums shook his head patiently. "Really, my dear. Those are things you can live without."

"No, I can't. I'm going home."

"Conveniences there may be in the future, dear girl, but who waits there to share those conveniences with you?"

Well, he had a point there. Abby scowled and remained silent. She was not going to let a cat, no matter how much she loved him, talk her into remaining in miserable old medieval England.

"Abigail," Sir Sweetums said gently, "Miles is a dashedly fine chap."

"He's a convicted heretic!"

"Abigail," Sir Sweetums chided, "you know the truth of that."

"Well, then . . . he's always trying to kiss me into submission," she finished, triumphantly. "It's barbaric."

"Consider his upbringing, my dear! The man is a knight. He is used to taking what he wants, when he wants it."

"And what if I don't want to be taken?" she said, feeling peevish. Peevish was good. It beat the heck out of feeling hurt.

"Then tell him so. But I rather suspect you would find you like it."

"I'm surrounded by chauvinists," she muttered—peevishly.

Sir Sweetums looked unruffled. "Think on the alternatives you've had in the past, my dear. What of Brett? Would he have fought for you? Exerted himself to do anything but help you spend your funds and deplete your pantry?"

"No," she admitted reluctantly.

"And what of those other insufferable fops you managed to find yourself keeping company with? Anyone there who had the spine to care for you?"

"Lord over me, you mean."

Sir Sweetums conceded the point with a graceful nod. "As The Miles does. Perfectly acceptable behavior for a medieval knight. A most modern medieval knight, if I were to venture an opinion. He's quite liberal-minded in his thinking, my dear. I've no doubt that you two will see eye to eye in the end."

"He has a big check mark in the Red Flag column," she insisted. "Running out is the kiss of death with me."

"Perhaps he had affairs to see to."

"It would have been nice to have been told, you know. How are we supposed to work things out, not that I'm sure I want to, when he isn't even around?"

"You've waited all this time for him, my dear. What are a few more hours in the grander scheme of things?"

Abby looked at her most beloved of cats and, in spite of herself, found she had to agree with him. Maybe Miles had left for a reason. A good reason.

"It'd better be a *damn* good reason," she muttered. "And he'd better come rolling back in here before long, or I'll give my second thoughts a second thought!"

A throat cleared itself from immediately behind her.

"Actually, my lady, there was very little rolling involved. I walked in quite well on my own two feet."

Abby whipped around to look at Miles, who was standing at the crook of the stairs. He climbed up another step or two. He smiled at her, then his gaze drifted across the gap to Sir Sweetums.

Miles sneezed.

"Likewise, I'm sure," Sir Sweetums said, with a swish of his tail.

Abby couldn't decide who to watch. Miles looked like he was going to faint again—she knew that look. She put out her hand to steady him.

"That's Sir Sweetums," she supplied.

"So I gathered."

"He's talking. But only until sunrise."

"How positively lovely," Miles managed.

Sir Sweetums grimaced. "Ye gads, boy, get on with this, won't you? 'Tis almost dawn. I'd like to see The Abigail comfortably settled before the night is out."

"Maybe I don't want to be comfortably settled," Abby interjected.

"Sir Miles?" Sir Sweetums prompted.

Miles came up another step and knelt. Abby stiffened her spine and reminded herself of all the reasons she had to be angry with him.

"Abby?" he said, quietly.

Oh, great. *Now* he decided to call her Abby. She scowled at him.

"This isn't going to work."

He looked at her solemnly. "Just what about me doesn't suit? My visage? 'Tis too ugly to be gazed at for the rest of your life?" He flexed an arm for her benefit. "Too scrawny? Too frail? Here, come sniff me."

She leaned close, then wrinkled her nose. "All right, so you don't smell too great. What have you been doing?"

"I've been riding hard since midday yesterday. Now, in what other thing do I fail?"

"You dress better than I do. A very important issue with me."

Miles plunked a small, jangly bag in her lap. "Hire a seamstress. Anything else?"

Abby fingered the money in the bag. She looked at Sir Sweetums, who was watching her silently. Then she looked up at the stars; she couldn't look at Miles.

"I want it all," she said, quietly. "Kids, a garden, Christmas." She cleared her throat. "And a husband who loves me."

"And I would not?" he asked.

She looked at him. "You left. What am I supposed to understand from that? I tell you what is most important to me, you ignore me, and then you leave."

"I went to fetch a priest."

She frowned at him. "Why? So you could have me exorcised?"

Miles smiled. "Nay, Abby, so he could see us properly wed."

She blinked.

"Wed?" she asked.

"Aye."

"I—"

He took her hand in both of his. "I want you, Abby, in my life and in my bed. I vow always to smell more poorly than you. I give you my solemn word that you will always have the majority of garments in our trunk." He lifted his hand and touched her cheek. "I want to give you what you want, Abby. I want to give you a home and a family."

She looked at him. It was hard, but she made herself look at him and ask about what meant the most to her.

"And what about love? Between us?"

He smiled, and the tenderness of it went straight to her heart. "I think I began to fall in love with you from the moment I first clapped eyes on you standing at my gates. Every breath I've taken since then has just convinced me that life with you is infinitely more joyful than life without you." He raised her hand to his lips. "My sweet Abby, how can you think I would offer you any less?"

"Oh, Miles," she said. It was all she'd ever wanted to hear. She threw her arms around his neck, closed her eyes and let her tears slip down her cheeks. "Oh, Miles."

"I want you to stay," he whispered, putting his arms around her and hugging her. "I'm half-afraid to ask you to give up the future for me." He pulled back and looked at her. "Will you? I haven't much to offer you, yet."

She looped her arms around his neck and smiled at him, feeling joy well up in her heart. "All I really want," she said, blinking back the tears that stung her eyes, "is you."

"You won't miss chocolate?"

"I hear making love is a good substitute."

Miles laughed. "Perhaps in our travels someday we'll learn the truth of it. Until then, can you make do?"

"Yes."

"And you'll wed me?"

"Yes."

"Finally," Sir Sweetums exclaimed, triumphantly. "Well done, Miles, old boy! Finally, someone to take care of my beloved Abigail!"

"I don't need to be taken care of—"

Miles kissed her.

"See?" Abby mumbled. She made a concentrated effort to pull away so she could point out that such barbaric practices were most definitely not in the agreement, but somehow she found herself mesmerized by the feeling of his mouth on hers.

All right. If he wanted to kiss her into submission, she'd let him. Now and then.

"Perhaps, Sir Sweetums," Miles said, when he let her up for air, "Abby might be more amenable to the idea of keeping me in line, rather than the opposite."

Sir Sweetums considered. "Well, Garretts *do* do that sort of thing."

Miles's eyes began to water. "The first thing she might do is remove me from your presence, my good cat. No offense, of course."

Sir Sweetums drew back at Miles's hearty sneeze. "Well, yes, perhaps that would be wise. I'll be on my way now."

"Oh," Abby said, holding out her hand, "don't go."

"But I must, my dear. You are safely settled. My task is finished."

"But," Abby said, "don't you want to see how our lives turn out? What if we have rotten kids?"

Sir Sweetums smiled again, a cheshire cat smile. "I'm a permanent member of the Guardian Feline Association, my dear. We're always about, lending a paw when needed. Now that you're here, I daresay I'll be popping into medieval England more regularly."

"Always on Christmas Eve," Miles said with another sneeze. "I doubt anything else during the year will give me quite the same start as watching you speak."

Sir Sweetums lifted a paw in farewell. "Until next year, then. God be with you, my dears!"

Sir Sweetums vanished. Abby looked at Miles with a watery smile.

"Hell of a cat, huh?"

Miles laughed. "Indeed, my love, he certainly is. Now, I believe you and I have some unfinished business below with a priest."

She followed him down the tight staircase to find the priest standing near Miles's inadequate bonfire, shivering. Abby took one last look around the hall and shook her head. The place was a dump. It made her apartment look like a four-star hotel suite.

Then Miles stopped, looked down at her, and smiled. He held out his hand for her.

Abby put her hand in his. The floor squished under her Keds as she let Miles lead her to the priest. Maybe she would ask for a shovel for Christmas next year. Why hadn't she thought to stuff a can of disinfectant in her jacket before she'd left the twentieth century?

Abby came to from her contemplation of Miles's floor to find the priest looking at her, waiting for her to give some sort of answer in the affirmative to the question of whether or not she wanted Miles and medieval England for the rest of her life.

She looked up at Miles. "Shouldn't your parents be here?"

Miles shrugged. "They'll learn of it soon enough."

Abby looked at the abbot, who seemed to be warning her with his eyes alone that she was sentencing herself to a life with a condemned heretic and shouldn't she really give it a few more minutes' thought.

"I'll take him," she blurted out.

Miles hustled the priest out the door before anyone had a chance to say anything else. Abby squished her way closer to the bonfire. She'd just gotten herself married to a man some seven hundred years older than she. Talk about a May-December romance! She shivered. Hopefully his family was as open-minded as he seemed to be. She heard Miles stomping his feet outside the front door and she took a deep breath. He didn't seem to be worried about what his parents would say. They would just have to cross that bridge when they came to it.

Abby rolled her eyes. Hadn't a bridge been what had started her entire adventure?

The front door opened and Abby gave up worrying about Miles's parents. She was married now and Garretts did do it after they were married. Frequently. With enthusiasm. Her grandmother had been very clear on that.

Abby stood up straight and planted her hands on her waist. No time like the present to get down to business.

And what wonderful business it promised to be.

Chapter Eight

MILES SAW THE abbot comfortably ensconced in the gate-house, then returned to the hall. He stood at the threshold and looked back over his bailey. Already, his mind was overflowing with ideas for improvement. He couldn't subject Abigail to life in these conditions. He would make Speningethorpe as modern as he could, for Abigail's sake.

He stomped his muddy boots to clean them, entered his hall, and closed the door behind him. Abigail was standing next to the fire, hands on her waist. Ah, so she was prepared to do battle again. Miles leaned back against the wood and smiled. Saints, what a woman he was blessed with. His life with her would be one joy after another.

After they survived the next few hours, that is. Miles folded his arms across his chest and contemplated his next action. They were wed legally enough. To be sure, he wanted to bed her, but was it too soon?

"Hey," she said, frowning. "Why are you over there?"

"I'm watching you," he replied, with a smile.

"I'm cuter up close."

Miles laughed as he crossed the floor. "You're fetching from any distance, my lady." He pulled her into his arms and held her close. "God bless that bloody Sir Sweetums for bringing you to me."

"I couldn't agree more."

Miles held her for several minutes in silence. After a time, he began to feel quite warm. He jerked away from Abigail and gave himself the once-over to make sure none of him was on fire. Abigail was looking at him as if he'd lost his wits.

"I was growing warm," he offered.

Her eyes twinkled merrily. "Nothing seems to be smoldering, Miles."

He looked at her, feeling exceedingly uncomfortable. What was he to say, that his warmth had definitely not come from any fire? Abigail tilted her head to one side and looked at him appraisingly.

"You shaved," she noted.

He nodded. "And had a wash outside," he added. "But I'm sure you still smell better than I do."

She laughed. "Thank you. I think."

Miles nudged a piece of slimy hay with his toe. "We could kiss." He looked at her from under his eyelashes.

"We could."

"I don't want to rush you, Abby."

She shook her head, with an amused smile. "You aren't. Garretts generally do it right after the ceremony. It comes from having to wait."

"I see—" Miles trailed off. Abby had stepped up to him and put her arms around him. What was she about?

"Don't worry," she whispered, still smiling. "I'm just going to lay one on you."

He realized, belatedly, that he wasn't prepared for her actions. He and Abigail had kissed often enough, but this kiss rocked him to the core. Perhaps it was because he knew it could definitely lead to other things. Miles threw his arms around her and held on.

Too soon, she allowed him to breathe. He blinked.

"I think," he managed, "I would like to have another of those laid on me."

She obliged him. Miles clung to her and hoped he wouldn't embarrass himself by having his knees buckle under him.

He'd planned to give her a goodly while to accustom herself fully to him, perhaps even a few days, but if she didn't stop kissing him thusly, he sincerely doubted he would be able to do much but hold onto the ragged edges of his wits. And, after all, Garretts did seem to have a schedule about these things. If Abigail wanted him now, who was he to say her nay?

He tore his mouth away. "I'm going to fall down soon, I think. Perhaps we could retire to the bed and go with the flow for a time."

Abigail laughed. "What is your family going to think when they hear you talking like a twentieth-century guy?"

"They'll think I've gone daft," he said, leading her to his bed and lying down beside her. "You should have seen the look the abbot cast my way at Seakirk when I told him to get the lead out."

"And where is the friar in question?"

"In the little room above the gatehouse," he said. He buried his hands in her hair and turned her face to his. He smiled. He'd been itching to get his hands in her hair for what seemed like years.

"Is he just a junior priest, then?" she asked.

"Nay. He's a powerful abbot."

She choked. "I see your nefarious reputation has its advantages."

He grinned at her. "Are you sorry you wed with such a one as I?"

"No, Dastardly Dan, I'm not," she said, tugging on his ear. "Come here and kiss me, you bad man."

How could he refuse? He kissed her as she wished, then he kissed her as he wished. Then he wished for less clothing between them.

"Oh, my," she said, when his hand trailed over her increasingly bare flesh.

"Indeed," he said with a shiver, as her cold fingers wandered over his chest. He would have to build better fireplaces. Perhaps he would raze the bloody keep to the ground and start over again. Abigail's hands found the warmth of his back and he yelped. Aye, more heat was surely a necessity he would see to as soon as possible.

When tunics had been discarded, he pulled her close to him and relished the feel of her bare skin against his.

"Oh, Abby," he whispered, closing his mouth over hers.

She was trembling. He hoped it was from passion and not fear. He knew it couldn't be from the cold. He was hotter than if he'd been standing in the midst of a pile of kindling.

He kissed and caressed her until both their breaths were coming in gasps. Then Abigail tore her mouth from his.

"Did you hear something?"

"Nay," he said, trying to recapture her mouth.

"It's a thumping noise, Miles."

"That's the blood pounding in your ears. 'Tis passion, Abby."

She eluded his lips. "Those are fists pounding on your gates, bucko. It isn't passion, it's company."

Miles lifted his head and frowned. "Damn."

Abigail froze. "Bad guys?"

Miles looked down at her grimly. "Knocking? Doubtful, my love. Enemies generally prefer a sneak attack."

"Then who could it be?" she asked, reaching for her tunic.

"My bloody sire, most likely." Why Rhys had chosen this precise moment for a visit . . . Miles growled. "I'm going to kill him for the interruption."

Her smile started in her eyes. "I really like you a lot."

He kissed her again, for good measure, then tore himself away and rose. He donned his tunic and waited while Abigail did the same.

"We may as well go let him in," he grumbled. "He'll pound all day if we don't."

"What are you going to tell him about me?" she asked. She looked very worried.

He shrugged. "We'll tell them you're from Michigan."

"Don't I have to be some kind of royalty to marry you?" she asked. She was starting to wheeze again.

Miles gathered her close. "As I'm hardly royalty myself, nay, you needn't be. But we can make you such, if you like." He pulled back and grinned at her. "What shall you be? Princess of Freezing Bluff?"

"I don't know why you think this is so funny," she said, her teeth chattering.

Miles laughed and kissed her. " 'Tis merely my sire, Abby. He will love you because you are you. We'll tell him you're from Michigan, which is a very long way away, and that you have no family nearby. You were out, lost your way, and wound up at my hall. That's truth enough for the moment. We'll worry about the rest later."

"If you say so."

"Trust me. Now, let's go let the irritating old man in."

He hadn't taken ten steps when the front door burst open

and not only his father, but his father and all four of his brothers burst into the hall, swords drawn, looking for all the world as if they'd expected a battle.

Rhys pulled up short and gaped. Robin, Nicholas, Montgomery, and John all did the same, piling up behind their father and almost sending him sprawling. Once the armored group of five regained their collective balance, a hush descended.

"So, 'tis as the abbot said," Robin whispered, in disbelief. "He *did* find a wench daft enough to wed him."

Rhys silenced his eldest son with an elbow to the ribs, then looked at Miles assessingly.

"I assumed I would come and find you overrun by ruffians, since you sent back your guardsmen."

"Nay, I am well," Miles said, fighting his smile.

Rhys nodded. "I can see why you wanted the hall to yourself."

"Aye," Miles agreed, "I daresay you can."

"Saints, she's fetching," Montgomery and John said together.

Miles scowled. His younger brothers were twins, and randy ones at that. He put an arm possessively around his wife.

"Aye, she is," he growled. "And she wed *me*."

"Poor girl," Robin said, with a regretful shake of his head. "Montgomery, go fetch Mother and the girls so they can offer Miles's bride some well-needed comfort. I've no doubt she's had a very *trying* day."

Miles growled at Robin. His eldest brother sent a nasty grin back his way. Miles turned his attention back to his sire. He watched his father chew on the facts for a moment or two and come to a decision. Rhys resheathed his sword and crossed the hall. He took Abigail's hand and raised it to his lips.

"Well met, daughter," he said, with a gentle smile. "My son smiles, so I must assume you have made him do so. Now, how does he sit with you? Tolerably well?"

"Oh," Abigail said faintly. "I think he's wonderful."

Miles beamed at his father. "She has excellent taste, Papa, don't you think?"

Rhys laughed. "Saints, Miles, here I thought I would find you shut up in this pile of stones like a hermit, and now I find I've interrupted the post-nuptial festivities."

"Aye," Miles said, remembering why he'd been irritated with his sire. "You timing is, as usual, very poor."

He would have said quite a bit more, but he didn't have the chance, for his mother, sisters, sister-in-law, and numerous nieces and nephews had entered the hall, along with the abbot, several people who weren't family but thought they were, and an army of servants. Miles groaned. Where was he going to put all these souls? And where was he going to find privacy with Abigail?

"Peachy," he muttered to Abigail, then threw his father a very disgruntled look. He received a wink and a hearty laugh in return. Miles scowled and turned to watch his mother come toward him. He had the feeling, much to his further disgruntlement, that once the introductions were made, it would be the last he would see of his wife for quite some time.

ABBY STAGGERED UNDER the onslaught of people. Once Miles's mother had entered the room, chaos erupted. If her beauty hadn't been enough to do it, the way she herded the men into work parties certainly would have. She was followed by at least two dozen people who were dressed very nicely, and at least a dozen who Abby surmised must be servants. Miles's mother came to her immediately.

"I'm Gwen," she said, "and I can see why Miles kept you a secret, for he would have been fighting his brothers to have you."

"Oh," Abby said, clutching Miles's hand, "I think I would have liked him best anyway."

Miles laughed and gave Abby's hand a gentle squeeze. "I think she loves me, Mama."

"How on earth were you fortunate enough to find her, my son?"

"Abby chased her cat into my moat."

Abby willed Miles to look at her, and he did—finally. He winked, then leaned down to kiss her.

"I'm afraid the only privacy we may have is in the stables. When I can get you away from the women of my family, that is."

"Shucks, what's a little hay between friends?"

"My thoughts exactly—"

And that was the last she saw of him for quite some time. Gwen took her in hand. Abby found nothing but affection and acceptance in Gwen's aqua eyes, and soon felt completely at ease with the woman. Gwen formally introduced her to Miles's four brothers, his twin sister, and his elder sister. Then there were the in-laws, which was confusing in its own right; grandchildren, and then non-family members who seemed to feel just like family. Abby promptly forgot everyone's name. Oh, the hazards of too many in-laws!

"Greenery!" one older boy yelled. "Where does it go, Grandmother Gwen?"

Gwen linked arms with Abby. "'Tis Abby's hall, Phillip. She'll tell you where she likes it."

"And we've things for you," said another in-law, a woman who looked like a younger version of Gwen. "I'm Amanda. Miles and I fight, but not as badly as I fight with Robin. Oddly enough, I had the feeling Miles would marry soon. I think I must have brought these with you in mind." She held up a basket filled with, of all things, solid soap, clean linen towels, and a comb. Abby sniffed the soap cautiously, then smiled in relief.

"Oh, *thank* you."

"Aye, and I've things for you, too," another young woman said. She had long, blond hair and dusty green eyes. "I'm Anne, Robin's wife, and I never fight with Miles. I think he's wonderful, even when he's being moody. I daresay you've already begun to tame him. He seems very cheerful."

"Well, I—" Abby began, then she was distracted by clothes that didn't look like Miles's hand-me-downs.

Then it was off to a corner behind a makeshift screen. She was given hot water and no privacy for a sponge bath, but the clothes more than made up for that. No sooner had she been properly dressed and coiffed than heavenly smells began to waft from the kitchen.

She came around the screen to find that the hall had been transformed. The floor had been freshened up, tables had been set up and covered with tablecloths, and food was starting to pour from the kitchen. Greenery had been scattered all over the hall and even a tapestry had been hung.

She looked for Miles. He was standing near the bonfire listening to his younger brothers, who seemed to be tumbling over each other trying to tell him some story. Then he caught sight of her. Abby blushed as Miles left his siblings talking to thin air and came directly across the room, pushing family and furniture out of his way to get to her. She smiled weakly.

"Like the dress?"

His mouth came down on hers. Well, that was answer enough. She clutched his arms as he finally lifted his head. Once she could focus again, she looked at him.

"I guess you do."

He smiled down at her. "Aye, I do." He stepped back a pace, made her a low bow, then offered her his arm. "Shall we partake of the festivities?"

Abby took his arm and let him lead her to the table. Within minutes, the table was overflowing with food. A small handful of musicians produced instruments and began to play. The festivities were soon going full swing. Abby had barely started to eat before she found herself being paid more attention to than the medieval celebration going on around her.

Toddlers toddled over to her. Children wanted to touch her hair and listen to her talk with her strange accent. And once they'd done that to their satisfaction, they simply wanted to be near her. Miles's family hovered around her, telling her stories about her new husband, asking her questions about her own life. His older brothers repeatedly asked why she'd settled for such a clod of dirt when there were two perfectly good de Piaget brothers still looking for wives.

After quite a while spent at the table, the company adjourned to chairs encircling the fire. Abby leaned back against her chair and looked around her, hardly able to believe the twists and turns life had sent her along over the past few days. She shook her head, marveling. Her grandmother's favorite saying had been "All in due time." That, of course, had always been preceded by a bout of serious headshaking. Abby understood completely. Who would have thought she would find the man of her dreams and the Christmas she'd always wanted seven hundred years in the past? Maybe *due time* had a sense of humor—but what a wonderful sense of humor! So Miles's hall wasn't exactly something Currier and Ives would have put to canvas; this was so much better because it was real.

Food abounded. Family was gathered around her, a family that came with helpful hands, warm hearts, and teasing smiles. She had a tree in the form of the greenery Miles's family had lovingly brought to spruce up his castle. The fire sparkled enough for hundreds of twinkling lights. And her best gift sat next to her, running his thumb over the back of her hand and looking at her with love in his eyes. He had given her so much more than a roof over her head, his own clothes to wear, and inedible stew. Abby smiled at him through her tears.

"Thank you," she said simply.

He smiled in return. "For all these appropriately Christmassy items? For my family?"

She nodded. "And, most especially, for you."

"God bless my surly and moody self," he said, with a gentle smile. He put his arm around her and pulled her close. "I love you," he whispered into her ear.

"I love you, too."

He pulled back and looked at her. "I don't know what my life would have been like without you . . . ha . . . ha . . . ha-hachoo!"

"Uncle Miles!" a young boy said, frothing at the mouth with excitement. "Look what I found outside!"

"Oh, kittens," Abby exclaimed. "How wonderful!"

"Won—wonder—hachoo!" Miles sneezed. "Dab cats!"

"Oh, Kendrick," Amanda exclaimed, following hard on the boy's heels, "put the kittens back outside!" She looked at Abby apologetically. "His father put him up to it, of course, the lout." She turned to the brother in question and glared. "Saints, Robin, you know Miles can't bear the smell of the beasties!"

Robin didn't appear to care. He was tipped back in his chair, laughing heartily. Or at least he was until Amanda marched over, put her foot on the front of his chair, and shoved.

"Out, now," Miles said, hauling Abby to her feet. "Before the war erupts."

"Where to?" she asked as he dragged her toward the door, away from his laughing family and bellowing brother.

"The stables. They'll never look for us there."

Abby fled with him outside and to the stables. They stopped finally in front of a stall. They hay was covered with a blanket and a candle had been left lit on a stool.

"My mother obviously thinks nothing of my horseflesh,"

Miles grumbled. "She could have burned the whole bloody place down."

"Your mother did this?"

He smiled down at her and drew her into his arms. "She was freshly wed once too. She likes you very much, else she wouldn't have bothered. Come to think of it, I like you very much too."

"How convenient," she said, smiling up at him.

"I thought so," he said, lowering his mouth to hers. "Now, where were we before my family overran our wedding bed?"

AND AS MILES made her his in that very chilly stable, Abby decided several things.

One, central heating just wasn't all it was cracked up to be.

Two, condemned heretics made mighty fine lovers.

And three, Sir Sweetums deserved a promotion!

Epilogue

SIR MAXIMILLIAN SWEETUMS reclined on a most comfortable cloud, contemplating his well-deserved repast. He brought a particularly plump Tender Vittle to his aristocratic nose and sniffed critically. Ah, the bouquet was excellent! He partook with relish.

"So, Boss, you finished up de job?"

Sir Sweetums was in such a fine mood, he didn't begrudge the bulldog his interruption of afternoon tea. "Yes, dear Bruno, my task is finished. The Abigail is well settled."

"Yeah, Boss, but dose kids she's gonna get." The bulldog shuddered. "Yikes!"

"Never fear, Bruno. I'll be there to aid her when she needs it. And I'll have a care for her little ones. All part of the job, you know."

Bruno struggled to scratch behind his ear. Once he managed to get his foot within range, he scratched thoughtfully.

"Dese jobs, Boss. Uh, don't you need some help sometimes?"

"Indeed, Bruno, it is a most taxing venture," Sir Sweetums agreed. "Never a moment to sit idly by."

"Den, uh, Boss, I was wonderin', you know, when . . . uh—"

The bulldog was positively aquiver with nervousness. Sir Sweetums looked at his loyal companion and felt compassion stir within his feline breast.

"Perhaps the next assignment, dear boy. It looks to be quite a tangle to unravel."

"Golly, Boss, really? I really get to go dis time?"

Bruno leaped up in joy, lost his balance and fell through half a dozen clouds before he remembered how it all worked.

Sir Sweetums sighed. It would be a very long unraveling indeed, with Bruno aboard.

"More cream, Boss?" Bruno bellowed happily from quite a distance. "Anything else I can get yous?"

"Perhaps something from a different galaxy, my friend," Sir Sweetums called.

Bruno bounded off enthusiastically. Sir Sweetums resettled himself to enjoy his peace and quiet. Yes, indeed, how happy The Abigail and The Miles were together. Sir Sweetums basked in the glow of a task well finished. The tranquillity was, of course, destined to last only as long as it took The Abigail to produce a child or two.

Bruno was, unfortunately, very correct about the offspring. Yikes! was the word indeed.

But never fear, dear reader, never fear! Sir Sweetums knew that The Abigail and her dashing Sir Miles would weather any storm together and love each other more for the surviving of it. In time he would, as a member of the Guardian Feline Association, have The Abigail's dark-haired, gray-eyed children to watch over. With any luck at all, they wouldn't inherit The Miles's propensity for sneezing at the slightest provocation. Sir Sweetums smiled.

It was indeed a wonderful afterlife!

The Three
Wise Ghosts

Prologue

THE INN SAT back, well off of the main road, nestled cozily on the hillside amongst rosebushes, hollyhocks, and delphiniums which had long since turned their minds to sleep for the winter. It was a comfortable abode fashioned of sturdy stone walls and a heavy, timbered roof. Well-wrought leaded windows found themselves surrounded by thick branches of climbing roses and wisteria. Light spilled out from the windows, beckoning to the weary traveler to enter and join in a companionable quaff or two of ale before retiring to the comfort of one of several guest chambers. At the moment a thin stream of smoke wafted up into the darkened sky from one of the fireplaces, as if to indicate that the innkeeper was indeed at home with something tasty on the fire.

At the sight of the smoke, a tall, elderly man quickened his pace up the way. His feet skimmed heedlessly over the finely laid brick pathway that wound through the slumbering garden. He hardly noticed the richly appointed entryway with its heavy beamed ceiling. He paid no attention whatsoever to the long hallway with its walls covered by pictures of famous (and infamous) former guests. His crisply pleated kilt flowed gracefully around him and his great sword slapped against his thigh as he strode down the passageway. There was trouble afoot. He could smell it from a hundred paces.

He came to an abrupt halt at the kitchen entrance. And then Ambrose MacLeod, Laird of the Clan MacLeod during the glorious sixteenth century, statesman of the most diplomatic proportions and thinker of deep, profound thoughts, stared at the sight that greeted his eyes, frowned a most severe frown, and wondered what in the blazes had ever possessed him to leave his beloved Highlands. Never mind that he had kin in the castle up the way who warranted looking after now and then. Never mind that the Boar's Head Inn boasted the most reputable and thorough hauntings on the isle—a distinction Ambrose had personally seen to at every opportunity. Those were things that could have sorted themselves out without him.

Nay, he decided as he observed the occupants of the kitchen, 'twas these two who had held him so long away from home. And damn the lads both if they weren't assorted family, making it just that much harder to leave them to peaceably killing each other!

"And *I* say," the first said, "he spends far too much time fiddling over those infernal gadgets of his."

"Better that than flitting from place to place, never staying more than a few months," the second retorted. "As *she* does."

"At least she has the imagination to do so."

"She's flighty," the second grumbled. "Changeable."

"At least she hazards a risk now and again. Unlike that stuffy, pebble-counting lad of yers!"

That final insult was delivered by the man on Ambrose's left. Ambrose looked at the ruddy-complected, red-haired former Laird of the Clan McKinnon (and Ambrose's cousin by way of several intermarriages), Hugh McKinnon. Hugh was done up handsomely in full dress, his kilt swinging about his knees as he bounced from one foot to the other, obviously anxious to inflict bodily harm on the man he faced.

And that man was Fulbert de Piaget, second son of the fourteenth Earl of Artane, and to Ambrose's continued astonishment, his own beloved sister's husband. Second son though he might have been, Fulbert carried himself with the complete arrogance of an Artane lad. Ambrose couldn't help but feel a faint admiration for that, especially considering the murkiness of Fulbert's claim to several other titles. Fulbert's finely embroidered doublet flapped about his legs as he gestured with his mug as he might have a sword.

"Pebble-counting!" Fulbert thundered, ale sloshing madly

over the edge of his cup onto the floor. "I'll have you know me nevvy does a proper day's work!"

"As does she!"

"When she can remember her place of employment!"

The two glared at each other furiously for a long, highly charged moment, then they lunged, bellowing clan mottos and other such slogans appropriate to the moment.

"Oh, by the saints," Ambrose exclaimed, striding out into the chamber and interrupting the fisticuffs. "Now's not the time for quibbling over tiny faults. We've serious work to do!" He turned a dark look on his cousin. "Hugh, cease with this meaningless bickering."

Hugh wanted to do anything but that—that much was apparent by the white-knuckled grip he had on the hilt of his still-sheathed sword.

"Hugh," Ambrose warned.

Hugh scowled, then ducked his head and gave his polished boots a closer look. "As ye will, Ambrose," he muttered.

Ambrose turned to his brother-in-law. "Fulbert?"

Fulbert looked to be chewing on a word or two, but finally nodded briefly and sought comfort in his cup.

"Then 'tis settled," Ambrose said, pulling up a chair and settling into it. "Sit, lads, and let us speak one last time of our plans. The pair's set to arrive on the morrow."

"Ha," said Fulbert, pursing his lips. "We'll be fortunate indeed if she manages to find her way—"

Ambrose held out his hand to stop Hugh from throwing his chair rather ungently in Fulbert's direction.

"Actually, Fulbert," Ambrose said, turning to him, "your brother's son—albeit many times removed—was the one I was most concerned about. He was particularly difficult to convince."

"And how would you know?" Fulbert demanded. " 'Twere me own sweet self that saw to getting him here. And I can't say as I blames him not wanting to come, what with all the important work he does." He cast a pointed look at Hugh. "Unlike that girl—"

"There's naught a thing wrong with me wee granddaughter," Hugh declared. He paused, looked faintly puzzled, then frowned. "I suppose I could consider her such."

"Indeed, you could, Cousin," Ambrose said, with a nod.

"And, to be sure, there is naught amiss with her." He ignored Fulbert's snort. "Now, lads, let us turn our minds back to the good work set before us." He looked at his kinsman. "You saw to the other establishment, did you not?"

"Aye," Hugh said, with a smile. "No room at the inn, as it were. Not that it was all that difficult, it being the season and all."

Ambrose nodded in approval. "I've seen to it that there will be none but the two reservations available here for the holidays and given instructions to Mrs. Pruitt on who shall receive them. All we must do is wait for the morrow and then lend a hand where needed."

"I still say we should have planned something in particular," Fulbert grumbled. "Perhaps a reprise of my performance for that Dickens fellow."

Hugh snorted. "'Twere bad fish he ate that gave him those foul dreams."

"Dreams? He bloody immortalized me Christmas visit in print!"

Ambrose suppressed the urge to throw his hands up in despair; it was a wonder he saw anything accomplished with these two underfoot. Even though the telling of tall tales went hand in hand with proper haunting, there was no time for such happy recollections now. If he allowed Fulbert any more room for speaking, they'd be listening to him boast till dawn.

"We're best served by seeking our rest," he said, rising. "We've a full fortnight ahead of us."

"But, wait, Ambrose," Hugh said, holding up his hand. "Ye never told us where ye went to find me wee one."

Those were memories Ambrose didn't care to discuss. After all, they had been surely the most traumatic events of his afterlife. He, Ambrose MacLeod, powerful laird of an even more powerful and noble clan, had taken his pride and courage in hand to do what no other laird (alive or otherwise) had done before him. His sires and grandsires who had passed on before him had no doubt held their collective breaths until his task had been accomplished.

"Aye," Fulbert said, suddenly perking up. "Just where was it you went to fetch that fidgety, harebrained—"

Ambrose cut him off by suddenly sitting back down. Why his sweet sister had chosen to marry an irascible Englishman, Ambrose would never know, but there it was. He took the mug Hugh handed him, and had a long swallow of ale, just to shore up his strength.

"Well," he began slowly, "it was a tad more difficult to track her down than I'd thought it would be."

Fulbert smirked. Hugh looked primed to say something nasty in return, so Ambrose quickly told the worst of it to distract them.

"I began in a Colonial fast-food establishment," he announced.

Both Fulbert and Hugh gaped at him, stunned into silence.

Ambrose took a firmer grip on his cup. "Indeed, I was forced to venture into more than one."

Gasps echoed in the kitchen.

"Failing to find her there, I searched further and learned that she had taken other employment." He paused. "In a theme park."

Fulbert tossed back the remaining contents of his cup and lunged for the jug. Hugh went quite pale in the face.

"Is there more?" Hugh asked, in trembling tones. "I beg ye, Ambrose, say us nay!"

Indeed, there *was* more, and Ambrose was loath to give voice to the telling of it. He looked about the chamber, just to avoid the eyes of his companions.

"I discovered," he admitted, his voice barely audible, "that she had been dressing up as a mouse."

"By the saints, nay!" Hugh gasped.

Fulbert made gurgling noises as he struggled to express himself. Finally he managed a word or two.

"You!" he exclaimed, pointing an accusing finger at Ambrose. "After all these years of proper haunting . . . consorting with cartoon characters! By the saints, Ambrose, what were you thinking!"

"I did what was required," Ambrose said stiffly. "And once she was found, I paid a short visit to her brother. He was quite willing to send her off on an errand here and more than happy to believe a healthy case of indigestion had given him the idea."

"Och, but the indignity of it all," Hugh breathed. "Traveling all the way to—" his voice trailed off meaningfully.

No one could voice the word.

California.

And, worse yet, the southern region of it! Aye, 'twas enough to give any sensible shade the shakes.

" 'Tis just that," Fulbert said darkly, "which leads me to believe that perhaps the lass is not quite—"

"The lass?" Hugh interrupted indignantly. "No matter where she's been—" He swallowed audibly and then pressed on. "At least she possesses some spark of creativity. *I'm* less than certain about that lad of yers—"

Fulbert leaped to his feet, cast aside his cup and drew his sword. "I'll not have me nevvy slandered by a man in skirts!"

"Skirts!" Hugh gasped, hopping up from his chair and flinging aside his goblet also. He drew his sword with relish. "Outside, ye blasted Brit. I'll need room fer me swingin'."

Ambrose gave one last fleeting thought to the peace and comfort of his ancestral home in the Highlands before he thundered a command for the lads to cease. He shook his head in disgust. "By the saints," he said, "have you nothing better to do than fight with each other?"

Fulbert looked faintly surprised. "Actually Ambrose, 'tis fine enough sport for me—"

"Aye," Hugh agreed. "Passes the time most pleasantly—"

Ambrose thrust out his arm and pointed to the door. "Begone, the both of you and leave me to my ale."

Fulbert opened his mouth to protest. Ambrose gave him the quelling look he'd given to more than one adversary over the course of his long and successful career. Fulbert shut his mouth with a snap and vanished from the kitchen. Hugh made Ambrose a quick bow and bolted as well.

Ambrose leaned back in his chair and sighed. Now that he finally had peace for thinking, he turned over in his mind the events of the past pair of months, gingerly avoiding the memories of his trip to the Colonies. Perhaps he shouldn't have meddled, but how could he have helped himself? Young Megan was his granddaughter—never mind how many generations separated them. Despite the personal indignities he'd suffered already in this venture, how could he not feel a certain responsibility to her and her happiness? And he had to admit Fulbert's lad was a good one, despite his preoccupation with modern inventions.

Aye, he would simply do all he could for them, then pray they had the good sense to finish falling in love by themselves.

Though, considering the pair due to arrive on the morrow, the only good sense to be found in the inn would be his own.

Chapter One

MEGAN MACLEOD MCKINNON stood on the side of the dirt road, stared at her surroundings, and wondered why in the world she'd ever agreed to any of this. She'd known the British Isles could be damp, but she'd never suspected they would be *this* damp. And what happened to that dry rain that supposedly fell strictly for atmosphere? Maybe she'd taken a wrong turn somewhere, like at Kennedy. She should have boarded that plane bound for Italy. How rainy could it be in Italy this time of year?

Of course, if things had gone according to plan, she would have been ensconced in a cozy inn, reading Dickens and sipping tea while toasting her toes against a cheery fire.

Instead she found herself trudging up a muddy road on the Scottish border in the middle of what had to be the worst storm in two hundred years. In December, no less. With only the clothes on her back.

This was not exactly a Currier and Ives kind of Christmas vacation.

She turned her face into the wind, picked her way around a puddle and kept walking. She wouldn't go home until she'd done what she came to do. She'd bungled every other job she'd ever had, but she wouldn't bungle this one. No matter how awful things got.

Rain began to leak past her collar. As her back grew increasingly damp, her thoughts turned to her brother. This was, of course, entirely his fault. If he hadn't been bitten by that search-for-your-ancestors bug, he never would have bought a castle and all that went with it, and he never would have sent her to look it over. Surely he should have known what would befall her on this ill-fated trip.

Hadn't he had an inkling that her row-mate on the flight over might be a screaming two-year-old? Shouldn't he have warned her that her luggage might vanish as she stood innocently in line to buy a train ticket north? Should there not have been some doubt in his overused brain that the weather in December might be a tad bit on the wet side? Hadn't he felt the slightest desire to rethink his plans for her as he booked her a room in a no-stoplight town at an inn that would subsequently lose her reservation?

Megan hopped over another pothole and gave her missing reservation more thought. Had it been merely missing or deliberately mislaid? Had the desk clerk taken one look at her bedraggled, luggageless self and come to a hasty decision about her desirability as a guest?

After making certain she understood there was no room for her at his inn, he had offered to make her a reservation at the only other hotel within miles. *A quiet place, just a wee bit up the road—conveniently near the castle,* he'd said. Megan had been overjoyed that there was actually another bed waiting for her within walking distance, especially since she hadn't seen anything resembling a taxi since the train had paused long enough for her to jump down onto the platform. Maybe Thorpewold didn't see all that many visitors.

She lurched to a stop, braced herself against the wind and peered into the mist. She frowned. Had she taken a wrong turn somewhere? Just how far was "wee" anyway?

Then she froze. Either the wind was revving up for a new round of buffeting, or that was a car approaching. She listened carefully. Yes, that was a car, and it sounded like it was heading her way. Megan stood up straighter and dragged a hand through her hair. No sense in not looking her best for a potential ride. The car came closer. She put on her best smile and started to wave. It was the Cinderella parade wave she'd perfected but never had the chance to use.

Even the headlights were now visible. Good. At least she wouldn't get run over before she could beg a ride.

"Hey," she shouted as the car materialized from the mist, "can I have a—"

She barely had time to close her mouth before the tidal wave struck. The car whizzed by, drenching her from head to toe. Megan looked down at her mud-splattered self, then blinked and looked up. The taillights faded into the drizzle.

She hadn't been seen. That was it. No one was in such a hurry that they would drive past a dripping maiden in distress and not offer so much as a "keep a stiff upper lip" in passing. Well, at least the car seemed to be going somewhere. That was reassuring. Megan wiped her face and continued on her way.

Fortunately it took her only minutes to reach civilization. The mist lifted far enough for her to see a sturdy, comfortable-looking inn. The lights were on and smoke was pouring from the chimneys; these were very good signs. Maybe she would actually be able to hold on to her reservation this time.

Her eyes narrowed at the sight of her errant would-be rescuer's car parked so tidily next to the inn. A tall figure headed toward the door and a horrible thought occurred to her. What if her room was the last one and this person sweet-talked his way into it?

She bolted for the steps. The man entered before her, but Megan didn't let that deter her. She grabbed the door behind him, then elbowed her way past him and sprinted to the little desk in the alcove under the stairs. She plopped her shoulder bag onto the counter then smiled triumphantly at the woman behind the desk. In fact, the thrill of victory was making her light-headed. She clutched the edge of the desk as she felt herself begin to sway.

And then, quite suddenly, her feet were no longer under her. She squeaked as she felt herself being lifted up by what seemed to be remarkably strong arms. She threw her arms around very broad shoulders—just in case her rescuer decided she was damp enough to warrant dropping. She let go with one hand to push her soggy hair back out of her eyes. She opened her mouth to tell him his actions would have been more timely had they occurred fifteen minutes earlier, then completely lost track of what she'd intended to say.

Maybe all that water had seeped into her brain. Or maybe she'd just never seen anyone quite this handsome before. *This* was the kind of man she wouldn't mind finding under the Christmas tree with a bow on his head.

His face was ruggedly chiseled, with only the fullness in his mouth to soften his features. His dark blond hair was, irritatingly enough, perfectly dry and casually styled, as if he'd just shaken it out that morning and it had behaved simply because he'd wanted it to. Megan stared into his bluish-green eyes and found that she was fanning herself. There was something so blatantly, ruthlessly handsome about the man that she felt a bit weak in the knees. All right, so his driving habits left a lot to be desired. The man had saved her from a possible faint and, considering how he looked up close, she thought she might be able to forgive him.

"Thanks," she managed, surreptitiously wiping a bit of drool from the corner of her mouth.

He only frowned back at her.

Even his frown was beautiful. Megan smiled her best smile. "Thanks," she repeated, wondering if it would sink in this time, "but I wasn't going to faint."

He pursed his lips and set her down well away from where she'd been standing.

"You were dripping on my laptop," he said, reaching down to give his computer bag a quick swipe. He looked back at her. "And you're also dripping on the carpet," he noted.

Megan blinked. That certainly didn't sound like an undying declaration of love, nor an offer to stuff himself in her stocking. Perhaps her current state of drowned-ratdom was getting in the way of his falling at her feet and pledging eternal devotion. She flipped her wet hair to the other side of her face, hoping to achieve a more windblown, ruffled look.

The man looked down at the new drops of water on his computer bag, then scowled at her.

"How did you manage to get so wet?" he demanded.

Megan frowned. Maybe hers wasn't the only brain that had taken on too much water. "You would know," she said.

He blinked. "I would?"

"You splashed me," she reminded him.

"I did?"

"With your car!"

"Hmmm," he said, then glanced down at his computer. Something must have caught his attention because he knelt down and started unzipping the bag. Megan watched as he pulled out a cell phone and fired it up.

Megan gritted her teeth. Somehow his manly good looks had distracted her, but she was feeling much better now. This was not the kind of man for her, no sir. No matter how finely made he was, if he couldn't remember his moments of unchivalry and apologize properly for them, she wanted nothing further to do with him.

She turned her back on him and his bad manners and planted herself resolutely in front of the little desk that seemed to serve as the check-in point. When he could tear himself away from work long enough to apologize, then she would think about forgiving him. Until then, he could suffer. She would ignore him until he begged her to stop.

That resolved neatly, she gave her attention to the matter at hand: throwing herself upon the mercy of the innkeeper. She took in the sight of the sad attempts at making the reception area seem dressed for the holidays, hoping to find something there she could gush over. A little buttering up of the proprietress couldn't go wrong. The desk was decorated with a few sprigs of holly and a ribbon or two. Megan looked up. Garlic hung in great bunches above the desk area, draped liberally on the overhang made by the stairs.

"Expecting vampires any time soon?" she asked the woman behind the counter.

The white-haired woman leaped to her feet as if she'd been catapulted out of her chair.

"Ye've no idea," she whispered frantically. Her eyes darted from side to side and she kept looking over her shoulder as if she expected to be attacked from behind at any moment.

Megan opened her mouth to suggest that perhaps the garlic might do the woman more good if she wore it around her neck, then thought better of it. The innkeeper looked as if one good push would topple her right over the edge as it was.

"Yer name, lass?" the woman asked, leaning forward as if to keep the walls from overhearing.

"Megan," Megan began slowly. "Megan McKinnon."

The woman's hand flew to her throat and she gasped. "A McKinnon in the house! The saints preserve us all!"

"This isn't good," Megan said, biting her lip. This was all

she needed, to be kicked out on account of her ancestry. "My mother was a MacLeod," she offered.

"Even worse!" the woman exclaimed.

"I'm from America," Megan said quickly. "Does that help? No, wait, don't say anything else. I don't want to know. Let's just get down to business and forget all the rest. Ye Olde Tudor Inn called over and made a reservation for me. You did get the call, didn't you, Mrs. . . . ?"

"Pruitt," the woman moaned. "And, aye, I've got yer roo—" her voice cracked, then she cleared her throat. "Room," she managed. "If ye're sure ye want it."

"Oh, I want it," Megan assured her.

"Ye've a private bath, too," Mrs. Pruitt added. "Up the stairs, down the hallway on yer left. If ye're certain here is where ye truly want to stay—"

A pen suddenly slapped itself down next to Megan's hand. Mrs. Pruitt screeched and leaped back, making Megan jump. Megan took a deep breath to calm her suddenly racing heart. Then she remembered the splashing one who'd been kneeling beside her, dusting off his precious computer. He'd obviously decided to interrupt Mrs. Pruitt's tirade by throwing his pen at her. Maybe he was antsy to get checked in. Megan turned toward him, ready to give him a lecture on not frightening potential hostesses.

Only he wasn't standing next to her anymore. He was talking on his cell phone, looking for a plug for the laptop he'd already unearthed from its case.

Odd. Megan looked back at Mrs. Pruitt. Maybe this quaking creature had produced the pen with a clever sleight of hand trick. But if she'd been the one to do it, why had she screeched like a banshee? Megan decided it was best not to give that any more thought. Mrs. Pruitt owned a hotel possessing a room with a private bath. At this point, that was all that mattered.

She signed her name and held out the pen. Mrs. Pruitt looked at it in horror.

"Okay," Megan said, setting the pen down carefully. "You don't seem to want this. I'm not sure why, but I'm certain I don't want to know. What I do want to know is if I can get dinner here."

"In an hour," Mrs. Pruitt blurted out. "In the dining room. The saints preserve us through it!"

"Okay," Megan agreed. "I'm sure it will be just lovely. Now, where do I go—"

"Up the stairs. Last door on the left." The woman practically flung the key at her.

Megan caught it neatly and gathered up her shoulder bag.

"Do ye need yer other bags carried up?" Mrs. Pruitt asked.

Megan paused. Her lack of luggage certainly hadn't aided her cause previously, but at least this time she had the key already in hand.

"My luggage was stolen," Megan admitted.

"Oh merciful saints above!" the woman exclaimed. "What'll happen next to ye?"

"It wasn't all that bad—"

"Ach, but ye've no idea," the woman interrupted, her eyes practically rolling back in her head. "No idea—"

"BY THE SAINTS, MRS. PRUITT, QUIT YER BABBLING. AND YOU, MEGAN, GO UP TO YER BLOODY BEDCHAMBER!"

Mrs. Pruitt gave vent to another screech and ducked down behind the desk. Megan whirled around with a gasp, incensed that a perfect stranger should speak to her so rudely.

"What did you say?" she demanded of the delectable hunk of manliness with no manners.

He didn't look up.

"Hey," she said, coming to stand next to him, "I asked you a question." She dripped on him for good measure.

He looked up and blinked at her. "Yes?" he asked, tipping his phone away from his mouth.

Megan looked at him with narrowed eyes. "Who said you could order us around like that?"

"I beg your pardon?"

"Hey," Megan said, wagging her finger at him, "don't give me that changing your voice routine either. Where'd that obnoxious accent go?"

There was a groan and a thump. Megan looked over to find that Mrs. Pruitt had fallen to the floor in a dead faint.

"I haven't the foggiest notion of what you're going on about," the man said, looking very perplexed. Then he turned back to his computer and said no more.

Megan looked from him to their fallen proprietress and then back to him. He was already entrenched in his business again. Obviously good looks and good manners did not necessarily come in the same package. She sighed. So much for a handsome stocking stuffer this year.

She turned and walked back across the foyer. It took only a touch on the arm to have Mrs. Pruitt roused from her swoon and screeching again.

"It's just me," Megan said, flinching. "I think you fainted."

"I'm f-fine," Mrs. Pruitt said, her teeth chattering like castanets. She accepted Megan's help in getting back to her feet. "Just go up to yer room, miss, quick as may be."

"But I think you might need help. Is there somewhere you could lie down? I'll fix you a cup of—"

"OH, BY ALL THE BLOODY SAINTS . . ."

Megan froze. She met Mrs. Pruitt's terrified eyes and swallowed, hard. Then she looked over her shoulder. The Corporate One was still gabbing into his cell phone, completely ignoring them. Megan turned back to Mrs. Pruitt.

"The wind?" she offered.

Mrs. Pruitt turned her around and pointed her toward the stairs. "I'll bring ye some dry clothes as quick as may be," she said, pushing Megan across the entryway. "Just go on up, lass. *Please*."

Megan hesitated at the bottom of the staircase. What sort of loony bin had she signed herself into? Men doing business in entry halls, innkeepers begging their guests to move along, voices coming from nowhere?

"I'm beginning to wonder if I should even stay," Megan said slowly.

The front door flew open and slammed back against the wall. The next gust of wind blew Megan up half a dozen stairs. Mrs. Pruitt fled around the desk and hid behind it. Megan saw the rude one rise, shut the door and then return to his hunched down position near the wall.

She shook her head, then turned and climbed slowly up the remaining steps. It was either stay here or head back out into the storm, and the latter was a very unappealing alternative. So what if everyone else in the house was bonkers? With any luck, her room would have a heavy-duty lock on it and she could bolt herself inside except for meals.

The front door must not have closed very well because the wind seemed to howl in spite of it. Megan shivered. Mrs. Pruitt's jumpiness was starting to rub off on her.

She let herself into her room and closed the door behind her. A hot bath awaited. She smiled for the first time in hours. Yes, indeed, things were certainly looking up.

Maybe the trip would be worth it after all.

AMBROSE MACLEOD SIGHED as he stepped into the fray and forcibly removed Hugh's fingers from about Fulbert's throat.

"Dinnae order me gel about!" Hugh thundered.

"She wasn't moving bloody fast enough to suit me," Fulbert threw back, rubbing his offended neck. "And she called me accent obnoxious!"

"Which it is, especially since we agreed not to converse with them unless absolutely necessary!" Ambrose exclaimed, glaring at Fulbert. "And you needn't have spoken to the child in such a coarse manner."

Fulbert scowled. "She should have gone straight up to her chamber instead of chattering on with that blasted Mrs. Pruitt. Besides, she kept adrippin' all over his confounded . . . ah . . . confounded scribbling machine," he finished, looking less than sure of his terminology.

"That's computer, dolt," Hugh snarled. "Any fool knows that—argghh!"

Ambrose applied himself this time to removing Fulbert's beefy fingers from about Hugh's throat.

"By the saints, cease!" Ambrose put one hand on Fulbert's shoulder and the other on Hugh's and held them apart. "How are we to do any proper matchmaking when all you two can do is go at each other? I'm of a mind to banish you both outside until the deed's done."

Fulbert folded his arms over his chest and clenched his jaw. Hugh scrunched up his face in what Ambrose readily recognized as his determined expression.

"I'm beginning to think neither of you wants to see this come about."

There was more clenching and scrunching. Ambrose knew it was time for drastic measures. He'd never see anything finished if he had to spend all his time reprimanding the troops.

"Very well," he said, with his sternest look, "I've come to a decision. Since Fulbert has had his turn urging young Megan along the proper path, 'tis only fair Hugh should have his turn with Gideon. I daresay he'll know what needs to be done first."

Hugh eyed the laptop with barely restrained glee. Fulbert huffed in outrage.

"He'll damage the boy's livelihood! The saints only know what'll happen to his person!"

Ambrose clapped Hugh on the shoulder. "He'll only do what he must. Perhaps you'll have a bit more care with Megan the next time."

Fulbert harrumphed and vanished. Ambrose smiled pleasantly at his cousin.

"I'm off for a stroll, Hugh. I'll expect a report on your progress before nightfall."

"Aye," Hugh said, advancing on Gideon.

Ambrose walked through walls and such until he came to the overgrown garden. He clucked his tongue at the sight. He'd have to have another chat with Mrs. Pruitt about her care of the inn. If she'd only stop screaming long enough for him to give her his list of instructions.

Truly, women could be so confounded irrational at times.

Chapter Two

THE HONOURABLE GIDEON de Piaget, president and CEO of Artane Enterprises, suppressed the urge to take his cellular phone and smash it through the wall.

"Put the fool on the phone, Humphreys," Gideon growled.

"I fear, my lord Gideon, that your brother is engrossed in a medieval text at the moment."

"I don't doubt it!" Gideon shouted. "Interrupt him!"

Humphreys tsk-tsked. "Really, my lord. Such displays of temper do not become you."

"I'll have you sacked!" Gideon roared.

"I believe Lord Stephen retains that privilege. Have a pleasant holiday, my lord," Humphreys said.

Gideon listened to the line go dead. Damn Stephen! As if this bloody holiday was actually going to relax him! He had mergers to contemplate, acquisitions to make, huge sums of money to move about. The entire company would go under in two weeks with Stephen at the helm. If he held true to form, he'd stay buried in some blighted old manuscript while billions of pounds floated merrily off down the Thames!

Gideon closed up his laptop and jerked the plug from the wall. He'd check in and then get down to some serious work in spite of his entire staff. And once this enforced holiday was over, he'd return and sack every one of them. Starting with his personal secretary.

Gideon ground his teeth at the thought of her. Alice had

taken Stephen's suggestion that she go on holiday without so much as a by-your-leave from him personally. And this only after passing on to the rest of the employees Stephen's instructions for the entire company to refuse Gideon's calls. Gideon scowled. They could refuse to talk to him, but they couldn't control what he did four hours away from London. He would hook up his modem and pretend he was at the office. Stephen would never be the wiser.

Go on holiday or I'll sack you.

Gideon grunted as he gathered up his gear. His brother had walked into his office two days ago and said those words, as if Gideon would actually take them seriously! Stephen had been inspired, he'd said, to send Gideon off to his own favorite retreat. It would do him a world of good, or so Stephen had claimed. Gideon had thrown his brother out of his office bodily.

Of course the board meeting the next day had been a little unsettling, what with Stephen having led a unanimous vote for Gideon's holiday on pain of termination. Protests had gotten him a signed motion requiring him to leave that day and hole up in some deserted inn on the Scottish border for a fortnight. Alice had been smirking as she'd taken notes. The old harridan had probably instigated the entire affair.

Gideon strode purposefully toward the reception desk. The woman behind the desk stood, looking quite frankly unsettled. Perhaps she wasn't used to her guests assaulting outlets in her entryway. Or, more likely, she was used to Stephen who retreated here once a year to do nothing more than ensconce himself in the blasted library and bury his nose in yet another book. Gideon looked at the proprietress.

"Mrs. Pruitt, I presume?" he said, dropping his suitcase with a thud. "I'm Gideon de Piaget."

"Aye, Lord Blythwood," she said, in shaky voice. "Your b-brother said you'd be arriving today."

"No doubt," Gideon said curtly. "And it was against my will, as it happens."

Mrs. Pruitt held out the key. Her expression was such that Gideon couldn't help but feel a faint fondness for her. She looked as if she were sentencing him to certain death.

"I couldn't agree more," he said, taking the key from her trembling fingers. "My room?"

"Up the stairs," she said, her very essence seeming to become more frantic. "First door on the right."

Gideon frowned. "You do have a phone in the room, don't you?" he asked. "And an outlet?"

"Aye, my lord."

What else did he need? Gideon attributed her actions to far too much inclement weather and not enough hustle and bustle. After all, what sort of mental stimulation could a sleepy old inn in the midst of nowhere provide a person? It was no wonder Stephen loved the place. He could read in peace.

Gideon started up the stairs, eager to finally get settled in and down to work.

He frowned as he fought to reach the upper floor. His bags weren't that heavy. He looked quickly behind him, but no one was there. He could have sworn someone was tugging on his laptop. Taking a firmer grip on his things, he leaned forward and applied himself to just getting up the steps.

And then, quite suddenly, he lost his grip. He made a frantic grab for the computer, deciding in a split second that his suitcase would better survive the trip back down to the entryway. The phone had flown upward and Gideon quickly positioned himself to catch it when it came back down.

And then he watched in complete astonishment as it flew past his outstretched hand, back down the stairs and smashed into the front door. Mrs. Pruitt screeched and fled. Gideon looked at the pieces of his phone scattered in the entry.

It just hadn't been his day.

He sighed deeply as he descended and retrieved his suitcase. He turned his back on the wreckage and climbed the steps. What good was his cell phone anyway? It wasn't as if anyone would talk to him.

He entered his room, tossed his suitcase on the bed and looked about for a desk. Espying a choice antique vanity, he removed all the paraphernalia and set up his machine. Miracle of all miracles, there was a phone nearby. He unplugged it and secured the modem cable. Finding an outlet wasn't as convenient, but he'd purchased an extra long cord for just such a situation.

He shrugged out of his mac, stripped off his stifling sweater and sat down to work in his shirtsleeves. He turned the computer on, then called in to his company server. He drummed his fingers impatiently against the wood of the vanity. Remote access was irritatingly slow, but he'd make do.

He typed in his password and held his breath.

And then he smiled for the first time in seventy-two hours. Stephen obviously hadn't been thinking clearly, else he would have locked Gideon out of the system. Gideon opened up his favorite spreadsheet program and pulled up a list of the week's transactions, already feeling his pulse quicken. This was what he was meant to do. Just looking at the columns and knowing he was responsible for their contents sent a rush of adrenaline through him. The sheer power of controlling these kinds of—

The room was suddenly plunged into darkness.

Gideon swore in frustration. Damned old inn. He heaved himself up from the chair, strode across the room, and threw open the door. To his surprise, there was a light coming from the end of the corridor. Perhaps only his room was acting up. He gathered up his gear and tromped down the hallway toward the light.

He opened the door and entered without knocking. A woman gasped and Gideon pulled up short. He recognized her as the one who had dripped all over his computer downstairs. He frowned at her.

"I need your outlet."

"What?"

"Your outlet," he said impatiently. "The power's out in my room."

"I'm trying to get dressed here," she said curtly.

Gideon wrestled his attention away from his outlet search long enough to verify that she was indeed standing there in only a towel.

The sight was enough to make him pause a little longer. He started at her toes, skimmed over nicely turned ankles and continued up. Then he stopped. She had freckles on her knees. For some odd reason, it made him want to smile. It was like seeing sunshine after endless days of rain. She obviously didn't use much sunblock, or she wouldn't have had so many sun spots. And what a shame that would have been.

Sunblock. He frowned. What was the status of that cosmetic company acquisition? He'd been on the verge of closing the deal when he'd been interrupted by that disconcerting board mutiny.

"I said, I'm trying to get dressed here."

"I won't watch," he said, scanning the room.

"I don't care if you won't watch!"

He flashed her a brief smile. "Then we're settled. You don't care and I won't watch. Lovely."

She took a menacing step toward him. Gideon fell back, instinctively clutching his computer to his chest. The woman pointed toward the door.

"Get out," she commanded.

Gideon followed her long, slender arm back over to her seemingly annoyed self.

"Hey," she snapped.

He blinked and looked up at her. She seemed to have an abundance of rather reddish hair, which at the moment was piled on top of her head. And then he looked at her face and he wanted to smile all over again. It was the sunshine effect, but this was even more potent than her knees. It wasn't that he'd never seen a more beautiful woman. Indeed, he had. But he'd never seen a woman whose beauty made him think of sun-drenched meadows and armfuls of wildflowers. He was certain he'd never loitered in a meadow, but looking at this woman made him want to.

He dropped his eyes and studied her figure. She certainly knew how to wear a towel to its best advantage. A model, perhaps? No, too friendly-looking. An executive? He took a quick look around her room but saw no executive trappings. Oddly enough, he suspected she actually might be on holiday to have a holiday. But why, when she looked so well-rested, as it was?

"Do I have to call the cops?" she demanded.

Ah, an American. He nodded to himself over that. Maybe that was why she looked so relaxed. Perhaps she was from one of those big middle states where they farmed a great deal and avoided the city rush.

The thought of Americans brought to mind a clothing company acquisition his executive VP had been working on. Adam MacClure had a knack for the American market. Gideon made himself a mental note to double-check how the numbers were running on that as soon as he was back online.

He strode purposefully to the desk, plugged himself in and began the logging-in process all over again. He heard a door slam behind him. Maybe his befreckled American neighbor had decided to dress in the bathroom.

Gideon sighed in relief once he'd accessed the server. Now maybe he could get some work done. He pulled up the file on Totally Rad Clothing and flexed his fingers. He'd missed his modem during the past few hours.

The computer beeped, then the screen went blank.

"Damn!" he exclaimed.

And then he realized the bedroom light was still on.

All right, perhaps just the outlets were on the blink. No wonder Mrs. Pruitt had wished him well. Had Stephen known? Was that why he'd been banished here? Gideon cursed his brother thoroughly as he retrieved his computer case from his room and hastened back to what appeared to be the only lighted bedroom in the entire place. He would just have to use up his spare batteries.

The woman with red hair was coming out of the bathroom. She was dressed this time, but Gideon wondered where she'd gotten her clothes. Her gown looked like something from a costume shop. Early medieval. Pity she hadn't tried it on before she rented it. The hem hit her well above her ankles, and she was positively swimming in the rest of it. Perhaps it had been fashioned for a much shorter, much plumper customer.

"Not exactly a perfect fit," he noted.

She looked down at herself, then back at him. "I lost my luggage," she said defensively.

"Nothing in your size?"

"Mrs. Pruitt brought it to me," she retorted. "What else was I supposed to do—run around naked?"

"Hmmm," he said, tempted to give that more thought.

Then he caught sight of the desk and remembered what his primary task was. He sat back down and slipped a newly charged battery into the computer. Then he crossed his fingers and plugged his battery charger, with its spare battery, into the outlet. He blinked in surprise as the charging light began to flicker. Now the outlet was functioning? The inn was a disaster. He was surprised the place hadn't burned to the ground long ago.

Gideon turned the computer back on and it sprang to life. He sat back and heaved a huge sigh of relief. He would run on battery power for awhile, just to be safe. It wasn't his preferred way—

"Would you mind telling me how long you're going to be using my outlet?"

Gideon turned. "I beg your pardon?"

"My bedroom," she said, with a wave of her arm. "My bathroom. My outlet. The space I've paid for for the next two weeks. How long are you going to be camping out in here? Dare I hope it won't be for long?"

Gideon frowned at her, then turned back to his laptop. "I don't know how long I'll be. I've important things to—"

The charger made an unwholesome sound. Gideon looked at it in alarm as smoke began to curl up from its sides. He blew on it, but smoke only began to pour forth more rapidly.

He dove under the desk for the outlet and unplugged the charger, but not before he'd heard an ominous pop, followed by a crackling sound. He whipped back up, smacking his head loudly against the front edge of the desk. He lurched to his feet, clutching the top of his head.

He stared down in horror at his laptop.

It was on fire.

Gideon stood rooted to the spot, unable to believe his eyes. His last link with civilization was going up in smoke right in front of him.

"Here."

He felt something wrap itself around his head. He unwrapped and found himself holding a sweatshirt. He used it liberally, smothering and beating until he was sweating and rather cross. Finally, he stood back and looked at the ruins of his working tools. He fanned his hand sadly over the smoking remains. It was a tragedy, really. He'd planned to put this fortnight to good use.

He looked at the sweatshirt in his hands, then unwadded it to see what was left.

"So sorry about Mickey's ears," he said, casting the woman an apologetic look.

She waved her hand dismissively, "Don't worry."

"I'll have another purchased."

"You can't. They gave it to me at the Kingdom when they canned me. In lieu of severance pay."

"The Kingdom?"

"Disneyland."

"You were sacked from Disneyland?"

She scowled. "I kept stepping on Dumbo's ears, all right? Can we move on to less painful topics? Your computer, for instance."

Gideon sat down heavily. It was just more than he could talk about.

"Can I make a suggestion?"

Gideon nodded.

"Take a vacation."

"You sound like my brother." He gave her a cross look. "He's the reason I'm stranded here. Told me he'd sack me if I didn't come."

"Hmmm," she said, "a workaholic, then."

"I have many responsibilities. I run the family business."

"Really? I'd hazard a guess that the family business runs you."

He looked at her narrowly. "You Americans are very outspoken."

She shrugged. "I call 'em as I see 'em. And I'd say you needed a vacation."

"It doesn't look as if I'll have much say in the matter. Unless," he said, an idea springing to mind, "unless I might find a computer for let somewhere here about."

She laughed. "Where, here in the boonies? You'd be better off with pencil and paper."

He shook his head and rose. "No, I fear a search will have to be made. I'm already behind on the Far East markets today."

"And I'm behind in my meal schedule, so if you'll go back to where you came from, I'll be going to the dining room." She looked at the sweatshirt in his hands. "You can keep that if you like. So you can carry your mess away," she added.

Gideon was recovered enough to take the hint. He gathered up the smoldering remains and nodded at his unwilling hostess.

"Thank you . . ."

"Megan," she finished for him. "Megan McKinnon."

He balanced his computer on one arm and thrust out his hand. "Gideon de Piaget. I run Artane Enterprises."

She took his hand and smiled politely. "What a pleasure to finally learn your name after all we've shared so far."

"You've heard of me?"

"No," she said slowly, "we just met, remember? Maybe you should get some distance from your computer. The fumes aren't doing you any good."

He shook her hand some more. "You've never heard of Artane Enterprises?"

"Sorry."

"We're an international company."

"How nice for you."

Gideon found, oddly enough, that he couldn't let go of her. He wondered if it might be because of something sticky from his battery charger, but nothing seemed to be burning his skin.

Except the touch of her hand, of course.

He looked at her searchingly. "The name doesn't ring any bells for you?"

She put her free hand to her ear, listened, then shook her head. "Nary a jingle."

"I'm the president of the company."

"Ah."

"A powerful CEO."

"I see," she said. Her gaze slid down to his ravaged computer, then back up. "Believe me, I'm impressed. I would have rushed to let you into my room if I'd only known."

"I don't think you're nearly as impressed as you should be."

She pulled her hand out of his and walked over to the door. "Beat it, business boy. I'm starving."

"Scores of people know who I am," he said, as she pushed him out into the hall.

"I'd take a shower if I were you. That scorched computer smell is starting to rub off on you."

The door closed behind him with a firm click.

Gideon stopped, sniffed and then began to cough. She had a point about the last.

He made his way unsteadily down the hallway to his room, the smell of burning components beginning to make him rather ill. He entered his room, shut the door behind him and set his burden down on the floor. He'd have to take it out to the trash. By the smell of things, his hard drive hadn't survived the fire.

Then he pulled up short. The lights were back on in his

room. Gideon shook his head. Perhaps one of Stephen's henchmen had been at the fuse box, flipping things on and off on Stephen's direct orders. Gideon snorted. That he could believe.

So Megan McKinnon had no idea who he was. Gideon scowled to himself over that thought as he pulled his suitcase off the bed, opened it on the floor and rummaged inside for his kit. Maybe he was looking a bit on the unkempt side. A shave might be just the thing to restore him to proper form and jar Megan's memory. Perhaps he'd drop a hint or two about his title. He rarely made mention of it, preferring to impress and intimidate with his wits alone, but she looked to be a particularly difficult case. His was a small barony, and one he rarely had the time to visit, but it was a bit of prestige all the same. Short of clouting her over the head with a copy of *Burke's Peerage,* it was the best he could do.

And once she was properly impressed, he would turn his thoughts to procuring some other kind of machinery. If there was a laptop within a hundred miles, he would find it.

He shaved quickly, then showered, hoping a good scrub would leave him smelling less like char. He tied a towel about his hips and dragged his hands through his hair, surprised at how much better he felt. Perhaps that was what he'd needed all along. He wiped off the fog from the mirror and stared at himself. A bit of a holiday now and then wasn't such a bad thing. Snatching the occasional half hour every few months for a bit of rejuvenation might improve his disposition.

He stepped out of the bathroom, humming cheerfully. Then he came to a teetering halt.

His suitcase was on fire.

Or, more to the point, the clothes in his suitcase were on fire.

"Damn it!" he exclaimed.

He whipped off the towel and leaped across the room to beat out the flames. It took more doing than he'd expected, almost as if the fire was determined to burn through every last article of clothing he'd brought with him.

By the time all that was left was a bit of smoke wafting lazily toward the ceiling, Gideon was sweating and swearing with equal intensity.

He stared down at the ruins of his clothes, ashes which of

course contained the clothes he'd been wearing earlier, and wondered at which end of his more colorful vocabulary to start. He had the pair of boxers he'd worn into the bathroom. Period.

He waved away more smoke. It was becoming a bad habit. He waved a bit more and considered.

"Hell," he said, finally, unable to find anything else that properly expressed the depths of his disgust. He folded his arms over his still damp chest and glared at no one in particular.

"Would anyone care to tell me what I'm supposed to wear now?" he demanded. "The bed linens?"

There was a small squeak from the wardrobe to his right. His gaze snapped immediately to it and he looked at it narrowly. Wonderful. No clothes, but likely a very large rodent. He strode over to the wardrobe and jerked the door open.

There was nothing inside but a pair of baggy yellow tights and a long green tunic.

Gideon stared, agog. Tights? There was no way in hell he was going to put on a pair of yellow—

The tights shook themselves.

Gideon frowned. There had to be some kind of hole in the back of the bloody armoire. With that kind of draft, Heaven only knew what sorts of things were making their nests inside.

The tights wiggled again, brushing the tunic and sending it dancing as well.

Well, it was either wear the blasted things or go naked. Perhaps Mrs. Pruitt could be persuaded to go out in the morning and procure him something suitable.

Gideon donned his boxer shorts, then retrieved the tights from the closet. He stuck his feet into the legs and drew them up. It wasn't a pretty sight. He took an experimental step or two, finding the way the tights scrunched up between his toes to be highly irritating. He swore and hitched the tights up forcefully.

Then he coughed and abruptly hitched them back down.

He put on the tunic. It felt more comfortable than he'd dared hope. He looked into the wardrobe again, wondering if by chance there might be something to put on his feet.

Oh, but there was.

He pulled out a pair of bright purple elf shoes. Indeed, they could be nothing but elf shoes. The toes curled up several times. Gideon looked at them askance. Just watching him walk would probably put any rational person into a trance. Perhaps he could use them to hypnotize Miss McKinnon, aiding her in recovering what memories she had to have of him.

Gideon put on the shoes, cursing over the renewed scrunching of tights between his toes. But he didn't hitch; he'd learned his lesson about that.

He jerked open his bedroom door.

"The court jester arrives," he groused. "Dinner can begin."

Chapter Three

MEGAN WALKED DOWN the hallway, feeling completely ridiculous in the King Arthur-era dress that made her look as if she expected the deluge to turn into a flood at any moment—and boy would she be prepared with her hemline halfway to her knees! If her own clothes hadn't been wringing wet, she would have put them back on and taken her chances with pneumonia.

Well, it wasn't as if she was out to impress anyone. And not that anyone in the vicinity would have forgotten about business long enough to be impressed. Gideon de Piaget was a man who needed to learn to relax. She could have taught him a thing or two about leaving work behind. Considering the times she'd done just that involuntarily, she could have written a book on the subject.

Megan descended the last of the stairs only to find that Mrs. P. was no longer at her post. Megan took that as a sign: either the woman had flipped out and left the inn for good or she had retreated to the kitchen to whip up something for dinner. Megan sincerely hoped for the latter. The taste of airline food still lingered in her mouth.

Not knowing where to go, Megan began opening doors. She found a sitting room boasting the same kind of comfortable clutter her own bedroom did. It was tempting to curl up in one of the overstuffed chairs and do her best to forget the last twenty-four hours. On the other side of the hall was a beautiful library with shelves stocked full of books, and a cheery fire burning in the hearth.

After searching through several more rooms, she opened up a double door and hit the jackpot. This room contained a long, elegant dinner table, chairs, a side buffet, and several other chairs sitting against the walls seemingly waiting for their turn to be needed. Megan took it all in, delighted by the atmosphere. Then she realized what had nagged at her from the start.

There were no places set. No fine linens, no silverware, no candles in silver candelabras. Maybe Mrs. P. had driven off all her helpers.

Or maybe she'd driven herself off and Megan would be left to fend for herself.

The thought was terrifying.

All of a sudden there was a terrible clang. Megan ran to the door at the back of the dining room, then stopped short. What if intruders had come in? She looked around, snatched a handy ornamental dagger from the wall and put her hand on the doorknob. Maybe those fencing lessons would finally be of some use.

She opened the door a crack and looked into the kitchen.

Mrs. Pruitt was doing battle with thin air. She held a lid up as a shield and waved a cleaver in front of herself, frantically fighting off something Megan couldn't for the life of her see.

"Nay, I'll not listen to reason!" Mrs. Pruitt shouted. "Ye bloody Scot, I'm sick to death of ye and all yer undead cohorts! I'll sign the bloody deed and be done with ye all!"

And then, quite suddenly, Mrs. Pruitt dropped her pot lid and her blade and clapped her hands over her ears. With a screech she turned and ran straight toward Megan. Megan jumped out of the way, then turned and watched, open-mouthed, as the woman ran the length of the dining room. Gideon stood at the far doorway, wearing a similar look of disbelief.

"Out of my way," Mrs. Pruitt said, giving him a healthy shove. "I'll not stay here another minute with these bloody old ghosts ahounding me!"

Megan watched Mrs. Pruitt disappear out into the hallway, then looked at Gideon, wondering what he thought it all meant.

Then she did a double take. Gideon was dressed in bright

yellow tights and an apple green tunic that barely covered, well, all the important parts. His sandy hair was mussed. His aqua eyes were blazing. And his tights were sagging at the knees. That didn't even begin to address his shoes.

Megan set down her dagger and clapped her hand over her mouth. She didn't clap fast enough: an errant giggle escaped before she could stop it.

Gideon's expression darkened considerably.

"Oh my gosh," she gasped, doubling over and wheezing. "If your board of directors could see you now!"

"Ah ha!" he said, striding forward and wagging his finger at her. "You *do* know who I am! I knew it would come to you soon enough. Perhaps you've seen me gracing the cover of *Fortune,* or clawing my way up the *Forbes 4*—"

Megan put her hand over his mouth. "Be quiet," she said, straining her ears. "I think a door just slammed."

"Wovwee," Gideon said. He took her hand away. "Lovely," he repeated crisply. "We likely have other guests arriving and here I am, impersonating Robin Hood."

Megan did her best to put on a sober expression. "I don't think Robin Hood would have been caught dead dressed like that."

Gideon looked at her archly. "At least what I'm wearing reaches where it's supposed—"

"Sshh," she said, "listen."

They stood, silently, listening.

"I don't hear anything," he whispered.

"Neither do I . . ." she began, then realized he hadn't let go of her hand.

It occurred to her, strangely enough, that she didn't mind. His hand was very warm. It was a comfortable sort of hand, the kind you would reach for across a dinner table or as you walked down a country road. Megan looked at her hand surrounded by his and was struck by the perfect picture it made.

She looked up at him to find a most thoughtful look resting on his face. In fact, for possibly the first time since he'd drenched her, he was looking at her and truly seeing her. Completely. Intensely.

It was enough to make her start fanning herself again.

Then she paused. Other than her own heavy breathing, there was no noise.

"Mrs. Pruitt," she whispered. "Oh, no, Mrs. Pruitt!"

"Wait—"

"She's not screeching anymore," Megan said, pulling Gideon toward the hallway. "We can't let her leave!"

Gideon seemed to be struggling to keep up with her. She spared him a brief glance. The toes of his shoes were flapping wildly as he dashed alongside her.

And then the unthinkable happened.

His curly toes curled together.

He went down like a rock.

Megan left him behind without a second thought. She fled into the hallway just in time to see Mrs. Pruitt come dashing out from the library. The woman bolted for the front door, her apron strings fluttering furiously behind her.

The front door closed behind her with a resounding bang.

"Help!" Gideon called.

Megan ignored him. She leaped the remaining few steps to the door like a champion long jumper and jerked it open. She clutched the door frame.

"Oh, no!" she exclaimed.

She heard Gideon thumping behind her. He lurched to a teetering halt on his knees at the threshold.

"Oh, no!" Megan repeated, pointing frantically outside.

"Oh, yes," Gideon corrected grimly. "There she goes, pedaling her bicycle off into the gloom."

"No other helpers?" she asked, looking down at him as he knelt beside her, staring off morosely after their former hostess.

Gideon shook his head. "My brother favors this inn for precisely that reason. Mrs. Pruitt is a widow and only hires in help from the village. There'll be someone in during the week to clean, but she does everything else. The place'll be dead as nails until then."

Megan looked off at the increasingly small figure of their innkeeper. "Think she just ran to the store for an egg?"

He shook his head slowly.

Megan looked out into the twilight and sighed. "We're stuck, then."

"It looks that way."

"Doomed."

"Very likely."

"We'll starve before they find us." She looked down at him. "I can't cook."

A faint look of panic descended onto his features. "You can't?"

"Hot chocolate is the extent of my skills," she admitted. "How about you?"

"I'm a powerful executive. I have a chef."

"Ah," she said, with a nod. "I was afraid of that. You know, I got a job a few months ago to try to learn, but . . ." She shrugged. "It didn't work out."

"It didn't? Not even for an edible few dishes?"

"Nope. Fast food is unhealthy. I couldn't cook it in good conscience."

"Sacked?" he asked kindly.

"As usual," she sighed.

He laughed softly. "Oh, Megan," he said, shaking his head.

Megan was so surprised by the sound that she had to look at him again, just to make sure he'd been the one to make it. And the sight of him smiling was so overwhelming, she had to lean back against the door frame for support.

"Wow," she breathed.

The smile didn't fade. "Wow?"

"You have a great laugh."

His smile was immediately replaced by a look of faint puzzlement. "Do I? No one's ever told me that before."

"They must have been distracted by your powerful and awe-inspiring corporate self."

"Ah *ha*," he said triumphantly, "you really *do* recognize me this time."

Megan rolled her eyes, pushed away from the door and started back to the kitchen. "Let's go see if Mrs. P. left us a cookbook."

"Wait," he said, maneuvering himself onto his backside. "I seem to have tangled my toes."

Megan watched him fumble with the spirals for a moment before she knelt, pushed his hands away and did the honors herself.

"Nicely done," he said, sounding genuinely impressed.

"I subbed for Snow White once. You'd be amazed what trouble dwarf toes can get into."

"Hmmm," he said, looking down at his feet.

Megan looked at him and felt something in the vicinity of her heart crumble. Just the sight of this intense and (by his own admission) powerful man sitting there with his sandy hair mussed, his tights bagging now around his ankles, playing with the toes of his purple elf shoes—well, it was enough to make a girl want to throw her arms around him and hug him until he couldn't breathe. That any man should look so ridiculous and so adorable at the same time was just a crime.

"Too much time in ears," she said, rising and shaking her head.

Gideon looked up at her. "I beg your pardon?"

"I spent too much time at Disneyland," she said. "It warped me. My judgment is clouded. My taste in shoes is skewed."

"Don't tell me you're acquiring a liking for fairy footwear."

And drooping yellow tights and aqua eyes and a smile that transforms your face into something even more breathtaking than usual.

"Nah, give me Keds every time," she said, making a grab for her self-control and common sense before they both hit the same high road her luggage had. "Let's storm the kitchen."

Gideon rose, keeping his feet a safe distance apart.

"Might I regale you with stories of my latest business coups whilst we prepare our meal?" he asked, reaching for her hand.

Megan found her hand in his and her common sense/self-control nowhere to be seen.

"Business coups?" she echoed, frowning up at him in an effort to distract herself. "I don't think so."

"Tales of exciting market trends and investment plans?"

She looked at him in horror. "You've got to be kidding. It'll ruin my appetite!"

"You sound annoyingly like my brother."

"He sounds like my kind of guy. Maybe he's the one who booby-trapped your computer."

"I'm beginning to suspect that might be the case."

"Well, then take your vacation. Getting fired is highly unpleasant."

"You seem to know of what you speak."

"Honey, you don't know the half of it."

And she had no intention of telling him the full extent of it. A few amusing anecdotes might make him smile, but he'd flip if he knew just how many times she had been canned.

But that wasn't going to happen anymore. She nodded to herself as she led him back to the kitchen. Thomas had given her a chance to be successful at something. After all, how hard could it be to get up to the castle, take a look around and tell him what he'd bought? It was a little chance, but one she had been desperate enough to take. She wouldn't fail. She *couldn't* fail. If she couldn't even do something this simple, there was no way she could show her face at home again. They all thought she was flaky as it was. She would head up to the castle first thing tomorrow. It couldn't be that far and it couldn't be that hard to find. She'd send home a report, then settle back and enjoy a well-deserved recuperation.

But first, dinner had to be made.

"Heaven help us," she muttered, as she and Gideon walked hand-in-hand into the kitchen.

She stood surveying the various pots and pans Mrs. Pruitt had left simmering on the stove, then looked at Gideon. He returned her stare, looking just as perplexed as she felt.

"Would you rather find a cookbook and read, or would you rather . . . *stir*?" she said, hoping a little subliminal suggestion might work on him.

"I'm a fabulous reader," he said promptly, commencing a search for a cookbook.

Megan stared back at the stove. Well, at least this would distract her from the deafening clamor her hand had set up at being parted from Gideon's.

"Bad hand," she said, frowning down at it sternly.

"I beg your pardon?"

Megan shoved her hand behind her back and smiled at Gideon. "Just giving it a pep talk in preparation for cooking. Find anything useful?"

Gideon held up a fistful of scribbled notes. "I think this might be it."

Megan sighed.

It was going to be a long night.

Chapter Four

GIDEON SAT AT the table, plowing manfully through his meal. The potatoes were scorched, the meat both raw and burned depending on what side of it faced up on one's plate, and the vegetables were unrecognizable in their mushiness. Somehow, his deciphering of Mrs. Pruitt's notes and Megan's stirring hadn't turned out the way it should have. At this point, Gideon didn't care. He was starved enough to eat about anything.

Once his nutrient-starved brain could function properly again, he looked over at his dinner companion. She was currently toying with her carrots, as if she thought they might provide the answers to life's mysteries. Gideon leaned over and looked at them.

"Don't see any answers there," he said, then met her eyes. "Do you?"

"Nope," she said. "Just overcooked vegetables."

"We'll do better next time."

"We'll starve to death," she said gloomily. "Surrounded by raw ingredients we can't put together to save our lives."

Gideon watched Megan's downcast face and wondered what troubled her. She couldn't think the disaster before them was her fault. He was as much responsible as she. Perhaps she was merely fatigued from her journey to the inn. While they'd cooked, she had told him of her harrowing experience with the thieves in London. Add that to her long walk from the village and it was no wonder she looked a bit on the peaked side.

Gideon couldn't deny that no matter how she looked, she still made him pull up short. There was something just so open and artless about her. He couldn't remember the last time he'd encountered another human being who didn't have some sort of agenda where he was concerned. Even his father, useless bit of fluff though he was, managed to tear himself from the races long enough to give Gideon a lofty earlish order or two. The only person who called him anymore without wanting something was his mother.

Megan didn't seem to have any expectations of him. She had no idea who he was and, distressing though it was to him, seemingly couldn't have cared less what he did. Not even blatant boasting about his title and manor hall at Blythwood had fazed her. She did, however, like his laugh.

He was beginning to wish some of her nonchalance would rub off on him. Just the sight of her left him with his head spinning. Having her undivided attention was almost more than he could take. Though he certainly wasn't having any of the latter presently. Her vegetables were enjoying far too much of her scrutiny.

Perhaps she was still put out with him? He'd apologized thoroughly for having splashed her. Secretly, he was relieved he hadn't plowed her over. He'd been trying to fix the blasted fax machine in his car. Another one of Stephen's insidious little assaults, no doubt.

Perhaps, then, she wasn't looking at him because she found the company dull. He frowned. He could be entertaining. Perhaps he should try out some of those skills he'd learned in that Don't Alienate Your Partner seminar his mother had coerced him into taking the year before. He'd done it to please her, because she asked so little of him, though he hadn't seen the point in it. He never alienated anyone unintentionally. Yes, he would trot out his hard-won skills and see if they were worth the sterling he'd paid for them.

"Tell me more about your family," he said. There, he was off to a smashing start. People loved to talk about their families. And there he was, fully prepared to listen to her. It was a foolproof plan. "You mentioned a brother? The one who sent you over here?"

"Thomas," she said. "He bought the castle up the way. He wanted something that had originally belonged to a McKinnon. He's always been big on the ancestral stuff."

"And he sent you here to study the terrain, as it were?"

She sighed and stuck her fork into a mound of carrots. "It was a charity gig. You know, after the mouse debacle."

"Poor Dumbo and his ever-lengthening ears."

"He kept pinching my tail. He deserved every bit of whiplash he got."

"Oh, Megan," he said, unable to do anything but shake his head and smile. Megan McKinnon was a business disaster.

"The rest of them are just like Thomas: all successful, all the brightest of stars, all settled into their careers and forging ahead, the obstacles be damned."

Everyone except me. Gideon didn't have to hear her say it to know it was exactly what she was thinking. He had no frame of reference for that. Everything he'd put his hand to had turned to gold. Schooling, sports, business. He'd never once been sacked, never once been told he wasn't good enough, never once questioned his direction or his purpose. He could hardly believe such things had happened regularly to the woman across from him. Surely there was something she'd done that was noteworthy.

"How did you fare at university?" he asked.

"I quit. I didn't like them telling me what to study."

Gideon mulled that one for a moment before turning to another possibility. "Your mother's clothing business—"

"Baby clothes are cute, but not for a life's work."

"The theater?" he ventured.

"I've done it all. Sewn costumes, painted scenery, worked lights, acted, danced, forgotten my lines. All in my sister's theater troupe."

Gideon looked at her in horror. "She didn't sack you, did she?"

"I did the honors myself."

Gideon reached over and took her hand before he knew what he was doing. And once he had ahold of it, he found he didn't want to let go.

"You just haven't found your niche," he stated firmly. "Something will turn up."

She looked at him and her eyes were bright. Gideon

suspected it might have been from the tears she was blinking away.

"Do you think so?" she whispered.

"I'm certain of it," he said, giving her hand a squeeze.

And then he understood what had been troubling her, why she'd said half a dozen times while stirring supper that she hoped the weather changed so she could pop up to the castle first thing. She needed a success.

And then a perfectly brilliant idea occurred to him. He would help her fix her career. His Don't Alienate instructor had specifically listed the fixing of partners on his list of Don'ts, but Gideon was certain that didn't apply to him. If anyone could fix Megan McKinnon's life, it would be him. And he would, just as soon as he had pried her away from her veggies so he could have her full attention.

"Let's escape to a tidier room," he suggested, rising. "We can talk more comfortably there."

"I can't leave the kitchen like this—"

"It will keep," he said, pulling her up from the table. "Maybe you can tell me a little about your career interests." He knew he was pushing, but he could hardly help himself. Business was his forte, after all.

"I don't have any career interests."

Gideon froze. "You don't?"

"Not in the sense you probably mean. I hate dressing up for work."

"You hate dressing up for work," he repeated slowly. "Yet . . ."

"I hate the corporate thing. Don't own panty hose. Don't want to own panty hose."

He lifted one eyebrow. "But wearing mouse ears and a tail didn't bother you."

"I didn't have to wear panty hose."

"I see."

"I think you do."

Gideon smiled at the way she looked down her nose at him. She was so adorable, it was all he could do not to pull her into his arms and kiss the freckles right from that nose.

Almost before he knew what had happened, he found himself doing just that.

She pulled away and laughed. And that was when he felt

himself falling. It was the first time he'd heard her laugh, and he'd been the one to bring it out in her. He was so taken aback by it, he couldn't stop smiling.

She was smiling back at him.

Gideon realized then that there was much more to it than just a smile. For the first time in his thirty-two years, he found the thought of standing right where he was and staring into green eyes to be the most important thing he could possibly do with his time.

Alarms went off in his head.

Gideon ignored them.

They sounded again, but with words this time. *Just what the devil are you thinking to stare at a woman's knees, then watch her destroy dinner, then want to kiss her?*

Gideon blinked.

Good heavens, he was losing it. He was supposed to be taking her in hand and repairing her life. He was not supposed to be feeling his knees grow unsteady beneath him. He was not supposed to be gaping at a woman he hardly knew and finding himself so charmed by her that he had to remind himself to breathe. It was all he could do not to haul her up into his arms and stalk off with her like one of those blasted barbarians from one of Stephen's medieval texts.

But the stalking sounded so appealing if it meant having Megan McKinnon in his arms.

He looked down at her again, considered his alternatives, then gave his common sense the old heave-ho. He took her face in his hands, stared down into her fiery green eyes, smiled at the silky touch of her riotous hair flowing over his fingers, then lowered his mouth and covered hers.

And for a blissful moment, the earth moved.

And then, just as quickly, Megan had moved—but not too far away because somehow his watch had gotten caught in her hair.

"Ow, ow, ow," she said, grabbing her hair with her hand.

"Wait," he said, following her with his arm.

She gingerly pulled strands of hair from his watchband. "I don't kiss on the first date," she said, staring intently at her hair.

"This isn't a first date."

"Then I *really* don't kiss, especially on the first non-date."

Half a dozen pot lids suddenly crashed to the floor. Megan screeched, a sound reminiscent of the recently departed Mrs. Pruitt, and threw herself into his arms. Gideon contemplated the positive aspects of this turn of events. He put his free arm around her and pulled her close. She clutched his shirt.

"Do you think . . ." she began, "I mean, do you think we might have a few—"

"Absolutely not."

"Mrs. Pruitt said the inn had them."

"Mrs. Pruitt left her sacred post at the stove without a backward glance. Her character and stamina speak for themselves."

"Maybe it's just the wind," Megan said, pulling out of his arms and working more frantically at her hair. "After all, there aren't any such things as gho—"

The lights went out in the kitchen and several more lids crashed to the floor.

Gideon found himself again with an armful of Megan McKinnon.

"I don't hug on the first non-date either," she squeaked.

"You might make an exception for this," Gideon offered. "The storm seems to have picked up again."

It was dark as pitch inside the kitchen, so he wasn't sure what her expression was, but he could tell she was mulling it over. She relaxed a bit in his arms.

"It *is* a pretty bad storm," she agreed. "What with all the wind howling and everything."

"Yes, indeed. Dreadful."

She released her death grip on him, but not by much. Gideon reached around her head, released his watchband and gingerly eased it from her hair.

Megan didn't move a muscle. "Should we find a candle or something? Or light a fire?"

"Smashing thought," he agreed. He released her, only after promising himself he'd find a way to have her back in his arms as soon as possible.

It took some doing, but after rummaging about for several minutes, he and Megan both were proud owners of lit candles.

Now it was time to get down to business. Perhaps he could find a way to put his arm back around her while distracting her with chatter about her choice of occupations.

"Shall we go talk about your career possibilities?" he asked brightly.

She looked at him and blinked. "My career possibilities?"

Damn. The proverbial cat was out of the bag now. Though he'd intended it to be a pleasant surprise, there was no sense in hiding his agenda now. They could fix her career, then move on to other things, such as getting the first date over with so the second could occur and she could see her way clear to kissing him again.

"I'd wanted to broach the subject more gently, of course," he began, steering her toward the door.

"Career possibilities?" she repeated.

"I'm the perfect one to help you, don't you think?" he asked. "After all, my résumé is quite impressive. I have hundreds of contacts and could likely find you any sort of employment you want."

"You want to talk to me about my *career possibilities?*" she demanded.

"Well, of course," he said.

She looked like she was going to hit him. Indeed, it was only by sheer instinct that he managed to duck in time to avoid her swing.

"You jerk!" she exclaimed.

He straightened and looked at her with wide eyes. "Me?"

She swung again.

Gideon jerked back. "Good heavens, Megan, have you lost your mind? I'm *helping* you!"

"I don't *want* your help, you big idiot!"

"But why ever not—"

She advanced and he retreated. Amazing how one could still see murder in another's eyes by candlelight.

"I can't believe you!" she exclaimed. "What in the world makes you think I need to be *fixed?*"

"Fixed? How did you—"

He ducked instinctively, prepared for another blow, but this one came at him from a different angle. Her foot connected solidly with his shin.

"Ouch, damn it," he said, jerking his candle. He wasn't sure what hurt worse, her shoe in his shin or the hot wax on his fingers. "Megan, I don't think you realize what you're turning down."

"I realize exactly what I'm turning down," she said, poking him in the chest. "You're just like the rest of them. I don't need to be worked on, I don't need to be a project and I don't need any damned career advice! If I want to keep getting fired from now until doomsday, that's my business!"

"But—"

"But nothing! Good night!"

And with that, she slammed out of the kitchen. Gideon heard her stomp across the dining room, then heard the far door slam.

Well, that hadn't gone off well at all. Gideon stood there with the wind making an enormous racket as it came through the cracks under the door and shutters, and wondered why he felt so flat. He'd only been trying to help. And who better to fix her career than him? The countless people he knew, the businesses he owned—why he was a veritable gold mine of corporate acumen and resources! Her reaction to his generous offer was insulting, to say the very least.

He studiously ignored the thought that he'd just made an ass of himself and bruised Megan's feelings in the process.

Well, it was a sure sign that he'd put his foot to the wrong path. It was time he took hold of his priorities and wrested his destiny back onto its original course.

"I don't have time to worry about this," he announced to the kitchen. "I have work to do. I don't need any of these feminine distractions. My life is full of important tasks."

The wind continued to howl.

What about love?

Gideon turned a jaundiced look on the door. "I'm certain," he said crisply, "when the wind starts blathering on about love that it's far past the time when I should be back at work."

He turned to the dining room door and held this candle aloft purposefully.

"Tomorrow," he said, taking a smart step forward, "I'll be on my way tomorrow!"

His candle flame went out. Another collection of pots crashed to the floor behind him.

"How many bloody pots does this inn have?" he demanded of the darkness.

The wind only growled an answer.

Gideon left the kitchen with all due haste.

"Holidays are useless wastes of time," he said as he made his way up the stairs. "I'll find myself a proper set of clothes in the village, then search for another laptop. I've already lost a day."

He paused on the landing as a most unsettling thought struck him. He tried to push it aside, but it came back to him, as if someone had whispered it to him.

I think, my lad, that you stand to lose much more than just a day.

Gideon felt chills go down his spine. He peered back down the stairs into the darkened entryway. It wouldn't have surprised him in the least to have seen someone standing there.

But the entryway was empty.

Gideon straightened. He was hearing things. He nodded to himself and opened the door to his room. He'd had a very long day and the wind was playing tricks on him. Either that or he'd spent far too much time looking at Megan McKinnon. She unsettled him more than the wind.

Freckles, he decided as he closed his bedroom door behind him, were hazardous to a man's good sense.

Chapter Five

"Nay, you'll not do it!"

"Out of me way, ye bloody Brit, and leave me to me work!"

"'Tis a brand new Sterling! This horseless cart cost me nevvy a bleedin' fortune!"

Ambrose put his head beneath the bonnet of Gideon's car and glared at his companions.

"Will you two cease with this confounded bickering!" he snapped. "We're here to pull the spark plug wires, not argue over who'll do it!"

Fulbert leaned heavily against the fender. "I don't think I can lend my aid. That pot banging last eve took all my strength."

"Ha," said Hugh, casting him a derisive sneer. "I flung a far sight more than ye, and look at me in the bloom o' health this morn."

"We're all under a great amount of physical strain," Ambrose said sternly, "but we'll have time enough to rest once the deed is done. Now, we've eight of these slim little cords to pull and precious little time to argue over the pulling of them."

"Eight's too many," Fulbert groused.

"I want no chance that the automobile will spring to life," Ambrose countered. "I've done a goodly amount of reading on the subject and know of what I speak. Now, we'll start from this end."

It took a great amount of effort, and there was much grunting and swearing given forth, as well as several bouts of condemning modern man for his ridiculous inventions that required more than oats and a good rubdown, but finally the deed was done. Ambrose stood back from the car and admired their handiwork.

"There," he said, with satisfaction. "Gideon will not be off today. As the rain seems eager to aid us in our task of keeping him here, I daresay he won't be venturing out on foot any time soon, either." He reached up to close the bonnet.

"I'll see to it," Fulbert said, suddenly. He did a little leap in the air. "I feel quite the thing suddenly."

Ambrose was quite frankly surprised at Fulbert's change of heart, but wasn't about to challenge him on it. Lifting things from the physical world was, as always, exhausting. There were but few hours before dawn. He would do well to rest before Gideon rose and gave them any more trouble.

"As you will, Fulbert. Come, Hugh. Let us seek our rest while we may."

Ambrose took a final look at the engine, then, satisfied his work was done properly, entered the house and sought his bed for a well-deserved nap.

FULBERT WAITED UNTIL Hugh and Ambrose passed through the door before he peered back down into the engine.

"They plucked too bleedin' many of these things," he muttered to himself. "I'll just put a few back. The saints only know what kind of damage could be done to the beast otherwise."

It was an intense struggle and he had to admit he couldn't quite remember how the rubber cords had been attached at the start, but he plugged five of them back in, crossing the cords here and there and stretching them when they didn't wish to go where he decided they should.

Calling upon the very last reserves of his considerable strength, he pulled the bonnet down home.

He made his way slowly inside and took up his post at the end of the upstairs passageway. It didn't take long before he'd sat, then stretched his legs out, then fallen asleep.

It had been a most tiring night's work.

* * *

THE HOUSE WAS silent as Gideon trudged down the stairs, elf shoes well apart to avoid toe tangleage, dragging his heavy suitcase with him. It contained, of course nothing useful. He'd decided, though, that he just couldn't leave his ruined computer and the ashes of his clothes lying about in the bedroom. The least he could do was find a rubbish bin somewhere and add to it.

He set his burden down and walked back to the kitchen. There were pots strewn all over the floor and the remains of last night's meal still on the table. Gideon looked down at Megan's fork still standing in her now congealed vegetables. The sight of that brought other, disturbingly distracting memories to mind: Megan in his arms; Megan's lips under his.

Megan mad as hell over his wanting to fix her.

He'd given her response to his innocent suggestion quite a bit of thought over the past sleepless night. He'd given even more thought to her successful family, and he could see where she might feel as if she didn't quite fit in. He wondered if they made it a point to point out her failures to her. The thought of that set his blood to boiling.

Actually, just the thought of Megan set his blood to boiling. He felt himself becoming distracted all over again.

"Work, work, work," he said, chanting his favorite mantra.

Damn. All he could think about was freckles.

"Price/earning ratios," he said, letting the seductive words roll off his tongue with a silky purr.

Freckled knees.

No, no, this just wouldn't do. Gideon planted his feet well apart, put his hands on his hips and smiled his favorite pirate's smile.

"Corporate takeovers!" he said, trying to infuse the term with its customary gleeful overtones.

Freckled nose. Flaming red hair. Sweet, kissable lips.

"Spreadsheets, annual reports, chats with my broker!" he cried out in desperation.

Megan.

Gideon clapped his hands over his ears, spun around and bolted from the kitchen. Maybe Megan's vegetables were starting to put thoughts in his head. It was best he escaped the whole place before he lost his mind.

He grabbed his suitcase on his way to the door. Perhaps if

he got some distance from the inn, his sanity would return. Yes, a little jaunt to Edinburgh would be just the thing. His first stop, however, would have to be to a tailor's shop. No one would take him seriously in his current dress.

He threw his suitcase into the boot, then got into the car. His footwear didn't fit all that well under the wheel, but he made do. He pumped the gas pedal once and turned the key. The car made a hideous, thunderous bang, then smoke began to pour forth from the engine.

Gideon could hardly believe his eyes. "Not again!" he exclaimed. He released the latch, bolted from the car and jerked open the bonnet.

His engine was on fire.

Why he was surprised, he didn't know.

The rain started up again with renewed vigor. Gideon looked up into the heavens with narrowed eyes. There was something afoot in the world and it seemed either bent on burning up everything he owned or soaking him to the skin.

The front door wrenched open and Megan appeared. Gideon looked at her helplessly. Her eyes bulged, then she disappeared. Gideon looked back up into the sky and wished for a stronger downpour than the one that drenched him at present. But no matter how large a downpour, it likely wouldn't put out the inferno beneath the bonnet of his brand-new Sterling.

The next thing he knew, Megan was wielding a fire extinguisher. When the dust settled, there were no flames, and hardly any smoke. And no serviceable motor.

"Hell," Gideon said.

Megan looked up at him. "Do these kinds of things happen to you normally, or are you just having an off week?"

"The elements are combining against me."

"Maybe somebody's trying to tell you something."

"Go on holiday?"

"That'd be my guess."

Gideon looked at her and considered. His car was ruined. He'd already tried the inn phone that morning and found it unresponsive. There he was, loitering in backwoods Scotland with no computer, no modem, and no cell phone.

And Megan McKinnon.

"Ah *ha*," he said, feeling the force of the moment reverberate through him.

What could it hurt to take a day or two and put work aside? It wasn't as if he could do much about it anyway, short of walking to the village and hiring a car. It would just be time wasted. Stephen might not be interested in the company, but Adam MacClure was. He could hold down the fort for a day or so.

Besides, Christmas was right around the corner. People all over the world were contemplating holidays with their families. There was food to be prepared, gifts to be wrapped, carols to be sung. He hadn't done any of that in years. Christmas had always seemed a perfect time to catch up on things at the office. Stephen had always thrown a lord-of-the-manor type of affair, doing his damndest to revive old customs. Gideon had thought it politic to just stay in London and not spoil Stephen's party.

But now he was, for all intents and purposes, prisoner on the Scottish border with only time on his hands and Megan McKinnon to admire.

Damn, but the holidays were shaping up brilliantly.

"I think," he said, reaching out and relieving Megan of the fire extinguisher, "that a holiday is just the thing for me."

She blinked. "You do?"

He shrugged and smiled. "I hear they're quite therapeutic. Perhaps you'd care to show me how they're done?"

He watched her look at him, and then her eyes narrowed. "Why?" she demanded. "So you can sneak in some fixing?"

Gideon shook his head. "I was wrong to even bring it up. I apologize."

"Well," she said, looking quite off balance. Gideon suspected she'd been bracing herself to really let him have it.

"Well," she repeated, "I just don't need to be fixed."

"No, you don't."

She looked at him suspiciously. "What's the deal with your new angle here?"

"No angle. No agenda. I've just come to realize rather suddenly that I'm the one who needs some fixing. I work too much."

She reached up and felt his forehead. "You're a little warm. Maybe you caught a bug from being out in the rain."

Gideon took her hand and pulled her back into the house.

He'd caught a malady and it had red hair and green eyes. He set the fire extinguisher down and shut the front door.

"I'm officially on holiday. What should we do first? Decorate the place?" He looked about the entryway. "We could investigate the nooks and crannies of the inn, or learn how to cook. Sing a carol or two in front of the fire." The more he thought about it, the more appealing it sounded. Perhaps he would stretch his holiday into three days instead of two. After all, Christmas was in three days and he certainly wouldn't get any work done then. "Read Dickens before the fire," he said, his head filling with ideas. "That Ghost of Christmas Past is one of my all time favorite characters. Why, I'm starting to think this will be brilliant," he said, beaming down at her.

"Can't."

He blinked. "I beg your pardon."

She smiled up at him. "I have to work. See ya."

And she turned and walked back to the stairs.

"Work?" he asked, aghast. *"Now?"*

She looked over her shoulder. "I'm here to work, Gideon. Remember? My brother's castle? I have to go take a look at it."

"But, surely that can wait . . ."

"Nope, I've got to get right on it."

"But—"

She waved at him over her shoulder as she mounted the steps. Gideon stared after her in shock.

"But it's Christmas!" he called after her.

She didn't stop.

Well, this just wouldn't do. Gideon watched her disappear upstairs and frowned. He tapped his foot impatiently, which generally provided him with stunning solutions. All it did now was make him dizzy. He shook his head. How could she be so consumed with work this close to Christmas?

"Work can wait," he said, trying the words out on his tongue. They felt, surprisingly enough, quite good.

"It isn't everything," he added.

That felt even better.

"Why, holidays are a *good* thing," he said, with enthusiasm.

It occurred to him, suddenly, that he was possibly responsible for Megan's desire to work through the holidays. Good heavens, had he been the one to drive her to this madness?

Well, he would rectify that. He had just recently seen the light and burned with the enthusiasm of the freshly converted. Holidays were good for a body. Too much work was hazardous to one's health.

And he would know.

Chapter Six

MEGAN TUGGED ON her leather jacket and shoved her feet back into her still-damp boots. It was raining outside anyway and she would get soaked within minutes, but it didn't matter. She had work to do. A little rain wasn't going to stop her because she'd be damned before she would fail at this job. She would show them all that she could follow through, do what she said she would, make things happen. Her family would finally think she was a success.

As would Gideon.

Not that she cared what he thought. No sir.

She stepped out into the hallway and shut the door firmly. No time like the present to start down the road to success. She put her shoulders back and marched smartly down the hallway.

"Damn the gel if she hasn't ruined him for decent labor."

Megan froze. Then she put her fingers in her ears and gave them a good wiggling. Surely there was no one else in the hallway. She was just hearing things.

"She may as well have gelded the poor lad!"

Megan whirled around. She would have squeaked, but she had no breath for it.

There, standing not fifteen feet from her was a man. A big man. A man wearing a sword. In fact, he looked to be wearing chain mail too, what she could see of it under his folded arms and knightly overcoat-like tunic. He might have looked like something out of a historical wax museum collection if it hadn't been for the disapproving look he was giving her.

Megan gulped. "Help," she whispered.

"Doin' a full day's work's no sin," the man grumbled.

"Help," Megan squeaked. "Help, help!"

"You're fillin' me boy's head with womanly notions!" the man exclaimed. He unfolded his arms and shook his finger at her. "I'd take it more kindly if you'd stop with it!"

"Gideon, help!" Megan screamed, backing up rapidly.

"Megan, good heavens!" Gideon called from a distance.

Megan heard him thumping up the stairs behind her, but she didn't dare take her eyes off the knight to look at him. She backed up into him and pointed down the hallway.

"Look," she whispered.

"Look at what?"

"There's someone in the hallway. Look, down there!"

"I can't see a thing," Gideon said.

"He's standing right there!"

"Who?"

Megan spun around, grabbed him by the tunic front and shook him. "There's a man at the end of the hallway wearing chain mail and a sword, you idiot!" she said. "Open your eyes and look!"

Gideon put his hands on her shoulders to steady himself. "Megan, you're thinking too much about work—"

"See?" the man behind her complained. "Look at what you've done to him, gel!"

Megan pointed back behind her. "He's talking to me. There at the end of the hall."

Gideon put his arms around her. "Now, Megan—"

"Don't you 'Now, Megan' me," she warned. "Mrs. Pruitt said there were ghosts and I'm telling you there's one standing at the end of the hallway!"

Gideon gave her a squeeze. "If it will make you feel any better, I'll go have a look."

Megan looked over her shoulder and squeaked at the new addition to the troops.

"Damn ye, Fulbert, dinnae scare me wee granddaughter like that!" a red-haired man in a kilt exclaimed in tones of thunder.

"I was only tellin' her—"

"I heard what ye said—"

"Wait," Megan said frantically as Gideon tried to move past her. "Now there are two of them!"

Gideon frowned at her. "I think you've been working too hard." He sidestepped her and started down the hallway.

Megan watched in horror as the kilted one drew a sword and waved it menacingly at the first.

"They're going to kill each other!" She leaped toward Gideon. "Duck," she said, jerking on his arm. "You're going to get your head chopped off!"

Gideon pushed her gently back into the doorway of his bedroom. "Megan," he said calmly, "there's nothing in the hallway. I'm going to go have a look in your room. You stay here until I get back."

Megan watched him turn and walk straight into the path of a swinging sword.

"Oh my gosh!" she exclaimed, clapping her hands over her eyes so she wouldn't have to watch him be decapitated.

"Megan?"

Megan paused, then peeked at him from between her fingers.

Gideon was standing in the middle of the hallway, unhurt. But the two swordsmen were going at each other with murder in their eyes, neatly fighting right around him.

"Don't you see them?" Megan asked incredulously.

"See who?"

"Those two men fighting? Right in front of your nose, Gideon!"

Gideon put out his hand, waved it up and down, side to side, then shook his head.

"Nothing."

Megan rolled her eyes. "I can hear them calling each other names." She paused. "And not very nice names, either."

"Enough!" a voice roared from her left.

Megan fell back against the door with a gasp. A man strode angrily up the stairs. He was wearing a kilt as well, along with a very long broadsword. His cap was tilted at a jaunty angle; the feather flapped madly as he leaped up the remaining steps. He advanced on the two fighters.

"By the saints, you lads are trying the limits of my patience today! You, Fulbert, leave young Megan be. She has enough to think on without you tormenting her."

"But look what she's done to me nevvy—"

"She's done nothing that didn't need doing. Now, be off with you!"

The first man shoved his sword back into its scabbard, threw Megan a disgruntled look, then vanished.

"And you, Hugh," the one seemingly in charge scolded. "I'm ashamed of you! Brawling in the passageway thusly!"

The red-haired one ducked his head. "I was just defendin' me wee one's honor."

"Well, I can't say as how I blame you," the other said, with a nod, "but it isn't seemly to hack at the blighter in front of her."

"Aye, Ambrose. Ye're right, of course."

"Then be off with you, Hugh."

The other put away his sword, then vanished.

Then Megan watched in astonishment as the commanding one turned and made her a deep bow.

"My deepest apologies for the disturbance, granddaughter. Please carry on with your day."

And then he walked through Gideon and disappeared into the closet at the end of the hallway.

Megan bolted after him and jerked open the closet door, fully expecting to see someone hiding inside. Instead she came face-to-face with stacks of bed linens. She clutched the door frame and came to a quick conclusion.

"I'm losing it," she announced.

"I think I agree," Gideon said, coming up behind her. "You need a holiday."

"What I need is some fresh air." She turned, pushed past him, and walked down the passageway. "Maybe I should go get some work done. That would probably snap me right back into reality."

"I've been a bad influence on you," Gideon said, trailing after her.

"No, I think you've been just the opposite," Megan said, thumping down the stairs. She reached the entryway well ahead of him and strode to the front door purposefully. A nice walk to the castle would be just the thing to clear her head of the surreal experience she had just had.

She opened the door and peeked out—into a hurricane.

"It's just a little rain," she said. She turned the collar up on her coat and steeled herself for the worst.

A large hand caught the door before she could open it any further.

"Megan, it's raining too hard to go out."

"I don't care," she said, putting her shoulders back. "I have work to do."

Gideon eased her back from the door and shut it. He turned her around and looked down at her gravely.

"There's more to life than work," he said.

"But," she said, gesturing toward the door, "I need to look at the castle—"

"It's been there for centuries. It will be there for another day or two."

She looked up at him with a scowl. "Why the sudden change of heart?"

He smiled and shrugged. "I've come to realize quite suddenly that there is more to life than work."

"You've got to be kidding."

"I've been distracted by freckles."

"Freckles?"

"Yours."

"Oh," she said. Then she froze and felt a blush creep up her cheeks. "Mine?"

"Oh, yes," he said, with a nod. "Enough to make a man rethink his priorities."

"Oh, really," she squeaked. She cleared her throat and dredged up the most uninterested expression she could. "Well," she said, her nose in the air, "there is more to me than my freckles. Attractive though they might be."

"You have my full attention."

"Hmmm, well," she said, quite at a loss for words. This about-face by a dyed-in-the-wool CEO was very hard to believe. "I would elaborate on my other desirable qualities if I had the time," she said finally.

"You have the time. It's too wet to go out right now."

She wanted to argue, but couldn't. It was just as nasty outside today as it had been when she'd walked to the inn and she had very vivid memories of that soggy trip. "I suppose it is a little on the rainy side," she said reluctantly.

"You can go after Christmas. The castle will keep until then."

He had a point. "All right," she conceded. "I'll wait until then."

"Good," he said. "Interested in breakfast?"

"If you stir."

"Done."

And then Megan watched as he took her by his comfortable, companionable hand and led her toward the kitchen. And she went with him, partly because it was too wet to go to the castle and partly because she had to see more of the Gideon-on-vacation side he seemed to be showing. And, lastly, she went with him because there was something about a man with bouncing purple curly cues on his toes that was just too much to resist.

Gideon stopped at the entrance to the kitchen and looked around, seemingly perplexed.

"I must admit, I haven't the vaguest idea where to start," he said, scanning the area.

"Clean-up first, then cooking," Megan said. "Here, I'll show you what to do."

Organizing was definitely one of her strong points and she used it to its best advantage. Once the kitchen was tidied, she turned to Mrs. Pruitt's notes. She flipped through until she found something she thought they might manage.

"Ever had bannocks?" she asked.

"They're tasty enough. I think we could manage."

"All right, here goes."

Megan did her best to decipher Mrs. Pruitt's scrawl while Gideon sifted and stirred to her specifications. Megan looked into the bowl.

"I think they're supposed to look like pancakes," she said, tipping the bowl this way and that. "This is too runny."

Gideon looked at her helplessly. "Should I stir more?"

"It says not to stir them too much." She looked at the bowl and rubbed her chin thoughtfully. "I think maybe we should add . . . um . . ."

"A wee bit more flour."

Megan squeaked and whirled around. The red-haired, kilted ghost from upstairs was standing directly behind her. He took off his bonnet with the feather stuck under the badge and clutched it in his hands. He made her a small bow and then straightened and smiled shyly.

"Hugh McKinnon, at yer service," he said, with another bow.

Megan backed into Gideon, hard.

"Megan?" he asked, putting his arm around her waist.

Megan shook her head with a jerk. "I'm okay."

Hugh scrunched his cap all the more. "I was quite the cook in me day," he offered.

Megan gulped and nodded, then turned and looked at Gideon. "A little more flour," she said.

Gideon added more, then stirred. "Well," he said, looking astonished, "that did the trick." He looked at her and smiled. "I'd say that time at McDonald's wasn't wasted at all."

"If you only knew," Megan said, under her breath.

"Well, now all we have to do is cook them," Gideon said, firing up the stove.

"Heaven help us," Megan said. She stole a look at Hugh, who had moved to stand behind Gideon. He leaned up on his toes to peer over Gideon's shoulder.

Gideon shivered and brushed off his right shoulder, as if trying to rid himself of an annoying fly. Hugh didn't seem to notice; he only peered more intently.

"Och, but he'll burn 'em with the fire up so high," Hugh said, casting Megan a look of concern.

"Maybe you should turn the heat down," Megan suggested quickly.

Gideon did so, then poured some of the batter into the pan. He waited, studying it intently. Then he eased his spatula under the flat cake and flipped it. The cooked side was a beautiful, golden brown. Megan peeked over Gideon's left shoulder. She exchanged a quick look with Hugh, who was leaning over Gideon's right shoulder, and received a nod of encouragement.

"I think it's done," she announced.

Gideon flipped it onto a plate.

"Perfect," Hugh said, beaming his approval on her. "I always ate them with a wee bit o' butter and a smackerel o' jam." He smiled crookedly. "Always had a sweet tooth, did I—"

"*HUGH!*"

Hugh gulped, plopped his cap on his head, made her a

very quick bow and then turned and fled through the pantry door. Megan didn't even bother to go after him to see if he was lurking inside with the tins of vegetables. She had the feeling he wasn't.

She took a deep breath and smiled up at Gideon.

"I hear butter and jam are good with these."

"Sounds delightful," Gideon said, holding out the plate. "Shall we share the first fruits of our labors?"

The bannock was very tasty and Megan put her newfound kitchen skill to good use by overseeing Gideon while he cooked more. Megan stole looks around the kitchen as she did so, but saw nothing else out of the ordinary. Hugh must have been able to escape the watchful eye of that distinguished ghost for only a few minutes.

"Megan, what are you looking at?"

She looked at Gideon and put on her most innocent smile. "Nothing."

"You're supposed to say," he said, plopping another bannock on her plate, "that you can't tear your eyes from me. You aren't thinking business thoughts, are you?" He looked at her closely.

"Not a one."

"A day or two's holiday won't hurt you."

"My, how the leopard has changed his spots."

Gideon smiled ruefully as he sat down with her at the table. "I like to believe I'm intelligent enough to recognize a better course when it comes along."

"And that better course would be?"

"The holidays spent with you, of course."

Megan rested her elbows on the table and propped her chin on her fists. "So," she said, "what do you have in mind, since we're stranded together in this haunted inn in the middle of nowhere?"

He smiled dryly. "I don't believe in ghosts."

A pot lid went sailing across the room and landed at the back door.

Gideon sat bolt upright in his chair.

Megan only smiled serenely. Maybe Hugh McKinnon had taken exception to that last remark.

"Just the wind," she said soothingly.

"Of course." Gideon jumped to his feet. "How about a fire in the library?"

"No talk of work? No fixing?"

He shook his head as he pulled her to her feet. "You don't need to be fixed." He cupped her cheek with his hand, leaned down and brushed his lips across hers. "I won't talk about my work either. We'll sit and gaze dreamily into each other's eyes."

Megan suppressed the urge to tell him he was starting to make her crazy. She'd come to the U.K. to be a success, not to find herself captured in the arms of some renegade CEO who for some unfathomable reason had decided that a couple of days' vacation really would be good for him. What would happen when he snapped back to reality?

She would never see him again, that's what would happen. He would go on his merry way accompanied by his business toys and she would be left with her heart in shreds. Too many more looks into those aqua eyes would just do her in.

"Megan?" He looped his arms around her waist.

It was too much. What could he possibly want with her? He was probably used to dating very successful, very rich women who could keep up with him at parties and things. She couldn't even keep a job for more than three months. How would he introduce her, "this is my wife, the queen of pick-up-your-paycheck-on-your-way-out-the-door"?

As if he'd even stick around long enough to decide he wanted her for a wife!

"I need to clean up the kitchen," she said, pulling away from him. "I can't look at this mess any longer. You go on ahead."

She turned to the table and started stacking plates, bowls, and utensils.

Gideon didn't say anything. Instead, he merely worked beside her as she scraped and washed and dried and put away. And when all she had left to do was twist a dishtowel into unrecognizable shapes, he took the cloth away from her, then pulled her into his arms.

It was the last place she wanted to be.

Unfortunately, it was suddenly the only place she wanted to be.

She closed her eyes and hoped she wouldn't make a fool out of herself by either crying or blurting out that she wasn't the kind of girl for a fling.

"I'm scared," she whispered instead.

She felt him swallow.

"So am I," he said, just as softly.

She jerked her head back so fast, it almost gave her whiplash. "You are?" she asked incredulously.

He looked as helpless as she felt. "Of course I am. You weren't exactly on my agenda."

"I didn't have an agenda. But," she added, "if I'd had one, you wouldn't have been on mine either."

"I see." He paused and looked at her solemnly. "I don't date, you know," he said, finally.

"Really? Me neither."

He continued simply to stare down at her. Well, maybe he'd said all he was going to say and it was her turn.

"I don't fling," she announced. She watched him closely for his reaction.

"Neither do I," he stated. He frowned suddenly. "If you don't date and you don't fling, when do you kiss?"

He asked it so earnestly, Megan couldn't help but smile.

"I like you," she said.

"I like you too," he replied. "And I feel certain a small kiss would be entirely appropriate at this point, but you seem to have a schedule about these things."

Megan slipped out of his arms. "Actually, I think there's an application involved."

Gideon blinked. "What?"

"And a résumé," she added, heading toward the dining room door.

"You can't mean that."

"And I'll have to check your references," she said, pushing open the door.

"You've got to be joking!" he exclaimed, hurrying after her. "You've applied for too bloody many jobs; it's ruined you for romance!"

Megan only smiled. She wasn't sure what his intentions were, but he didn't date and he didn't fling. As for anything else, she would just wait and see. At least they were on the same shaky footing. Time would sort out the rest.

She was halfway through the dining room when she heard an *oof,* then a substantial *whump* behind her. She turned to find Gideon flat on his face.

"Damned shoes!"

Heavens, how could she resist such a man?

Chapter Seven

THE NEXT MORNING Gideon sat in an enormously comfortable overstuffed chair in the library and watched Megan do marvelous things with the pitiful decorations Mrs. Pruitt had left behind. And as he sat there, he came to two conclusions: Stephen didn't read because he liked books, he read because he was basically a hedonistic blighter who liked overstuffed chairs; and, Megan MacLeod McKinnon was a magical creature who had completely stolen his heart.

After his abrupt reunion with the floor after breakfast the day before, she had tied his toes into little knots so they wouldn't tangle anymore. She had drawn from him his innermost secrets and dreams during a rousing game of Truth or Dare, then she had taken those words in her hands and crossed her heart as she vowed not to repeat them to anyone—especially Stephen, who might poke fun at him. She'd beaten him at chess, exacting a kiss for every man she took—and he hadn't even had to fill out an application or cite references.

They had explored most of the inn the previous afternoon. Gideon had watched in amazement as Megan had identified obscure works of art, styles of furniture and patterns of lace and china. Her employments might have been short-lived, but they hadn't been failures.

And when he'd walked her to her door very late in the

evening, he had been completely surprised by how wrong it seemed to have her go inside alone and shut the door, leaving him outside. He'd stood there with his arms around her, gazing down into her lovely, befreckled face and wondered what she would do if he proposed on the spot.

Likely have dashed off for the thermometer.

So he'd kissed her sweetly, then retreated to the library to read for most of the night.

No wonder Stephen buried himself in books.

"Well, I've taken this about as far as I can. We'll have to go to town if I want to do more."

Gideon blinked at Megan. Those were almost his exact thoughts. Though whilst she no doubt spoke of Christmas decorations, his thoughts were more along the lines of procuring a marriage license.

"Hey, look at this."

Gideon wanted to get out of the chair, but it seemed reluctant to let him go. "I fear I'm trapped."

Megan walked over to him, her eyes glued to a document she'd picked up from off the desk in the corner. She held out her hand and hauled Gideon to his feet.

And then she started to shake. She looked up at him. "I can't believe this."

Gideon looked at her blanched face and immediately threw his arms around her. It seemed like the proper precaution to take when your beloved looked as if she might fall down in a dead faint.

"Read it!" Megan exclaimed, shoving it in his face.

Gideon read. And then he reread. And then he shook his head in wonder.

"I'll be damned."

"This can't be legal!"

"It certainly looks as if it is. All you need do is sign. I can witness it for you."

"Gideon, Mrs. P. left me the entire inn! What am I going to do with a haunted inn? I don't know the first thing about cooking, or cleaning, or advertising—"

Gideon pulled her close and rubbed his hand soothingly over her back as she continued to list in great detail all the things she could not do. He smiled into her hair as he scanned the rest of the deed. It was all quite legal and quite binding. And he knew without a doubt that Megan would do a positively smashing job at all of it.

"I'll be stuck out here all by myself for the rest of my life with the rain and the ghosts—"

Gideon paused, then stroked her back more thoughtfully. That was a problem. After they married, she wouldn't be able to be here full time. In fact, he didn't know how she could spend more than a week or two here during the year. His business was in London. AE, Inc. would collapse without him overseeing it every day. Good heavens, his vice presidents couldn't tie their shoelaces without Gideon giving them a memo on it!

Well, there had to be a solution to the dilemma. Gideon was known for his creative solutions to impossible tangles. He'd fixed other things, he could fix this too.

"—probably doesn't even have a washing machine. I'll be washing things on a rock in the river. All right, so my nails aren't in great shape anyway. Can you imagine what they'd look like after a few months of that?" She pulled back and looked at him. "Well? Can you imagine?"

Gideon took her by the hand and led her over to the desk. He put the deed down, found a pen and handed it to her.

"Sign," he commanded.

"Oh, I just don't know—"

"Sign, Megan. It will all work out for the best."

She leaned over the document, then looked at him from under her eyebrows. "Will you," she paused, then cleared her throat and looked away, "will you come visit me now and then? When you take another vacation?"

"Oh, Megan," he said, surrendering his heart to her all over again. "Of course I will."

She started to cry. She dragged her sleeve across her eyes and looked at the deed. "You know, I'll probably end up just as batty as Mrs. Pruitt. At least she was a Mrs. She hadn't been stuck here alone her entire life."

"Megan, sign the deed," Gideon said, forcing himself not to blurt out his intentions. He wanted his proposal to have the proper romantic setting; popping the question while his bride-to-be sniffled liberally into her sleeve was not it.

Megan signed, then buried her face in her hands and wept.

Gideon witnessed her signature, then pulled her into his arms and held her.

"Megan, you just acquired a lovely little getaway. These should be tears of joy."

"Oh, I'm just thrilled!"

"The place could stand a little sprucing up, of course."

"I'm broke!"

"You're forgetting whom you're drenching. I'm the extremely powerful CEO, remember?"

She froze, and then looked up at him. "But, I don't want your money."

"I'm not going to give you any money." *You'll just take it out of our joint account,* he added silently. "I'll just help you get a business loan," he lied.

She worried a loose thread on his tunic. "And you'll show up now and then?"

"Probably more than you'll want," he said, fishing heavily for a compliment.

"I could use help with the cooking," she said, looking no further up than his chin. "And maybe the decorating. You know, British input and all that."

He laughed softly and tipped her face up to kiss her. "Of course, Madame Proprietress. My proper British tastes are at your disposal." He smiled down at her. "Well, shall we go ransack Mrs. Pruitt's room and see what other surprises she left for you? Then perhaps we should head down to the village and stock up for the Christmas feast."

"It will be a quick trip," Megan said as he pulled her toward the library door. "My savings account isn't exactly padded."

"I'll buy—"

"No, you won't" she said, digging in her heels.

Gideon frowned down at her. "Megan—"

"No, Gideon. I don't want your money."

"Ah, but seeing my hands prune up from too much dish washing appeals to you."

She smiled up at him so brightly, he almost flinched.

"Exactly," she said.

"Are you going to be this stubborn for the rest of our lives?"

She blinked. "The rest of our—"

The front door slammed, making them both jump. Gideon pulled her behind him. "Let me go first."

"Oh, brother. It's not a burglar."

"Humor me."

"Maybe it's another guest," Megan said suddenly. "Hurry, Gideon. Maybe he'll pay in cash up front."

Gideon stumbled out into the entryway, thanks to Megan's hearty push. It was a good thing his toes were tamed, or he would have embarrassed himself.

A young man stood there, soaked to the skin. His jaw dropped.

"We're in costume," Gideon said, gritting his teeth. No sense in pummeling any of Megan's potential customers.

"I was sent for Lord Blythwood. Is he—?"

"I am he," Gideon said, swallowing a feeling of dread. "What is it?"

"An urgent message from a Mr. MacClure. The phone's out up here so I was sent to give it to you. Lord Blythwood," he added in a tone that said volumes about his opinion of Gideon's manner of dress.

"What was it?" Gideon demanded. Heaven only knew what kind of disaster Adam had landed them in. Gideon cursed himself thoroughly. He never should have given up so easily on staying connected with the company.

"He said it was something of an emergency, and a long, expensive one at that. They need you in London as soon as you can get there."

"I knew it, damn it," Gideon said, dragging his hand through his hair. This was what he deserved for thinking to take a holiday. And when the company collapsed, Gideon would personally hold Stephen responsible.

"All right," Gideon said, striding to the door, "let's go. Are there any cars for hire in the village? I suppose the train might be just as fast. Or maybe a flight from Edinburgh. Well, come on, lad. Don't just stand there."

Gideon strode out the front door into the pouring rain and swore. The boy had come up on a motorbike. Well, perhaps it was fitting to end his ill-fated holiday soaked to the skin, since it was how he'd begun it once his car had caught fire. The car likely would have exploded if Megan hadn't been so quick with the fire extinguisher.

Megan.

Gideon froze in mid step, then turned around. Megan was standing in the doorway.

Gideon strode back to her and put his hands on her shoulders. "I'll ring you soon."

"Sure."

"I will," he promised, "And I'll arrange for some help to come up. I'm sure there is someone in the village who'll hire out for the holidays."

"It's okay," she said, pulling away.

"I'll send a decorator too. Maybe a chef to get things rolling. We have an advertising division at AE. I'll have someone ring you after Christmas with some ideas—"

"Gideon?"

He closed his mouth on the rest of his plans. "Yes?"

"I'll be okay on my own. Really."

"But I can help," he said.

She shook her head. "I don't want your money."

"But—"

She backed away. "Just go do your business thing."

"Megan—"

"It was fun." She smiled, but her eyes were too bright. "I'll see you around."

And with that, she shut the door in his face.

Gideon stood there on the porch and felt worse than he'd ever felt in his entire life. Not even blowing the entire U.K. telecommunications market had left such a sinking feeling in his gut.

"My lord?"

Gideon turned. It was all he could do to put one foot in front of the other.

He climbed onto the back of the motorbike. It was an unpleasant ride to the village, but it was probably just what he needed to bring himself back to his senses.

He would straighten things out in London and ring Megan the first chance he got. He would fly her down and they could resume their relationship in town. He could come home earlier at night, in time for a late supper, perhaps. Maybe he would give thought to taking a few hours off on Sundays to devote to her. Things could work out remarkably well.

He had Adam on the line within moments of arriving in civilization.

"What?" he barked. "Were we robbed? Scooped in the Far East? Did the infrastructure of the company collapse?"

"No," Adam said, sounding confused, "but the stock was off ten points today in New York."

"And?"

"What do you mean 'and'?" Adam exclaimed. "It was off *ten* points, Gideon!"

"Stocks dip."

"What?" Adam gasped. "The last time it dipped *two* you dragged us all out of bed for an emergency board meeting!"

"It will bounce back."

"It will bounce back," Adam echoed, disbelief plain in his voice. "Gideon, have you lost your mind? This is a disaster!"

"Adam, relax—"

"Relax?" Adam bellowed. "I'm sprinting through the halls, bloody frantic about this and all you can say is 'relax'?"

Gideon whistled softly. "I think you need a holiday."

"What did they *do* to you up there?" Adam yelled.

Gideon paused, wondering where to begin. Normally he would have gone on about equipment failures and the time it had cost him, but now he saw clearly that business went on in spite of him. Even the few hours he had spent fretting and stewing had been nothing but a waste of time.

And then quite suddenly a most amazing thought occurred to him.

"Adam, I think I understand."

"Understand what?"

"What she wants."

"Oh, no," Adam moaned. "Tell me there isn't a she involved!"

"I'll call you in a few days. Maybe after the new year."

"Gideon, wait—"

"Go home, Adam. It's Christmas Eve. You need a holiday."

"What I'm going to need is a trip to hospital—thanks to the chest pains you're causing—"

Gideon hung up the phone and lowered himself onto a handy bench. Realizations of this magnitude were better digested while sitting. Yes, it was all becoming clear. He wondered why he hadn't seen it before.

He looked up at his dripping chauffeur. "Are there any shops still open? I need ingredients for a modest Christmas dinner and a few of the trimmings."

The boy nodded, his eyes wide.

"Then let's be off, shall we? I won't spend much. That isn't what's important."

And now he knew what was.

Chapter Eight

MEGAN LOOKED AT the rain beating incessantly against the window. She'd been watching it from the same position for most of the day. Part of it was she couldn't seem to get out of Gideon's chair, and part of it was she just didn't have the heart to move.

It being shattered and lying all around her in pieces as it was.

Well, it was getting close to dark now. Probably time to go and see what was in her kitchen. Somehow, she just couldn't get enthusiastic about the thought of it being hers. She would never go into it that she didn't see Gideon standing over the stove, coaxing his bannocks to cook properly and not scorch themselves.

"Get over it, McKinnon," she commanded herself sternly.

She clawed her way out of the overstuffed chair and dragged herself through the entryway and down the hallway to the dining room. She walked over the place where Gideon had planted his face more than once. Then she gave herself a good shake. She couldn't walk through the house and see him at every turn. He'd made his decision and it was blindingly clear that his priorities didn't include her, despite his brief about-face. He was a workaholic. There was no changing him.

She put her hand on the door, then froze. There was someone in the kitchen. More than one someone, if her ears weren't deceiving her. She grabbed her trusty ornamental dagger from off the buffet and eased the door open the slightest bit.

"I'll go after him," a voice said, in less than friendly tones. "I'll teach him to break me wee granddaughter's heart!"

"Leave him be, ye blighted Scot! He's regained his senses and gone off to do his manly labors!"

"Och, and what more manly a labor is there than having a wife and bairns?" the first voice demanded. "Pebble countin' ain't the way to happiness!"

There was a sudden ruckus and a great deal of gurgling. Megan feared murder, so she shoved open the door and leaped into the kitchen, her dagger bared and ready.

"Eek!" the ghost dressed in knightly garb said, leaping back and tripping over his chair. He landed ungracefully on his back-side.

Megan froze, her eyes glued to the scene before her. There were three men in her kitchen, two of whom were dressed in kilts, one in chain mail. And she recognized all of them.

"Ah," she said, lowering her dagger and straightening up from her lunging position, "um, hello."

Hugh smiled and waved. The knight heaved himself to his feet with a grunt and frowned at her. Megan looked at the third ghost, the one with the commanding presence and very fancy kilt. A huge brooch of emeralds and silver fastened a scarf-like bit of cloth to his shoulder. Megan felt completely frumpy in her dress that was six inches too short. She gave the chief ghost a little wave.

"Hi," she said, whipping her hands behind her back to hide her dagger, "I'm Megan." She wished she had a pocket to stash the knife in. It looked ridiculous compared to the swords the ghosts were packing.

The head ghost made her a low bow. "Ambrose MacLeod, Laird of the Clan MacLeod, at your service."

"Okay," Megan said slowly, giving in to the urge to drop a little curtsey.

"He's your granddaddy," Hugh said, "on yer mama's side."

"A bit removed," Ambrose said modestly.

"I see," Megan said, wondering if her eyes were bulging as far out of her head as she thought they might be.

"And I'd be your granddaddy on your papa's side," Hugh added proudly. "A wee bit removed," he added, darting a glance at Ambrose.

Ambrose nodded to Hugh, then turned and nodded to the knight who had plunked himself down into a chair. "This is Fulbert de Piaget. He's Gideon's uncle."

"Several times removed," Megan surmised.

"Aye," Fulbert grumbled.

Megan leaned back against the door frame. "Well, he's off to do his business. Aren't you happy about that?"

"Of course I am," Fulbert retorted, scowling. "He does mighty important work, missy!"

"And he misses out on life because of it," Ambrose said, sitting down heavily. "Come, Megan, and join us. We've puzzled our heads sore trying to understand the lad and I've no more mind to speak of him. We'll speak instead of your plans for the inn."

Megan soon found herself sitting in a circle with three hale and hearty ghosts, listening to them discuss what could be done with the inn now that a member of the family finally had it back in her possession.

"Then you don't mind?" she asked Ambrose.

"Mind?" Fulbert snorted. "Missy, we saw to the deed ourselves!"

"And *you* don't mind?" she asked, turning to Gideon's grumbly ancestor.

Fulbert looked at her from under his bushy eyebrows. "I'm wed to your blasted aunt, gel. I'll learn to put up with you soon enough."

Hugh whipped out his sword. "Keep a civil tongue, ye blighted—"

"It's okay," Megan said, holding up her hand. "He doesn't have to like me. Maybe it runs in the family."

Hugh looked at her and his bright blue eyes filled with tears. "I think Gideon liked ye fine, Megan lass. He's just a bit off in the head."

Even Fulbert seemed to have nothing to say to that.

"Plans for the inn," Ambrose broke in. "What do you think, my dear, about this modern fascination with the past? I daresay we could make use of it. After all, we're quite conversant with many decades of traditions."

"I don't doubt it," she said, feeling the faintest glimmer of enthusiasm. "You mean, period costumes and traditional holiday celebrations?"

Hugh elbowed Fulbert. "She's a quick one, she is. That's *me* wee granddaughter, ye stubborn Brit."

Megan smiled at him, then turned back to Ambrose. "It would have to be small scale, until I have more money to invest in it."

And with that, they were off and running. Megan listened to ideas fly between her ancestors and wished she'd had a tape recorder. She hardly had time to wonder if they could *be* recorded before she found herself swept into a maelstrom of ideas. And if she only put into practice a fraction of them, she would be busy for the rest of her days.

Which was a good thing, since she would have all that time on her hands.

She refused to think about Gideon. And about how much she would have loved to share this with him. And about how adorable he would have looked in a kilt.

And just before she was tired enough to lean her head back against the chair, she looked at Ambrose and decided, based on the twinkle in his eye, that he had been the one to rustle up the purple elf shoes.

And that was almost enough to make her fall asleep with a smile on her face.

SHE WOKE LATER, stiff and sore. The kitchen was lit with a single candle burning low on the table. There was no sign of the chairs that had been occupied by three spirits earlier, nor was there any sign of their silver mugs or the keg Fulbert seemed to have produced from thin air. Megan blinked. She was tempted to think she'd dreamed it all, but the memories were too fresh in her mind. At least her relatives cleaned up after themselves.

She stretched, then froze. Was that a noise?

"Hugh? Ambrose?" She looked over her shoulder. "Fulbert?"

There it was again. And it wasn't coming from the kitchen.

Megan took her dagger in hand and went out into the dining room.

"Anyone here?" she asked.

The noise stopped abruptly.

That was enough to spook her. She peeked out into the

dimly lit hallway. There, over the McKinnon coat of arms was
a sword reminiscent of Hugh's. It would be a far sight more
protection than the little unsharpened dagger she held. She
slipped out into the hallway, laid the dagger on the reception
desk and tiptoed over to the sword.

She eased it down. And the point immediately made a
whumping noise as it fell against the carpet. It was, however,
not as heavy as she feared. She hoisted it, took up the stance
she'd seen Hugh and Fulbert take when they'd been trying to
decapitate each other upstairs, then walked softly to the library.

Something was shuffling inside.

Megan didn't give herself time to think. She flung open the
door and jumped inside, brandishing her blade.

Gideon whirled around in surprise, stumbled backward,
and went down heavily into a Christmas tree.

"Ouch, damn it! I'm being poked everywhere!"

Megan tossed the blade onto the couch and ran to help
him. She pulled him up, then turned him around and picked
out bits of ornament and tree parts that had somehow found
their way into his backside.

"You scared me to death," he exclaimed. "You could have
cut my head off with that thing!"

"Nice to see you too," she said, with a scowl. "How was I
supposed to know you weren't a burglar?"

"Decorating?"

Megan tried to resurrect the tree Gideon had sat on. It had
been a rather small one to start with and Gideon hadn't done it
any favors. She let it flop back to the ground, then stared down
at it.

"It was a nice thought," she said quietly.

"It took me a long time to find the right one," he said, taking her hand. "A very long *time*."

She met his gaze. "It did?"

"It did." He led her over to the chair of no return, snagging
a shopping bag on his way. He sat and pulled her onto his lap.
"Here. These things will explain it better than I could." He
reached for his bag and dumped its contents into her arms. He
held up an unwrapped umbrella, then set it aside. "You didn't
need to open that. It's just to get you up to the castle, so you
can put that job behind you before we start on the inn."

Before we start on the inn. Megan was just certain she'd heard him wrong. She frowned.

"What about your emergency?" she demanded.

"I took care of it."

She frowned some more, just to let him know where she stood. "Did it take all afternoon?"

"It took about five minutes. The rest of the time I was looking for things for you."

"Well," she said, feeling rather at a loss. There she'd been griping about him to her ancestors, and he'd been hunting up presents. "That sheds a different light on things."

"I thought it might." He smiled. "Aren't you interested in what I got you? And the humiliation I went through whilst shopping in yellow tights and purple shoes?"

Megan felt her heart soften even more. Gideon had tried to spruce up the library with his little tree and he had left his dignity behind to shop for something to put under it for her. It merited at least a second glance at what was piled in her lap.

There were four packages of various sizes. She immediately zeroed in on the very small, very ring-like looking box, then forced herself to look at something else. It couldn't be what its size screamed it might be. Megan looked at Gideon from under her eyebrows and saw a twinkle in his eyes, as if he had an impressive secret he couldn't wait to share.

Taking a deep breath, she opened up a long, slender package—and held up a paintbrush.

"To use in our redecorating," he said.

"*Our* redecorating?" she asked.

"I told you I'd offer my humble services, didn't I?"

That was before he'd hiked right on out of there—but then he'd hiked right back in again. Megan held up the brush and considered.

"It's a really small brush, Gideon."

"Then I guess it will take a long *time,* won't it?"

"Hmmm," she said. On the surface that looked good, but what was his definition of time spent? Would he be there for two or three days, consider his decorating contribution fulfilled, then toddle off merrily to London? She set the paintbrush aside. No sense jumping to any conclusions quite yet.

She chose another hastily wrapped gift, convinced Gideon had done the wrapping honors himself.

"Interesting," she said, holding up rubber gloves.

"So I don't get dishpan hands while I'm washing up after supper," Gideon said, with a smile.

"Well," she said. A man didn't buy yellow rubber gloves if he didn't plan on using them, did he? And these weren't the wimpy kind that supermarkets sold; these were heavy-duty, dabble-in-toxic-waste-and-not-ruin-your-fingernail-polish kind of gloves. These were gloves meant for more than just a handful of dips into sudsy water. Did he plan on doing dishes for more than just the weekend?

"And this is a cookbook," Gideon said, relieving her of the gloves and handing her a heavy package instead. "I perused the index already and I think there are several things we could actually succeed in making. I was somewhat alarmed by the quantity of raw ingredients required, but I decided that together we might have a go at it. What do you think?"

"Ah," Megan said, stunned, "um, well." She unwrapped in a daze. Based on their previous forays into the kitchen, the gift of a cookbook was not something to be taken lightly. Especially one that required them to make things from scratch. "It sounds pretty time-consuming," she said. "Not exactly a single weekend project."

"I know," he said, smiling widely. "It will be brilliant fun, don't you think? All that time together in the kitchen, bonding over bouillabaisse?"

Megan clutched the cookbook, looked at her errant business mogul and wondered if one too many equipment disasters had finally forced him to relinquish his tenuous grasp on sanity.

"Gideon," she said slowly, wanting to make sure he understood each word, "when in the world are you going to have time for all of this?"

"I'll make time."

"You can't. You're the president of an international company."

"I'll manage it."

"You hobnob with billionaires!"

"I know."

Megan gritted her teeth. He was wearing a cheesy grin,

and that annoying twinkle was still stuck in his eyes.

"You don't have time to cook," Megan said. "That's why you have a chef."

"We'll send him on holiday."

It was time for the killing blow. He would have to admit his true intentions sooner or later, and this was guaranteed to force him to face reality.

"You wouldn't last a week up here," she said. "You can't live without your laptop."

Gideon calmly took her face in his hands, leaned up and kissed her softly.

"Yes, I can," he said, his smile sweet and gentle. "I realized when I left that what I was heading toward was far less important than what I'd left behind."

It started to sink in. He was serious. Megan felt her eyes begin to water.

"I can live without the company, Megan, but I can't live without you."

He proceeded to hand her the little box she'd been so carefully avoiding. Megan clutched it. She didn't dare open it.

"A new marble for my collection?" she asked, trying to smile.

Gideon only laughed. "Hardly."

Megan looked at him and saw nothing but love in his eyes and tenderness in his expression. He covered her hand with his own comfortable, companionable hand and gave her a reassuring squeeze.

"Open it, please," he said softly. "Quickly, so I'll know if I've just made a great fool of myself."

Megan opened the box to reveal a slim gold band. At least she thought it was a slim gold band. She could hardly see it for her tears.

"Oh, Gideon."

"It's just a placeholder," he said. "Thorpewold isn't exactly a buzzing metropolis."

"No, it's beautiful."

He ducked to catch her gaze. "I can't guarantee I'll be perfect," he admitted, "but you've seen quite a bit of me at my worst. I'll still have to work, but I'll work less. Much less." He put his hand under her chin and lifted her face up. "I know you won't marry me for my money or my title, and that will confuse my father greatly, but," he said, with a smile, "will you marry me for my time? I'll make it worth your while."

"Somehow, I imagine you will," she said, returning his smile. "And yes," she added, "I will marry you."

And then she learned just how much time he planned on lavishing on her as he took many, many minutes to kiss her breathless.

"If we could get out of this damned chair," he said, when he came up for air a very long while later, "we could adjourn to another room and see how much more time we could spend at this. I mean, after all, we're engaged now, and there really isn't any reason . . ."

"Why, there'll be none of that!" Hugh gasped. He appeared behind the chair and looked down at Gideon with marked disapproval. "Imagine that! The thought of visitin' me wee one's marriage bed 'afore the ceremony!"

Gideon blinked. "What did you say?"

Megan shook her head. "I didn't say anything."

Gideon scratched his head, then shrugged. "Well, what do you think—ouch, damn it!"

Hugh had given Gideon what Megan could only term a thorough boxing of the ears.

Gideon looked down at her hands that were captured handily enough in his own, then raised his gaze to hers slowly.

"You didn't do that," he stated.

"'Fraid not."

He lifted one eyebrow. "I don't suppose you would know who had, would you?"

"I suppose I would."

Gideon shivered. "All right," he said, to the middle of the room. "I take the hint."

Hugh harrumphed and disappeared. Gideon looked at her and laughed uneasily.

"I don't suppose we'll have any privacy on our wedding night either."

"I think they know where to draw the line." Or so she hoped.

"Will I pass muster if I limit myself to kissing you? After all, it is Christmas Eve. I think it's tradition."

"And we wouldn't want to break with tradition," she said, the moment before she found much more interesting things to do with her lips besides form words.

And between kisses, Gideon briefly described the makings for Christmas dinner he'd found. He polled her opinions on what other holiday traditions she thought they could indulge in to distract themselves until they could arrange a wedding.

"Yule log," he offered, then kissed her thoroughly.

"Bing Crosby on the stereo," she managed when he let her breathe again. "Counts as Christmas caroling."

"Wassail and other trappings," he said, winding his fingers through her hair.

"It's a Wonderful Life," she suggested.

He smiled. "It certainly is."

Megan started to tell him that he didn't understand what she meant. Then she saw the look in his eye and realized he understood completely.

And it certainly was.

IT WAS VERY late when the fire had burned down and Megan woke, only to realize she'd fallen asleep in Gideon's arms. He was sound asleep, still fully trapped in the chair's embrace. Megan blinked as she saw Fulbert come up behind the chair. He gave her a scowl that wasn't as scowly as his former expressions, then plopped a red bow on top of Gideon's head. He huffed something under his breath, then turned and went to join Hugh and Ambrose who were standing next to the fireplace. Hugh was beaming. Ambrose looked perfectly satisfied with his work.

"Stocking stuffer," Ambrose clarified.

"Thank you," Megan said, with a smile.

"Hmmm?" Gideon said, stirring.

Megan kissed him softly. "Nothing. Go back to sleep."

Once he had drifted off again, Megan looked at the small collection of gifts on the floor next to the fallen tree, gifts that represented the time Gideon intended to commit to their relationship. The last glowing embers from the fire sparkled against the thin gold band on her hand, a symbol of love found in the most unexpected of places.

Then she looked at Gideon and decided that he was by far the best Christmas gift of all—even if he was too big to fit into her stocking.

She tucked her head into the crook of his neck and closed her eyes, content.

Epilogue

AMBROSE MACLEOD, GRANDFATHER several generations removed, escorted his granddaughter down the aisle. Her sire
walked on the other side, preoccupied with not tripping over
his daughter's flowing medieval gown.

"Good grief, Megan, where did you come up with all this
medieval hoopla?" her father muttered.

"Oh, Dad," Megan said, with a little laugh, "the inn just
seems to inspire it."

Ambrose looked down at her and felt pride stir in his
breast. Of all the places he could have been, this was the best.
Of all the posterity he could have matchmade for, this lass was
the sweetest. She looked up at him and smiled brilliantly. Ambrose returned the smile proudly.

He turned his gaze to the front of the chapel. Gideon stood
there already, resplendent in his medieval finery. Fulbert stood
to one side, his hand on his sword, Artane pride etched into his
very bearing. Fulbert had made his peace completely with
Megan over the past month, once he'd realized she actually increased Gideon's capacity for proper labor. The office Gideon
had installed in the inn had satisfied them both. Ambrose knew
he would miss Megan when she and her love made for London,
but Gideon had given his word they wouldn't stay overlong. Of
course, Gideon had been looking in the wrong direction when
he'd said as much, but Ambrose had accepted the gesture just
the same. The lad's vision would clear up soon enough.

Hugh stood next to Megan's sisters Jennifer and Victoria, clutching a beribboned nosegay of conservatory flowers. Megan smiled fondly at him. Hugh pulled a snowy linen cloth from his sleeve and blew his nose into it with a honk.

Gideon jumped half a foot and whipped his head around to stare straight at Hugh.

Then he seemingly caught sight of Fulbert's blade and jerked around to stare at him.

"Uh oh," Megan said, looking up at Ambrose. "The jig's up."

Ambrose felt Gideon's eyes on him and he returned the lad's startled look.

"Come on, Dad. Gideon's going to faint if we don't hurry up."

Ambrose stood back and let her hasten to her blanched groom's side. It was rather touch-and-go until Fulbert barked for the lad to stand up straight. At that, the boy stiffened as if he'd been skewered up the spine.

Ambrose didn't relax truly until the vows had been spoken, the rings exchanged and the kiss given. Then he sat down wearily next to Megan's father and his own kinswoman.

"Where does she come up with these things?" the man asked, shaking his head. "All this medieval hocus pocus. Look at me, Helen, I'm in a kilt!"

"Yes, dear."

"It's that damn MacLeod blood, Helen."

"Of course it is, dear. It's a family trait."

Ambrose smiled at his daughter, many times removed, then blinked in surprise as she looked straight at him and winked.

"Well, I'll be damned," he whispered.

IT WAS SEVERAL hours later that Megan and Gideon were sent off on their honeymoon, the guests were all put to bed and Ambrose could finally relax in the kitchen. Even Hugh and Fulbert seemed at peace. They were only hurling mild insults at each other. No blades were bared.

"I say we turn our sights to those two sisters of hers," Hugh said, clutching his cup. "I'm thinkin' they'll be a far sight easier to see settled."

Fulbert snorted. "Didn't you mark that Victoria? By the saints, Hugh, she's a bleedin' garrison captain!" He shivered. "I wouldn't cross her if me life depended on it."

"Ambrose?" Hugh prodded. "What think ye?"

"I'm leaving it up to you two for a bit," Ambrose said, rising and stretching.

Hugh and Fulbert gaped at him.

"Where're ye off to?" Hugh asked.

Ambrose stared off into the distance thoughtfully. "The Highlands, I believe."

"But ye can't," Hugh gasped.

"We've more matches to make," Fulbert spluttered.

Ambrose smiled fondly at his two compatriots. "They'll keep well enough until I return."

"But—"

"How can you—"

"Lads, lads," Ambrose said, shaking his head. "A well-earned rest is nothing to take lightly."

"A holiday?" Hugh's ears perked up.

Fulbert tossed his mug aside. "I'm for France." And he vanished.

"The Colonies," Hugh announced, standing and tilting his cap at a jaunty angle. "I'm feeling quite the risk-taker at the moment." He made Ambrose a quick bow and disappeared.

"And I'm for the Highlands," Ambrose said, feeling his pulse quicken at the very thought.

Home.

And, of course, the precise area Megan and Gideon had chosen for their getaway.

After all, a grandfather's work was never done.

Ambrose smiled, set his mug on the table and made his way from the kitchen, turning out the lights behind him.

And the Groom
Wore Tulle

Prologue

IAN MACLEOD LAY in the Fergusson's dungeon and, not having much else to do, contemplated life's many mysteries.

How was it that the Fergusson could be so hopelessly inept at growing grain or raising aught but stringy cattle, yet have the knack of producing such a fine, healthy crop of rats? Ian would have been annoyed by this if he'd had the energy—especially given the fact that one of the rats was currently making a nest in his hair while the rodent's fellows sat in a half-circle around Ian, apparently waiting for the nest maker to finish and invite them to have a closer look at his building skills—but Ian didn't have the energy to even shake off the offender, much less muster up a good frothy head of irritation.

Secondly, he gave thought to the location of his sorry self. It wasn't often that a MacLeod found himself in a Fergusson hall, much less in his pit.

It wasn't as though his kinsmen hadn't made attempts to liberate him from their bitterest enemy's dungeon. They had and he had appreciated their efforts, even though they'd been to no avail. He would have liked to have forgotten about the entire affair, and the accompanying indignity of it, but he was, after all, the one sitting amongst the vermin, so thinking on it was almost unavoidable.

And then lastly, and by no means the least of any of the things clamoring for his attention, he thought he just might be dying.

That, however, was the only good thing to come of the past two months.

Ian settled back against the wall—or pretended to, as there wasn't much movement in his once finely fashioned form anymore—and gave thought to the whole business of dying. It was actually the only thought that had cheered him in days. His time in 1313 was obviously over and no one would miss him if he perhaps managed to elude death's sharp sickle and sneak off to the forest near the MacLeod keep. And if by some miracle he reached that forest and happened to find the exact spot that would carry a man hundreds of years into the Future, well, who would begrudge him that? What would one fine, manly addition to the Future hurt? It was either escape to there or toast his backside against the fires of Hell.

Unfortunately, Ian had no illusions about his sins. He'd spent too much time at the ale kegs, wenched more than any man should have without acquiring scores of bastards, killed with too much heat in his blood, and—surely the most grievous of all—wooed Roberta Fergusson to his bed and cheerfully robbed her of her virginity.

It was the last, of course, which had earned him a place in Roberta's father's dungeon.

It wouldn't have mattered so much had Roberta possessed any redeeming qualities besides her virginity. More was the pity for Ian that she sported a visage uglier than a pig's arse and the temper of an angry sow. Her guaranteed virtue had been her only desirable trait and she possessed that no longer.

Ian suspected that her new unmaidenly condition didn't trouble her overmuch. After all, he had taken great care with her and spared no effort to make the night memorable for her. 'Twas rumored, however, that her father had been less than enthusiastic upon learning of the evening's events. Ian had known there would be retribution. He also knew that 'twas almost a certainty that the Fergusson was in league with the Devil, which left him wondering what conversations the two had already had about him.

Best not to think on that overmuch.

He turned his mind quickly from the contemplation of Hell and settled back instead for speculation about where he would have gone had he had the choice.

The Future. Even the very word caused his pulse to

quicken. He knew as much about the distant future as a man in Robert the Bruce's day should—likely more. He'd had a young kinsman travel to the Future and return briefly to tell of its wonders. And then another miracle had occurred and a traveler from the Future had arrived at the MacLeod keep. She had married the laird Jamie and carried him home to 1996 with her. Ian had grieved for Jamie's loss, for he was Ian's closest friend and most trusted ally, but he'd been afire with the idea that one day he too might travel to a time when men flew through the skies like birds and traveled great distances in carts without horses. At the time Jamie had forbidden him to come along with him to that unfathomable point so far ahead, telling Ian that his time in the fourteenth century would not be over unless he escaped certain death.

Ian was certainly facing death now.

Ach, but if that wasn't enough to make Ian ache for the chance to walk in the MacLeod forest, he didn't know what was. Ian dreamed of how it might have been had he managed to gain the Future. He would have been dressed in his finest plaid, with his freshly sharpened sword at his side and a cap tilted jauntily atop his head. Future women would have swooned at the very sight of him and Future men would have envied him his fine form and ability to ingest vast quantities of ale yet still outsmart his shrewdest enemies—and all this, mind you, before even breaking his fast in the morn.

He would have searched for his kin soon after his arrival. Jamie would have been pleased to see him, and Ian would have been pleased to see Jamie. First he would have hugged Jamie fiercely, then planted his fist in Jamie's nose—repeatedly.

Jamie being, of course, the reason Ian found himself wallowing in the slime.

Ian found the energy to scowl. If he and Jamie just hadn't been in that one tiny skirmish together, Ian might have avoided having a rat fashioning a home upon his head. Jamie had caught William Fergusson's son scampering off to safety, boxed the lad's ears in annoyance, then filled them full of a message for the boy to take to his father. Of course, Jamie had informed the lad in the most impressive of details just how thoroughly Ian had bedded Roberta, then wished the family good fortune in finding a mate for her.

Ian's fate had been sealed.

Ian tried to shake the rat off the top of his head, but found that all he could do was sit in the muck and give a grim thought or two as to whether or not he should be repenting while he still could. Perhaps Saint Peter would have pity on him and let him squeak through the gates. Ian spared a thought as to whether those heavenly gates swung inward or outward, and the means of defending them if it were the latter, then he found that even that was too taxing a thought to ponder.

Death was very near.

Ian mustered up the energy to give one last fleeting thought to the Future. Perhaps if he vowed to leave off his wenching ways and settle down with one woman. Aye, that he could surely do to earn himself a place in heaven. . . .

Suddenly a piercing light descended and blinded him. He closed his eyes against it, fearing the worst. Apparently not even his last-minute bargain was enough to save him. From behind his eyelids he could see that the light flickered wildly.

Damn. Hellfire, obviously.

Ian sighed in resignation and took one last deep breath.

And then he knew no more.

"DID YE GET him?"

"Aye."

"Sword too?" the first asked.

"Aye," the second said, hefting his burden over his shoulder with one hand and holding onto the blade with the other. "Ye can see I've both."

"Is he dead, do ye think?"

"Dunno." The second would have taken a closer look, but his burden was heavier than he should have been after all that time in the pit. "Looks dead to me."

"Well, then," the first said, apparently satisfied, "take him and heave him onto MacLeod soil. Sword too. The laird wants it so."

The second didn't need to hear that more than once. Best to do what the laird asked. He had no desire to see the bottom of the Fergusson's pit up close. The riding would take all night, but 'twas best seen to quickly. He would return home just as quickly, for he had no desire to be nearby when the clan MacLeod discovered their dead kinsman.

"Was that a moan?" the first asked suspiciously.

"Didn't hear it," the second said, walking away. Dead, alive, he couldn't have cared less in what condition his burden found himself. He'd do the heaving of the man, then be on his way. If the MacLeod fool wasn't dead now, he would be in a matter of hours.

"Leave the sword near the body!" the first called.

"Aye," the second grumbled, tempted to filch it. But it was a MacLeod blade and he was a superstitious soul, so he turned away from thoughts of robbery and concentrated on the task before him. He'd return for his payment, then find a dry place to lay his head, hopefully with his belly full of decent fare and his arms wrapped around a fine wench. He'd do it in honor of the almost-dead man he prepared to strap to the back of his horse. The man might have been a MacLeod, but he was a Highlander after all, and deserved some kind of proper farewell.

The second man set off, his mind already on his supper.

Chapter One

JANE FERGUSSON SAT with her chin on her fists, stared at the surroundings of her minuscule cubby at Miss Petronia Witherspoon's Elegant Eighteenth Century Wedding Fashions, and contemplated the ironies of life. There were a lot of them and her contemplating was taking up a lot of time. But that wasn't much of a problem, mainly because she had a long weekend stretching out in front of her and no beach house to retreat to. No, what she had was herself trapped in Miss Witherspoon's shop with only her imagination to keep her company.

What a waste that was. There she was in New York, city of designers, and she had the talent and ambition to design ultra funky clothes in a rainbow of colors. She had her health. She had panty hose in her drawer without any nail polish stemming the tide of runaway runs. She even had an apartment she could afford. Surely with all those things in her favor, she should have been working at a fashionable house designing incredible things for only the long-legged and impossibly thin to wear.

But where did she find herself?

Trying to keep her head above the water line while drowning in vats of faux pearls and more lace than a Brussels seamstress could shake a seam ripper at—all for use in the design and construction of wedding gowns.

The problem was, Jane didn't particularly like bridal gowns.

In fact, Jane wasn't even sure she liked brides.

She sighed, closed her eyes, and let her mind drift back to how it had been in the beginning. She had come to New York with her head full of bold, energetic designs and her suitcase full of funky, short things in black. She'd heard that the truly chic of New York dressed all in black and she had cheerfully pitched every colored item she owned on the off chance that the rumor was true.

She had hoped for a place with someone big, really big; someone who was so ultrahip that even her stuff would look a little frumpy by comparison.

It was then that her course had taken a marked quirk to the left.

She'd been pawing through an upscale antique store's selection of vintage fashions, on the lookout for the elusive and the unusual and muttering to herself about how she would have designed the gowns differently, when she'd felt the imperious tap of a bony finger on her shoulder.

"Are you a seamstress, dear?"

The term alone should have sent up a red flag, but Jane had been so thrilled that someone might think her something akin to a designer that she'd bobbed her head obediently and waited breathlessly for some other gem of recognition. And when she'd been offered a place at Miss Witherspoon's salon, she'd leaped at the chance.

Little had she known that she would wind up designing wedding gowns for a woman who made *Oliver Twist's* Fagan look like a philanthropist. And not only was she designing all those eighteenth-century wedding gowns, she was watching Miss Witherspoon's niece take credit for it. It was pitiful.

Jane planned to leave. She'd been planning to leave for almost three years, but what with one thing and another—mostly rent and food—she found herself staying. After all, she was actually doing a great deal of designing, and that wasn't something she could turn her back on lightly.

So she invested a lot of time trying to ignore the fact that she was basically an indentured servant. That invariably led to questions about where her Prince Charming was hiding his white horse. Surely there was someone out there who would rescue her from the acres of tulle she'd gotten herself lost in.

She sighed and turned her mind away from the rainbow of colors she could be working with to more productive thoughts—such as if hari-kari were possible with dressmaker's pins. Before she could do any experimenting, the phone rang, making her jump. She was, of course, the only one left at the shop, having been assigned the task of closing up for the three-day weekend. She picked up the phone.

"Hello?"

"Jane, dear," Miss Witherspoon said, sounding rushed, "just a few last-minute things before we visit yet another royal residence. So many beautiful gowns preserved for the discriminating eye, you know. Remember that we'll be hopping back over the Pond on Tuesday."

Yeah, on the Concorde, Jane thought with a scowl.

"Europe has given Alexis such glorious design inspiration . . ."

Not even Europe will improve her stick figures, Jane thought with a grumble.

". . . Christy and Naomi will be in early next week, so you'll want to be sure to remain behind the scenes. Alexis will do the showing of the gowns, of course, for we all know she has the beauty to complement them while you do not!"

Jane had no reply for that, so she merely rested her chin on her fist and thought Gloomy Thoughts about her less-than-arresting face.

"Oh, and one last thing, dear. I want you to check in the workroom immediately. There was a rat heard frolicking about there this afternoon."

Rats. What else? Jane put the receiver back in its cradle, her head down on her desk, and sighed. Miss Witherspoon never would have asked Alexis to check out a rat rumor. Alexis wouldn't have been any good at rat patrol anyway. Alexis was from California. If they had rats, which Jane doubted they did in Alexis's neck of the woods, they were no doubt tanned, relaxed, and unaggressive. Alexis was not up to the New York rat, a hearty, belligerent beast. Jane, however, was unafraid.

At least that's what she told herself as she picked up a yardstick and headed for the back room.

She opened the door, flicked on the light, and spared a brief moment to look at her creations hanging so perfectly on the long racks against the wall. Every pearl in place, every tuck just so, every drop of lace dripping as if it had been poured that way. Jane had to admit that even though she wasn't all that fond of bridal wear, the gowns were beautiful. She had taken the styles of the period and put as much of her personal stamp on them as she could get away with. It wasn't much more than an unexpected tuck here or an unusual bit of lace there, but at least it was something.

It was then that she was distracted by the sound of crunching.

She glanced down and saw a trail of junk food wrappers leading over to the corner.

And she muffled a squeak of fright.

Well, it was obvious that the rat wasn't dining on satin, so what was the use of chasing him out right then? Jane let the benevolence of the moment wash over her as she quickly retreated from the room. She left the light on and shut the door. Maybe the light would convince the rat that he'd wandered into the wrong place and he would abandon his designs on the workroom.

That sounded much better than trying to convince him to leave by means of a flimsy stick.

She quickly packed up her bag, put on her sneakers with the rainbow shoelaces—not chic maybe, but definitely colorful—and hurried out into the Manhattan evening. The colors and smells of the twentieth century assaulted her, assuring her that she wasn't trapped in a Victorian sweatshop. She took a deep breath, slung her bag over her shoulder, and set off down the street to her sublet, thoughts of rats temporarily forgotten.

BY THE TIME she reached her building, she was sweating and cross. She trudged up three flights of stairs, stood outside her door until her breath caught back up with her, then shoved her key into the lock and welcomed herself home to her glorified attic apartment. She turned on the lights, then closed the door behind her and leaned back against it, letting her bag slide to the floor. A quick survey of her surroundings told her she was indeed in the black-and-white space she had created for herself upon her arrival in New York. She had been convinced a monochromatic scheme was perfectly in keeping with her chic, designer self and would do nothing but enhance her creativity.

Lately she had begun to have her doubts that this was good for her state of mind.

She pushed away from the door with a sigh and headed toward her bedroom to exchange her requisite working uniform of anything black—heaven forbid we should compete with the brides, dear!—to something at least in a comforting sweatsuity shade of gray. She usually found her bedroom, with all the purity of its white contents, soothing. Today it just felt sterile.

Jane quickly took stock of what she'd consumed that day, decided that the M&M's had pushed her over the edge, and vowed with a solemn crossing of her heart to stay away from the vending machine at some point in the very near future. Perhaps before she turned forty, in another decade or so.

There was one deviation from her color scheme and that was the hope chest her parents had insisted she take with her. It was a beautiful, rich cherry and it sat under her tiny window and beckoned to her with all the subtlety of a lighthouse beam at close range. Jane knew what was in the trunk.

She was tempted.

But she also knew where looking would lead, so she turned sharply away and rummaged in her dresser for something appropriate for her *aprez* work Friday night activity of watching an old movie.

Once she'd shed her Witherspoon image for something more comfortable, she made herself a snack and settled down with the remote. She couldn't afford cable, but the public broadcasting system always had something useful on Friday nights.

"Great," she groused, tuning in and getting ready to tune out. "Sheep."

Ah, but it was sheep in Scotland and that was enough to keep her thumb off the remote. Scotland and all those sheep who worked so hard to donate all that wool. Jane's fingers itched at the very thought of it. Truth be told—and it was something she didn't tell anyone at work lest it ruin her image as a user of already woven goods only—put a pair of knitting needles in her hands and she could work miracles.

And yarn came in such a rainbow of colors.

She watched until she knew more than she wanted to about sheep and their habits, then she turned off the TV and crawled into bed.

And she dreamed of Scottish sheep.

Chapter Two

And back in the workroom . . .

IAN LIFTED HIS sword and plucked from the end another of the bags of food he had gathered. He broke open the outer coating and reached inside for some of the crunchy inner meat. While he ate, he looked at the words engraved upon the outside of the pouch. Cheetos. He nibbled, then looked with concern at the orange residue left upon his fingers. It only added to the acute alarm he felt. He continued to chew, certain he would need whatever nourishment he could have, and contemplated the direness of his situation. He was dead, obviously, for he was surely no longer in the Fergusson's pit. It concerned him, however, how much his mortal frame still pained him. He'd been certain he would have shed his body on his trip to the afterlife. But possess it he still did, and an uncomfortable thing it was indeed.

He looked about him. He was in a chamber full of white gowns. He hadn't seen them at first, as he had woken to complete darkness. Then a faint light had forced its way through a window, leaving him with the knowledge that he was no longer in the Fergusson's keep. He'd heaved himself to his feet in a desperate search for food and water.

It was then he'd espied the little box full of pouches. Drink he'd found there too, in little boxes and tasting of strange and exotic flavors. The drink he had enjoyed. The food, less so.

He'd staggered back to his corner and settled down for a rest when a light so bright it burned his eyes blazed to life before him. He'd been so stunned, he hadn't moved at first.

Heaven? he had wondered. Or perhaps a chamber assigned to those who awaited their journey to Hell. He couldn't be certain, but he strongly suspected that he had somehow, while being out of his head with weariness, escaped the Fergusson's guards and landed himself in a chamber containing gowns for future angels. There were, after all, all those garments in white to consider. And those little black machines on the tables. Ian hadn't dared touch them, but he'd read the words inscribed on them easily enough. Singer. If that didn't cause a body to think of singing angels, he surely didn't know what would.

But there had been no angels roaming about fingering the gowns so Ian had been left to ponder other alternatives. He'd eventually come to the conclusion that he wasn't in either Heaven or Hell, he was in Limbo, that horrible place between the two. The food alone should have told him as much. He looked about him at the remains of what he'd consumed. Cheetos, Milky Way, Life Savers—and aye, he could have used those in truth—all in colors he hardly recognized and tastes he'd never before set his tongue to. All in all, he couldn't help but wish heartily that he were back in Scotland braving the fare at his clan's table.

Then another more disturbing thought occurred to him. Perhaps the powers that were deciding his fate were still struggling to make up their minds about him.

He looked about him and frowned at the leavings scattered here and there. He'd had to remove the slippery outer coatings of the food—once he'd discovered those outer shells weren't fit to eat, that is. Perhaps 'twould make a better impression on Saint Peter's gate guards if Ian tidied up his surroundings. He struggled to his feet, using his sword to help him get there, then merely leaned upon his sword and caught his breath. Never mind where he was; what he needed was a decent meal and a fortnight's rest to recover from his stay in the Fergusson's keep.

Ian started to bend down to see to his clutter when a door at the far end of the chamber opened. He froze, afeared to draw attention to himself when he was looking less than his best.

A demon walked in. It could be nothing else. It was dressed all in black, its hair pulled up and pinned to its head with half a dozen sticks of wood. Ian spared a thought about what kind of pain that must have caused the beastie, then realized that it likely felt no pain. Dwelling in such a place as this would surely numb the senses.

The creature looked over the angels' gowns, thumbing through them with the air of one familiar with such things. The gowns hung on shiny poles in a most magical manner and Ian spared a bit of appreciation for such a finely wrought manner of hanging the clothing. Perhaps Limbo was a more advanced place than he'd thought at first.

The demon finished with its work, then turned his way. He watched its eyes roam over the chamber, then watched those eyes widen. The shebeastie, and he could now divine that it was a she and not a he, opened its mouth to speak—but no sound issued forth. Ian took the opportunity to assess his opponent before she spewed forth things he likely wouldn't care to hear.

Her face was unremarkable, but fair enough, though Ian wasn't of a mind to examine her too closely. She was passing skinny. Perhaps she was only allowed to make a meal of her victims on an occasional basis. Ian was almost curious enough to ask her, but he was interrupted by the low whine that suddenly came from her. It started out softly enough, then increased in volume until it became a most ear-splitting shriek. Ian threw his Cheeto-encrusted fingers up over his ears until the beastie's mouth closed. Then he hesitantly took his hands down. The beastie blinked, shook her head, then blinked again.

"Only in New York," she said in a particularly garbled tone. "This could only happen in New York."

She repeated that as she turned and left the chamber by the door Ian hadn't dared open before.

New York? Was that what they called the place, then? Ian reached up to scratch his chin over that piece of news, then realized how unkempt he must have appeared to her. Then a more disturbing thought occurred to him. What if she had gone to tell the Deciders of His Fate about his less-than-pleasing appearance? By the saints, with the way he looked at present, the very last place they would think to send him was up the path to the Pearly Gates.

He looked about him frantically for aid. He had been

strengthened somewhat by the ghoulish fare and felt certain that he had the vigor to make himself more presentable. Perhaps if he looked the part of an angel, they might mistake him for one and send him along on his way.

'Twas nothing short of a miracle what he was surrounded by. Angel gowns.

He set his sword aside, peeled off his plaid and shirt, and set to work looking for something in his size.

JANE WALKED INTO her office, very proud of herself that she was still breathing normally. It wasn't every day that a woman saw a filthy, swordbearing, bekilted man six inches taller than she loitering in her workroom. Her hand was very steady as she reached for the phone and dialed 91—

Her finger hovered over the last number. What was she going to tell the cops anyway—*hey, there's a grubby guy standing in the middle of junk food wrappers in the room down the hall?* For all she knew, they would come get *her* and haul her away. She slowly set down the receiver and took stock of the situation.

It was the Saturday before Memorial Day and given the fact that Miss Witherspoon had given the entire staff the long holiday off—except Jane, of course—it was a safe bet that she would be the only one in the salon until Tuesday.

Alone with a crusted-over Swamp Thing.

Jane looked around her for a weapon. Damn, nothing but a handful of dressmaker's pins—and she had already determined their lack of usefulness in inflicting fatal wounds. It looked as if her only option was to beat a hasty retreat and face the remains of the mess on Tuesday with everyone else.

Her hand hadn't gone halfway to her bag before she realized that wasn't an option either. The best gowns in that workroom were one-of-a-kind creations that she had put together herself. She had spent hours rummaging through estate sales, garage sales, and dusty antique shops to find the unique bits and pieces that went into making her additions to the salon truly special. Could she really allow those creations to be ruined because she'd been too cowardly to face the man nesting in the workroom? Besides, he really hadn't looked too steady on his feet. Maybe he needed help.

She squelched the Florence Nightingale thoughts before they could bedazzle her common sense, then gathered up what she hoped was defense enough: a Bic pen and a pair of very long, very sharp dressmaker shears.

"Here goes nothing," she muttered as she left her office and tiptoed down the hallway to the workroom.

She stopped outside the door and put her ear to it. Damned old metal things. Where was a good old-fashioned hollow core wooden door when a girl needed one? With one last deep breath, she flung open the door and stepped inside.

Swamp Thing squeaked in surprise and spun around to face her, his skirts rustling loudly in the sudden silence. Jane would have squeaked as well but she was too dumbfounded by what she was seeing.

He was wearing the most modern of their gowns, a nineteenth-century Southern Belle special. It was an off-the-shoulder number with dozens of hand-placed pearls and enough lace encrusting the bodice to turn the upper half of the dress into the stiffest noncorseted creation ever worn by anyone who'd ever said "y'all."

Well, at least he wasn't toting the matching parasol.

Jane felt her mouth working, but she found that all sound refused to come out. There was a man in her workroom wearing a bridal gown. It was too small by several sizes, the hem hitting him midcalf. His relatively hairy arms poked out at an awkward angle through the sleeve holes and the neckline barely reached midsternum. Jane decided right then that men with any amount of body hair at all were not meant for shoulderless, sleeveless bridal fashions.

And then Swamp Thing spoke.

"Would ye perrrchance be one of Saint Peterrr's ilk," he began, sounding rather nervous, "or are ye belonging to the . . . errrr . . . Deevil's minions?"

His r's rolled so long and so hard, they almost knocked her down. It occurred to her that he was a Scot, which explained what had looked like a kilt before, but it didn't explain what he was doing in Miss Witherspoon's shop.

And then it sunk in what he had asked her.

"Huh?" she said, blinking at him.

He took a deep breath. Then he put his shoulders back—no mean feat given his attire. "Be ye angel," he asked, "or demon?"

She was sure she'd heard him wrong. "Angel or demon?"

"Aye."

"Well," she said, wondering what planet he'd just dropped down from, or, more to the point, what asylum he'd escaped from, "neither, actually."

"Neitherrrr," he echoed.

That Scottish burr almost brought her to her knees. Jane put her hand to her head to check for undue warmth there. There was a lunatic standing ten feet away from her and she was getting giddy over his accent.

He gave his bodice a hike up and scratched his matted beard. "Limbo, then," he said with a sigh. "And here I am, having taken such pains to look my best."

"Look your best," she said, watching him lean wearily against one of the worktables. "Is that why you put on one of the dresses?" *Wacko,* she decided immediately. And one for the books.

He nodded, then explained, his r's rolling and all his other vowels and consonants tumbling and lilting like water rushing over rocks in a stream. Jane was so mesmerized by the sound of his speech, she hardly paid attention to what he was saying.

"So, I was thinking that if you were indeed someone keeping watch for Saint Peter that perhaps I'd make a better impression if I wore something that would make me seem more angelic"—and here he flashed her a smile that just about finished off what his r's had done to her knees—"and spare me a trip to Hell." He sighed and rubbed his eyes. "But if you're trapped in Limbo as well, I can see my efforts were for naught."

"Limbo," she repeated. "Why do you keep talking about Limbo?"

He looked at her as if she was the one who was seriously out of touch with reality. "'Tis the place between Heaven and Hell, and you know nothing of it? 'Tis worse for you than I feared."

"Pal, we aren't in Limbo, we're in New York."

His expression of resignation turned to alarm. "New York? Is that closer to Hell, then?"

"It's actually closer to Jersey than Hell, but we try to forget that bit of geography, except when the wind's from the south, then it's an inescapable fact." She tucked the pen into her hair and loosened her grip on the shears. "Look, let's try to get you back to where you came from, okay? You tell me how you got here and I'll help you get home." That sounded reasonable enough.

He leaned more heavily against the table. "How can I go home? I'm dead." He shifted and a snootful of his aroma hit Jane square in the nose.

"Nope," she said definitely, "you're not dead. I told you, you're in New York. Different state of being entirely."

He looked very skeptical, but she pressed on.

"Do you have any family?"

"I've kin in the Highlands," he said. "I've also kin in the Future, but I daresay I've bypassed them to get to here."

A wacko with delusions of time traveling, she noted. She'd read those time-traveling romances and knew all about how it worked. Standing stones, faery rings, magical jewelry—those were all devices necessary for the time traveler. Since there were none of the above in the vicinity, it was a safe bet the guy was kidding himself. Jane wasn't familiar with any of the local sanitariums, so she decided to ignore that alternative for the moment. She took a different tack.

"You got family in the area?" she asked. "In Manhattan? Queens?"

"I'm first cousin to the laird of my clan," he said wearily. "But I fear there are no queens amongst our kin."

Jane opened her mouth to ask him what he meant, then shut it and shook her head. Better not to know.

"Okay," she said slowly, "how about your name instead."

"Ian MacLeod."

That was a start. "Birth date?"

"Allhallows Eve, 1279."

"Right," she said, starting to feel like Joe Friday. Maybe if she could get just the facts. "Whoa," she said, holding up her shears, "let's fix that. What year did you say?"

"The Year of Our Lord's Grace 1279," he repeated absently, looking around in something of a daze.

"All right," she said, putting that tidbit into the "Really Wacko" column. "Let's move on. What about your family?"

"All left behind in 1313," he said, plucking at his skirts with grimy fingers. "Save my cousin Jamie, of course, but he's in the Future."

Okay, we'll play it your way, she thought. "The Future? What year would that be?"

"1996," he said, leaving fingerprints behind on the antebellum gown. "That was the year he said they would hope for."

"Wrong," she said, shaking her head and hoping the motion would dislodge the rest of his words. The year they would hope for? What kind of babble was that? "1996 is the past, buster," she continued. "We're in 1999. Just a blink until the new . . . um . . ." She found her voice fading at the look on his face.

"1999?" he whispered.

"Yes."

"1999, not Limbo?"

She was sure she had never before seen such a look of dreadful hope on anyone's face. She nodded slowly.

"1999," she confirmed. "That's the year, New York is the place."

His eyes suddenly filled with tears. Before she could ask him why, he had fallen to his knees.

"Ach, merciful Saint Michael," he breathed, his hands clasped in front of him. "I escaped . . . I escaped in truth!"

Escape. Now there was a word she didn't really want to hear from him. It conjured up thoughts of bars and breakouts and maimed guards. But before she could tell him as much, he had begun to teeter on his knees.

"Um, Mr. MacLeod," she said, holding out her hand, "maybe you'd better . . ."

He looked up at her with a smile of such radiance, she almost flinched.

Then his eyes rolled back in his head, his eyelids came down, and he pitched forward, landing with his face on her toes.

She looked down, speechless.

A passed-out nutcase lying on her feet. What else could happen this weekend?

She was fairly sure she didn't want to know.

She stared down at the unconscious and very fragrant Ian MacLeod sprawled at her feet and wondered what in the world she was going to do with him now. And then she noticed the condition of his back revealed so conveniently by the zipper he hadn't been quite able to get up. She could have been mistaken, but those scabs looked an awful lot like Hollywood's rendition of healing whip marks.

Just what kind of trouble was he in?

And why was he so thrilled to be in New York in 1999?

Somehow, and she certainly couldn't have said why, she had the niggling suspicion that he was just as rational as she was and that he had never seen the inside of an asylum to escape from.

But that was a hunch she really didn't want to pursue. Instead, she turned her rampant thoughts to the matter at hand—namely getting Ian MacLeod out of Miss Witherspoon's workroom on the off chance that someone else was feeling exceptionally diligent and decided to come in for a little unpaid overtime.

Moving him without his help was out of the question. She wasn't a great judge of those kinds of things, but she hazarded a guess that he was several inches over six feet, certainly tall enough to get a kink in his neck while looking down at her. He was heavier than she was by far—even taking into account those last many pounds she hadn't managed to get off in time for bikini season. Dragging him out, even if she could manage it, would do nothing but leave grime on the carpet and ruin the gown. Short of dumping cold water on him, probably the best thing she could do was wait for him to wake up and hope he hadn't left too much of himself on the Scarlet O'Hara dress.

So she took a deep breath, sat down with her shears, and waited.

Chapter Three

IAN WOKE WITH difficulty. It seemed to him as if he struggled up from his dreams like a man struggling to escape the embrace of a pond lest he drown. He knew there was a reason to wake, but he couldn't remember what it was. He only knew he had cause to open his eyes and soon, else he would lose what he desperately wanted.

He opened his eyes and realized he was still in the white room. He lifted his head to find the woman who had delivered the glad tidings sitting a few paces away from him, holding onto her strange weapon.

A Future weapon, by the look of it.

Ian smiled, a smile so fierce it hurt his face to do it. He had done it! He had escaped the past and landed himself precisely where he had dreamed of being for years.

By the saints, it was a miracle.

"How're you feeling?"

Ian looked at the woman and realized that he would have to do a great deal of work on his speech before he sounded as she did. He'd learned English, of course, being the laird's cousin and all and potentially in line for the chieftainship, and he'd practiced a bit with his cousin Jamie's wife while she was with them. Hopefully it would suffice him until he could master the new tongue.

"Well enough, mistress," he said, with as much dignity as

he could muster, being face-down on the floor before her. "I fear I never asked your name."

"Jane," she said. "Jane Fergusson."

"Fergusson?" he croaked.

She waved her hand dismissively. "We've got a Scottish ancestor way up in the branches of the family tree."

"Well," Ian managed, "as long as he's not likely to drop from that tree upon me presently."

"He died a long time ago, I'm sure."

Ian decided on the spot to let the past stay in the past. No sense in punishing this girl for what her kin had done. For all he knew, she wasn't directly related to the Fergusson. As Ian's back twitched from a remembered flogging, he certainly hoped not.

Jane Fergusson rose to her feet. "We need to get you out of here."

Ian immediately felt her urgency become his. "Why? Is it a bad place?"

"You're in Miss Petronia Witherspoon's Elegant Eighteenth Century Wedding Fashions, and believe me when I tell you Miss Witherspoon would not be pleased to find you wearing one of her bridal gowns in your . . . um . . . present condition."

Ian heaved himself up. It took some doing, and he tangled himself soundly in his skirts before he managed to gain his feet. Even then he had to hold onto the table for a moment or two until the stars ceased to swim about his head. He looked sideways at Jane and tried to smile.

"I've been a bit . . . er, detained for the past pair of months."

"Detained?"

She looked less than eager to hear the entire tale, but Ian felt he owed it to her.

"I was in an enemy's dungeon. I fell asleep dreaming of Hell."

"And woke up just yards from Jersey," she said with a nod. "Makes sense."

Ian wasn't familiar with the place called Jersey, but he had the feeling he'd be well to avoid it. He continued, trying to piece together what must have happened. "I think they mistook me for dead and pulled me free," he said. "Perhaps they carried me to our land and left me there." He shrugged. "I've no idea, truly, but I'm grateful to be here." He smiled, to show her how grateful he was.

She looked less than convinced. Maybe she didn't believe his tale. Perhaps she would believe him when he found Jamie and Jamie could vouch for the truth of it.

"Dungeon?" she asked. "Here in New York?"

"Nay, in Scotland. In the Highlands. In 1313." He straightened and tried to look as trustworthy as possible. He truly didn't expect her to believe him immediately, but she would in time. Or perhaps she would merely take pity on him and help him find Jamie whether she believed him or not.

Assuming Jamie was in the Future. Ian had seen Jamie and his wife Elizabeth ride off into the forest. He'd even gone to the place where he knew the doorway into the Future to be and made certain they hadn't been overcome by beasties or brigands. There had been no sign of them. Ian had been convinced Jamie had found his way to 1996.

He most assuredly did not want to contemplate what a sorry state he would be in if he was wrong.

"Hmmm," she said, fingering her weapon. "1313?"

"I need to find my cousin, James MacLeod." There. Just saying the like made him feel more confident. Jamie had to be here. Ian would accept no other alternative. He put all doubts from his mind and concentrated on the task at hand—mainly remaining upright.

"Maybe you'd better clean up first," she countered. "You really don't want to go around dressed like that now that you don't need to make an impression on Saint Peter anymore."

He looked down at the dress and frowned at the less-than-pristine condition of it.

"I fear I've ruined the frock," he said apologetically.

"Forget it. It wasn't one of my best anyway."

He looked up at her. "Yours?"

"I designed it." She looked around the chamber. "I designed all of these."

Somehow she didn't sound overly enthusiastic about it. Ian, however, was impressed. He'd fingered the majority of the gowns looking for something he could use. Jane was a fine seamstress indeed to have done so much work.

"They're passing fair," he offered. "Bonny, truly."

"For bridal gowns," she conceded. "Now," she continued briskly, "let's figure out what to do with you."

He made her as low a bow as he could manage without landing himself upon her toes again. "I am in your hands, my lady."

He looked out from under his eyebrows to see the effect his words had had on her. She was looking at him with pursed lips and he straightened with a sigh. So she was resistent to his charms. Ian remembered his hastily made vow that he would mend his ways and settle with one woman. Perhaps Jane was not the woman for him. After all, he had the entire Future to choose from. No sense in not looking them all over before he made his choice.

But that didn't mean that Jane didn't deserve his most gallant self. It was the least he could offer, given his current condition.

A SHORT WHILE later he found himself riding, trapped, in what Jane called an elevator. All he knew was that the floor was falling from beneath his feet and he thought he just might shame himself by crying out. To take his mind off the interminable ride, he fingered the buttons of the raincoat he'd been given to wear over the remains of his plaid. His feet were bare and his sword was wrapped in a sheath of white fabric. He'd seen the wisdom of not parading about with his weapon until he was more familiar with the conditions of the day.

He'd just prided himself on surviving the torture of the little descending box when he found himself outside Miss Petronia's dwelling, standing on strange ground that fair burned the soles of his feet. The heat rose in waves from the hardened ground and beat down upon his person so strongly, he thought he might expire on the spot.

"Are you certain this isn't Hell?" he asked Jane, wiping his grimy brow.

She put her fingers to her mouth and whistled so loudly, he clapped his hands over his ears.

"Nope," she said, when he pulled his hands away cautiously. "Welcome to New York in summer. It's hot as hell, but still a different place entirely."

And then Ian noticed everything else. There were those little boxes on wheels—nay, those were the cars he'd heard tell of. He looked at them in astonishment, amazed at their speed and their braying calls as they surged by one another. Their drivers leaned out of them, shouting and swearing. He jumped as he heard one screech to a halt a mere finger's breadth from the back of another.

Then there were the people who hastened past him without marking him. He was pushed and jostled as more souls than he had ever seen in the whole of his life swelled around him.

The confusion, the noise, the heat and the mass of humanity were almost enough to bring him to his knees weeping with uncertainty. He struggled to regain his courage—something he had never had trouble with in the past. But who could blame him? By the saints, this was a world he'd never expected, full of sights and sounds he could hardly digest. He clutched his hands together only to realize he was clutching Jane's hand between the both of his. He looked at her to find she was staring at him with something akin to pity in her eyes.

"I . . . I fear . . ." His voice cracked. "So many people," he managed.

She smiled, a gentle smile that almost had him kneeling at her feet in gratitude.

"We'll take a cab to my place," she said, giving his hand a squeeze. "You'll feel better once you've had a shower and something decent to eat."

Eat was the one thing he did understand at present, so he nodded over that and let her lead him into a little yellow car that suddenly stopped in front of them. He sat on the strange bench and closed his eyes as the car lurched forward, the driver swearing and bellowing his displeasure at those around him.

Ian began to pray.

It seemed to take forever until the car stopped at their destination. Jane handed the man pieces of paper that Ian surmised served as payment. Ian followed her from the car and into a tall, bricked keep. He sighed in relief at the sight of steps. At least there would be no more torture in the little box that went up and down.

"You'll probably want to eat first," Jane said after they had climbed the steps and she had led him through a doorway she had opened with a key. "Stand here and don't move."

Ian stood and he didn't move. He didn't dare. Her dwelling was a curious mixture of only black and white and he feared to soil anything he might touch. He watched as Jane came from another part of her house carrying a goodly bit of cloth. She spread it over a strangely cushioned bench, then motioned for him to sit.

"I'll bring you something to eat, then I'll go see if I can round up some clothes for you. You're not going to want to wear what you've got on much longer."

"Aye, it could bear a washing."

She looked skeptical that such a thing might suffice, but he didn't argue. His belly was nigh to burning a hole in his middle and he didn't want to distract her from her errand in the kitchen.

Within moments, Ian was holding a strange, round trencher with something called a BLT piled atop it. It was very edible and he ingested several, depleting Jane's loaf of bread, but unable to apologize for it. It had been a very long time since he'd had anything fit for a man to consume. After they had eaten, Jane took away their trenchers and headed toward a black box in the corner.

"Here's the television. You can change the channel if you want to. I'll be back in about an hour."

Ian started to say "fine," then gasped in surprise as Jane touched the box. It sprang to life, or rather the people trapped inside the contrivance sprang to life. Ian could only gape at the poor souls, unsure if he should try to rescue them or not.

"Ian? You okay?"

Ian looked up at her, still speechless.

"I know," she said with a sigh. "Saturday afternoon TV. It's pretty bad, but it'll keep you entertained. Here's the remote."

And with that, she left.

He was alone with the television.

By the saints, 'twas almost as frightening as contemplating another trip into the Fergusson's dungeon.

At the thought of that, he felt his eyes narrow of their own accord. Jane was a Fergusson, no matter how far removed she was. Had she turned on the beast to torment him?

He sat on the soft bench in her house and pondered that. Then he looked at the black sticklike thing she had placed into his hand. He pressed upon it and jumped at what happened inside the television. It was too horrifying to be believed. He pressed what he'd pressed before and, by the blessed saints, the group of players trapped inside changed yet again.

He wished somehow that Jane hadn't left him alone.

"Dolt," he muttered to himself. He was a score and fourteen, surely old enough to have lost his fear of things he didn't understand. This was a Future creation. There was no dark magic about it. It was just another marvel the men of the Future had invented to entertain themselves—the saints pity the poor fools they had shrunk and trapped inside the box to provide the amusement.

Could he rescue them? He gave that serious thought before deciding that perhaps that was what he needed to do. He leaned further up on the edge of the bench. The television paid him no heed. He rose slowly and approached as quietly as he could. His body was still battered, but he felt better than he had before. Another fortnight, and he would be fully himself again—if he survived an afternoon alone with the beast in front of him.

The television gave no sign of having marked his approach, so he moved even closer. Ian reached out to touch the smooth surface and jerked his hand back as the beast bit him with invisible teeth.

Ian sucked upon his fingers. As tempted as he was to do a bit of rescuing with his sword, he decided that perhaps patience was a virtue he could practice that afternoon. He retreated to his square of cloth and sat down again, eyeing the television with disfavor. Cheeky beast. Then he realized the players inside were speaking in Jane's English and he saw the benefits of paying close attention to them.

But despite himself, he couldn't help but wish Jane would hurry with her errands.

Chapter Four

JANE STOOD IN her bedroom several hours later, leaned on her dresser and stared at herself in the mirror, and wondered if she would be better off to lock her door and forget what lay outside it. Somehow, though, she suspected locking it wasn't necessary to keep the non-native out. He didn't particularly seem up to turning the handle. Either he was a complete wacko, he was from a different planet, or he was from where he said he was.

Scotland, the Year of Our Lord 1313.

But she didn't want to think about how that could be possible.

Unfortunately, it was a conclusion she was having a hard time avoiding, and that had everything to do with the afternoon and evening's events. She'd never considered herself a Sir Gallahad type, but she had done more rescuing in the past eight hours than Sir G. had likely done in his entire life.

Jane had initially—and with no small bit of trepidation—left Ian at home to watch television. She'd warned him under pain of death not to touch anything. She wouldn't have been surprised in the least to have returned and found her building belching smoke and fire into the afternoon air. She'd been relieved to find Ian in the same place she'd left him: gaping at the TV. He'd jumped half a foot when she'd touched his shoulder. She'd then found herself standing stock-still with a sword at her throat.

Whatever else she could say about Ian MacLeod, she had to admit he was apparently a helluva swordsman.

Once she'd been able to breathe again, she'd ushered Ian to the bathroom. She'd soon heard a serious clanking noise and had hurried to investigate only to find he had peed in the sink and was in the process of taking apart her plumbing. She'd saved him from being bonked over the head with her showerhead—by her. The last thing she needed was to have to call the super and ask him to come put her powder room back together. Deciding that perhaps Ian's next foray into the bathroom could wait, she'd taken him back to the kitchen for a second lunch.

That had precipitated his sudden love affair with the chrome toaster. Jane had barely managed to throw together a tuna casserole before she'd had to announce "stop" in a very loud voice to keep him from completing his investigation of the toaster's insides with a sterling silver butter knife. He'd transferred his attentions to the outlet, necessitating a stern command that he park himself at the table with his hands empty and in plain sight.

He had subsequently looked at what had come out of the oven as if he'd never seen anything like it before in his life. She was the first to admit she was a lousy cook, but surely her offering hadn't merited such tentative pokes with a fork into the depths of the casserole dish. Apparently Ian's appetite was less threatened by her potato-chip crust than Ian was, because it induced him to wolf down the entire thing without missing a beat.

She'd headed him back into the bathroom again with grooming aids that hopefully wouldn't get him into too much trouble, and left him to it. Then she'd come into her room, leaned on her dresser, and looked at herself, wondering what had possessed her to bring Ian home. And that brought her back to her initial problem of determining his origins: loony bin or fourteenth-century Scotland. She fervently hoped there was a difference.

Well, there was no sense in postponing the inevitable any longer. She would have to go out, find out the truth, and then figure out what to do about it. Maybe she could help him find his family and get him out of her life so she could get back to darts and gathers.

Somehow, though, after what she'd been through in the past eight hours, producing wedding gowns just didn't sound all that exciting anymore.

She took a deep breath and walked to her bedroom door. The apartment was minuscule, but it was hers alone. It had reminded her of drafty servants' quarters in some bad eighteenth-century penny novel and that had seemed so appropriate, she hadn't been able to pass it up. That and she could afford it. The down side was that there wasn't some long, elegant hallway separating her from the living room so she would have its length to get a good grip on herself.

She opened the door and stepped out into the living room/dining room/kitchen combination and for the second time that day found herself gaping at Ian MacLeod. Only this time terror had nothing at all to do with her speechless condition. He had risen to greet her and stood in front of her couch with his hands clasped behind him, a grave smile on his face. She was greatly tempted to swoon, a good, old-fashioned, antebellum kind of swoon. Instead, she shut her mouth and commanded her knees to remain steady.

He'd shaved. She noticed that right off. Amazingly enough, beneath that ratty beard lurked a granitelike jaw, chiseled cheekbones, and a full, pouty lower lip that had her biting hers in self-defense. She wondered if fanning herself would give the skyrocketing of her blood pressure away. And then there were his eyes, a vivid blue that made them seem as if they leaped from his face. They were eyes she could have lost herself in for centuries and not cared one bit about the passage of time.

His shoulders were impossibly broad and she was vaguely disappointed that she'd bought him an extra-large tee shirt. *Should have picked up that medium,* she thought with regret. It wouldn't have been as good as a wet tee shirt, but she wouldn't have quibbled. All in all, Ian MacLeod was the most handsome man she had ever laid eyes on in the whole of her twenty-nine years. Something nagged at her, but she shoved it aside in favor of more lusting. She looked lower and saw that his jeans hugged him most securely—and then it hit her what was so dreadfully wrong with the picture.

He was wearing boxer shorts.

On the outside of his jeans.

She looked up, startled, only to find that he'd turned himself around to look at a noise from the kitchen end of the living room and she got an eyeful of his long, glorious dark hair—tied back with a bright pink bow. The only relief she felt was knowing it was something he'd unearthed from one of her bathroom drawers.

But before she could say anything else, he'd turned back to her and given her another of his smiles, only this one wasn't grave. It was a heart stopper.

"My thanks for the clothing," he said, with a little bow. "Passing comfortable, these long-legged trews." He pulled at his jeans, then lovingly caressed the boxer shorts with the smiley faces on them. "Very cheerful and pleasing to the eye."

Jane didn't have the heart to tell him he had them on in the wrong order. Besides, it was New York. No one would look at him twice.

"Do you perchance have a map?" he asked, his lilt taking her for another roller-coaster ride. "I've a need to find my cousin as soon as may be and I'd best know where I am now. I'm not familiar with New York."

"Sure," Jane said. She had an atlas. She'd bought it her first month at Miss Witherspoon's, based on her certainty that she'd be traveling to all the fashion hot spots soon and it would be best to know where she was headed.

It was, unsurprisingly, still in shrink-wrap. It had been, after all, a very expensive atlas.

But who better to use it on than a lunatic sporting a pink bow and wondering where New York found itself in the grander global scheme of things? Jane got the atlas and sat down next to Ian on the couch. She opened up to the world and then looked at Ian to see if anything was ringing a bell for him yet.

He was looking at it blankly.

Jane pointed carefully to the British Isles. "Scotland," she said. "I think the Highlands are up there."

Ian looked the faintest bit relieved to see something that was apparently familiar. "Aye," he said with a gulp. "And there's Inverness, Edinburgh. Those places I know. Now, where are we? Lower down?"

"A bit to the left," she said, sliding her finger across the Atlantic and stopping on Manhattan. "We're on a little island here."

Ian gaped. "Across the sea?"

"Across the sea."

"But," he spluttered, "how did I come across the sea?"

Jane looked at him carefully. "That's a very good question. How did you come across the sea?"

Ian closed his eyes and she watched him swallow very hard. It seemed to take him a moment or two to regain control of himself before he opened his eyes and looked at her.

"I live in Scotland," he managed. "How I came to be across that vast sea, I know not. But I must go home." He looked bleakly at the map. "I must go home."

There was a wealth of longing in those words and in spite of herself, Jane was moved. She recognized the feeling. She wanted to go home, wanted it more than anything, but home wasn't a return ticket to Indiana. She loved her family, but they were solid, dependable people with solid, dependable dreams. Jane, despite her solid, dependable name had never been one of them, never shared in their dreams. They wanted accountants and bankers; Jane wanted a sheep farm, a spinning wheel, and dyes in vibrant, breath-stealing colors. Her dream home was a little house in the Scottish Highlands where she could weave in peace and never again look at a bridal gown, never again be bound by white and ecru, never again wear black unless someone had died.

Home. In a place she'd never dreamed of.

And with a person she'd never expected.

"I have to go home," Ian repeated.

She nodded. "I understand."

"Can you help me?"

She took a deep breath. "I can. In fact, let's start now. We'll call information and see if we can't get your cousin on the phone."

"The phone?"

She picked up the cordless and handed it to him. He was giving it the same look of intense interest he'd given the toaster, so she took it away from him.

And she couldn't help but wish he'd look at her that way. Maybe women hadn't changed enough since the Middle Ages for her to be all that much of a novelty.

She shook her head as she went to look for the phone

book. "Maybe I'm the one who needs the asylum," she muttered under her breath. "I'm starting to believe him!"

Within moments, she was sitting next to him on the couch, connecting with international information. She asked for a listing for James MacLeod in the Highlands.

"There are scores," the operator said with asperity. "Can you be a bit more specific?"

Jane put her hand over the mouthpiece. "Can you be more specific? A specific town?"

Ian peered at the map. "Well, 'tis a half se'nnight's journey from MacAllister's keep, but less from the Fergusson's. We've a forest nearby and the mountains are behind us."

He traced the map with his finger and as he did so, Jane made a decision.

"Thanks," she said to the operator and hung up the phone before she could change her mind. What she contemplated was possibly the stupidest thing she'd ever contemplated, but she was tired of her safe existence. Here she had the perfect opportunity to pick up and do something, well, colorful. There was every reason not to, but none of those reasons was appealing, so she ignored them. She looked at Ian. "We'll just fly over and you can get there by landmarks. You can do that, can't you?"

"Easily. But this flying . . ."

"In a plane. You'll love it."

"I will repay you—"

She held up her hand and cut him off. She didn't want to talk about money. It wasn't why she was doing it.

"I will," he insisted. "It isn't proper that you spend what you've earned on a stranger."

"We'll deal with that later."

He looked at her, then shook his head. "The journey will be very long. Your work—"

"I hate my work," she said, then shut her mouth when she realized what she'd said. Hate was a strong word. She took a deep breath. "It really won't take very long and I have some vacation time coming up anyway."

"I couldn't—"

"Please." She hadn't meant to say it, but it slipped out of her mouth just as surprisingly as had the other things. "I would very much like to see Scotland," she amended. "I hear it's beautiful."

Ian took her hand and squeezed it. "You're very kind, Jane Fergusson. You have my gratitude."

She would have rather had his unrestrained passion, but gratitude wasn't a bad start.

"How about a movie?" she asked, pulling her hand away before she did something stupid, like leave it in his. "We'll do popcorn, too."

"A Future tradition?"

With the way he said Future, she couldn't help but capitalize it in her mind. Whatever Ian's mental state, he certainly was enthusiastic about everything she suggested.

"Definitely," she answered him. "Maybe we'll do ice cream later." She'd already put her foot to the slippery slope of breaking out of her normal routine. Might as well go for the full trip.

Her only hope was that she had some heart left for beating in her chest once Ian was safely delivered home.

THREE HOURS LATER, Jane huddled in her bed, wondering if she shouldn't have chosen a romantic comedy instead of an alien thriller. A tap on her door almost left her clinging to the ceiling.

"What?" she croaked.

The door opened a crack. "Jane, might I perchance sleep up here with you? On the floor, even."

More of Ian inched through her door, clad in boxers and dragging a blanket behind him.

"Well . . ." she began.

"I saw an alien in the garderobe."

She might have argued with him, but she was almost certain she'd seen the same thing in her closet.

"All right," she said slowly. *I am insane,* she thought. An unknown quantity coming to sleep on the floor next to her bed. It would be just her luck to wake up throttled, or worse. She wasn't sure what anyone else might think would be worse than a throttling, but she could come up with a few things.

"A peaceful rest to you, my lady," came the deep whisper from beside her bed.

My lady. Well, how could you not feel just a little more relaxed with that kind of talk coming your way?

Jane closed her eyes, sighed, and then another thought occurred to her.

"Ian?"

"Aye."

"Do you have a passport?"

"Passporrrt?" he echoed in a sleepy burr.

"You know, papers to get you through customs and all?"

"Future customs," he murmured, smacking his lips a time or two. "Must learn those right away."

"Did you leave it at home?"

Her only answer was a snore. Besides, she thought, if he'd entered the country through the normal channels, surely he would have had it on him when he'd arrived in New York.

In Miss Witherspdon's salon, wearing filthy rags and spearing bags of munchies on the end of a sword.

She sighed. Wonderful. What she had was a wacko without the necessary documents to deposit him back on home soil. Why couldn't she have had a cousin in some illegal kind of import-export business?

Then again, there was Frank at Miss Witherspoon's. He dressed like an aging urchin, bathed with the regularity of an eighteenth-century chimney sweep, and always had the faint hint of cannabis clinging to him. If anyone might know where to come up with a passport for Ian, Frank would. It was something to hope for. She closed her eyes and to her surprise, immediately and quite peacefully drifted off to sleep.

And she dreamed of Scotland.

Chapter Five

IAN SAT BEHIND a strangely fashioned table in what Jane called her broom closet at Miss Whitherspoon's workplace and marveled at the fineness of the fabric surrounding him. It was all white, of course, but the variety and the beauty of it was truly a wonder. He picked up the Future weapon Jane had originally faced him with and saw that its jaws opened and closed with great precision. He reached for a swath of fabric to try it out upon. He hadn't but begun to close the teeth when he heard a screech that fair sent him scampering for cover.

"Stop!"

Ian stopped in mid-closing and looked up to find Jane teetering at the doorway.

"Don't cut that," she said, reaching out and taking the weapon from him. "Come with me. Frank wants to take your picture."

Ian followed her obediently through the empty hallways. Frank, he understood, would provide him with the necessary things he would need to return to Scotland. He wasn't exactly sure why he had come to New York in the first place, but he suspected there was something quite magical about the city that drew seekers of all kinds.

Or wackos, as he heard Jane occasionally mutter under her breath.

Within moments, courtesy of another claustrophobic ride in the elevator, Ian faced a small black box and was subsequently reeling from the shock of having a bright light explode in his eyes. He looked at Jane and blinked several times until his eyes cleared. He sincerely hoped whatever Frank intended to do for him was worth what he'd just faced.

"He can do this thing?" Ian asked her, rubbing his eyes.

"I know a guy," Frank said, busily attending to the torture device he'd just used on Ian.

"He knows a guy," Jane said, taking Ian by the arm and pulling him from the chamber. "Now to go beg for some vacation time," she said with a sigh. "This should be fun."

With the way she said it, Ian wasn't sure *fun* was something he wanted to be involved in. He put his shoulders back and tried to look his most confident. He didn't want to get in Jane's way as she negotiated for temporary freedom from her employer. It was more of a sacrifice than he was truly willing for her to make, but she seemed determined to come with him. And, if the truth were to be told, he wasn't sure he could get himself to Scotland of the Future without her.

Or, strangely enough, that he even wanted to.

He was almost certain it wasn't just misplaced gratitude, though he had enough of that and to spare. How he ever could have survived his arrival in the Future without Jane having been there, he surely didn't know. She had fed him, clothed him, and given him a place to lay his head. There was much to be said for that.

And then he quite suddenly lost track of all his thoughts as the elevator doors opened, he stepped into the passageway, and his rather starved libido caught an eyeful of the women who had suddenly filled Miss Witherspoon's place of commerce.

Too skinny by half, most of them, but passing beautiful. Tall, willowy, in all colors and shapes. Ian could only gape at them, stunned mainly by the looks they were giving him, looks that said they would be more than willing to engage in whatever activity he might suggest. He knew the look. He'd seen it before and he'd certainly taken advantage of it before.

"Models," Jane threw over her shoulder as she plunged into the midst of them. "They wear the bridal gowns for the customers."

Brides? He could hardly believe it, for none of them looked nervous enough to be contemplating their first night with a man. Just as well. Ian was acutely aware of the last virgin he'd tutored and where that evening's instruction had landed him. It was far better to indulge in one of these. Or several.

His conscience gave him a sharp poke, reminding him that at one point in the Fergusson's dungeon he'd made a last-minute plea for forbearance based on the promise of pledging to one woman.

He looked at Jane as she parted the way before him. She was dressed all in black again and Ian wondered if that was so she would fade when compared to the other creatures circling him like carrion birds dressed in white. Her hair was confined the same way he'd seen it at first, all bunched at the back of her head with a handful of sticks poking from it. They were pencils he knew now, but they still looked odd to him. She was almost as tall as the other women but not nearly as slender, though her shape was a fine one.

One woman.

Or the score he currently waded through.

Jane, or a variety of delicacies he thought he just might want to sample.

He felt a smack on his backside and he yelped as the hand lingered. Ian couldn't tell who had done it, but there were several standing about him who looked capable of such an intimate gesture. Jane turned around and frowned at the lot of them.

"Down, girls. He's out of your league."

One of the women snorted. "As if he's in yours, Janey."

It was at that point that Ian began to suspect that beneath all the beauty and seductiveness might lie less-than-nice souls. He also cared not for the quickly hidden flinch he'd seen Jane display. These women knew nothing of her and yet she allowed them to wound her? Ian stepped up to Jane's side and took her hand.

"Let us be off," he said, casting the disparaging woman a look of disapproval. Jane didn't pull her hand away, but Ian felt her fingers fluttering nervously. It was as if he'd caught a butterfly. It was not the hand that would take liberties with an unknown man's backside.

"Models," Jane muttered with distaste. "They're very dangerous."

"So I see," Ian said, rubbing his abused backside with his free hand.

"And what we're going to face is even more dangerous. We're almost there." She looked up at him. "Try to look helpless and pathetic. We're going for the mercy vote."

As you will Ian had planned to say, but before he could get the words out, the door to Miss Witherspoon's office had been opened and he'd gotten a complete eyeful of Miss Witherspoon.

"Oh," Jane said, sounding less than pleased. She pulled Ian behind her into Miss Witherspoon's private chamber. "Where is she?"

"Out," the vision purred, coming to her feet from behind the impressively large table, revealing impressively large proportions herself.

Ian could only gape at the woman, speechless. This was obviously not the stern and unyielding employer Jane had told him about.

"And who do we have here?" the young woman continued.

"A friend of mine," Jane said. "Ian, this is Alexis, Miss Witherspoon's niece. Alexis, Ian."

Ian had never seen such lush curves. He suspected he'd never even dreamed of such a form, impeccably rounded in the proper places and impossibly slim everywhere else.

"Aahh," he attempted.

And then she held out her hand and he looked down to see blood dripping from all her fingers.

"Ach!" he cried, jumping back.

Alexis only stretched and smiled like a satisfied cat, practically clawing the air with her daggerlike hands. "Just nail polish, silly. They're my own nails, of course."

Ian could see that and he was afraid. He knew what kind of marks a Fergusson whip could leave. He could only imagine how a man's back might pain him after a night abed with those.

"Oh, Jane dear, I see you've finally arrived."

Ian found himself pushed aside by a solidly built woman well past the prime of her life. She cast him a practiced look of assessment before she turned her attentions back to Jane.

"Alexis drew some wonderful ideas on the way back. You'll see them mocked up as soon as possible."

"Well," Jane began.

Ian looked down to find that Alexis had sidled up to him and was placing her considerable charms beneath his nose for closer inspection.

"I design all the gowns, you know," she whispered, reaching up to tap his chin with one long nail. "No matter what you've heard. Jane just does the sewing." She slid her finger down and began to toy with one of the buttons on his shirt. "I'm going to be a famous designer one day."

Ian vowed he would believe anything she said to him if she would just cease with her descent down the front of his chest.

"I need my vacation time," Jane said calmly. "Ian needs to get back to Scotland and I've volunteered to get him there."

"No."

Ian looked to Miss Witherspoon. She hadn't bothered to look up from what she was doing.

"I'll take him," Alexis offered. "I've always wanted to see Scotland."

"I've already offered," Jane said.

Miss Witherspoon shoved a handful of pages at Jane. "Get to work on these. I want mock-ups done before next week."

Ian watched Jane take the pages, then he caught sight of the drawing upon the topmost sheaf. And he suspected that even he might be more successful at creating a bridal gown than the woman who had done the depictions before him.

It was then that he began to understand.

"Get to work on my stuff," Alexis said, giving Jane a little push toward the door. "We'll take good care of Ian."

Ian watched Jane hold onto the pages and consider. And for a moment, he thought she just might do as she was bid. Then he watched her put her shoulders back.

"I have three years' worth of vacation time coming," she said firmly, "and this is something of an urgent situation. I'm sorry I can't give more notice, but it's imperative that Ian return to Scotland as soon as possible and he needs me to help him get there."

Alexis made a scornful sound, then looked up at Ian. "I can take him places you couldn't even imagine in your wildest dreams."

Ian was afraid to ask where those places might be and what

Alexis might to do him with her claws if he let her escort him there.

"I said no and I meant it," Miss Witherspoon said sternly. "Now, get to work on those, Jane. I don't have any more time for your foolishness."

Ian saw Jane begin to falter and he cleared his throat. "I beg your pardon, my lady Witherspoon, but I do indeed need her assistance. If you would be so kind—"

"Alexis can accompany you," Miss Witherspoon said with a curt nod. "I have no more time for either of you."

"Alexis is not accompanying Ian anywhere," Jane said. "I want to go to Scotland. I've wanted to go to Scotland for years."

"Have you?" Ian asked, surprised. He hadn't realized the desire was so firmly planted in her, though he could well understand the like.

"Lots of sheep there," Jane said shortly, then she turned her attentions back to Miss Witherspoon. "We're leaving on Wednesday. I'll be back—"

"You'll go nowhere," Miss Witherspoon said, the edge in her voice as cutting as any blade Ian had run his fingers across. "Those designs must be fleshed out."

"That's right," Alexis said, turning to glare at Jane as well. "You can't go."

"It's only a couple of weeks," Jane said firmly. "You'll survive that long without me finishing up your homework for you."

Alexis gasped as if she'd been struck and Miss Witherspoon looked as if she might reach out and slap Jane. Ian fumbled for his sword, then realized he'd left it at Jane's home.

"You'll stay," Miss Witherspoon commanded, "and you'll apologize to my niece!"

Jane laid the drawings on Miss Witherspoon's desk and stepped back. "I'll be back in two weeks."

"If you walk out that door," Miss Witherspoon said angrily, pointing at Jane with a trembling finger, "you're fired."

"Yeah," Alexis added enthusiastically. Then she blinked a time or two, turned, and looked at her aunt in dismay. "But then who will—"

"Fired," Miss Witherspoon repeated. "Do you hear me?"

Jane took a deep breath, then shrugged. "Have it your way.

You owe me for six weeks' vacation. I expect to find the check in my mailbox when I get home. Come on, Ian. We've got to go pack."

And with that, he found himself being towed behind her out of Miss Witherspoon's presence and down the passageway back to the broom closet.

"Stupid job," Jane was muttering under her breath as she stomped down the hall. "Didn't like it anyway."

Before much time had passed, Ian found himself loaded down with all manner of odds and ends from Jane's little working chamber. He followed her out into the passageway only to find Alexis blocking his path.

"You can't take anything with you," Alexis said with a sneer. "Take nothing—which is what you came here with."

"These are my personal things," Jane said, brushing past her.

Ian gave Alexis's hands a wide berth and hastened down the passageway after Jane.

ONCE THEY REACHED her dwelling, Jane obtained by messenger a foodstuff called pizza. She hardly partook, though, before she excused herself and shut herself into her private chamber. Ian couldn't see letting the food go to waste, so he finished off what was left and felt himself as full and satisfied as he ever had after a meal at Jamie's table. He placed the pizza container in the kitchen then paused in the television chamber, wondering what he should do. It was then that he heard the sound of weeping.

He went to press his ear to Jane's door. The sounds were muffled, but he hazarded a guess that the weeping was not of the joyous kind. He tapped on the door and the snuffling abruptly stopped.

"What?"

"How do you fare?" Ian asked through the wood.

"Nothing's wrong," came the answer. "Really."

The last was accompanied by a mighty sniff. Ian knew enough about women to know that such a sound could only mean more tears to follow. He didn't wait for permission to enter, he merely turned the knob on the door and poked his head in the chamber. And what he saw took his breath away.

There was color everywhere. Balls and skeins of yarn in every imaginable color littered the floor where Jane sat. She had obviously unearthed these things from some hidden trunk. Ian walked over to her and knelt down amidst the riot of color. He picked up a ball of particularly vibrant purple, then looked at Jane in surprise.

"I had no inkling," he began.

"I pull them out to make myself feel better," she said, dragging her sleeve across her eyes. "But not very often, because it never makes me feel better."

"I had no idea you cared for such color."

"Yeah, well, I've got plenty of time to do all I like with it now." She looked at him bleakly. "I can't believe I lost my job. It wasn't a great job, but at least it allowed me to eat."

Ian gestured to the yarn. "Have you made aught with these things?"

She nodded, then pointed to the trunk Ian hadn't noticed before. He reached over and drew out a heavy tunic woven of thick, deep red yarn. It was something that would keep any man warm even in the hard winters of the Highlands. Then he pulled out a blanket woven of so many strands of differing colors that it almost hurt his eyes to look at it. It too was made of heavy wool.

"Beautiful," he said, stunned by the sight of the rich colors.

"The yarn was imported from Scotland." She fingered the blanket absently. "Lots of sheep there, you know."

"Aye, I do," he said, fingering the wool.

"I could see myself in a little cottage on the side of a hill, spinning and weaving to keep myself busy."

To his surprise, so could he. He looked at her with her slender hands and could easily picture those hands spinning and weaving.

And tending the small joys and sorrows of a handful of children as well.

He didn't know where it had come from, that thought, but he knew it was a good one. He reached over and pulled the sharp sticks from her hair, watching as the wavy strands fell about her shoulders. Even still wearing her black clothing, she looked much more at peace, much freer than he'd seen her before.

Aye, he thought, here was a woman who could share a hearth with him and not mind the keeping of it.

She began to put her things away and Ian stopped her by taking her hand.

" 'Tis a pity to waste your gift only on white," he said.

She shrugged. "It's what bridal gowns are made from."

"In my time, a bride wore the colors she found near her home."

"Then your brides were a lot more fun to design for than mine," she said with another sigh. She looked around her at the remaining piles of yarn. "Maybe I can start over again in Scotland."

"Aye—"

She interrupted him with a half laugh that contained no humor whatsoever. "Who am I kidding? I don't have the money to start over. I don't even have the money to go back home to Indiana."

Yet Ian had heard her talking into that magical telephone contrivance, promising to pay for both her and his travel to Scotland. Was that the last of her funds? He couldn't allow her to spend all upon him.

On the other hand, he had to get home.

He picked up a ball of yarn and handed it to her. "I'll find a way to repay you," he pledged. "Or perhaps you can remain with us for a time until Miss Witherspoon regains her senses and takes you back."

"Hrumph," she said with a scowl. "Poverty or indentured servitude. I don't know what's worse."

Ian looked again at the fragments of her dreams laying in lumps around her feet and thought perhaps that returning to Miss Witherspoon's was the very last thing Jane should be doing.

A little cottage was starting to sound better by the moment. Hopefully they would travel to Scotland and find Jamie there. There was no guarantee Jamie would have returned to their clan home, but Ian couldn't imagine him doing anything else. What other place on earth would call to Jamie but their keep in the Highlands?

Nay, Jamie had to be there and Ian would find him.

And then he would find some way to make Jane's dream come true.

Chapter Six

JANE STUMBLED OFF the plane wishing she had somehow managed to acquire a Valium or two before embarking. She looked at Ian who walked beside her, his eyes burning with a feverish light.

"Ach," he purred like a satisfied cat, "now *that* was a proper rrrush."

"Too much television," she chided, ignoring those blasted r's of his.

"We must do it again. I'll pay for the privilege next time."

I'd rather go by boat, she almost said, then realized that was likely what half of the *Titanic*'s passengers had said.

"Sure," she said aloud, "only next time let's go first class."

"First class?"

"Bigger seats. Better food."

As those had been his two complaints about that ride, Ian only nodded in agreement. Jane didn't let herself think about the fact that the odds of her ever traveling again with Ian MacLeod were practically nil. He would find his cousin and be merrily off on his way while she was left to return to the States and face her nonlife. Maybe she could beg Miss Witherspoon for her job back.

She almost pursued that thought when she realized it was out of the question. She'd spent half a night fondling skeins of vibrantly colored wool and fantasizing about what she would make from it. She could knit. She could weave. Surely she could make a living doing that. Or maybe she would take those colors, have cloth dyed to match, and design her own clothes. That was what she'd started out to do anyway, before money for rent and food had gotten in the way.

Jane would have given that more thought, but she suddenly found herself facing the rental car and realized that there was no wheel on the driver's side where it was supposed to be. She looked at Ian, but he was too busy peering into the outside mirrors to give any indication that he found the wheel placement unusual.

"Well, here goes nothing," she said, going around to the right side and sliding in under the wheel. She pulled down the sun visor and was greeted with bold letters reminding her to Drive On The Left. "When in Rome," she said, waiting until Ian had clambered into the passenger seat before she turned the car on. She looked at him. "You don't know anything about this driving on the left business, do you?"

He looked at her blankly. "We were accustomed to letting our mounts go where they willed."

"That's what I was afraid of."

THE NEXT THREE days were an endless, relentless exercise in trying to remember which side of the wheel the turn signals were on and spending most of her time turning on the windshield wipers instead. By the time they reached Inverness, Ian had familiarized himself with all the workings of the dashboard doodahs and had apparently decided that bagpipes were much preferable to top forty on the radio. He seemed to have no trouble understanding the unintelligible news reports she couldn't decipher. He spent a great deal of time grunting, as if he couldn't believe what he was hearing.

They left Inverness and headed north. Jane did the best she could with the roads available to follow Ian's homing beacon. By the time they reached roads that had continually shrunk in width and increased in incline, she was convinced they were hopelessly lost. She stopped in a little town and found the first bed and breakfast—which wasn't hard, as it was a very small town indeed—and pulled in.

"Enough," she said, turning the car off and putting her head down on the steering wheel. "I can't drive anymore today."

"I could drive."

She turned her head and looked at him out of one eye. The light of intense desire was visible even in the twilight.

"Not a chance," she said, resuming her position. "We'll get going first thing in the morning. I need dinner and some sleep."

She heard Ian get out of the car, then felt a brush of cool air as he opened her door. He unbuckled her seat belt, then took her arm and gently pulled her out. Before she knew it, she was enveloped in a warm embrace.

"I have driven you hard," he said, running his hand over her back, "and I beg pardon for it. I am anxious to see my home and know if there is aught left of it."

And to see his cousin, no doubt. Though she hadn't heard him say as much since they'd left the States, she knew he was worried that he wouldn't find what he was looking for. That she was even considering the ramifications of his missing his family because they had landed in different centuries only indicated how very tired she was.

"It's okay," she said with a yawn. "I can understand the feeling." She would have pulled away, on the off chance that such a thing might have gotten her dinner sooner, but she found that she just couldn't move. It was the strangest thing, but for the first time in her life she was content. Content in spite of a blinding headache from too much concentrating on the road, too little sleep, and continually doing her best to ignore what she was going to do when she returned to the States and faced the shambles that was her life.

"Food," Ian announced, "then a bed if they have one. I'll find some means of working for our keep this eve. Surely they have a handful of odd things needing to be done. Perhaps wood to be gathered for the fire or animals to be tended."

The thought of Ian manhandling a chainsaw sent shivers down Jane's spine. She pulled back to look up at him.

"I can pay for it."

"Nay, you cannot."

"I have enough left on my credit card."

His lips compressed into a tight line. "This does not sit well with me. Already you have done more than you should have."

"And if the shoe had been on the other foot?"

"How was that?"

"If I had been popped back to the"—and she had to take a deep breath to keep from stumbling over the very words—"fourteenth century, what would you have done?"

He sighed. "Given you food and shelter, then seen you home."

"What's the difference, then?"

"The difference, sweet Jane," he said as he smoothed his hand over her hair and smiled down at her, "is that being unable to provide for such needs wounds my manly pride."

Jane wasn't sure about the condition of his manly pride, but she was sure about the condition of her knees, and that was completely unstable. She had never considered herself anything but fiercely independent. The thought of anyone, her family or a man, doing anything remotely akin to taking care of her was something she had avoided at all costs.

But somehow, standing in the Scottish twilight in a tiny town on the edge of the sea with Ian MacLeod's arms securely around her, the thought of allowing someone else to provide for her for a change wasn't so hard to stomach.

She savored the moment as long as she could, then pulled away.

"I am starving," she admitted reluctantly. "For all we know, they won't even take a credit card or traveler's checks and we may very well be relying on your ability to chop wood."

Ian kissed her gently on the forehead, then pulled back and took her by the hand. "Perhaps I will have the chance to repay you."

"Perhaps you will. We could head back to the fourteenth century." she offered.

He laughed. "You would find it a very primitive place indeed. No airplanes, no automobiles, and no MTV."

"Ugly," she agreed, and she tried not to enjoy overly the feeling of her hand in his. It was more delicious than she would have suspected and she could hardly keep herself from wishing such hand-holding might continue far into the future—say for the next fifty or sixty years. Or maybe for the rest of forever.

She put her free hand to her forehead. No fever. Maybe insanity didn't begin with an overheated brain. Just a gradual slip into believing things that couldn't possibly come to pass—such as sharing a life with a man who claimed to be from the year 1313.

The B and B did take credit cards and they also didn't pass up Ian's offer to do a few chores as the proprietress was very pregnant and her husband had been laid up for several weeks with a back injury. Jane figured it was the perfect situation. She got to eat and watch Ian strip off his shirt all in the same twenty-four hours. Life just didn't get much better than that.

LATE THE NEXT morning, after a pair of hours watching Ian soothe his manly pride, Jane crawled behind the wheel of the car again and suppressed a groan. If she'd even suspected Ian might have the wherewithal to negotiate a stick shift, she would have turned the keys over to him happily. He'd tried to convince her he was capable, but he'd come close to plowing over half a dozen flowerpots on his way out of the driveway when he'd offered to demonstrate his skill. She'd taken the keys away and promised him a driving lesson somewhere less dangerous.

"Direction?" she asked, turning on the car.

"North."

North, north, and evermore north. Jane drove without hurrying and she wasn't sure exactly about her reasons for her leisurely pace. She told herself she was just meandering so she could enjoy the scenery. It was true that the mountains and forests were breathtaking. And every time they passed a little hamlet that deserved to be immortalized on some postcard, she couldn't help but imagine how life would be if she lived there.

And she sure as heck didn't imagine living there alone.

The drive was, needless to say, very hard on her heart.

Hours had passed and Jane's imagination, and her bladder, had taken just about all they could take. Espying a choice place to pull off, she did so before Ian could protest. She shut off the car and sighed.

"I don't think this map is accurate," she began. "Maybe it's all this driving on the wrong side of the road, but I don't see anything familiar. . . ."

"I do."

The tone of his voice sent shivers down her spine. She looked at him.

"You do?"

He nodded and pointed out the window. "There's the loch. We're a day's ride southeast. By horse," he added.

"Shouldn't be far in a car, then," she said slowly.

"Shouldn't be."

She pulled back out onto the little two-lane road and continued slowly. They passed through a good-sized village and Jane slowed to a crawl.

"Recognize this?" she asked, then realized the answer was written in Ian's astonished expression. "I take it this wasn't here the last time you rode through."

He looked visibly shaken. "Nay, it wasn't."

She decided that any lightness was completely inappropriate, so she managed a bathroom stop before they continued through the village. The road then took a sharp turn west.

"Wait," Ian said, pointing to a very sketchy-looking road leading more northward still. "Take that."

"But it doesn't look—"

"It's the right direction."

"Whatever you say," she said, following the one-lane road away from the village. She could only hope no one would come flying down it the other way without honking first.

And then suddenly and without any warning at all, the road stopped in what could have been termed a cul-de-sac if one had been feeling generous terminology-wise. Jane hadn't taken the car out of gear before Ian was reaching over to pull the keys from the ignition.

"Come with me," he said, heaving himself out of the car.

"Bags?" she asked, following him.

"We'll come back for them. 'Tisn't far."

Never mind what kind of shape he'd been in when she'd first met him. A week of rest and her cooking, pathetic as it was, combined with the substantial meals they'd had in Scottish pubs, had restored him to a walking form she could barely keep up with. She just held onto his hand and ran to keep up with him as he strode first over a field and then plunged into a forest. It was perfectly quiet in amongst the trees and profoundly chilly despite the time of year. Ian continued to hurry until they were both almost running.

And then, without warning, the forest ended and they practically fell forward into a meadow. Jane hunched over with her hands on her knees and sucked in air until she thought she might be able to stand upright. Then she looked up, and felt her jaw go slack. She held out her arm and pointed.

"That," she spluttered, "that . . . is a castle." She'd seen plenty of them on their way, but this one was so . . . well . . . perfect.

Ian looked down at her, a smile of satisfaction on his face.

"Home," he said simply. He took her hand, hauled her into his arms, and kissed her full on the month before he threw back his head and laughed. "By the saints, Jane, we're home!"

Before she could decide how she felt either about a medieval-looking castle being given such a cozy moniker, or about being kissed by someone who had a sword strapped to his back, she found herself being pulled once again into a flat-out run.

Ian skidded to a halt some two hundred yards farther. "The village," he said in astonishment. " 'Tis gone."

"Well," she panted, "at least the castle is still there."

Ian looked at it suspiciously as well. " 'Tis in a far better state of repair than it was the last time I saw it."

Jane knew that had been something to concern him. They had seen enough ruins along the way to make Jane wonder how any medieval castle survived its trip through the ages.

" 'Tis a mystery we'll solve later," he announced, continuing on the way up the meadow. "Jamie will know the answer to this."

"Think your cousin's here?" she asked with a little wheeze.

"I hope so," Ian said somewhat grimly.

And then he seemed to find just getting to the castle to be taxing enough on his verbosity, because he said nothing else as they trudged toward a dwelling that was starting to give Jane the willies. She'd never seen a castle that looked that authentic and that lived-in. Admittedly, her experience in the British Isles was limited to their drive from Edinburgh, but this was still spooky.

"New gate," Ian remarked as he pulled her through it and across the small courtyard to the castle itself.

Jane didn't have a chance to say anything before he'd marched them up the steps and was pushing on the door. It didn't open, so Ian took his sword and banged on the portal with the hilt. Jane started to say that maybe he shouldn't, then she decided that arguing with a large man with a sword in his hands wasn't a very good idea.

The door finally opened and a young man looked out.

"Yeah?" he asked.

Jane judged him to be in his mid-twenties, exceptionally fine-looking, and obviously home alone based on the carton of milk he held. Bachelor, she deduced by the lack of glass in his hand.

"I am Ian MacLeod," Ian announced, as if that should have clarified everything for the guy.

Apparently it did, because his jaw went slack. "Jamie's cousin Ian?" he asked, looking with wide eyes at Ian's sword.

Ian threw Jane a look of supreme relief, then turned back to the young man. "And you are . . . ?" he demanded.

"Elizabeth's youngest brother," Elizabeth's youngest brother managed. "Zachary."

"Ah, Zach the Brat," Ian said, thrusting forward his hand. "I heard many tales of your escapades from your sister."

"I'll bet you did," Zachary said, stepping back a pace. "You may as well come in. Jamie and Elizabeth aren't here right now, which means there's nothing in the fridge, but you can make yourselves as at home as you can." He looked at them as if he'd just noticed them. "You guys are traveling light. Don't you have any bags?" He looked at Jane. "Are you fourteenth-century too?"

Jane shook her head with a smile. "Nineteen seventies vintage."

Zachary frowned. "How did you find Ian?"

"He showed up in my bridal salon."

"Figures," Zachary said.

Jane looked at Ian, then looked at Zachary. "You believe all this time-traveling business?"

Zachary gave her a world-weary yawn. "You live long enough in this place, you see it all. I believe just about anything anymore," he continued, turning and heading off to what Jane could only assume was the kitchen.

Ian shut the door, then looked down at her. "Do you believe me now?"

"I think I believed you from the start."

" 'Tis a miracle."

"You don't know the half of it," she said as he took her hand and pulled her through a large gathering room of some sort. Too much more holding hands with the guy and she'd start to believe in all sorts of miracles.

No, she decided as she walked across the huge room, it was already too late. She'd begun to believe the moment she'd seen Ian in an antebellum gown in Miss Witherspoon's workroom.

Now, she was completely lost—in Scotland, in a medieval-looking castle, holding onto a man from a century far in the past.

A miracle?

Maybe they were possible after all.

Chapter Seven

IAN STOOD ON the steps leading up to the great hall, stared out into the morning light of his first full day back at the MacLeod keep, and sighed a sigh of pure contentment. He was home, in an entirely different century, but home nonetheless. It was nothing short of amazing.

He had a chamber that had been reserved for him. He'd been surprised when Zachary had told him the like, but apparently Jamie had been either suffering from a serious bout of sentimentality, or he'd known Ian would somehow find his way forward in time. Ian hadn't even used the bed. He'd given it up to Jane for the night and slept in Jamie's thinking chamber. There was one of those strangely padded benches there for his pleasure and he'd found it comfortable enough. Saints, he would have slept in marshy rushes for the pleasure of being home again, except this time with a toaster nearby.

He heard a light footfall behind him and turned to see Jane in the doorway. The sight was so arresting, he had to turn fully to better appreciate it.

She was wearing jeans and a black sweater—he reminded himself to do something about the latter as quickly as he could—and her hair was flowing freely about her shoulders. He wasn't sure what had happened to her since arriving at the castle the day before, but it had been a happy transformation. Perhaps she would never possess the kind of beauty that caused a man to stop in his tracks and gape. Hers was a loveliness of a rarer kind, one that only showed itself upon closer examination. Ian had had the luxury of closer examination over the past se'nnight and he suspected he saw what others might miss. And today, not only was she lovely, but she looked perfectly content, as if she had found the peace she'd been seeking. Unbidden, the vision of her sharing hearth and home with him came to him.

By the saints, this was not what he'd expected to find so soon.

Was it too soon? Was it just the shock of the past se'nnight? Should he wait to see what other souls he might encounter?

Then she smiled.

And he thought he just might be lost.

"You have beautiful mornings here," she said.

"Oh, aye," he managed, jamming his hands into the pockets of jeans before they did something foolish, like grab her and never release her. He cleared his throat. "Would you care for a ride?"

"In the car?"

He smiled. "On a horse, actually. I understand Jamie's mount is going to fat in the stables from lack of activity. We could filch something from the kitchens and roam for the day."

"Sounds heavenly."

"If I see to the horse, will you forage for food? I fear I don't recognize most of what's available."

"Neither do I," she said with a laugh. "Zachary's diet isn't exactly stellar, but I'll see what I can do."

Ian nodded, smiled, then turned away and whistled as he headed toward the stables. He had the feeling it might turn out to be quite a wonderful day indeed.

NOT TWO HOURS had passed that he wasn't congratulating himself on being such a successful seer. Astronaut, Jamie's horse, was as well behaved as he had been the last time Ian had borrowed him for a quick getaway. The weather was perfect, sunny with a bit of a chill wind from the north. The food was actually better than he had hoped.

'Twas the company, however, that gave him the most

pleasure. Who would have thought that showing a woman from the Future all the places he had roamed in his youth and fought in the years of his early manhood would have given him such pleasure and puffed his chest out so far?

They spent the middle of the day at the flat top of Jamie's meadow, looking down over the castle and the forests flanking it. Ian told Jane of battles won, cattle lifted, enemies routed and sent home in shame. It was passing odd to see places he'd tramped over in his youth and realize how many years had passed since then. The landscape had changed, but not so much that he couldn't recognize his favorite retreats.

Then he rolled over onto his belly and watched Jane as she told him of her dreams. He'd expected to hear of grand schemes to see her designs made all over the world. Surely she had a gift for it.

But she told him instead of her wish for a little cottage on the side of a hill and a spinning wheel by the hearth. He watched a faraway look come into her eye when she spoke of the colors she would use and the objects she would make with her hands.

It was then he began to wonder if Fate hadn't had a hand in his delivery to the Future. Surely he could provide her with her wishes. They were modest things surely, but he had the feeling that in her hands, they would be grand things indeed.

Once she was finished, he looked down the way and saw a place where such a thing could be built perfectly.

"Care you for that spot over there?" he asked casually, pointing to a little clearing above the western forest. The remains of a crofter's hut sat on the face of the land in the place he gestured to. It wouldn't make much of a house, but it could be used to build something else.

He looked at her from under his eyelashes as she contemplated the location. He didn't want to assume too much, but he could have sworn he saw a bit of longing sweep over her face.

"It's very beautiful," she said softly.

"Is it?" he mused. "Aye, 'tis pleasing enough, but yours is the beauty that holds my gaze."

She looked at him as if he'd lost his mind. Then she looked away, apparently dismissing his words.

"I'm in earnest," he insisted.

"No models around for competition," she said lightly.

Ian shuddered. "I care not for that kind of beauty. Rather, give me a woman whose loveliness runs true to her bones."

"Hmmm," she said, but she looked unconvinced.

So it would take him a while to persuade her. Fortunate he was then, to have the rest of the Future in which to do it.

He reached for her hand. "Stay here in Scotland for a bit," he said. *Stay forever,* he added silently, realizing as he thought it that it was indeed something he wanted very much.

She looked at him, then looked around her. It took no great powers to divine that she wanted to remain.

"Well," she said slowly, "the scenery *is* beautiful."

He smiled. "Thank you," he said modestly.

She laughed. "I suppose you are part of the package." She paused and sighed. "Well, my rent is paid up through next month. I guess I could get Miss Witherspoon to send my check here. Do we have an address to send it besides 'Jamie's castle'?"

"I'm sure Zachary will know."

She paused again. "Will your cousin mind if I stay?"

"'Tis as much my home as his," Ian said.

"Really?"

"'Tis our family home. One more addition, and such a fetching one at that, will not trouble him."

That earned him a bit of a blush from her and he was relieved to see that she wasn't entirely immune to his charms.

"All right," she conceded.

"Good," Ian said. He stretched out on the blanket and held open his arms. "I'm in need of a small rest after all that sentiment. Will you join me?"

She did. Ian closed his eyes, wrapped his arm around Jane Fergusson, and felt more at peace than he had the whole of his previous life.

He fell asleep with the sun shining down on his face.

JANE AWOKE, CHILLED. Obviously the sun had just gone behind a cloud because she found herself in shadows.

Then she realized it was only a single shadow and it came from a man looming over them. She sat up with a shriek.

And then everything happened too fast for her to do anything. Before she'd finished with her shriek, she found herself behind Ian, who was now on his feet with his sword drawn. There was, she decided, something to be said for having a medieval clansman as a boyfriend.

Boyfriend? She shook her head, deciding to give that more thought later. Now her time was probably better used wondering if she was going to die in the next three minutes.

Well, no blood was being spilt, so Jane took a good look at their attacker so she'd know who to finger in the lineup.

He was tall, perhaps even a bit taller than Ian, and definitely broader. She had to give Ian the benefit of the doubt, given what he'd been through in the past couple of months, but the guy facing him was in very good shape. He had dark hair, a commandingly noble face, and the most piercing pair of green eyes she had ever seen. These she noticed only because he had turned a bit to face Ian more squarely and the sun was shining down on him. And it was as she saw him fully illuminated that she realized what seemed wrong with the picture.

He was dressed—and she could only surmise this to be the case—in full pirate gear. His black boots gleamed. A long saber hung down alongside a leg that, along with the other leg, wore black-as-sin pants that poofed a little as they tucked themselves into the boots. A snowy white shirt, along with a red bandanna draped around his head in true pirate fashion, completed the picture. The only thing that seemed out of place were all the ruffles on his shirt, ruffles completely incongruous with the man's formidable frown.

And it was then that she thought Ian just might get them both shot with the gun the other man was toting so casually on his hip.

Ian reached out with his sword and flicked up a bit of lace.

"Lace?" he drawled. "Have you enough of it, or might there yet be a scrap of your shirt that isn't adorned with it?"

"Ian," Jane whispered fiercely, "shut up!"

The other man only folded his arms over his chest and frowned. "'Tis pirate clothing, you fool."

"You look like a woman."

"But I still fight like a man. Would you care to test it?"

Then Ian, to Jane's consternation, tossed aside his sword. Well, if he was going to be that stupid, she would have to make up for it. She hauled herself to her feet and made a grab for the blade. It wasn't as heavy as she feared, but it wasn't exactly a pair of pinking shears, either. She managed to get it and herself upright only to find that instead of killing each other, the two men were exchanging a gruff embrace complemented by a great deal of hefty backslapping. It went on for a few minutes, then suddenly the two pulled apart and began to punch each other in the arms and pummel each other on the chest.

Jane rolled her eyes. Men.

"Ian, you randy whoreson!"

"Jamie, you bejeweled peacock!"

Jane let the point of the blade slip down. Jamie? This, then, was Ian's cousin? Dressed like a pirate, no less. She wondered if it was too late to hop in the car and drive off. She was beginning to have serious doubts about the rest of Ian's family and their taste in clothes.

Jamie pulled away and grinned. "Took you long enough to get out of the Fergusson's dungeon."

Ian gave him a healthy shove. "I wouldn't have found myself *in* his dungeon if it hadn't been for your wagging tongue."

Jamie rubbed his hands together gleefully. "Ah, but what a tale it had been to tell. How could I have resisted?"

"You could have clamped your lips together and remained silent, that's what!"

Jane found herself suddenly being scrutinized and she suppressed the urge to check to see if her clothes were on straight. After all, it wasn't as if she and Ian had been doing anything besides sleeping. Jamie made her a low bow.

"James MacLeod, your servant," he said. "If I might have the pleasure of your name, mistress?"

"Jane F—"

"She's from New York," Ian interrupted. "A very fine designer of bridal wear."

Jamie slapped Ian on the back again. "You didn't waste any time finding yourself a woman, cousin." Jamie winked at Jane. "Never lacked for a handsome wench did this one."

Jane found herself with the distinct urge to use Ian's sword. On Ian. Apparently Ian could see what she was thinking because he flinched visibly, then turned and gave his cousin another healthy shove.

"I've mended my ways."

"When hell freezes over!" Jamie laughed.

"It fair did to get me here and I tell you, I've changed."

"A last-minute bargain with Saint Peter?" Jamie asked in a conspiratorial whisper. "I can only imagine how the discourse proceeded. You always did have an excess of fair speech frothing from your head."

"The difference between you and me is," Ian said tightly, "that I know when to cease babbling and you do not!"

"I never babble."

"You do! That's what landed me in the Fergusson's dungeon, you babbling fool!"

"Fergusson?" Jane echoed. "What's this?"

"William Fergusson," Jamie said, scowling at Ian. "Our bitterest enemy. Ian helped himself to Roberta's—"

"Never mind what I helped myself to," Ian interrupted. He looked at Jane. "'Tis in the past."

"But, Ian," she said slowly. "I'm a—"

"It matters not."

Jane found herself under Jamie's scrutiny again. She put her shoulders back. "My last name is Fergusson. I'm probably related to that William."

"And you've more than made up for William's lack of hospitality," Ian said, taking his sword away from her.

"Ian, I don't know . . ." Jamie began.

"Aye, generally you don't," Ian said, then he firmly planted his fist in Jamie's face. "That's for the last time you babbled without thinking. Try not to do it again this time and foul up my future."

Jane would have checked to see if Jamie planned to get up off the ground from where he'd been knocked, but she found that she was being dragged by the hand down the meadow toward the castle. She had to run to keep up with Ian's furious strides.

"Hey, slow down," she panted.

Ian sighed and stopped. Then he stared off into the distance for several minutes while she caught her breath and he apparently worked every tangle possible out of his hair. At least that's what she thought he was doing, dragging his hands through it that way. Then he cleared his throat.

"I should likely tell you," he said, looking down, "of why I found myself in that dungeon."

She shook her head. "I'm getting pieces of it, and I don't know that I want to know any more."

"Jamie will tell you if I do not." He sighed again and looked heavenward. "I robbed a woman of her virtue."

Jane felt a chill come over her. "Forcefully?"

Ian looked so shocked, she immediately relaxed. "Saints, nay," he said, with feeling. "I did it cheerfully, for it made her father's life very difficult, but I wouldn't have done it had she not been willing." He smiled a little smile. "Willing is perhaps not a strong enough word. She knew who she stood to wed with and I daresay she considered me a more pleasant prospect for her deflowering."

"Was she very beautiful?" Jane asked wistfully.

Ian laughed. "Saints, nay. She was passing unpleasant, both of face and humor. And she threatened to unman me should I not do my work well."

"I take it you did your work well."

"Well enough," he said briskly. He looked very uncomfortable all of a sudden. "Now, must we discuss this further?"

She shrugged. "You brought it up."

"Aye, well, I did and I'm sorry for it. I daresay you don't want the details."

"Don't I?"

"You do not."

"Why not?"

"Because you and I . . . well . . ."

"Yes?"

"You and . . . er . . . I . . ."

From out of the blue an unexpected warmth began in her heart. Jane had the most ridiculous idea creep up on her that Ian might actually be talking about her and him. Together. As a . . . well . . . couple. She found herself beginning to smile. "Yes?"

He frowned at her. "The past is dead and buried—"

"Yeah, I'll say it is. About seven hundred years buried."

"—and I'd prefer it stay that way," he finished with a darker frown. "I've mended my ways, though Jamie will likely never let me forget them. One does not discuss his past lovers with his future . . . er . . ."

"Yes?" She could hardly believe she was indulging in this word game, because she could hardly believe he might truly be interested in her, but there was that warmth in her heart. And he was definitely frowning. That could mean any number of things, but still . . .

Ian looked at her with narrowed eyes, then took her by the hand and pulled her along behind him to the castle. "I'm finished with this discourse."

"I'll just bet you are," she said, but she was very tempted to smile. His future what? Could he have been prepared to use the word *friend*? *Bride* would have been the expression she would have chosen, but it was still early yet. Maybe she would spend a few more days with Ian and decide that she really didn't like him. Maybe she would decide that Scotland wasn't really the place for her and she would scurry back to New York and throw herself on Miss Witherspoon's mercy.

Or maybe she would take Ian up on his offer and stay in Scotland for a little while. Who knew what might happen if she did?

Chapter Eight

TWO WEEKS LATER, Jane found herself sitting on a bench with her back against the castle wall waiting for Ian and Jamie to indulge in a little swordplay.

"And he clouted me in the nose!" Jamie was saying to his wife Elizabeth as they came onto the field. "Just reared back as casually as you please and took his fist to my sweet visage!"

Elizabeth only sighed lightly. "Yes, Jamie, we've heard all about it for the past two weeks. Go use Ian up in the lists to soothe yourself."

"Never should have named my bairn after him," Jamie grumbled, as he kissed his wife and walked away. "What possessed me to do the like?"

Jane had watched Ian's face when he'd first been introduced to his little cousin Ian, and watched the emotions that had crossed that face when he realized how he'd been honored. It had resulted in more backslapping with Jamie, but no apology for the condition of Jamie's nose. Jane suspected Ian was still suffering from very vivid memories of his time in the Fergusson's dungeon.

That she had begun to accept the time-travel story as fact had ceased to surprise her. Maybe it was the Scottish air. Maybe it was the countless walks and rides she'd been on with Ian where he spoke so easily of events in the past. It also could have been watching Jamie and Elizabeth together and hearing them talk so easily of events that they claimed had happened hundreds of years ago.

Or maybe it was just watching Ian, who was no slouch in the sword department, practice against the supposed former laird of the clan MacLeod, who was even less of a slouch when it came to swordplay.

"Ian's still getting his strength back."

Jane looked at Elizabeth who had sat down on the bench next to her. Jane had come to like Jamie's wife in the short time she'd known her. Elizabeth somehow managed to keep equilibrium in her life despite a very strong-willed husband and a rambunctious toddler. She managed the two quite well, seemingly kept up a writing career, and remained a hopeless romantic all without breaking a sweat.

"I think that couple of months took more out of him than he wants to admit," Elizabeth continued. "Especially to you."

Jane paused, considered the far-fetchedness of that, then shook her head. "Ian couldn't care less about my opinion."

Elizabeth looked at her so appraisingly that Jane felt herself begin to squirm.

"Well," Jane began defensively, "he really couldn't."

"I think," Elizabeth said slowly, "that you give yourself too little credit. And you give Ian even less. He wouldn't lead you on. That makes him sound shallow, and that's the last thing I would call him."

Jane felt her cheeks begin to burn and for the first time in a long time, she felt ashamed. "I know he's not shallow. I didn't mean that."

"Then why don't you trust him to know his own heart?" Elizabeth asked with a gentle smile. "He's old enough to have figured out what he wants."

"He hasn't seen what's available this century."

Elizabeth laughed. "Well, he saw more than his share in the past, so don't feel too sorry for him. Ian was something of a—"

"Free spirit?"

"Lothario was more what I was going for," Elizabeth said with a grin, "but how could he help himself? He was a MacLeod minus the grumbles. Women were always throwing themselves at him."

"And he rarely resisted," Jane finished.

"No cable TV," Elizabeth said, as if that should have proven beyond doubt that there was little else to do besides give in. "And it was a hard life. Men died young. It wouldn't have made sense to them to refuse a willing woman."

"Why didn't Ian ever marry?"

"Well, you were here and he was still there," Elizabeth said slowly. "What else could he do?"

Jane leaned her head back against the cold stone. It was so very tempting to believe such a thing when one was surrounded by Scottish countryside. Almost anything seemed possible there. "Hope is a terrible thing," she said with a sigh.

"I think Ian's gone way past hope. He was haggling with Jamie last night over his share of the MacLeod fortune, and that's no small sum."

"Really," Jane said.

Elizabeth nodded. "Jamie unloaded some family treasure he found in the fireplace. I think Ian wants to have a house built before winter. I suspect he doesn't intend to live there alone."

"You're one of those happy ending kind of girls, aren't you?"

Elizabeth only laughed. "Guilty." She smiled at Jane. "Don't you believe in fate?"

"Ian asked me the same thing."

"Did you ever wonder why?"

Jane didn't know how to answer that, so she turned to watch the spectacle in front of her. She suspected that even once Ian got his complete strength back that he might still never be exactly the same kind of swordsman that Jamie was, though she had no doubts he could protect her quite nicely if the need arose. Ian was just, well, less intense than Jamie seemed to be. She couldn't see Jamie loitering by a fire with his feet up and a book in his hands while Elizabeth spun wool into thread. Then again, she couldn't imagine Elizabeth spinning, so maybe it was a good match there.

But she was a weaver herself.

And Ian enjoyed a hot fire and a good book.

"It's all true," Jane said softly. She turned to Elizabeth. "Isn't it?"

"Oh, yes," Elizabeth said, just as quietly. "All of it."

"You lived in the fourteenth century and married Jamie there."

Elizabeth nodded.

"And Ian was there, too."

Elizabeth nodded again.

Jane rubbed her eyes. "The funny thing is, I'm starting to believe it's true, too. Not that I'd want to go back in time and see for myself," she said quickly. "I'll opt for the cable TV, thanks."

"And you know Ian isn't about to give up the possibility of more plane rides."

Jane nodded, trying to put that thought out of her mind. If Ian had his way, they would be flying from one corner of the world to the other on a regular basis, just for the fun of it. She'd been heartily disappointed to find that Jamie had a private jet. Jane had the feeling that if she did intertwine her life with Ian's, she would be flying the friendly skies more often than she wanted to.

But if she had Ian's hand to hold, what was a little turbulence now and then?

She folded her arms over her chest, then looked down at the sweater she was wearing and felt herself smile. It was the most colorful of the sweaters in the local woolen shop and Ian had made her change into it the minute after he'd bought it for her. He'd also bought her a pair of boots for hiking and spent half an hour diligently threading her rainbow-colored shoelaces through the eyes.

If she hadn't loved him before, she thought she just might have begun to then.

"Uh-oh," Elizabeth said, shaking her head. "They're reverting to the native tongue for insults now. Once the Gaelic begins, it's all downhill from there." She looked at Jane as she rose. "Going to stick it out?"

Jane nodded happily. "Wouldn't miss it."

Elizabeth smiled a half smile. "It's easier to watch when you know it's just them keeping in shape, not them preparing for battle."

She invited Jane to come in later for cookies, then walked back around the corner to the front door. Jane turned the thought of Ian going off into battle over in her head for a while as she watched him and Jamie go at each other with their swords. She'd spent ample time studying the two and had come to recognize when Jamie was pushing his cousin and when he wasn't. Ian had long since stripped off his shirt and his back was a patchwork of healing stripes.

It was a chilling sight.

"Bad ancestor," she muttered under her breath, wishing she could give William Fergusson a piece of her mind. "Bad, bad, ancestor."

But despite Jamie's well-rested self and Ian's back, Ian was indeed something amazing to watch. She had no doubts that every one of his boasts about his successes in battle was true. She was only relieved that she hadn't known him then to worry over him. Talk about turbulence!

And then talk about turbulence.

"Where is she? Where is that girl?"

The imperious tone that had the power to etch glass cut clearly through the midday summer air. Jane felt her teeth begin to grind of their own accord. And then her jaw went slack as she realized she was hearing Miss Petronia Witherspoon in person. Well, maybe that was what she deserved for even alerting Miss Witherspoon to her whereabouts.

Even the two combatants in the yard turned to look as Miss Witherspoon rounded the corner of the castle like a battleship in full regalia, all sails unfurled. Alexis, clad in a painted-on leopard-print catsuit, came trotting behind her in her wake, loaded down with a couple of bolts of fabric and a pair of dressmaker's shears in her arms. Miss Witherspoon clutched a rolled-up drawing in her hand and brandished it like a sword.

This was not good.

Jane watched Alexis come to a dead stop when she saw both Ian and Jamie in skirts, wielding swords. Jane was used to the sight of them fighting in their plaids. She couldn't decide if Alexis was more shocked by the sight of bare knees or bare chests. Then she took a look at the men and decided it was the latter—definitely the latter.

Miss Witherspoon, however, seemed unmoved by the sensational view in front of her. She gave Jamie a cursory glance, did the same to Ian, then turned and fixed Jane with what Jane always called her eighteenth-century, bring-your-sorry-indentured-servant-butt-over-here-this-instant look.

"Jane! Jane!" Miss Witherspoon said this with an imperiousness that even Queen Elizabeth likely couldn't have mustered on her best day. "Jane!"

Jane looked at Ian to see how he was taking all the name-calling. He'd impaled the dirt in front of him with his sword and was resting his hands on the hilt, all the while watching with a smile playing around his mouth. She'd become very familiar with the look. It meant he found something vastly amusing but didn't want to spoil the fun by sticking his oar in where it might not be wanted. That was the thing about Ian. He always seemed to find something delightful about what was going on around him. Jane liked that about him. She especially liked that about him now that Miss Witherspoon was waving a bony finger in her direction and screeching her name. After having spent many days in Ian's company, she too could appreciate the absurdity of what to her had been life or death—like rent and food money—to her but a short three weeks ago. Ian had been talking to Jamie about his share of the MacLeod inheritance. Who needed Miss Witherspoon's paltry offerings?

Assuming he intended to see to the care and feeding of the both of them with that inheritance.

Well, if Elizabeth was worth her salt as a romantic, Ian intended to do something along those lines. In honor of that, Jane slouched back against the wall, and propped an ankle up on the opposite knee in a very un-eighteenth-century pose.

"Miss P.," she said with a little wave, "what's shakin'?"

"You disrespectful chit!" Miss Witherspoon said shrilly. "Without me you would be wallowing in the gutter!"

She had a point there, but Jane wasn't ready to concede the match. She went so far as to put both feet on the ground and stand up. She nodded her head in proper servant-like fashion, but refused to curtsey.

"You're right," Jane said with another nod. "You took a chance on me. I wouldn't be where I am if it hadn't been for you." *And I never would have found Ian.* That alone had been worth three years of slavery.

"I should say not!"

"Your showroom wouldn't be where it is without me, either," Jane said pointedly, "as you cannot help but admit."

Miss Witherspoon, surprisingly enough, was silent, but Jane could hear her teeth grinding from twenty paces.

"Alexis as well has benefitted from my skills," Jane continued.

"Alexis is a brilliant designer," Miss Witherspoon said stubbornly.

"Then why are you here?" Jane asked.

"She needs a wedding gown," Miss Witherspoon said briskly. "You'll sew it. She wants, and I cannot understand this for he certainly is not the man I would choose for her," and she drew in a large breath and released a heavy, disappointed sigh that almost blew Jane over, "but she wants *him.*"

The bony finger lifted, spun around like a needle on a compass, and pointed straight at Ian.

Ian's smile disappeared abruptly. His glance dropped to Alexis's red fingernails and he emitted a little squeak.

"I like him," Alexis said, raking her claws down the bolt of tulle. She fixed Ian with a look that made him back up a pace. "Do you always carry that sword?" she purred.

"By the saints," Ian said, backing up again. "I want nothing to do with this one."

"Of course you do," Miss Witherspoon said briskly. "Jane, come here and take the materials. Get started right away."

Jane walked past Miss Witherspoon, pushed Alexis out of the way, and stood in front of Ian.

"Get lost," she said. "The both of you. I found him first and I'm keeping him."

"I want him," Alexis protested. "Auntie said I could have him."

"Auntie was wrong," Jane said, pointing toward the gate. "Beat it."

"Wait," Ian said, putting a hand on Jane's shoulder and pulling her to one side.

Jane looked at him in astonishment. "Wait?" she echoed.

"Aye," he said, looking in Alexis's direction with what could have been mistaken for enthusiasm. "Wait."

"But you just said you didn't want anything to do with her," Jane said. She shut her mouth abruptly, amazed that the words had come out of it. As if she should point out to Ian where she thought his eyes should and shouldn't be roaming!

"Aye, well, let us not be so hasty," Ian said, continuing to study Alexis closely.

Jane felt her face go up in flames, taking her heart with it. She couldn't believe she'd misread Ian so fully, but apparently she had. He wouldn't look at her, which convinced her all the more that somehow she had overlooked the fact that he was a rat.

A rat. Hadn't it all started that way? She should have known.

"Let me see the design," Ian said, holding out his hand to Miss Witherspoon.

He unrolled it and looked it over. Jane didn't want to look, but her curiosity got the better of her. She snorted at the sight. One of her designs, of course, and one Alexis had no doubt swiped from her office. It wasn't Miss Witherspoon's normal fare. It was gauzy and flowing and like nothing Miss Witherspoon or Alexis had ever imagined up in either of their worst nightmares.

Ian held up the drawing and compared it with Alexis, as if he tried to envision how it would look on her. Then he looked over the materials she'd brought with her. He fingered, rubbed a bit against his cheek, then fingered some more. Alexis had begun to salivate. Jane wanted to barf and she was on the verge of saying as much when Ian spoke.

To her.

"Make this," he said, gesturing toward the drawing.

Jane was speechless. She could only gape at him, wondering where she was going to find air to breathe again since he'd stolen it all with his heartless words. It was bad enough he was dumping her for Alexis. To demand that she make the wedding dress was just too much to take.

"I have my measurements written down for you," Alexis said, baring her teeth in a ferocious smile. She shoved the material at Jane.

Jane had just gotten that balanced when Ian placed the drawing on top. It was the killing blow. Jane felt the sting of tears begin to blind her.

"If you think for one moment," she choked, "that I'm going to do any of this—"

"Of course you'll do it," Ian said. "The gown is perrrfect."

Jane had the distinct urge to suggest he take his damned r's and wallow in them until he drowned.

"But," he added, reaching over and placing the point of his sword down in the dirt between Alexis and her, "'tis the wrong color entirely, that fabric."

"Huh?" Alexis said.

"Huh?" Jane echoed, looking up at him. Damn him if that little smile wasn't back.

"White isn't your color," he said, the smile taking over more of his face, "but I suspect you'll look stunning in blue. A deep blue, perhaps. We'll find the dye for the cloth and then you'll make up the gown."

Alexis stamped her feet, setting up a small dust storm. "Blue is *not* my color!"

"Aye," Ian said with a full-blown grin, "I daresay it isn't. But 'twill suit Jane well enough."

"But . . . but . . ." Miss Witherspoon was spluttering like a teakettle that couldn't find its spout to vent its steam.

Ian waved his sword in their direction and sent both Miss Witherspoon and Alexis backing up in consternation.

"Off with ye, ye harpies," he said, herding them off toward the gate with the efficiency of a border collie. "Ye've made my Janey frrrown and I'll not have any morre of it."

Jane stood in the middle of James MacLeod's training field, her arms full of her future and could only stare, speechless, as Ian threw her tormentors off the castle grounds. Then she looked at Jamie who was rubbing his chin thoughtfully. He made her a little bow.

"I'll see to a priest," he said, then he walked away.

Jane watched him go, then continued to stand where she was, finding herself quite alone.

It had to be something in the air. Or the water.

"I think," she said to no one in particular, "that I've just been proposed to."

No one answered. The clouds drifted lazily by. Bees hummed. Birds sang. The wind blew chill from the north, stirring her hair and the material in her arms. The castle stood to her right, a silent observer of the morning's events. It seemed disinclined to offer its opinion on what it all meant.

And then Ian peeked around the corner, startling her.

"Well?" he asked.

Jane looked at him, noted the grin that was firmly plastered to his face, and considered the possibilities of this turn of events.

She tilted her head and looked at her potential groom.

"Will my little stone house have indoor plumbing?"

"For you, my lady, aye, I'll see it done."

"Electricity?"

"If it suits you."

Well, Ian had lived most of his life without it. It was a certainty that he'd probably live a lot longer if he didn't have any outlets to stick metal implements in.

"I'll give it some thought," she allowed. "How about cable TV?"

That brought him around the side of the castle and over to where she stood. Before she could find out how he felt about television in general, he'd put his hand behind her head, bent his head, and kissed her.

And then before Jane could suggest that perhaps it might be more comfortable if she put the material and sundry down, Ian had wrapped his arms around all of her and her gear and pulled her gently to him. He smiled down at her before he kissed her again, a sweet, lingering kiss that stole her breath and her heart.

By the time he let her up for air, she was convinced he intended that her heart be permanently softened and her knees nothing but mush. If she hadn't been such a good designer, she probably would have lost her grip on the material. As it was, she was sure she'd lost her grip on her sanity because she was seriously considering marrying a medieval clansman who kissed like nobody's business. Heaven help her through anything else he might choose to do.

"Wow," she gasped, when he finally let her breathe again.

He smiled down at her smugly. "We won't need TV."

"I guess not."

His blue eyes were full of merriment and love and dreams for the future. "A spinning wheel, though," he said. "And a hearth large enough for us to warm ourselves by in the evenings."

"And to gather the children around to hear glorious stories of their father's conquests in battle?" she asked, feeling her heart break a little at the thought.

"Aye, that too," he said gently, then he kissed her again. "That too, my Jane, if it pleases you."

She would have told him what pleased her, but he kissed her again and the sensation of having her toes curling in her boots was just too distracting to remember what it was she'd meant to tell him.

Then he put his arm around her and led her back to the castle. He was already planning their future out loud and she suspected she wouldn't get a word in edgewise until he was finished. But since his dreams included her, she wouldn't begrudge him his plans. She was a weaver and he was a storyteller. She would weave her strands in and out of his dreams and he would tell everyone who would listen how it had been done.

And somehow, she suspected they would live out their lives in bliss, quite likely by candlelight.

When you had a fourteenth-century husband, things were much safer that way.

Epilogue

Ian MacLeod sat in a comfortable chair in front of a large hearth, toasting his toes against the warmth of the fire, and contemplated life's mysteries. They were many, but the evening stretched out pleasantly before him, so he had the time to examine them at length.

The first thing that caught his attention and qualified for an item of true irony was that he warmed his toes against a fire in a little stone hut when he had a perfectly good manor house up the way with all the modern amenities a goodly portion of his money could buy. His toes could also have been enjoying a fine Abyssinian carpet and his backside a well-worn leather club chair. Even more distressing was the thought of the stew simmering in the black kettle in front of him when there was a shiny red Aga stove sitting in the kitchen waiting for him to pit his skill against it.

By the saints, he might as well have still been in the Middle Ages for all the advances he'd made in his living conditions.

The sound of a spinning wheel distracted him and he found himself smiling in spite of his longing to test out a few new electrical gadgets. He looked to his left and saw the most wonderful of life's great mysteries.

There she sat, the woman of his dreams, the woman he had searched for all his life and never would have found had it not been for a twist of time. She was born and bred in an age far removed from his, yet she was at her most peaceful when they retreated to a place that could have found itself existing comfortably several centuries ago.

Jane's spinning was soothing with its rhythmic sounds and Ian found himself relaxing as he watched her be about her work. Firelight fell softly upon her sweet visage and caressed her long, slender fingers as she fashioned her strands of wool. They were tasks belonging to another age. There were times during he evenings they spent at the cottage when Ian would have to go to the door occasionally to assure himself that his shiny red Jaguar still sat in front of the door.

Ian had discovered that he liked red.

He had also discovered that he liked going very fast.

He leaned his head against the back of the chair and looked at his wife, noting the changes. Her long skirt was a riot of colors. Her sweater was a rich, vibrant red that brought out the strands of flame in her hair and the fine porcelain of her skin. Whatever wildness had resided under her constrained hair and black clothes had found full freedom in the Highlands. Ian found himself smiling. How changed Miss Witherspoon would have found her.

"You're smirking."

Ian looked at Jane, startled by her voice. "How can you tell?" he asked, moving his feet closer to the fire.

She didn't look up, but instead continued with her work. "I can feel it."

"You're guessing," he countered.

She looked at him then and smiled. The sight of it smote him straight in the heart. Aye, this was where she belonged and he praised every saint he could think of with his few poor wits that he'd had the good sense to wind up in Miss Witherspoon's shop on Jane's watch.

"What were you thinking?" she asked with another smile.

"I was just wondering what Miss Witherspoon would say at the changes in your appearance."

Jane laughed. "She'd have heart failure on the spot. I think color makes her nervous."

"We could go to New York and show your colors to other designers," he said, for surely what had been the hundredth time in the past year. "The apple is a large place."

"That's the Big Apple, Ian. And no," she said, holding up her hand, "I'm not all that interested in going back right now."

She looked around the hut with satisfaction, then smiled happily at him. "I like it here."

Ian couldn't blame her, for he felt the same way. It had taken them a year to see their two dwellings built and furnished to their satisfaction. Fall was already hard upon them and perhaps it wasn't the best of times to travel. And what need had they to venture forth when so many things came to their door? Ian had come to look forward to the afternoons when he managed to snatch the mail away before Jane could retrieve it first and hide all the catalogs from him. Shopping by Her Majesty's postal service was another of the Future's great inventions that Ian had discovered he enjoyed very much.

"I can sell enough of my work in the village to keep me happy for now," she continued. "And you have a new batch of students coming in before January."

"Aye, there is that," he agreed. His students were souls who came to him for lessons in swordplay. Through the connections of various kin and partly due to fool's luck, he'd managed to meet a pair of men of the Hollywood ilk who needed a swordmaster for their filming in Scotland. Ian had taken on the task and found himself with a new and goodly work to do. Perhaps it wasn't as exhilarating as battle, but 'twas a great deal less hazardous to his health.

"Perhaps in the summer, then," he said. "A journey to the States."

She shook her head. "You'll be busy in the summer."

He frowned. "I've no students then."

"You'll be helping take care of a baby."

"Elizabeth is with child?" Jamie would be pleased, but Ian suspected Elizabeth's days of traveling would be over for the foreseeable future.

Jane stopped her spinning and looked at him. "No, Elizabeth is not pregnant."

"But who . . . else . . ." He stopped and looked at his wife who had turned a bright shade of red. Ian liked red very much. Indeed, the color had begun to swim before his vision, along with a chamber full of stars.

And then he found himself with his head suddenly between his knees.

"Breathe," Jane commanded, with her hand on his neck.

Ian did as she bid until he thought he might manage to get to his feet and remain there successfully. He stood, gathered his lady wife into his arms, and looked down at her, feeling a great sense of awe.

"You didn't tell me," he whispered.

"I wanted to be certain before I did."

"A son," he said reverently.

"It could be a girl," she pointed out.

"A wee lass," he said, petrified. By the saints, the young men he would have to slay to keep her safe from their clutches!

And then another thought occurred to him. He looked at Jane sternly.

"'Tis too cold here for you," he said firmly.

"In Scotland?" she asked incredulously.

"In this cottage," he clarified, feeling a thrill of electricity rush through him. Finally he would investigate the mysteries of man's inventions to his heart's content. "We'll repair immediately to the house where it's warm."

"I'm suspicious of your motives," she said, but she smiled as she said it.

"Be suspicious after you've warmed up. I'll return later for supper and the spinning wheel."

He pulled the door firmly shut behind him and herded his wife efficiently toward the marvels of the Future that awaited him at home.

IT WAS VERY much later that Ian lay in his exceedingly comfortable feather bed with his lady sleeping sweetly in his arms, and gave thought not to the ironies of life, but to the sweet mysteries. There were no angry clansmen who stood to break down his door any time in the foreseeable future. He wouldn't find himself woken from a deep sleep with the necessity of being on his feet with his sword in his hand prepared to fight in any future he could envision. His greatest danger would likely come from machines that wouldn't stop merely when he said "whoa" in a loud voice. That he could live with, especially when the reward for it was the finding of his love and—the saints aid him to be equal to the task of fatherhood!—a bairn.

He surely had no desire to thank William Fergusson for the hospitality of his pit, but Ian couldn't deny that it had certainly been a path to his future and he couldn't help but be grateful for it.

He closed his eyes, sighed, and fell asleep to the comforting click of the radiator.

And he dreamed, for a change, of the Present.

The Icing on
the Cake

Chapter One

IT HAD BEEN the morning from hell.

Samuel MacLeod carefully avoided the last chuckhole, turned the engine off, and unclenched his teeth. He carefully leaned his throbbing head against the steering wheel of his once clean and shiny Range Rover and let out a long, slow breath.

"I am," he said to no one in particular and with a distinct edge to his voice, "too old for this."

He should have known from the start that it would have been a day better spent in bed. He'd had a lousy night's sleep and was suffering from an incredible case of writer's block. He could have made a soufflé, put his feet up on the coffee table, and wallowed in eggs and spectator sports. Or he could have propped his feet up on the fat leather ottoman in front of the picture window, settled back into the matching leather chair, and stared out into the wilderness surrounding his rented cabin. The deep green forest could have held his attention, as could any number of critters that might have used the front yard as a hiking trail. Fall was his favorite time of year, and fall in Alaska was like nothing he'd ever before experienced.

Yes, he could have been comfortable. He could have been warm. He could have been entertained by wild things.

But instead of following his better instincts, he'd risen at five, determined to work out the kinks in his plotline. He'd planned to finish chapter twenty by ten o'clock, leaving him plenty of time to get to town and back.

The way the lights had been flickering should have told him it wasn't a day to be tempting the Fates.

First had come the power spike at eight, wiping out three hours of irreplaceable prose. He'd gone outside to check the generator and heard the distinct, unwelcome sound of a locked door closing behind him. Breaking in through the window had left him with cuts on his hands and his sweats. He'd headed back outside, determined not to let his rented house get the best of him this time.

Fixing the generator had gone rather well, though he didn't have a clue as to what he'd done. Banging it a couple of times with a wrench and threatening it had seemed to do the trick.

Unfortunately, that had been the only success of the morning.

He'd tried to ignore the lack of hot water midway through his shower. He'd laughed off the small kitchen fire that had resulted from a misbehaving toaster. He'd even kept a smile on his face, insincere though it might have been, when he discovered he'd forgotten to turn on the dryer the night before and all his clothes were soaking wet. He'd simply put on dirty jeans and headed out to the garage to warm up the car—

Only to encounter a creature of indeterminate origin who glared evilly at him before hiking its leg and relieving itself on Sam's tire. Sam had made it into his four-wheel-drive sustaining no damage to himself. Of course, that had been rectified nicely after he'd had a flat on the way into town and been forced to change said tire.

And, heaven help him, it was only noon.

He clambered out of the Range Rover, casting an eye heavenward to check for falling satellite parts, and stepped kneedeep into one of the chuckholes he had so carefully tried to avoid. He saw stars. He indulged in a few choice swearwords before he uttered what summed up his feelings about the past three months of his life.

"I hate Alaska."

Of course, the blame for that—though he was loath to admit it—was something he could lay only at his own feet. He could have been back in New York, hobnobbing with the well-heeled and dabbling in his artistic pursuits. He could have been worrying about a date for the opera, struggling to decide who to take to a gallery opening, wracking his brains for a suitable miss to gaze adoringly at him while he listened to an obscure poet read even more obscure poetry.

He also could have been listening to his family ridicule his two passions: writing and food. They couldn't fathom why a man with a perfectly good eight-figure trust fund seemed to find it necessary to ruin his manicure with manual labor.

He'd pointed out to them that somewhere back in their family tree there had been a MacLeod or two doing plenty of manual labor on Scottish soil—likely in the form of cattle raiding and sword wielding. His father had hastened to inform him that they were kin to a long, illustrious line of Scottish lairds, and that stealing beef and waving swords around didn't count as manual labor.

Sam had tried to explain his driving need to put words on paper by reminding his kin that the first American transplant from their ancestral clan had made his living as a newspaperman. His older sister had ruined that excuse by pointing out that said newspaperman had actually been an "editor in chief and very wealthy newspaper owner."

Sam had given up trying to probe any further back into his well-documented genealogy for examples to back up his arguments. He'd settled for informing his family that not only had he been writing, he'd also been studying with one of New York's most famous chefs. His mother's week-long attack of the vapors upon hearing that news was what had finally driven him to seek sanctuary as far away from New York as he could get and still remain on the same landmass.

Sans his trust fund—and that by his own choice, no less.

"Alaska," he grunted.

He was an idiot.

He sighed and reminded himself why he was there. Alaska was the last vestige of untamed wilderness and he was a MacLeod. Sword wielding wasn't all that legal anymore, but he could do mighty things with a pen and the occasional spatula. He could do those things on his own terms and by the sweat of his own brow.

But there were times when he wondered if Southern California wouldn't have been wilderness enough. He suspected a ramshackle house on the beach would have been a great deal easier to manage than his rented cabin with its accompaniment of deer, bears, and other sundry and perilous wildlife.

He sighed deeply, then tromped across the mud and up the worn steps to the general store. Smith's Dry Goods and Sundries seemed to be the precise center of whatever hubbub was going on in Flaherty, Alaska, population three hundred. The store was the gathering place for anyone who was anyone to discuss everyone else. Sam suspected he'd had his share of space on the gossip docket. He opened the door and stepped inside, avoiding the rotting floorboard near the door. No, sir, he wasn't going to put his foot through that twice in a lifetime. He wasn't a greenhorn anymore.

He ambled over to the counter and nodded to the usual locals holding court next to the woodstove, chewing the fat and their tobacco. Sam pulled out his neatly made supply list and handed it to Mr. Smith, the proprietor. It was a lean list, of course, because he was still living on the proceeds from a couple of articles he'd sold to a cooking magazine. He was beginning to wonder now if he would have been better off to have traded out for six months of groceries.

A throat near the stove cleared itself, coughed, then hacked into the brass spittoon. "Yer the writer fella?"

Sam identified the speaker as an old-timer he'd never met before, a grizzled man who probably hadn't had a haircut since World War II.

Sam nodded, smiling slightly. "That's right."

There was a bit of low grumbling. There was always low grumbling after he admitted to his vocation. Since he didn't like to hunt, fish, or chew, he had left the Clan very unimpressed. Sam would have liked to point out to them that his great-great-great-grandfather had come across the sea and cut a swath through Colonial America that even the Clan would have been impressed by, but then he might have been questioned about his own deeds and he didn't dare admit the kind of soft life he'd left behind in New York. He suspected that in Alaska lynching was still an acceptable means of population control.

"Heard yer up at the Kincaid place," another bearded octogenarian demanded. "That right?"

"That's right," Sam agreed.

The grumbling rose in volume until it reached outraged proportions. The spokesman rose and stomped to the door.

"Just ain't right," he growled. "It just ain't right."

The rest of the group departed after giving Sam disapproving looks. Sam looked at Mr. Smith, an older man with a merely rudimentary sense of humor.

"What did I say?"

Mr. Smith shrugged. "Reckon you'll find out soon enough."

Sam wondered if that could possibly be anything he would want to investigate further. Then again, forewarned was forearmed. He took a deep breath.

"Care to translate?" he asked.

Mr. Smith shook his head. "Better to let you find out for yourself."

Sam leaned against the counter and tried not to let the ambiguity of that statement unnerve him. With the way things were going, finding out for himself could be downright dangerous.

The door behind him opened and shut with a bang.

"Joe, when are you going to get this damned floorboard fixed?"

Well, now the sound of *that* voice was almost enough to make all the misery of the past three months worth it. Sam leaned heavily on the counter while his knees recovered. It was a voice straight from his most favorite lazy Saturday-morning dreams, the voice that belonged to his warm and cuddly football-watching partner. He was tempted to whip around immediately and make sure, but he resisted. Surely the sight that awaited him was even more luscious than the sound of her voice. Better to let the anticipation build for a bit. Sam closed his eyes and gave free rein to his imagination.

Maybe she would be a Nordic type, with legs up to her ears and pale hair streaming down her back. Or perhaps she was a brunette, petite and lovely with a mouth just made for kissing. A redhead? Sam considered that for a moment or two, wondering just what kind of fire a redhead could really produce when put to the test. One thing was for sure: Whatever awaited him had to be a ball of sultry femininity, no doubt bundled up in a nicely done fake-fur coat and boots. He straightened, unable to wait any longer. He would look. Then he would investigate. Then he would likely invite her out to dinner. He put his shoulders back, then turned around, afire with anticipation.

He looked.

Then he felt his jaw slide down on its own.

The creature before him was covered with something, but it wasn't a fake fur. It looked more like mud. The dirt was

flaking off her coat in layers while clinging to her hat and
scarf with admirable tenacity. And not only was she filthy, she
smelled. The fact that he could ascertain that from twenty
paces was truly frightening. It wasn't anything a gallon of
Chanel No. 5 couldn't cure. Sam stared at the apparition, unable to believe it was a woman.

"Good to see ya, kid," Mr. Smith said with an indulgent
chuckle. "Roll in this mornin'?"

"And not a moment too soon," the swamp monster grumbled. "You should see what's been done to my—"

"Boy, here's your things," Mr. Smith interrupted, shoving
Sam's box of supplies at him. "You'd best be headin' home. I
have the feeling there's going to be a storm brewing right
quick."

Sam didn't need to hear that twice. The last storm that had
brewed had left him stranded in twelve inches of mud in the
middle of the road to his rented cabin. If the Tenderfoot Patrol
hadn't come to rescue him, he would have starved to death.
He grabbed his box and made a beeline for the door, slipping
twice on the mud the creature had dragged in with her, but
skillfully avoiding the rotting floorboard by the front door.

"'Bye, Mr. Smith."

"See ya around, boy. Better batten down those hatches."

Sam didn't bother to say anything to the woman as he
passed her. He was far too busy holding his breath so he didn't
have to inhale her fragrant Pig Pen-like aura.

He pulled the door shut behind him and let out the breath
he'd been holding. He paused to clear his head, giving it a
shake for good measure. Nothing like a little fresh air to bring
a man back to his senses. He carefully negotiated a path to his
car, threw the supplies in the back, and mucked his way
around to the driver's side. Twenty minutes and he'd be home.
Maybe he'd go back to the old standby of writing on a legal
pad with a smooth, round number two pencil instead of playing power-surge roulette with his computer. That would certainly save him some aggravation. Then he'd make a filet for
supper. He'd hole up in his nice warm cabin and weather
whatever storm Alaska saw fit to throw at him.

Chapter Two

SYDNEY KINCAID STOOD in Smith's Dry Goods and Sundries and praised the wonders of civilization. She pulled off her filthy knit hat and dragged her fingers through her hair. She'd never felt so dirty in all her life, and it had been her boarder's fault. Damn the woman if she hadn't left the garage door open. The remains of a critter invasion were readily obvious to even the most plugged of noses. A broken window and no hot water had been the last straw. Well, that and the fact that the place was clean. It had taken her almost a half an hour to make it feel like home again.

But now home was comfortably strewn with clutter, and her stomach was about to be filled with something besides trail mix. Life was improving all the time.

"So, Syd," Joe said, pulling out another box and beginning to fill it with Sydney's standing order of just-add-water suppers. "How'd it go?"

"How does it ever go?" Sydney grumbled as she crossed the store to toss her hat on Joe's counter. "I've spent the last four months pulling one city boy after another out of places they never should have been looking at in magazines. Don't people realize this is *wilderness* up here?"

"Reckon they don't," Joe said, rearranging a few cans of stew.

"If that wasn't bad enough," Sydney continued, irritated, "I go home to find my house clean. Just what kind of neat freak did you rent my extra room to, anyway? I thought you said she was a writer. I expected lots of crumpled-up balls of typing paper hiding under the coffee table."

"You could have done worse," Joe offered. "Tidy isn't bad."

"I don't like it," Sydney groused, reaching into Joe's candy jar and helping herself to a piece of licorice. "I didn't see any curlers in the bathroom, but I'll bet she's just as lily white and frilly as they come. She's a baker, too, can you believe it?"

Joe pushed Sydney's box at her. "Hurry on home, girl. There's a storm brewing, and I wouldn't want you to miss out on it."

"You mean be out in it, don't you, Joe?"

"Reckon so."

Sydney pulled out another piece of licorice. "Who was that man?" she asked casually. He might have been a potential tour-guiding customer, and she wasn't one to miss out on a business opportunity.

"What man?" Joe asked, blinking innocently.

Sydney chewed even more casually. "You know, that city guy. Old man Anderson was grumbling about him being a writer or something."

Joe reached under the counter and pulled out a magazine. "There's a piece in here of his. Read it myself. It wasn't bad, if you like that sort of thing."

Sydney looked at the cooking magazine and dismissed it as something she'd be interested in only if hell froze over. She turned her attentions back to the matter at hand. "Is he planning on staying?" Or course, she wasn't *truly* interested, but she could appreciate a fine-looking man as well as the next girl.

"I wouldn't know what his plans are. I suppose you could ask him the next time you see him."

Sydney shook her head. "We're attracting these writer types like flies up here. The next thing you know, we're going to need a stoplight or two."

"We just might," Joe agreed.

Sydney shoved the magazine in her box and made her way out to her mud-encrusted Jeep, trying to put the man out of her mind. She'd probably never see him again, so there wasn't much use in worrying about it. Especially since she wasn't a girl on the lookout for romance. She had her father's trail-guide business to keep running, and her own reputation to maintain. City boys with eyes as green as spring leaves and hair the color of sable just didn't fit into her plans. The man probably couldn't put a match to a handful of dry kindling and get anything but smoke.

She drove home slowly, tired to the bone. Four months of being out in the wild, going into Anchorage only to wash her clothes and pick up another group of greenhorns, had left her aching for home and hot showers. Of course, her shower today might not be hot, thanks to whatever damage Samantha had done, but that could be fixed in time. First a shower, then maybe she'd come out and find a hot meal waiting for her. The cake sitting on the counter had been delicious. Sydney hadn't meant to eat all but one slice, but she hadn't had a decent meal in weeks. Sam was good for something, even if just for cooking. Joe had been annoyingly closemouthed in his letters, not dropping a single hint about what Sam wrote.

Sydney braked suddenly, sending the Jeep into a skid. It settled to a stop, and she looked off into the distance, feeling dread settle into the pit of her stomach. Sam was a Samantha, wasn't she? It really was possible that two writers had moved into Flaherty over the summer, wasn't it?

She knew all she had to do was pull out the magazine Joe had given her and check.

She shook her head. Joe wouldn't have rented out her house to a man. He was a terrible matchmaker, but even he had to draw the line somewhere. Besides, it was a food magazine. What kind of guy would write for a food magazine?

Sydney put the car back into gear and eased the clutch out until the tires caught. Sam was no doubt pleasingly plump and terribly maternal—just the kind of roommate Sydney had been looking for. If she could be convinced not to try to fix anything else electrical, that was.

The door to the garage was closed, and Sydney took it for granted that Sam had parked her car inside. A lecture about keeping the door closed could wait until after dinner. No sense in upsetting the cook. Sydney'd had enough trail rations over the past few months that she was willing to keep her mouth shut in exchange for some real food.

She left her Jeep in the gravel pit that served as a driveway,

then walked into the house, dropping her muddy coat on the
floor and discarding her hat, gloves, and scarf along the way to
the basement. She went down and made a few minor adjust-
ments to the water heater. Someone had been trying to turn it
up and turned it down instead. Sydney shook her head in disbelief. She'd have to put her foot down about Sam loitering
anywhere but the kitchen. It could be hazardous to their health.

She discarded the rest of her clothes on the way to the
bathroom. Sponge baths in the privacy of her tent just hadn't
cut it for her. Already she could feel the hard spray washing
away the layers of grime, taking the tension with it. Baby-
sitting helpless executives was hard on a woman. Maybe Sam
would hear her washing up, take the hint, and start dinner.
Maybe she would even warm up the last piece of that chocolate cake and top it off with some ice cream.

The guest room door opened, and Sydney hastily reached
for a towel to cover her otherwise naked self. She'd say a
quick hello, then duck into the bathroom for her well-
deserved shower. After all, she wasn't exactly dressed for a
long conversation.

Sydney looked at her housemate.

Then she blinked again, just to make sure she wasn't imag-
ining things.

Yes, she recognized that hair the color of sable, those
spring green eyes, and the rugged, handsome face. Worn
jeans hugged slim hips and long, muscular legs. A long-
sleeved rugby shirt revealed muscular arms and a broad
chest—and probably hid a nice, flat belly. It was a hard body,
one she had only glimpsed in the general store, one she had
actually thought might serve as tasty dream fodder later in
front of the fire.

And then full realization hit.

Sam was anything but a Samantha.

"You!" she squeaked.

"*You!*"

Sydney fled into the bathroom. "What in the hell are you
doing here?" she shouted.

"Me?" the man yelled back. "What in the hell are *you* doing here?"

Sydney locked the door. Then she put the clothes hamper
in front of it for good measure.

"This is *my* house!"

"Your house?" her unwelcome greenhorn responded, sounding more annoyed than he should have, given the circumstances. "Lady, you're losing it. You might be Sydney's girlfriend, but you can still haul your butt right out of that bathroom and get moving because he's not here right now to clean you up!"

Sydney couldn't believe her ears. "You idiot, *I'm* Sydney Kincaid and this is *my* house."

"You're Sydney Kincaid? But Joe told me—"

Sydney wanted to scream in frustration. It was pure frustration, not fear. No, she wasn't afraid. She was never afraid. She'd faced down three grizzly bears, four groups of chauvinistic city boys, and an army of wilderness inconveniences and come out on top. A tenderfoot writer from New York was nothing compared to what she'd been up against. She pulled the rifle down from its hook over the commode, loaded it with the shells hiding in the empty can of Noxzema, and pointed it at the door.

"Joe's an old fool and I'll give him a piece of my mind just as soon as you get out of my house so I can get dressed," she said, putting her no-nonsense-now-boys edge in her voice. "Beat it."

"Look, lady, I've got rent paid up through December—"

"I'll give it back." She didn't want to say it, because she certainly couldn't afford to be without a boarder over the winter. And damn Joe if he hadn't given Sam a cut rate that guaranteed Sydney would have to keep him on or starve. Her guide services were pricey, but not pricey enough to feed her much past February. She took a deep breath. "Just get your stuff and go."

"I'm not going anywhere," came the annoyed growl. "And since I'm going to be staying, I suggest you start wearing a few more clothes on your way to the bathroom."

Sydney clamped her teeth together and swore silently. She cursed some more as she propped the rifle against the side of the tub and started the shower. She cursed her father for having put only one bathroom in the cabin. She cursed whatever quirk of fate had brought Samuel, not Samantha, MacLeod to Alaska to move his annoying self into her house. She cursed her situation, because she would most definitely have to make

Sam go and that would leave her wallowing in very dire straits indeed.

And she finally, and most thoroughly, cursed Joe for allowing Sam into her house.

Because, despite his convenient cover as owner and operator of Smith's Dry Goods and Sundries, Joe was first and foremost a matchmaker.

And she knew she was number one on his hit list.

Chapter Three

"DAMN WOMAN," SAM grumbled as he flipped a chunk of butter into the pot of drained potatoes. "First she tracks mud in this morning"—he dumped in a splash of milk—"then she leaves all her gear stinking up the front room"—he jammed the beaters into the mixer—"then she does a strip-tease with clothes that ought to be burned, not washed." He turned the mixer on and savagely beat the potatoes to a pulp. "As if I had time to baby-sit a barbarian!"

"What are you still doing here?"

The voice was as smooth and husky as whiskey and immediately brought to mind the vision of a cozy evening spent cuddling in front of the fire on a fur rug. Sam turned off the mixer and shook his head, amazed that such an appealing voice could belong to such an unappealing woman. He wanted to get to know Sydney Kincaid about as much as he wanted to get to know the porcupine that ambled across the front yard every now and then. He turned, prepared for battle.

And forgot every word of the speech he'd thrown together over the past half hour.

It was no wonder she hid under all that mud. Her hair was as dark as midnight, her skin flawless and not needing a speck of makeup to enhance its beauty. Sam put down the mixer and walked over to her, mesmerized. He couldn't remember the last time he'd been so affected by the sight of a woman in a ratty bathrobe. Without thinking about it further, he put his hand under her chin, lifted her face up, and bent his head to kiss her.

And then he froze at the feel of something hard against his belly. He really wanted to believe it was the belt of her robe. Really.

"Get your hands off me," she said in a low, rather unnervingly calm voice.

"Sure thing," he said, lifting his hands and backing away slowly. "Don't shoot. That thing isn't loaded, is it?"

"Want to find out?"

He smiled weakly. "I'm right in the middle of cooking dinner. Filet mignon. Know what that is?"

The sound of the gun being cocked echoed in the stillness of the kitchen.

"I guess you do," he conceded. "Are you hungry?"

"Starved. And I get kind of cranky when I'm starved."

"Yes, I can imagine that's true," he said, wondering how in the world such a good-looking woman could have such a bad temper. He backed up until the counter stopped him. "Think you could put that gun away?"

She gave him an assessing glance. "Why would I want to? It isn't as if you've been very gentlemanly."

"Well, how does 'I can't cook under stress' sound?"

Her eyes narrowed. "Did you make that chocolate cake I saw today, or did you buy it?"

"I made it."

She considered, then lowered the gun. "You won't try anything?"

The barrel was level with his groin. He looked quickly at her face and knew she realized just where she was pointing her weapon. He shook his head vigorously.

"Wouldn't think of it."

The gun was uncocked, then lowered. "Well, then. I'm going back to change. You finish cooking."

"Yes, ma'am."

With a toss of her shoulder-length, unbelievably silky looking hair, she walked out of the room. Sam leaned back against the counter and blew out his breath. Sydney Kincaid was definitely not what he'd been expecting.

He finished the mashed potatoes, pulled the steaks out from under the broiler, tossed a salad, and hastily set the table. He was just pouring water into glasses when Sydney came back into the room. She sat down at the table and started to eat. Sam couldn't believe what he was seeing. He walked around the counter and plunked down a glass of water in front of her.

"Haven't you ever heard of waiting until everyone is sitting at the table before you start eating?"

"Got to get it while it's hot," she said, her mouth full. "And before anyone else gets to it. It's the only way to survive in the wild."

"Well, this is civilization. We can reheat things in the microwave here."

She ignored him. Which was just as well, to Sam's mind, because he was still trying to figure out just what in the hell he was going to do for the next three months, living with a woman whose face said "touch me" and whose actions said "do it and I'll geld you." Oh, why had he ever decided Alaska would be a nice place to hide and write?

He really should have headed for California. Nice, warm beaches overflowing with women whose come-hither looks probably meant come hither. Trying to second-guess Miss Wilderness was too complicated for his poor overworked brain. All he wanted was to go back to his room, turn on his computer, and deal with characters he had control over. The character sitting across from him was way out of his league.

"This is all there was?"

Sam blinked at the sight of her empty plate. He looked at his housemate and blinked again.

"Where did you put it all?"

"I haven't eaten a decent meal in almost four months. Are you going to finish yours? No? Well, I'll do it for you."

Sam watched as his plate was removed from under his nose. She finished his supper, then sat back with a sigh.

"I'm going to sleep now," she said, putting her hand over her mouth and yawning. "Don't be here when I get up."

"Look," he began, "I signed a contract . . ."

"You also let a who knows what into my garage, screwed up my water heater, and cleaned my house. If that wasn't breach of contract, I don't know what is."

"You've got to be kidding."

"I never kid." She rose. "I sleep with a gun, so don't think about trying anything funny."

"I'd rather waltz with an angry polar bear."

Her mouth tightened into a thin line. "I'm sure you would. Which is just fine with me, mister. You can stay the night, but you sure as hell better be gone when I wake up."

And without a single compliment about dinner, or even a thank-you, she left the room. Sam gritted his teeth at her rudeness. No wonder Mr. Smith had laughed so gleefully when Sam had signed his name on the dotted line. Sam had never thought to wonder why no one had wanted to board at the Kincaid house. It had been a cabin straight from one of his Sunday-morning, lots-of-snow-on-the-ground snuggling fantasies. How was he to know the snugglee would rather be snuggling with a rifle than him?

Sam sighed and rose, cleaned off the table, then made himself a peanut-butter-and-jelly sandwich. Though he was tempted to stay just to irritate Sydney, he knew he was probably better off cutting his losses and leaving. But not until after Friday. He needed Sydney's kitchen for his day job. She could put up with him for a while longer.

He cleaned up the kitchen, then headed back to his room. He sat down and turned on his computer, ready to dive into chapter twenty-one.

And then he found himself staring blankly at the computer screen, distracted by the image of a beautiful woman with dark hair and pale eyes. He sighed and turned off the machine. Creation would have to wait until morning. He needed to go to bed before the day could hand him any more surprises.

Though he doubted the Fates or Mr. Smith could top what he'd been handed already.

SYDNEY WOKE, DISORIENTED. Then she realized she was in her own bed, under a toasty-warm comforter, and she smiled. There was nothing quite like coming home. It was one of the reasons she enjoyed her work so much. She never appreciated home more than she did after three or four months out in the wild.

She fumbled for her watch, wanting to know the time and the date. She flopped back on her bed and groaned. Twenty-four hours gone without a trace. She vaguely remembered a trip or two to the bathroom, trips made without encountering her housemate.

She sighed deeply and burrowed back down under the covers. Much as she wanted to kick Sam's arrogant, overbearing self right out the door, she knew she couldn't afford it. Though she was just as good a guide as any man out there, city boys were reluctant to use her. She'd had to cut her fees drastically just to get business. It was the reason she'd decided to rent her spare bedroom. Joe had assured her he would find a suitable renter. Damn him, anyway.

Well, it was either keep Sam or starve. She couldn't give him back the rent money he'd paid all up front because she'd already spent it. She hated the thought, but it looked like she was stuck with him until December.

She rolled out of bed and pulled her robe around her. She rubbed her arms vigorously as she left her bedroom and made her way to the kitchen. She was used to traveling in the dark, when necessary, and had no trouble finding her way. Or spotting the creation that sat cooling on the counter.

Cake. Sydney's mouth began to water at the sight. She wanted it to be warm, but no, that might be too much to hope for. She got a knife, for the sake of propriety, and cut herself a generous slice right out of the bottom tier. Whatever else his flaws, Sam certainly could bake rings around Sara Lee. Sydney closed her eyes and brought the slice up, then opened her mouth to bite.

"Stop!"

Her eyes flew open. She squinted into the beam of a flashlight.

"Don't move."

Sydney stood, frozen to the spot, as the flashlight approached. The cake was very carefully and gingerly removed from her hand.

"Hey—" she protested.

"Quiet," Sam growled. "You just ruined six hours' worth of work, lady, so right now it would be a very good idea for you to just wash your hands and go back to bed."

"It's just cake—"

"It's a wedding cake!" Sam exploded.

"You're getting married?" This guy was certifiable.

"It's not for me! It's for Eunice and Jeremy. Tomorrow afternoon at one o'clock."

His face was illuminated by the flashlight he held between

his forearm and chest as he carefully set the slice of cake onto a plate. And she wanted to laugh.

"You make wedding cakes?"

"It pays the bills. Turn on the light. I've got major surgery to perform here."

Sydney obediently turned on the kitchen light, then she caught an unobstructed view of Sam's face—and his furious expression. She backed up a pace in spite of herself.

"Uh, I'm sorry . . ."

Sam reached behind her and jerked a cake knife out of the pottery utensil holder sitting on the counter. He didn't spare her a glance.

"I didn't realize . . ." she began.

Sam was pulling ingredients out of her cupboards, strange things she didn't usually keep, like flour and sugar. He didn't respond as he got out a bowl and started mixing these foreign substances together.

"Look," she began, his silence starting to make her uncomfortable, "can't you just fix it? Patch it together? It would probably take a lot of time to rebake it."

Sam stopped and turned his head slowly to look at her. "Too bad you couldn't have thought about that before you ruined it."

"I didn't mean to!"

"That hardly matters now, does it?"

"I didn't ask you to come live here," she said, sticking out her chin stubbornly, struggling to find some way to defend herself.

"That really isn't the point, is it, Sydney?"

Sydney felt lower than the lowest grubworm. So she bristled even harder.

"You should have told me not to touch it."

"You've been asleep for twenty-four hours. I didn't want to wake you and find myself without my family jewels." He turned and reached into the refrigerator for a plate encased in Saran Wrap. He handed it to her. "Roast beef sandwich. Here's a can of pop. Go eat it somewhere I don't have to look at you."

"This is *my* house," Sydney said in a last bid to save her pride.

"Yeah, well, this is *my* kitchen at the moment and I don't want you in it."

Sydney clutched the cold can in her hand and walked out of the kitchen with her head held high. No, she wasn't upset. Sam's kindness in making her dinner didn't hurt her. His anger didn't bother her. His assurance earlier that he'd rather dance with an angry bear than touch her didn't trouble her either. After all, she was Sydney Kincaid, wilderness woman. She was every inch her father's daughter, bless his crusty old soul. She'd survived on her own since her seventeenth birthday, since Sydney the elder had died on his way back in from the woodpile. She didn't need anyone. She'd made it all by herself, and damn anyone who tried to imply differently. The very last thing she needed in her life was a man, especially a man who would probably starve to death five yards from the house unless someone showed him the direction back to the kitchen.

She shut and locked her door, put the supper Sam had fixed for her on her nightstand, then threw herself onto her bed and tried to burst into tears.

It didn't work. So she rolled over on her back and looked up at the ceiling. She hadn't cried in thirteen years, not since before her father's funeral. If she hadn't cried then, a simple snubbing by her housemate certainly wasn't going to bring tears to her eyes now.

She ignored her supper and crawled back under the covers. Tomorrow was Eunice and Jeremy's wedding. If she didn't go, the town would think her a chicken and the Clan down at the store would grumble about her cowardice. If she went, the women would shake their heads sadly and pity her that she couldn't find a husband.

Not that she wanted one; no, sir.

No, she reminded herself again as she drifted off to sleep. The very last thing she needed was a man.

Especially one as handsome and useless as Sam.

Chapter Four

THE NEXT AFTERNOON Sam stood in Flaherty's dilapidated Grange hall and felt as if he'd been transported to another planet. His mother would have succumbed to another fainting fit if she could have seen his current surroundings. He found, however, that the place was growing on him. There was something good and solid about the beat-up wood under his feet. He looked around at the reception guests and felt the warmth increase. These were good, honest people. At least he never doubted where he stood with them.

"Oh, Sam," Eunice gushed, "you're *so* talented!"

"It's just a hobby," he said modestly. But if the bride was happy, then so was he.

"Well, I've never seen anything so fancy," she said, looking adoringly at the three-tiered wedding cake adorned with icing flowers. "And look, Jeremy, there's already an indentation where you should cut the first piece. Sam, how in the world did you bake it that way?"

"That's my secret," Sam said pleasantly. He looked over Eunice's head for the culprit. He and Sydney hadn't come to the wedding together, which was no doubt safer where she was concerned. He had the feeling he would have been tempted to strangle her if he'd had her alone in a car in the middle of nowhere.

"You know," Eunice continued, "Mother has already recommended you to all her friends. I'm afraid you'll soon have more business than you can handle."

Sam grimaced. He would spend his mornings baking and his evenings repairing whatever damage Sydney did to his creations. He could hardly wait.

Besides, he already had more business than he could handle. Though the Clan at the general store seemed to find him somewhat lacking, the mothers of Flaherty did not. He was certain it was that author mystique. It would pass. But hopefully not before December. Baking cakes for the local Ladies Aid Society provided him with spare cash and free lunches every Wednesday. A guy couldn't ask for much more than that.

His mother was, however, apoplectic over the news that he was making a living elbow-deep in flour.

His older sister periodically sent him papers to sign that would transfer his assets to her account, on the off chance that his dementia extended to his signature.

Sam turned his thoughts away from his family and back to the wedding guests. It was shaping up to be an afternoon for the annals.

First he was accosted by Estelle Dalton and her eighteen-year-old ingénue daughter, Sylvia. Sam took one look at Sylvia and decided against it. No matter that he was thirty-five and almost old enough to be her father; the girl looked like she couldn't fix a broken fingernail, much less a leaky sink. They would drown within a month.

Then there was Ruth Newark and her daughter, Melanie. No, definitely not. Both of them looked like they'd just stepped out of the pages of *Vogue*. Sam had visions of watching his royalty checks be spent faster than he could haul them in. Then Ruth announced that she fully intended to live with her daughter and future son-in-law. Sam wondered why. Then Ruth pinched him on the behind when Melanie's back was turned, and he understood. He fled to a safer corner of the reception hall.

Next there was Bernice Hammond and her daughters Alvinia, Myra, and Wilhelmina. Sam immediately had visions of the women dressed in breastplates, brandishing swords and making him listen to Wagnerian opera for hours at a time. Not that having a handywoman around the house wasn't an appealing thought. But a quartet of Amazons just wasn't for him. These were mountain women. They needed mountain men.

He didn't want to grow a beard, and he wasn't all that fond of plaid flannel shirts—his ancestry aside. No, these gals were not for him.

Sydney walked through his line of vision, and he felt a scowl settle over his features. Now, there was definitely *not* the right woman for him. She was irritating. She was selfish. She had no manners at the dinner table. It was no wonder she was still single.

"Well," a smooth voice purred from beside him, "would you look at that?"

Sam looked down and gulped when he saw Ruth Newark sidling up to him. He suppressed the urge to cover his backside.

"What?" he asked, not really wanting to know the answer.

"Sydney Kincaid. Have you ever seen such a pitiful creature?"

Sam looked at Sydney. She was wearing jeans and a dark blue sweater. Not exactly wedding-reception attire, but it certainly suited her. She must have felt him looking at her because she turned around. She looked at him and smiled weakly. He started to smile back, then remembered how annoyed he was with her. He scowled at her. She turned away.

"Joe's been trying to set her up for years," Ruth continued. One of her hands disappeared behind her back. Sam took a step to his left, moving his buns away from certain trouble.

"Oh?" he managed.

"No one will take the bait. Why would they? She can't cook, she can't keep house. Perfectly worthless as wife material." Ruth turned to him and put her hand on his chest. "Poor Sam, stuck out at the Kincaid place with that creature. Why don't you move in with us, honey?" She dragged her fingers down his chest. "You can have my bed. I'd be more than willing to sleep on the couch just to get you out of that wild woman's house. Or maybe we could share the bed. If you want."

Sam watched Ruth's hand slide down his belly, over his belt. He hastily backed away with a muffled yelp.

"Now, Sam," Ruth coaxed, "don't be shy."

Sam had never considered himself a coward; rather, he was

a man who knew when to cut his losses and run. So he ran, straight for the men's room.

He hid out there until the men who came in started to look at him strangely. He knew better than to hang around any longer. His reputation was tattered enough as it was. So he crept back into the reception hall, keeping his eyes peeled for Ruth the Bun Molester.

The Clan from the general store stood huddled near one end of the buffet table. They looked terribly uncomfortable in their Sunday best, but Sam noticed they didn't let that stop them from noting everything that went on around them. The reception would no doubt provide fat for them to chew on for quite some time.

The Ladies Aid Society stood at the other end of the buffet table, probably discussing the Clan. Then again, maybe they were discussing the Jell-O salad Mrs. Fisher had brought. Sam had overheard someone say she'd used regular marshmallows instead of the mini variety. The ensuing uproar had been enormous.

The rest of the population stood around in groups, dividing themselves up by age. Sam felt comfortable with none of them, so he remained against the wall, hoping he could blend in with the woodwork.

The bride and groom stepped up to the table, and the cake ceremony began. As Eunice made a comment about Sam's cake-cutting-guide indentations, Sam searched the room for his misbehaving housemate, determined to give her a few more glares before the afternoon was over.

He found her without much trouble. She was at the far side of the reception hall, leaning back against the wall in the same way he was. She was alone and watching Eunice and Jeremy with an expression he didn't understand right off. When he finally figured out what it was, he felt like someone had slugged him in the gut.

It was hunger. It wasn't envy, it wasn't disdain; it was hunger, plain and simple.

He watched people drift past her. Men her age ignored her. Women her age gave her looks that would have made most women break down and weep. Sydney did nothing, but her spine stiffened with each look. Even from across the room,

Sam could see that. The Ladies Aid Society snubbed her with a thoroughness that made Sam's blood pressure rise. Not even the Clan came to her rescue.

Sam's scowl faded into a thoughtful frown. This was something he hadn't expected. If there was one thing he wouldn't have figured on, it was that Sydney Kincaid would be vulnerable. But there she was, looking so lost and forlorn that he could hardly stop himself from striding out into the middle of the room and blasting the general population for ignoring her. Sydney might be irritating and pigheaded, but she didn't deserve this. The men should have been fighting among themselves to get at her. Instead, they avoided her like three-day-old fish.

Then Sydney met his eyes. She pulled herself up to her full height and threw him a scowl that would have only infuriated him ten minutes earlier. Now he understood exactly why she was glaring at him.

But there was no use in letting her in on his realization. So he glared back while his mind worked furiously, trying to assimilate what he'd just learned and understand what he wanted to do with that knowledge. Was it pity he felt? No, he didn't think so. It was something that went far deeper than that. Seeing Sydney vulnerable, watching her draw her dignity around her like a cloak, had touched something deep inside him, something he'd never felt before.

When he realized what it was, he had to lean back against the wall for support.

She had awakened his chivalry.

It was frightening.

It was obviously a latent character flaw that had been lurking in a forgotten corner of his Scottish soul. He wondered if there was some ancestor he ought to be cursing for it.

But as he turned the notion over in his mind, he found that the waves of noble sentiment that coursed through him were irresistible. He wanted to stand straighter. He wanted to find a sword and wave it around his head in an Errol Flynn-like manner, scattering enemies like leaves. The thought of rescuing Sydney Kincaid from injustice was tantalizing beyond belief.

Assuming she wanted to be rescued.

He shook aside that niggling doubt and put his shoulders back. He would rescue her. In fact, he was going to make the best damn knight in shining armor she'd ever seen.

Carefully, of course. He had fond hopes of fathering a few children in the future. No sense in getting Sydney's trigger finger itching too badly at first.

He took a deep breath. Then he fixed his most formidable frown on his face and crossed the reception hall to her, threading his way through the dancers, skirting the Ladies Aid Society and the Clan, and rounding the buffet table to where Sydney stood against the wall, looking as if she were going to run at any moment. But she stood her ground. He smiled to himself. Yes, sir, Sydney Kincaid would never back away from a fight.

He slapped his hand against the wall next to her head. "I suppose you heard about my cake-cutting guide."

Her pale eyes flashed. "What of it?"

"You just about ruined my reputation. I'd say that means you owe me."

"I don't owe you anything—"

"The Clan tells me your father always paid his debts. A pity his daughter doesn't have the same sense of honor."

Ouch, that had to have stung. He waited for her to slap his face, and he knew he would have deserved it. Instead, she started to wilt right there in front of him. And that he couldn't bear. He had to do something drastic.

"Giving up already?" he demanded.

Well, that took care of the withering. The fire immediately came back to her eyes. "All right. What do you want?"

"I've already paid up through December. I'm moved in and I don't want to move out. The way I see it, you owe me a place to stay." She started to balk, and he quickly continued. "You wouldn't want word to get around that you're a chicken, would you?"

"That's blackmail," she snarled.

He nodded.

She gritted her teeth and looked away. Sam watched the wheels turn, wondering what she wrestled with.

"I won't bother you," he said, in a low voice. "I'll be a perfect gentleman. You won't even know I'm there," he lied. He fully intended to give her no choice but to notice him. And he had the feeling he knew just how to do it.

"You'll cook?" she asked.

Bingo. "You bet."

"Cakes?"

"Whatever you want."

She looked back up at him and frowned. "Don't break any more windows. And don't mess with the water heater."

"Done." He held out his hand. "Truce?"

She ignored his hand. "Get out of my way. I've had enough of this wedding garbage. And come home soon. I'm ready for dinner."

Come home soon. Sam rubbed his fingers over his mouth to hide his smile. Maybe there would come a day when Sydney Kincaid would say those words and mean them in an entirely different way.

Now all he had to do was figure out how to convince her that she *wanted* to mean them in an entirely different way.

Because, whether he wanted it or not, he had just fallen head over heels in like with the orneriest woman west of the Hudson.

Chapter Five

SYDNEY BROUGHT IN an armload of wood and shivered as she dumped it in the bin next to the fireplace. It had taken her an entire week to chop enough to last until the new year. On Monday she'd been a bit irritated that Sam wasn't coming out to help her. On Tuesday she'd been completely annoyed with him. Either she wasn't very good at hiding her emotions, Sam was very bright, or he had begun to feel guilty, because he'd come out Wednesday morning, dressed in sweats and sneakers, ready to help.

He'd succeeded only in almost chopping off all the toes on his right foot.

Sydney had decided right then that chopping the wood herself was far less aggravating than watching over Sam while he helped. So she'd sent him back inside to play on his computer while she worked like a dog.

Well, at least they'd be warm for the next couple of months. The cabin was actually centrally heated and had two backup generators in case the main power supply went out. The wood served as merely a last resort, as well as something of a luxury. There wasn't anything Sydney liked better than to turn off all the lights, sit in front of the fire and dream she was sitting there with an attentive man. He didn't have to be gorgeous, or built like a football player; he just had to be nice. Of course, if he was gorgeous and built she wouldn't argue.

And just such a man was living with her.

She brushed her hands on her jeans and walked out of the house. She had to get out. Fast—before she started to let her imagination run away with her. She backed her Jeep out of the double garage, then got out to close the door. Sam bounded out onto the porch.

"Where're you going?"

"Town," she said shortly. *Please don't say you want to come along.*

"I want to come along. Wait for me, Syd."

She closed her eyes briefly and prayed for strength. It wasn't that he was handsome. It wasn't that he was built like a linebacker without the excess pudge around the middle. It wasn't that he could cook up a meal like a trained chef.

It was the way he said her name.

She got into the Jeep and slammed the door shut. She closed her eyes and rested her head against the steering wheel. Letting Sam stay had been a very bad idea. Guilt was a very bad thing. She would have kicked him out if he hadn't held that stupid cake over her head.

The passenger door opened, the car dipped slightly and the door closed.

"Hey, what's the matter?" His low, husky voice washed over her like a soothing, warm wave. "Want me to drive?"

"No, I'm fine." She lifted her head and rubbed her eyes. "I'm fine."

"You've been working too hard." Strong fingers were suddenly working their way under the collar of her coat to massage her neck. "I should have helped you with the wood. I'm sorry, Sydney."

"You would have lost a limb by the end of the week," she said, pulling away. "I just haven't been sleeping well."

Sam retreated back to his side of the Jeep. "You'll have to come home and take a nap before dinner. Let's get going."

Sydney eyed the package on Sam's lap as they drove toward town. "What's that?"

"First draft. My agent thinks I've been doing nothing but napping all summer." He flashed her a smile that made her knees weak. "She has a rather inaccurate impression of my manliness, I'm afraid."

Sydney doubted that. No woman with eyes could have

formed an inaccurate impression of Sam's manliness. Sydney concentrated on the road.

"Do you ever read espionage novels?"

"Never," Sydney fibbed firmly. "I haven't got the patience for them."

"Romances?"

"Not those, either," she lied. Wow, two lies in the space of ten seconds. With any luck, Sam would never look in her room and see what filled her bookshelves. "I've only got time to read up on work stuff. You know, trail information and things. Wilderness studies. Hunting techniques."

"You're such a stud," he said with a laugh.

Normally, that kind of comment would have stung deeply. But the way Sam grinned at her took all the sting away. She smiled weakly.

"I have a reputation to maintain."

"I hear you're the best."

"Oh?" Now, this was news. "Who from?"

"Mr. Smith. The Clan. Even Mrs. Fisher, who doesn't know when it's polite to use regular marshmallows and when it isn't. She was complaining Wednesday at the Ladies Aid meeting that someone needs to marry you and saddle you with a dozen kids before you run her sons out of business. A backhanded compliment, of course, but it was still a compliment."

"She's an old biddy," Sydney grumbled. Secretly, she was pleased. Maybe things were starting to look up.

Then why did the thought of half a dozen sable-haired, green-eyed children running around her house seem more appealing than showing dozens of spoiled executives the beauty of her land?

The general store saved her from speculating about that disturbing thought. She pulled to a stop and turned off the engine.

"Anything you want inside?" she asked.

"I have a list. I'm just going to run to the post office, then I'll come meet you." He tapped the end of her nose with his finger. "Don't leave without me. I'm making apricot chicken tonight."

"I'm convinced."

He looked at her with a strange little smile before he got out of the car and made his way across the street to the post office in his high-top sneakers. Sydney shook her head as she walked up to the porch of the store. She needed to think about something more practical than Samuel MacLeod's smiles.

His feet. Yes, that was the ticket. Sam needed boots. Maybe Joe had an extra pair lying around. If not, he could order a pair. Sam wouldn't survive the winter without them.

She walked into the store, nodded to Joe, and approached the Clan. They grunted a greeting. Sydney jammed her hands in the pockets of her jeans and bestowed a rare smile on them.

"What's new, fellas?"

"Kilpatrick's heading south," Zeke grumbled. "I said he'd never make it up here. Born and bred in California. No spine at all."

"*I* said he'd fold," Amos said, leaning over to deposit a hefty bit of spit into the spittoon. "Guiding's a man's job. Ain't that so, Sydney?"

"You bet, Amos," Sydney said, rocking back on her heels. It was no easy feat in her boots, but she'd had plenty of practice. "Not for cowards."

Zeke looked up at her with a disapproving frown. "Still got that writer fella out at your place, Sydney?"

"He's paid through December," Sydney said defensively.

"I heard Ruth Newark offered him a place. He shoulda taken it. Ain't right to have him out at your house, Sydney. Your pa wouldn't have liked it."

Sydney frowned right back at him. "He's paid through December," she repeated. "Money's money, Zeke."

"And he's a single boy, Sydney."

Sydney felt her good humor evaporate. "It isn't as if he wants anything to do with me," she said sharply, then spun around and walked over to the counter. She shoved her list at Joe and pretended a mighty interest in the contents of Joe's glass case. She could name all the flies there and could tell which ones were best for what kind of fishing. Yessiree, that was certainly the kind of knowledge she needed to attract a man.

She looked up as the door opened, expecting to see Sam. Instead, she saw Melanie Newark and Frank Slater. Frank was the only male in Flaherty who had ever given her the time of day. He thought it was great that she had her own business, and he had even asked her out on a date. Once. Her one and only date.

"Hey, Sydney." Frank smiled, coming over to her. "How's it going?"

"Great, Frank. How are you?"

"Frank, stop," Melanie hissed.

Frank threw Melanie a faintly annoyed look. "What?"

"What are you doing, you idiot?" Melanie spluttered.

"Well . . ."

"Frank, you come away from her."

"Now, Melanie . . ."

"You know she's desperate for a husband. Or maybe she isn't. Either way, you don't want to stand too close. And I certainly don't want you talking to her. It will ruin your reputation. Mother says no self-respecting man would get within ten feet of Sydney Kincaid."

"Sure, Melanie," Frank mumbled, moving away. "I guess you're right." He didn't spare Sydney another glance.

Sydney looked back down at the case, blinking furiously. She didn't care what Melanie thought, or Frank for that matter. They were just stupid. Stupid, idiotic, ignorant jerks who didn't have a kind bone in their bodies.

"Here's my list, Joe," a deep voice said directly behind her. "Alphabetically, just how you like it. Sydney, did you give Joe your list?"

She nodded, keeping her head down, mortified that Sam had probably heard all of Melanie's diatribe.

"Why, Sam," Melanie purred, "how nice to see you again."

Sydney peeked to her right in time to see Melanie shove Frank out of her way so she could get closer to Sam.

"Mother wanted me to invite you out for supper tonight."

"Hey," Frank complained, "I was coming out for supper—"

Melanie glared briefly at Frank, then smiled at Sam. "What do you say, Sam?"

It was the last straw. Sydney knew when to concede the battle. Not that she wanted Sam. No, sir. But he was her housemate, after all. She couldn't help but feel a little proprietary where he and his chocolate cakes were concerned. She backed up, intending to make a clean getaway before Sam started discussing his dinner plans.

She backed up straight into Sam's hard body. He grabbed a fistful of her jacket and held her immobile.

"Can't," he said cheerfully. "Sydney's going to teach me

how to fish this afternoon, then we're going to fry up our catches tonight."

Sydney turned around, as best she could with him still clutching her coat, and gaped at him.

"Isn't that so, Syd?"

She could have sworn he winked at her. She couldn't even manage a reply. He pulled the hood of her coat up over her hair.

"Why don't you go out and warm up the Jeep? I'll get Frank to help me out with the goods. And, Syd, do you think I need boots for the winter? Joe, have you got any boots? Get moving, Sydney. We haven't got all day. The fish will be asleep by the time we get out to the river."

Sydney got help to the door. Sam kept up a steady stream of nonsense conversation as he steered her past the booby-trapped floorboard and pushed her out the door.

"Go start the car," he said in a low voice. "I want a quick getaway before Melanie's mother gets here. Move it."

Sydney moved it. She walked out to her car, crawled in under the wheel, and started the motor. Then she put her head down on the steering wheel and tried to cry. It didn't happen. She steeped herself in the humiliation she'd just been through, repeating Melanie's words over and over again in her head. No tears were forthcoming. Not even the knowledge that Sam had wanted to leave quickly not because of her but because of Melanie's mother brought any tears to her eyes. As if he would actually want to stick up for her!

Though he had. Rather nicely, too. She shook her head. He hadn't meant it. He was just a nice person. He wanted nothing to do with her. He probably felt the same way all the other men in Flaherty felt. Sydney Kincaid wasn't good wife material. A woman who couldn't cook or keep house was a bad bet for marriage. Best stay away from her. Wouldn't want to ruin your reputation or anything.

The driver's side door opened. "Keys."

Sydney didn't move, so Sam reached in for the keys. She listened to him load their supplies into the back. By the sound of it, the supplies were numerous enough to last them through the winter. It was just as well. It would start snowing soon enough, and they'd be trapped together. Alone in her house.

Too bad nothing would happen.

"Move over, sugar."

Sydney looked up at Sam—handsome, kind Sam who stood inside the open door.

"What?"

"I'm driving home. Move over."

"But—"

He picked her up in his arms, carried her around to the other side of the car, unlocked the door, and put her in. He buckled the seat belt, returned to the driver's seat, and started up the motor. And he said nothing, all the way home. Sydney grew more miserable with each mile that passed. Maybe he was having second thoughts. Maybe Melanie had talked him into coming out to dinner. Maybe he was going to stay once he got there. She wasn't sure why it bothered her as much as it did, but there was no denying it.

She unloaded the groceries with Sam, then helped him put them away. And when they were done, he plunked her down on the counter as if she'd been a rump roast and slapped his hands down on either side of her.

"We've got a problem," he said, looking her square in the eye.

She could hardly swallow. "You're going to dinner at Melanie's?"

"Hell, no. Her mother fondled me at Eunice and Jeremy's reception. At the reception, mind you. No, I am definitely not going to dinner at Melanie's house."

Sydney couldn't stop a small smile. "That's really a compliment, you know. She doesn't grope just anyone."

"I'd rather be snubbed. Which brings me to what I want to discuss."

Sydney's smile faded. He was leaving. He was leaving and she was stupid enough to want him to stay.

"The way I see it," Sam continued with his hands still resting on either side of her, "we both have what others would consider a problem."

"We do?"

"We do. I can't find a wife because I can't tell one end of a hammer from the other. You can't find a husband because you can't cook. That about sums it up, doesn't it?"

She nodded slowly. "That's about the size of it."

"So," he said, clearing his throat and looking at something

behind her, over her right shoulder, "I figure we can help each other. You can help me become mechanical and I'll help you learn how to cook. Of course, this means I'll have to stay here with you longer than I'd planned. Probably three or four months more." He sighed. "I'm really hopeless when it comes to fixing things. It might take you that long to rectify my lack of studliness."

He was staying. Sydney blinked back the tears that should have been there at his announcement.

"You think a man wants a woman who can cook?"

"Absolutely. And not just cook. She has to be a fabulous cook. It'll take me at least six months to teach you what you'll have to know. Maybe more if you really want to become marketable. Especially since I'll have to keep working on my revisions."

"So you won't be able to help me every day?" *He was staying.*

"We'll see. What sorts of things do you do during the winter? Will you be busy a lot?"

"I just read. And watch television." She paused and looked at something behind his left shoulder. "I could fix you lunch and things while you work. Just to practice," she added hastily.

"Of course," he nodded, just as hastily. "All right, let's have a plan. We'll get up in the mornings and make breakfast together. Can you scramble eggs?"

"If it doesn't come prewrapped and precooked, I can't deal with it."

Sam smiled. "Eggs first, then. Once we've finished breakfast, you can teach me something to increase my machismo. I bought boots today, so I don't have to worry about losing any toes."

"Good point."

"Then we'll make lunch. Then I'll either work on my book in the afternoon while you read up on your trail-guiding studies or I'll teach you how to bake. How does that sound?"

"Fair enough," she said. In reality, it sounded like bliss. Maybe if she were exceptionally inept, Sam would stay until spring.

Or summer.

Or fall.

Or forever.

He tapped the end of her nose. "Go take a nap, sweetheart. Your eyelids are already at half-mast. I'll wake you up in time for dinner."

"Apricot chicken?"

"What else?"

She hopped off the counter and pushed him out of the way. "I suppose this is a good thing," she said, trying to sound businesslike. "I guess it's about time I got married, and I'm sure not attracting any prospects the way I am."

He smiled. "We're doing each other a favor. All I'm getting is my butt pinched the way I am now. I'd like to be respected for my prowess in the tool shed."

Sydney nodded and left the kitchen. She was happy. For the first time in years, she was happy. And that happiness lasted until she closed her bedroom door and flopped down onto her bed. Then her happiness was replaced by hollowness. How many nights had she lain in that very bed and dreamed of a man who would want her? Too many to count. She'd pretended it hadn't hurt her feelings. Men were stupid, and she hadn't wanted any part of them.

Until Sam. He was handsome and funny and kind. And he couldn't stand Melanie Newark's mother. That said a great deal about his character. He wasn't afraid to bake mouthwatering cakes. He couldn't start a fire on his own, and she half wondered how he managed to work the oven without help.

But she wanted him to want her. She wanted him to look at her with those leaf-green eyes, smile that secret little smile of his, and say, "Yes, Syd, I think you're perfect and I want you." And if he thought the perfect woman was a woman who could cook like a French chef, then that's what she would become.

She closed her eyes and fell asleep, dreaming about flour and sugar.

Chapter Six

SAM CAME OUT of the bathroom a week later to the sound of pots clanking and a certain wilderness woman cursing. He walked through the living room and stopped just shy of the kitchen, curious as to what Sydney was up to. The smell of burnt eggs immediately assaulted his nose.

"Damn it, anyway, I'm going to burn all the winter supplies before November if somebody doesn't start cooperating right now! Go down the disposal, you ungrateful little sonsa—"

Sam indulged in a grin. It was no wonder Sydney had such a tough reputation as a trail guide if she talked to her city boys the way she talked to her breakfast ingredients. The woman was adorable. Sam could hardly stop himself from striding into the kitchen and kissing her senseless.

No, that wouldn't do. In the first place, he'd promised to be a gentleman. In the second, he had the sinking feeling that she had her heart set on Frank Slater. Why, Sam didn't know. The guy was a wuss. All right, so he wasn't exactly a wuss. He could hunt and fish and do all those Alaska things, but he couldn't tell the infinitive form from the subjunctive, and Sam had his doubts he knew what a pronoun was. And he was dating Melanie. If that didn't say something about his character, and his intelligence, Sam didn't know what did. No, Frank Slater wasn't for Sydney.

Now to convince her of that.

Carefully.

Sam cleared his throat and entered the kitchen.

"Hey, Syd, what's for breakfast?

"Oh," she said, blinking innocently, "eggs. Just like you taught me, Sam. I'm just getting ready to cook them," she added, waving the pan around, probably to make the smell of burned eggs dissipate.

"It sounds great. Want me to make the toast?"

"No. You just go on in and sit down in the living room. I'll call you when it's ready."

Sam let her off the hook and went to hide in the living room. After a week of lessons, Sydney still couldn't scramble eggs to save her life. They were either too runny or too dry. Sam didn't care either way. One day she'd be making runny eggs just for him, and he'd eat them with just as much gusto then as he did now.

Half an hour later, he sat facing a plate of quivering eggs. It was a lucky thing he usually liked his over very easy or he might have been slightly sick at the prospect facing him. Sydney looked like she wanted to cry, so he ate not only his breakfast but hers, then he made her some unburned toast. And he started to gird up his loins for his humiliating part of the bargain: his wilderness-man studies.

He didn't care about hammers. He didn't care about wrenches or screwdrivers or power tools. He didn't care about what made the generator tick. It provided light and heat, and power for his computer. He didn't want to know where that power came from or what to do when the power was off. Sydney would be around for that.

But today was different. He was going to learn how to fish. Sydney promised him she would teach him what kind of lures lured what kind of fish. Sam could thread a needle about as easily as he could jump over the moon, so he anticipated a great deal of difficulty in hooking the lures to the string. Fishing line. Whatever they called it, he knew it was going to give his fingers fits and Sydney would have to give him a great deal of help.

And if that wasn't enough to make a man grin, he didn't know what was.

He buzzed through four chapters of the revisions his agent had requested, then cheerfully waited in the living room for

Sydney to go get their fishing gear. She came in with a tackle box and two rods. Sam opened the box the moment she set it down and peeked inside. He held up a little silver fish with three hooks hanging from his underbelly.

"Cute," he noted.

"No, not cute," Sydney corrected. "Clever. Efficient. Practical. Lures are never cute, Sam."

"I'll keep that in mind. Whatever happened to salmon eggs? Or worms?"

"Minor-league stuff," Sydney said, reaching for a rod. "You're fishing with the big boys now."

"Do your city boys know all about this when they come up?"

She shrugged. "Some do. Some would like to think they do."

"Why do I have the feeling they don't like hearing what they're doing wrong from a woman?"

"Because you're very bright, Sam. Now, pay attention. I'm going to explain the parts of the reel to you."

He leaned back against the couch and moved just the slightest bit closer to her. "I'm listening."

"This up front is the drag knob. It adjusts the tension. Then we have the spool. See how the fishing line is wound around it, then fed through the guide?"

Sam nodded obediently.

"Now when you're casting, you release the line here, by pressing this button. Then you drag the lure back toward you by cranking the handle . . ."

Sam stopped listening after that. It wasn't that he wasn't interested in fishing. He didn't mind salmon, barbecued with lots of lemon on it. He found he just couldn't concentrate. Sydney was just so doggone beautiful. He wondered why in the world every male in Flaherty over the age of ten wasn't beating a path to her door. Frank Slater probably was. Sam didn't care for that thought.

"Sam?"

He blinked and realized she was looking at him. Her pale blue eyes were wide and her lips parted just slightly. Sam had the overwhelming urge to bend his head and capture her mouth with his.

"Sam, you look flushed. Did my eggs do you in?"

"I'm fine," he said. But his voice sounded suspiciously hoarse, even to his ears.

"Do you want me to go back over the parts of the rod?"

"No. Keep going."

She launched into a discussion of lures, and Sam did his best to follow. But her perfume kept getting in his way. He couldn't decide if it was something she'd put on, her shampoo, or the dryer sheets he'd used in the last load of wash. He leaned closer for a better whiff and bumped his chin on her shoulder when she suddenly leaned back.

"Sam!"

"Sorry," he said, rubbing his jaw. "I was just moving in for a closer look."

"Here, let's put the tackle box on your lap. It'll be safer that way."

Sam let her put the heavy box on his lap, then he sniffed unobtrusively when she leaned over to pull out a lure. Could have been shampoo. Could have been the dryer sheet. Whatever it was, it was sexy as hell and it was making him light-headed.

"Sam?"

"I'm just a little dizzy," he said, drawing his hand over his eyes. "It'll pass. I must have stayed up too late."

"Oh, no," she said, lifting her arm and sniffing her wrist. "It's that insect repellent I put on. I'll try not to get it under your nose again." She met his eyes. "Then again, maybe I should go wash it off."

He felt himself falling. And then he felt himself falling. Literally. Sydney caught the tackle box.

"Sam!"

"Oh, this is bad," he moaned as he lunged to his feet and ran for the bathroom, where he summarily lost both breakfast and lunch.

"Sam, open up!" Sydney shouted, pounding on the door.

Sam flushed the toilet, then rinsed out his mouth in the sink. He looked at himself in the mirror and smiled weakly at the pale shadow that stared back at him.

"Sam, good grief, what happened?" Sydney had pushed open the door and caught sight of his face. She blanched to about the same color. "I did this to you," she whispered.

"Bad eggs. Not your fault. Just help me get to bed."

She put her arm around him and helped him into his room. Well, now, this had been one way to get her there. Not exactly how his chivalrous self would have planned it, but drastic times called for drastic measures.

"Oh, Sam, I'm so sorry."

"Honey, it wasn't you," Sam said, sitting down gingerly and willing his stomach to stop churning. "It might not have been the eggs. It could have been the chicken from last night."

She looked like she just might cry for real this time. Sam took her hand and squeezed it.

"Syd, this is going to give you a great chance to hone your pampering skills. Every man loves to be pampered. I'll show you just what to do."

"You're right," she said, sounding relieved. "Let's get you comfortable, and then I'll wait on you hand and foot until you're better."

And whoever said food poisoning couldn't be fun?

Chapter Seven

THIRTY-SIX HOURS LATER Sydney sat at Sam's bedside and prayed she hadn't killed him.

First had come twelve hours of staying out of Sam's path to the bathroom. She had decided he looked mighty fine in a pair of red-and-blue-plaid boxers.

Then had come half a day's worth of shivers, when she'd piled every blanket she owned on top of him and he still begged her to turn up the heat.

Then his fever had raged and he'd wanted nothing on him at all. She'd had to fight to make him leave his underwear on.

Now he was sleeping peacefully. He looked like hell and she felt like hell. She had done this to him, laid this beautiful man low with one turn of her spatula. It was no wonder she couldn't find a man to marry.

She leaned forward and brushed an unruly lock of hair back from his face. He opened his eyes and smiled at her.

"Hi," he croaked.

She couldn't return his smile. "Sam, I'm so sorry."

"Hey, you're doing a great job of pampering me."

"Oh, Sam . . ."

He took her hand and pressed her palm against his cheek. "It wasn't your fault, sugar. It was Joe's fault for selling us rotten eggs. We'll bake him some brownies with laxative frosting in a few days as repayment."

She pulled her hand away. "I'm never setting another foot in that kitchen."

He pulled himself up against the headboard, wincing as he did so. "Oh, yes, you are. When you fall off a horse, you get right back on. Go take a nap, Sydney, while I clean up. Then we'll make soup for supper and find a good movie on television. Tomorrow we'll start over. You promised to teach me how to change the oil. I don't want to miss out on that."

"The Ladies Aid Society thinks I killed you," she said in a small voice.

Sam laughed softly as he swung his legs to the floor. "I'll set them straight next week. Now git."

Sydney rose, then stopped at the door. "I can make soup." She met his eyes. "It comes in a can, you know."

"Then you go make soup. I'll be out to eat it in half an hour."

She nodded and closed his door behind her. At least soup wouldn't kill him. Saltine crackers would be a nice addition, especially since someone else had cooked them. And ice cream for dessert. Yes, Sam would certainly be safe through dinner.

Half an hour later, she heard the TV go on in the living room. She brought out a tray with two bowls of soup and a package of crackers. She set the tray down and watched Sam try to start the fire. When he started to swear, she knew the time for aid had come. She knelt down next to him and smiled.

"You're pitiful, you know?"

"Yeah, that's what I hear."

"Try kindling under the log, Sam. Newspaper and twigs. Works every time."

He used too much paper and wasted half a dozen matches getting the blaze going, but she didn't complain. He sat back on his heels with a smug smile.

"Piece of cake."

She nodded solemnly. "Of course. Now come eat your dinner before it congeals."

He followed her over to the couch and sat down, looking at the tray on the coffee table. "It's a feast!"

"Well, at least it won't kill you."

Once dinner was consumed, she cleaned up, then went back into the living room. Sam was relaxing on the couch with his feet propped up on the coffee table and a blanket over his legs. He smiled when she came in.

"There are so many channels, I don't know where to start."

She sat down on the opposite end of the couch. "Pick whatever you want. It doesn't matter to me."

Sam started to flick through the channels, then he slid a glance her way.

"You know," he said, "we're missing out on a perfect opportunity."

"How's that?"

He shrugged nonchalantly. "For snuggling practice. It's my understanding that the skill can never be too refined."

"Really." Was that her voice sounding so breathless?

"From what I understand."

"I'm sure Melanie already knows how to snuggle."

"I'm not interested in Melanie."

Sydney didn't want to know who he was interested in. But her mouth had a different idea.

"Are you interested in someone else?"

Sam looked away. "Yes."

"Oh," Sydney said. Funny how there was that little cracking sound when your heart broke. She'd never expected to have it hurt so badly.

"What about you? Planning on making Frank Slater a wonderful wife?"

She looked up and met blazing green eyes. She blinked.

"Frank?"

"Yes, Frank, damn it."

"I'm not interested in Frank."

"Oh." He looked taken aback. "Then, are you interested in anyone?"

"Yes."

He looked like she'd slapped him. Then he started to scowl.

"Whoever he is, he isn't good enough for you. I want to meet him. What's his name?"

"That's none of your business."

"It sure as hell is my business. Who is he?"

"What do you care?" she retorted.

He growled. And he scowled some more. Then he thrust out his hand.

"Come here. We might as well get on with this snuggling business. I'm sure the fool will appreciate it eventually."

"I think he might." If Sam only knew!

He took her hand and hauled her over to him. Sydney found herself pinned between his heavy arm and his hard chest. He dragged her arm across his waist and pushed her head down against his shoulder.

"This is snuggling," he grumbled. "And that's *Singing in the Rain* on TV. I hope you like both because I'm not giving you a choice about either."

Sydney didn't care what was on television. They could have been watching a televised correspondence course in advanced calculus and she would have been perfectly content. After a few minutes, Sam relaxed, and she relaxed against him. She closed her eyes and sighed as he began to trail his fingers over her back. She snuggled closer to him and pressed her face against his neck.

"That feels good."

He cleared his throat. "Compliments are, of course, always appreciated. As are comments about the snuggling partner's warmth."

"You're very warm, Sam."

"Yes, like that," he said gruffly. "You're getting the hang of it."

"No, not quite yet. I think it might take another couple of hours."

She could hardly believe the words had come out of her mouth, but it was too late to take them back now.

"Yes, well, it might." Sam sounded positively hoarse. "We'll see how it goes tonight. We might have to do this often. Just so you perfect your technique."

"Of course."

"And so you can please Sasquatch. Or whatever the hell his name is."

"Right," she agreed.

"I don't want to know who he is."

"I wouldn't think of telling you."

She felt the weight of Sam's head come to rest against hers. "Are you comfortable, Syd?" he murmured, the annoyance gone from his voice.

"Very," she whispered. "This is nice. Thank you, Sam."

He sighed deeply. "It's the least I can do for the woman who's going to take her life in her hands and teach me how to change the oil in my Range Rover."

"You'll do a great job."

He said nothing, but tightened his arms around her.

Sydney closed her eyes and smiled. She didn't think about whoever it was that Sam was interested in. *She* was the one in his arms at present, and if his embrace was any indication, he didn't want to let her go.

There was a nagging doubt at the back of her mind about the identity of Sam's woman, but she pushed it away. There would be time enough tomorrow to be irritated and miffed.

For the moment, Sam was hers.

Chapter Eight

SAM SWUNG THE axe down, and it split the wood with a satis-
fying crack. Yes, there was something therapeutic about chopping wood. Especially when you could do it and not worry
about losing toes in the process. He didn't need to chop any
wood, but it was keeping him busy. And it was certainly the
only positive thing in his life at present. His revisions were
worse than the first draft, and his plan to woo Sydney was
turning out worse than his revisions.

And it had everything to do with her mystery man.

He finished his stack, put the axe back in the shed, and
walked into the house. Sydney was lying on the couch, her
nose stuck in a book on trail guiding. He wished for once she
would read something else. Something he'd written maybe.
The woman claimed she wanted to learn how to cook. A little
foray into a cooking magazine wasn't too much to ask, was it?

She looked up as he clomped by. He glared at her. She returned his look coolly.

"Ready for our lesson?" she asked, her tone as icy as her
look.

"I can hardly wait. Let me shower first."

"Please do."

He slammed all the doors he could on his way to the
shower. It had been a week since their snuggling lesson on
the couch. Sydney had awakened the next morning in a sour
mood, one that matched his perfectly. He'd lain awake all

night wondering just who the hell this man of hers was. Sydney didn't know any men. Was he some New York investment jockey with plans to take Sydney to the Big Apple? The thought of Sydney Kincaid being yanked out of her native environment rankled. The thought of someone else besides him doing the yanking just plain infuriated him. If anyone was going to be doing anything with Sydney, it was going to be him.

He had no idea why she was so angry. Maybe she was reacting to him being such a jerk. He didn't know. He almost didn't care. Damn her, she was the one making him miserable, not the other way around. She knew he didn't have any ties. He never received mail or phone calls except from his agent. She sure as hell couldn't imagine that he was after Marjorie.

He took a shower that used up every bit of hot water in the tank. Then he went into his room and scowled for half an hour.

Love sucked.

He finally walked out into the living room. Sydney was asleep. He hauled her up without warning. She threw her arms around him in self-defense, so he picked her up and carried her into the kitchen.

"Cookbook," he barked.

She rubbed her eyes as she reached for it and handed it to him.

"Pay attention," he growled.

"Stop being such a jerk," she growled back, the sleep fading from her eyes, to be replaced by anger.

"Me?" He threw up his hands. "Women! Go figure."

He grabbed his keys off the rack and slammed out the front door. Might as well go check the post office box while he was out acting like an adolescent. He drove to town and found nothing in his box. Frustrated, he made his way to Smith's Dry Goods for a cold root beer. He thought about taking up smoking, then discarded that idea. No sense in taking more years off his life than Sydney had already taken.

He leaned against the counter and sipped his root beer. "Joe, does Sydney date much?"

"Reckon she doesn't," Joe said, polishing a shiny lure.

"Has she dated much in the past?"

"Once," Joe said. "Frank Slater."

Sam gritted his teeth. Frank Slater. It figured.

"Only one time, though," Joe said conversationally. "Her pa wasn't much on seeing her married."

"Just one time? You gotta be joking."

"I never joke."

Sam didn't have any trouble believing that. "But she says she's in love with someone. Some Sasquatchy mountain man."

"I reckon she's lying," Joe said, unperturbed.

"Then who could she possibly be in love with? Some city boy?"

Joe looked at him. "Now that's a thought."

Sam frowned. "Do you know who she's been taking around this summer? Names? Phone numbers?"

Joe held the lure up to the light and buffed it a bit more. "I'd look a little closer to home if I were you, Sam."

"Then I'll need a map of Flaherty and names of who lives where. And ages of the men, if you have them."

Joe gave an exasperated snort. "You don't need a map, boy. Just go back home and see if you can't figure it out from there."

Back home? Well, Sam supposed it wouldn't take all that long to plow through Sydney's copy of the phone book.

Then the proverbial light bulb went on in his head.

Home?

"You're joking, right?" he said in disbelief.

Joe looked at him and pursed his lips.

Sam held up his hands. "I know, I know. You don't joke."

Joe took away Sam's root beer bottle. "Go home, Sam. And don't you dare hurt her. You are planning on staying in Flaherty, aren't you? Permanently?"

Sam thought about it for the space of ten seconds, then he realized there was nothing to think about. He didn't have to live in New York to write. He could take Sydney down to Seattle or San Francisco for a few weeks every now and then so he could do his research. There was absolutely no reason to leave. His mother, his sisters, and his trust fund would survive quite nicely without him.

"Yep." Sam nodded. "I am."

"Then get on home, boy. And see what you come up with if you look hard enough."

Sam took Joe's advice and headed home. He wasn't quite

ready to accept the fact that he was the one Sydney was interested in, but there certainly wasn't anyone else in her neck of the woods. He'd go home and keep an open mind about things. Who knew what he would find out?

HE ENTERED THE house quietly and immediately sensed that Sydney was in the kitchen. He followed the sound of her curses and walked in to find her in the middle of the biggest mess he had ever seen. Every bowl in the house was dirty. There was flour all over the floor, the counters, and the cook. And the cook was furious.

"What," he asked in a strangled voice, "are you doing?"

"I'm cooking," she snapped. "What does it look like I'm doing?"

It looked like she was making a mess, but he wisely chose not to point that out to her. He crossed the room and put his hand under her chin, tipping her face up. He gently wiped the flour from her cheeks.

"What are you making?"

"A cake. But it isn't going well."

"Want some help?"

"Yes."

"Let's clean up first. It'll be less stressful if you start with a clean kitchen."

Sydney wasn't much better at cleaning than she was at cooking, but he had to admire her enthusiasm. He kept back the necessary bowls and put the rest in the dishwasher. Then he opened the cookbook, laid out all the ingredients, and proceeded to show her what to do.

"It says 'fold in the dry ingredients.' What does that mean?" she demanded.

"Here, turn the mixer back on," he said, standing behind her. "Take the spatula in your right hand and the bowl of flour in your left. Just dump in a little at a time and let the mixer do the work."

"But that's mixing, not folding."

"Same thing."

"Then why doesn't it say the same thing?"

"I don't know." He didn't. All he knew was that Sydney Kincaid was standing in the circle of his arms, concentrating on something else, leaving him free to concentrate on her. The fragrance of her hair wafted up and forced his eyes closed. He breathed deeply, savoring the smell.

"Now what do I do? Sam, are you falling asleep?"

"No."

"The cake's folded. What do I do now?"

"Preheat the oven, then pour the batter into the cake pans."

He leaned back against the counter and listened to her hum as she poured the batter into two pans, then slid them both into the oven. She set the timer, then turned and smiled.

"Now what?"

"Now you come over here and listen to me apologize for being such a jerk these past few days."

Her smile faltered. "You weren't, Sam. I'm not the easiest person to live with."

He reached out, took her hand and pulled her across the floor. "We're going to practice making up now, Syd. An important part of any relationship. I'm going to say I'm sorry. You're going to listen, forgive me, then hug me. Got it?"

She nodded.

"I'm sorry."

"I forgive you."

"Now, hug me."

"But . . ."

"Hey, I need the practice, too. For Miss Sasquatchette. It's as easy as snuggling, only you can do making-up anywhere."

She moved closer to him, slowly. When she was close enough, Sam put his arms around her and drew her close. And he closed his eyes and sighed. Yes, he'd come home.

"Where did you go, Sam?" she asked softly.

"To have a root beer down at Joe's."

"I was worried about you."

Sam smiled into her hair. "I'm sorry, Sydney. I won't go like that again." He stroked her back. "I'll stay right here for as long as you want me to be."

"Miss Sasquatchette won't be angry?" Sydney asked, her voice muffled against his shirt.

"Somehow, I just don't think so."

"Then you'll hold me for a few more minutes?"

"I sure will."

He held her for forty-five more minutes, to be exact. And

he cursed the timer when it went off and pulled Sydney away from him. Her toothpick came out clean, and she grinned as two perfectly baked rounds were pulled from the oven. Sam showed her how to put the cake on a cooling rack, then she made frosting. They waiting for the cake to cool, then Sam leaned against the counter and watched her frost her chocolate cake. He had to smile at the concentration on her face.

Then she stood back and admired her handiwork.

"It's beautiful," she said reverently.

"No," he said, taking her hand and pulling her closer, "*you* are beautiful."

"Sam . . ."

He put his finger to her lips. "You're going to practice taking compliments. It's a skill I'm sure will come in handy in the future."

"You think so?"

He nodded. "I do." He put one arm around her shoulder and pulled her closer, then smoothed his hand over her hair. And he tried to find the words to say to tell her just how beautiful she truly was and what fools the men of Flaherty were never to have seen that. How could they have overlooked those haunting eyes, or that exquisite face? Her hair was soft and luxurious, hair that a man could bury his face and drown in without too much trouble. He met her eyes and saw the hesitancy there.

Or was it desire? He honestly couldn't tell, but there was one surefire way to find out. He lowered his head until his mouth was a mere inch from hers.

"May I kiss you?" he whispered.

"More lessons?"

"Definitely."

"If you think it will come in handy in the future."

His only answer was to cover her mouth with his own. He pulled her closer to him as he explored her lips. By the time he was finished, Sydney was shaking like a leaf. And it occurred to him, accompanied by the most Neanderthal rush of pleasure he had ever felt, that she had probably never been kissed before.

"Are we finished?"

Sam opened his eyes. Sydney's teeth were chattering.

"Do you want to be finished?"

She shook her head.

"Are you afraid?"

"Me?" she squeaked. She cleared her throat. "I've faced down grizzlies bigger than you and not broken a sweat."

"Well," he said with a smile, "that says it all, doesn't it?"

She rubbed her arms. "I think I'm cold."

"I'll build you a fire. I'm getting pretty good at it, you know." He took her hand and led her out into the living room. He built the fire quickly, then took off his shoes and pulled a blanket down in front of the fireplace. He looked up at Sydney.

"Join me?"

"Shouldn't I start dinner?"

"We'll have sandwiches later. We'll practice our cuddling tonight."

"Cuddling?"

"A completely different technique than snuggling," he said with a nod. "So get comfortable. We could be here a very long time."

The thought was singularly appealing.

Chapter Nine

SYDNEY PICKED UP the nail, then straightened, certain that Sam's eyes were raking her from the heel of her cowboy boots to the waistband of her jeans. She doubted he got much further than that, but she didn't care. She turned slowly, savoring the feeling of power she had somehow acquired over him in the past couple of days.

"This," she said, holding the item out for inspection, "is a nail. We don't leave these lying around on the floor. Someone might step on them, and that would hurt. Oh, look. There's another one." She bent right in front of him and brushed his chest with her forearm on her way up. "We have to be careful out here in the workshop, Sam. Safety is no laughing matter."

Sam grunted in answer. Sydney smiled sweetly and turned back to the pegboard. She set about explaining all the various tools and giving him possible uses for each. In reality, she had no idea what she was saying. All she knew was Sam was standing only inches behind her and he was paying as little attention to what she was saying as she was.

Three days had passed since he'd kissed her in the kitchen, and she was fast learning that he was determined that she practice kissing as often as possible. If he could be persuaded to work at all, he was never in his room for more than ten minutes without coming out to check on her.

And Sydney loved it.

She didn't want to speculate on his reasons. He didn't want to discuss Miss Sasquatchette, whoever she was. Sam never got personal calls, and Sydney was desperately hoping that he didn't have anyone waiting for him in New York.

"Oh, Sam," she said, pointing at a crescent wrench to her right, "would you get that for me? I can't seem to reach it."

He muttered something under his breath and reached out to take it down. Sydney slid her hand up his forearm and over his hand to take the wrench from him. She could have sworn she felt him shiver. She definitely heard him curse.

"Oh, not this one," she purred. "The one higher up." She leaned back against him as he reached, thoroughly enjoying teasing him. Never in her life had a man looked at her with anything besides impatience or disdain. Sam looked at her with lust, plain and simple. Oh, there were those other looks, those looks that a less sensible girl might have mistaken for love. But Sydney was nothing if not sensible.

"Maybe the one higher up," she said, pointing. "Yes, I think that's the one . . ."

She jumped as Sam grabbed a rag, swiped it over the bench surface, spun her around, and plunked her down on the wood with enough force to make her teeth rattle.

"All right, enough is enough. You can only tease me for so long before I snap. And I'm snapping."

"Tease?" she said, putting her hand over her chest and blinking in surprise. "Me?"

"Your jeans are so tight that I doubt you can breathe, your shirt is unbuttoned far enough to give you pneumonia, and you're wearing makeup. Which you don't need, by the way."

"I don't—"

He covered her mouth with his and cut off her words. Well, he certainly was effective when it came to making a bid for a little silence. He kissed her until she forgot what she'd been about to say, then she forgot her name, and she came close to forgetting to breathe. She had only enough presence of mind to notice the last because the lack of air was starting to make her ears ring.

She froze. That wasn't her ears ringing. It was the doorbell!

"Sam," she gasped frantically. "Let me go."

"No," he murmured, holding her more tightly.

"Someone's at the door!"

Sam stiffened, then lifted his head. His eyes were wide. "Oh, no."

"Oh, no, what?"

"I invited the Ladies Aid Society over for lunch."

"Sam!" she wailed.

"I forgot," he said, releasing her and stumbling back. "You go answer the door. I'll be right there."

"Me?" she screeched. "I look kissed!"

"And I look aroused. Give me five minutes to let things, ahem, settle down." He smiled at her hopefully. "Please?"

She jumped down off the bench and tried to resurrect her hair. It was useless, so she dragged her fingers through it and straightened her clothes. Putting her shoulders back, she tried to recapture some of her dignity.

"Syd?"

She turned at the door. Sam was staring at her with a gentle smile.

"I love you."

She froze. Then she gestured to the bench. "Because of—"

He shook his head sharply. "No."

"Oh, Sam."

"Go answer the door, honey. This is going to be the shortest Ladies Aid meeting in history."

Four hours later, Sydney was ready to throw the Ladies Aid Society out of her house without any regard to where they landed. Sam ushered them out with his usual charm, and Sydney went in to start the dishes. One thing she could say for Sam—he'd taught her how to keep a clean kitchen.

She jumped when she felt arms go around her.

"Only me."

She leaned back against him. "Did you mean what you said before?"

"Yes." He took the last dish out of her hand, stuck it in the dishwasher, then turned her around. He smiled down at her. "Let's go snuggle on the couch. I'm beat, how about you?"

"The Society is exhausting."

"But very impressed with your brownies."

"I couldn't care less."

Sam laughed. "I know. And that tickles me." He kissed the end of her nose. "Let's go."

She grabbed a magazine off the counter as they went into the living room.

"What's that future Pulitzer Prize-winning article you have there?" Sam asked.

Sydney smiled. "Yours, of course."

"I thought you didn't read cooking magazines."

"I lied. Joe gave me a copy."

"And do you like it?"

She smiled at the way he wouldn't meet her eyes. "I loved it. You're great, Sam."

He stretched out on the couch, then smiled up at her. "Those were the magic words. Come down here, gentle reader, and let me kiss you in gratitude for preserving my delicate author's ego."

Sydney let him draw her down next to him on the couch and then sighed as he kissed her.

He lifted his head and smiled at her. "Come with me to the Ladies Aid Society dance Friday. I want to rub this in Frank Slater's nose. And Sasquatch's. Whoever he is."

"He's you, silly. Who did you think he was?"

"I had no idea. Joe told me to look close to home. I figured he was some mountain man, hiding in your woods."

"No, he's a writer, hiding in my kitchen."

"Speaking of kitchens, do you want dinner?"

"Only if I don't have to cook it."

He sighed and rose. "A man's work is never done. If I have to go, you have to come. The least you can do is praise me while I work."

It seemed a fair trade to her.

Chapter Ten

WHEN FRIDAY NIGHT arrived, Sam found himself pacing in the living room, waiting for Sydney to come out of the bathroom. He paced for other reasons as well. He'd spent Wednesday night snuggling with her on the couch while she'd slept contentedly in his arms. Yesterday they hadn't spent a moment apart. Sam had the feeling he was going to have to move to a hotel until the wedding.

Assuming, that is, that Sydney wanted to get married.

He stopped his pacing once he caught sight of her standing near the fireplace. His jaw went slack.

"Oh, no," he said, shaking his head. "You aren't going anywhere dressed like that."

Her face fell immediately and she turned away. Sam strode across the room and caught her. He turned her around in his arms and tipped her face up.

"You're stunning. Breathtaking. Exquisite. And by the time the evening is over, I'm going to be bruised, bloodied, and broken from fighting off all those wilderness men who'll want you. Where is that gunnysack I found for you?"

She smiled hesitantly. "You like this?"

"Sydney, you look sexy in jeans, but this?" He stepped back and looked her over from head to toe. She was wearing a long navy blue dress and no-nonsense work boots. He was quite certain he'd never seen anything like it in New York. He was even more certain he'd never seen anything sexier. He sighed deeply. "You knock my socks off."

She didn't look all that convinced. "I don't know how long I can take this whole dance thing. We don't have to stay long, do we?"

"We'll only stay as long as you want to. You say the word and we're out of there."

THE TOWN HALL was filled with Flaherty folk of all ages, and the band was already warming up with a few golden oldies. Sam greeted the Clan and his Ladies Aid Society. Sydney greeted the Clan and Joe. And then she and Sam went out to dance and they didn't pay attention to anyone else.

Sydney was asked to dance by plenty of men. She refused each one. Sam avoided being pinched by Ruth Newark and made it plain to hopeful mothers that he was off the market. As if they couldn't have told that by the way he was holding Sydney as they danced. Even the Clan seemed to accept it. Grudgingly, of course. Joe was simply beaming.

Sam couldn't take his eyes off the woman in his arms, and he found that he couldn't let go of her either. But he'd already made up his mind that she deserved a wedding before anything else, so dancing with her in public seemed the safest way to hold her and not get carried away.

He geared himself up on the way home to pop the question. His palms were sweaty. His heart was racing. In fact, his chest hurt so badly he feared he might be having a heart attack. A man didn't make it to the ripe old age of thirty-five without having had a healthy aversion to that "Will you marry me?" question.

He took a deep breath. His chest pains were from something he'd eaten at the dance. His palms were sweating because he didn't want Sydney to say no.

"All right," he said, with another deep breath. "Sydney, will you marry me?"

There was no answer.

Did she have something stuck in her throat? Had her powers of speech been swiped by aliens? Sam scowled as he looked to his right to find out why in the world she hadn't answered him.

Her mouth was open. Her eyes were closed. Her head was lolling back on the headrest.

Great. He let out the breath he'd been holding and turned his attention back to the road. This probably hadn't been the most romantic way to do it, anyway. He would gird up his loins yet again the next day and see if he couldn't pop the question while the lady in question wasn't drooling.

And he hoped this wasn't a sign.

THE NEXT MORNING Sam stumbled out into the kitchen to find Sydney standing over the stove, making pancakes. She looked incredibly well rested. Sam felt his eyes narrow, which wasn't all that difficult since he hadn't slept a wink.

Sydney turned and smiled at him. "Sleep well?"

"No."

"Okay," she said slowly. "Would breakfast help?"

"I doubt it."

"What's your problem?"

Sam dug his fists into his eyes and rubbed vigorously. "Lots on my mind. It's nothing that concerns you."

Sydney's spatula dipped, and she looked as if he'd slapped her. Sam found, to his faint dismay, that he couldn't seem to find anything to say to fix that. He'd spent the night going back and forth, wondering if he'd lost his mind or his heart.

He wanted to marry her.

But would she want him? Or would she just chalk up his devotion to too much cabin fever beginning to prey on his overworked imagination?

The phone rang. Sam had never been more grateful in his life.

"I'll get it," Sydney said, but he reached it first.

"Hello?" he said.

"Sam, I'm at the airport," a crisp voice announced with all the diction that six generations of finishing-school attendees could instill in their posterity's genes.

Sam blinked in surprise. "Marjorie?"

The sigh from the other end of the phone almost blew his hair off his scalp. "Who else? I've come to see about the condition of your revisions."

Revisions? Sam frowned. Marjorie would hardly make a

trip all the way to Alaska to check on his revisions. She was obviously on a mission to see what he was up to. But there was no sense in going into that over the phone. "All right," he said, resigned. "I'll come get you."

"Hurry," came the demand. "I'm appalled by the dander floating in the air—inside the building, mind you."

Sam hung up the phone before he said something he would regret. Marjorie was his agent, after all, and she was reported to be a very good one. She was also his sister, which meant it would be very embarrassing to be dumped as a client.

He looked at Sydney and wondered what she would say when she learned about the life he'd left behind. And then he looked at her and really saw her. And he knew all over again why he loved her.

Because she loved him. Samuel MacLeod, struggling writer, respectable cook, and pitiful handyman.

He took her by the shoulders, hauled her to him, and kissed her smartly on the mouth.

"I've got to go get my agent. But I'll be back as soon as I can. I have something to ask you."

She blinked. "Okay."

"I'll find her a hotel, then come home."

"Oh, she can stay here," Sydney offered. "If you want."

Sam paused. He wasn't sure he wanted them in the same enclosed space before he had a chance to explain a few things to Sydney, but maybe it was best to get all his cards on the table before he asked her to marry him. He smiled weakly.

"She won't stay long. I promise."

"It's fine. Really."

"I'll kick her out in thirty-six hours, forty-eight max. Can you put up with her that long?"

"Of course."

"I'll be back late," he said.

"It's supposed to snow. Maybe you should stay overnight."

An evening alone with his sister? The thought was terrifying, but even more terrifying was the thought of getting stuck in a snowdrift with her.

"All right, tomorrow," he agreed. "I'll miss you."

She nodded and held him tightly. "Can Marjorie cook?"

"She studied cooking with some of France's finest chefs." Why that was okay for Marjorie but not him was something he'd never understood, but getting all riled over the sexism of it wouldn't do him any good at the moment. "She can make a soufflé that'll just knock your socks off."

He hurried and packed an overnight bag, gave Sydney one last kiss, and headed off toward Anchorage. This was a good thing. He'd get some input from his agent, get his life out on the table with his future wife, then get on with things.

SYDNEY WATCHED SAM drive away, and her heart sank. She had no idea who Marjorie truly was. Sam said she was his agent. Was she also an old girlfriend? Sydney couldn't bear to think about it. All she knew was that Marjorie used to be a chef. She was probably beautiful and she was from New York.

Sydney began to pace. Marjorie and Sam had probably been lovers. He probably had plans to go back to New York and sleep with her some more.

Sydney almost cried.

Then she stiffened her spine and marched herself into the kitchen. A soufflé, was it? She pulled out a cookbook and looked up the recipe. And she frowned.

Eggs. Her old nemeses.

Well, they wouldn't get the best of her this time. She'd make a damn soufflé if it took her the next twenty-four hours to do so. Then Sam would see Marjorie had nothing on her.

And then he would stay.

Chapter Eleven

SAM DROVE BACK to Flaherty, skillfully avoiding the potholes. He'd managed to do the same with the verbal land mines that his sister had scattered in front of him—up till now. But he sensed his luck was about to run out.

"Just what are you so mysterious about?" Marjorie asked tersely.

There was no sense in postponing the inevitable any longer. Sam took a deep breath. "I'm in love."

"Oh, please, Sam," Marjorie said, rolling her eyes with enough force to stick them up in her head permanently. "Please be serious."

"I am serious, Marj. She's the best thing that ever happened to me—"

"She runs a trail guide service, Sam. She's out alone in the wilderness with horny executives for months at a time."

Sam fixed his blond companion with a steely look. "Watch it, Marjorie. I have no qualms about letting you out right here and watching you hoof it back to Anchorage. Now, if you can't exert yourself to be civil, let me know so I can pull over."

"Now, Sam, don't get testy. All this country living has certainly put you in a foul humor." Marjorie looked at her long, manicured nails. "You really should come back to the city."

"I'm moving here. Get used to it."

"Mother will have a fit."

"I couldn't care less."

"She'll cut off your trust fund."

"Marj, the trust fund is under my control. I never use it, anyway. Keep up with the times."

"Of course not. You bake those ridiculous cakes."

"I'm very good."

Marjorie gave a very unladylike snort. "I don't understand this compulsion you have about working. You've got gobs of perfectly good money sitting in accounts all over the world. Why dirty your hands?"

"You work," Sam said pointedly.

"I represent the current century's literary geniuses," Marjorie said haughtily. "It's a service to mankind."

Sam snorted. He knew Marjorie's true reasoning. If publishing had been good enough for Jackie O. and John Jr., then it was good enough for her. Unfortunately, her attention span was short, and she couldn't spell to save her life, so editing was out of the question. Fortunately for Marjorie, the rest of her mind—the part not in charge of putting letters in the right order—was like a steel trap, and the survival instinct flowing through generations of Scottish Highlanders had been honed to a fine killing point in her. In short, she was a barracuda in half-a-year's-salary skirts who could dissect a contract faster than an eighth-grade boy could dispatch a frog. Her clients loved her, editors feared her, and other agents envied her.

Sam was, of course, her pity case.

But he was realist enough to know that it wasn't easy to get published and that maybe being a good writer might not be sufficient. If his sister could get him a read or two that he might not get on his own, she would be worth her fee.

"She's probably not a virgin, you know."

Then again, maybe throttling her would be more rewarding than being the recipient of any of her called-in markers. Sam slammed on the brakes and the Range Rover skidded to a halt.

"That's it," he snarled. "Get out."

"Now, Sam . . ."

"Don't you now-Sam me, you cynical socialite. You're dead wrong about Sydney—"

Marjorie gasped. "You slept with her?"

Sam gritted his teeth. "No. But I know her."

"Thank heavens," Majorie said, sounding vastly relieved. "To propagate the species this way . . ."

"Have you ever considered the fact that I might want to have children?"

"And pass on your father's gene pool? Definitely not."

"He's your father, too. And just because he considered selling his seat on the Exchange—"

"Oh, Sam," Marjorie gasped, "please don't bring up that painful memory!"

"That doesn't make him a bad person," Sam finished. "You're a snob."

"And you're an incurable romantic." She turned the full force of her pale blue eyes on him. Sam was almost certain his head had begun to smoke from the laser-beam intensity of her stare.

"Come home to New York," Marjorie said with a compelling tone of voice that any vampire would have been proud to call his own.

"No."

"You can stay at my place until you find something suitable."

"I'm happy here."

"I cannot imagine why."

"Exactly," Sam said, deciding that there wasn't any point in discussing things further. Besides, Marjorie hated the silent treatment, and he was enough of a younger brother to relish giving her a little of it.

Sam put his 4X4 back in gear and eased back out onto the road. He ignored Marjorie all the way home, then left her to bring in her own luggage while he ran up to the house and banged on the door. He owed it to Sydney to prepare her for what she would soon face. He should have done it sooner.

Sydney opened the door, then walked away before he could hug her. He followed her into the kitchen and pulled up short. There were at least a dozen egg cartons on the counter, as well as what could have been mistaken for a soufflé.

Had it risen, that is.

"Sydney?"

"I was trying to make a damn soufflé, all right?" she snapped. "I couldn't do it. Satisfied?"

"Good heavens, what is this mess?"

Sam threw Marjorie a glare over his shoulder. "Shut up, Marj."

"And this must be your country girl," Marjorie said, extending her hand like she was a damned queen and holding a handkerchief to her nose delicately. "How quaint."

"Marjorie," Sam growled.

"Attempts at a soufflé, my dear? How charming. But don't you just eat grits and things up here? Or is it raw bear meat right off the bone?"

"Marjorie!"

Sydney fled from the kitchen. Sam threw up his hands in frustration.

"You *shrew*," he exclaimed. "I love her, damn it!"

"Now, Sam," Marjorie said, unperturbed. "Don't be so rude."

"You're fired," Sam bellowed.

"You can't fire me. I'm your sister."

"You're a pain! Get out of my house."

Marjorie peered out the kitchen window. "Oh, Sam, I do believe your little bumpkin is driving away. Does that mean I can stay for dinner? What time do we eat out here in the country, anyway?"

Sam ran out of the kitchen and back to Sydney's bedroom. On her bed was a note, along with an envelope. He grabbed the note.

> *Sam, I know I can't compete. Here's your rent money back. I'll stay away until Saturday. That should give you time to move out. I hope you have a happy life.*
> *Sydney.*

"Marjorie!" Sam roared.

"Yes, darling," she called.

"How are your clerical skills?"

"Nonexistent, my love. Why?"

"Better brush up," he yelled. "You're going to have to get a real job when I get you blackballed in the city!"

Sam drove his sister/former agent into Flaherty and paid one of the Clan members a hundred dollars plus gas to take her back to Anchorage. He watched with narrow-eyed satisfaction as Marjorie bumped off in a truck that didn't look like it would get five miles without breaking down. Her luggage had been dumped in the truck bed and would probably be covered with dog hair and a nice thick layer of compost by the time it reached the airport. Sam couldn't have been happier about it.

After assuring himself that Joe had no idea where Sydney had gone, Sam retreated back to the house to plan.

And prayed that Marjorie hadn't ruined everything.

SYDNEY CREPT BACK to her house Saturday afternoon. Sam's car was gone. She knew she should have been relieved, but she wasn't. She was heartbroken. All it had taken was one look at Sam's "agent" to see that there was no hope of winning Sam away from her.

And so she'd run. She'd scampered off with her tail between her legs like the coward she was and spent three days licking her wounds. She had the feeling that no amount of licking would heal them.

The house was empty when she entered. She didn't bother to check Sam's room. She sat down on the couch and tried to cry. It was a futile effort. If she hadn't cried before, she certainly wasn't going to cry now.

She sat there until the darkness was complete. The days were growing shorter all the time. Soon there wouldn't be much light at all. Fitting. She would spend the winter in the gloom.

She flicked on the light in the kitchen and pulled up short.

There, on her very own counter, was the top of a wedding cake. It was the most beautiful thing she had ever seen. It must have taken Sam hours to finish. And there was a note beside it. She picked up the note with trembling hands.

> *My beautiful Sydney, you have two choices: you can either eat this cake or you can go to the refrigerator, pull out the rest of the frosting, and fill in the blank. And if you're brave enough to come down to the reception hall, you just might find someone waiting with the rest of the cake, someone who has a few things to explain to you and something to give you.*
>
> *Love, Sam*

Sydney pulled out the bowl of frosting, then closed her eyes briefly before she looked at the top tier of the cake. It said: Congratulations, Sam and . . .

Oh, what did he mean? Why had he left the cake blank? Did he want her to fight for him?

Wasn't that what she'd been trying to do with the soufflé before she'd chickened out?

Sydney reached for the cake-decorating kit laid out conveniently close to the cake and spooned some frosting into the pouch. She could hardly spell her own name but that didn't matter. Her courage returned with a rush. She loved Samuel MacLeod and damn Marjorie if she thought to steal him away. A man didn't take his life in his hands to learn to fly-fish if he didn't love you, did he?

She carefully lifted the cake top and ran out to her car. Sam was waiting for her. She couldn't get to the reception hall fast enough.

And so, like clockwork, she got a flat tire.

It took her over an hour to fix it because she was so upset. By the time she was on the road again, she was filthy. And she was weeping so hard she didn't notice she was drifting off the road until her Jeep went front-end-first into the ditch. Sydney got out of the car, cursed fluently, then grabbed her precious cake top and started to walk.

And, of course, it started to rain.

It couldn't have been snow, so she could have died a very pleasant death from exposure. It had to be rain, which soaked through her coat, plastered her hair to her head, and left her with no choice but to tuck the cake top inside her coat.

She started to sob.

She wasn't sure how long it took her to get to town, but she felt certain it was half an eternity. She stumbled into the reception hall just as things looked like they were about to be packed up. Sam was standing in the middle of the room, looking defeated. And then he turned and saw her.

And he smiled.

Sydney didn't know where all her tears were coming from, but there was a whole new batch handy for this round of weeping. She threw herself into Sam's arms, squishing the cake top between them.

"I got a flat t-tire," she hiccuped, "then the c-car slipped off the r-road."

Sam wrapped his arms around her tightly. "It's okay, sweetheart. I've got you now."

"I crushed the cake," she wept. "I even put my name on it."

"The rest of the cake is here, honey," Sam said soothingly. "We'll eat it without the top. Or I'll make you a new one after we get home. Will that make you happy?"

She lifted her face and choked on her tears. "Y-yes, it would." She clung to him. "Oh, Sam, I thought you loved Marjorie."

"She's my ex-sister," Sam said, wiping the tears and rain from her cheeks. "I have a lot to tell you."

"She can make soufflés," Sydney blubbered.

"I'll tell you a secret," Sam said, bending his head to press his lips against her ear. "I hate soufflés. I think I even hate eggs."

"Oh, Sam!"

He gave her a gentle squeeze. "I want a woman who can change the oil in my Jeep and can tell the difference between a flat screwdriver and a Phillips. Now, if you'll tell me you've been waiting for a man who could bake with the best of them, we'll go in and get married."

She lifted her head and smiled up at him. "I love you."

"I love you, too. Does that mean you'll marry me?"

"It does."

"Then let's go."

"But I have cake smashed on the front of my sweater."

Sam unzipped her parka, then hugged her tightly.

"Now, we're both wearing it." He grinned down at her. "You look wonderful. Let's go."

She couldn't argue with a man who ruined his tux with wedding cake just to make her feel more comfortable. So she took his hand and let him lead her into the chapel.

And she became Mrs. Samuel MacLeod, wearing not only her cake but a smile that she was certain would never fade.

It matched Sam's perfectly.

Chapter Twelve

SAM SIGHED AND stretched, then saved the last chapter of the second book in his espionage series. He turned off the computer and stood, wondering what Sydney was up to. He looked down at his calendar, just to assure himself that it really was the last week of August and all her little city boys and girls would be going home soon. He could hardly wait to have his wife to himself again.

He walked out on the porch and looked over the front yard. He couldn't see the new addition to the house on the opposite side of the garage, but he knew it was there. It was conveniently far enough away that he could work in peace, but close enough so the inhabitants could be rescued at night if the need arose. Which it did. Often.

Camp Alaska was Sydney's baby. Sam had encouraged her and funded her, discreetly at first, until the application checks had started to roll in. Joe had called in a handful of favors, and the addition on the house had been constructed in May and June, then filled with six city children who had come up for two months of the wilderness life.

Sam had also come clean about the life he'd left behind, but Sydney hadn't been all that impressed. As she said, all that money didn't mean much if it was just stuck in a bank. Sam suspected they would eventually do something with all his loot, but they were still discussing how best to use it. She promised to go to New York with him eventually, but neither of them was in any hurry to leave Alaska.

Sam leaned against a porch post and smiled as his very own wilderness woman shepherded her children across the lawn.

"Will Sam fry up the fish for us?" one of the boys asked. "We'll clean 'em for him."

"No, Sydney, you cook them," one of the girls said, holding Sydney's hand. "Then maybe Sam will make us brownies. Do you think he will?"

"If you ask him, he just might," Sydney said, looking up and catching sight of Sam.

A little blonde darted away and threw herself up the stairs and into Sam's arms. "Will you, huh, Sam? We let you write all day long, didn't we? We stayed out of your hair, didn't we?"

Sam laughed and gave Jennifer a hug. "Yes, you did, sweetheart. And I'll make you brownies if you run on in and get out all the ingredients. Doug, you're in charge. Don't let anyone mess up my kitchen."

"Sure thing, Sam," Doug said. He was fourteen and took his leadership responsibilities very seriously. "Come on, brats, let's get moving. No, Chrissy, you can't stay outside with Sydney and Sam. They probably want to do something gross, like kiss."

There was a chorus of gagging sounds and childlike laughter that disappeared into the house. Sam rolled his eyes as he gathered his wife into his arms.

"How did it go today?"

"Nobody drowned. I call that a success."

Sam laughed and kissed Sydney softly. "You're great with them. It's going to be very hard next year to choose from all the applicants. We may have to build on a few more rooms and bring some of these kids back as camp counselors or something."

Sydney trailed her finger down the front of his sweater. "Yes, we might have to do that." She looked up at him. "Build on another room or two."

Sam kissed her, his heart full of love for the passionate, beautiful woman in his arms. He thanked his lucky stars that the men of Flaherty had been too stupid to see what was right under their collective noses.

"About the rooms, Sam," she said, looking in the vicinity of his chin. "I know we've got the loft, but we're going to have to build something else too. On the ground floor."

"Whatever you want, Sydney."

She met his eyes. "Sam," she said patiently, "don't you want to know why we need more rooms?"

"More campers?"

"No, Sam."

"You aren't letting Marjorie move in, are you?"

"Sam, sometimes you really aren't very bright."

He stiffened. "You aren't inviting any of the Clan in, are you?"

"Sam, I'm pregnant!"

"Oh," he said, with a smile.

Then he choked. "A baby!"

Sydney smiled serenely. "A baby. Maybe two."

"Oh, Sydney." He gathered her close and hugged her tightly. "Oh, Syd."

"Tell me you're happy about it."

"I'm thrilled."

"I didn't think you had enough headaches with just the kids during the summer," she whispered in his ear. "I thought a few distractions year-round might make you happier."

He lifted his head and looked down at her. "Did you say two?"

"The doctor in Anchorage says no, but Doc Bolen says he's sure it's twins. Sort of a variation on the spit-in-Drano test." She smiled up at him serenely. "He's never wrong."

"Oh, heaven help me. Twins."

"Maybe triplets. He wasn't quite sure."

Sam started to laugh. He leaned on his wife and laughed until tears were running down his face. Then he kissed her soundly.

"Oh, Sydney, you never do anything halfway, do you?"

"Never."

He pulled her inside, then made her sit while he gave his camp cooking and baking lesson for the day, then he pitched in with his six little helpers and cleaned up the dishes and the kitchen. Then he tucked them all in and tried not to get misty-eyed thinking about how he would be tucking in his own children in a few months.

And so he practiced once more by tucking his wife in. Then he un-tucked her and slid in beside her. He made love to her slowly and sweetly, then they shed a few tears of happiness together. Sam gathered Sydney close and counted his blessings. They included every chuckhole he'd ever bounced his Range Rover over, every minute on the Clan gossip docket, every Wednesday afternoon spent with the Ladies Aid Society to give his report of his and Sydney's activities and, last but not least, every bit of matchmaking Joe had done on their behalf.

Yes, it had been a match made in heaven.

And as he drifted off to sleep with his love in his arms, he promised himself he would check Joe for wings the very next time he went to town.